She felt the lightest touch against her nape. Fingers, lifting her hair, softly, gently. She closed her eyes and smiled.

Finn had awakened. He was behind her.

That was his ritual. He would come to her. Stand in silence. Touch her hair, lift her hair, press his lips against the flesh of her nape. She felt him touch her, then. The hot moisture of his lips, the warm, arousing moisture of his breath. In seconds, his arms would come around her. He would tell her that he loved her.

She felt his hands, sliding over her robe, beneath it, touching her flesh . . .

His touch fell away. She thought she heard him breathing . . . waiting. Waiting for her to turn into his arms, melt into them as she always did.

"Finn . . ."

She spun around, ready to do just that.

He wasn't there.

She was alone on the balcony.

The breeze suddenly turned colder. The eerie blue fog was rising from the street, moving quickly, coming higher, as if it were eager to engulf her.

**Don't miss any of Heather Graham's
Alliance Vampire novels**

Published by Kensington Publishing Corporation

HEATHER GRAHAM

THE AWAKENING

ZEBRA BOOKS
KENSINGTON PUBLISHING CORP.
http://www.kensingtonbooks.com

ZEBRA BOOKS are published by

Kensington Publishing Corp.
119 West 40th Street
New York, NY 10018

All Kensington titles, imprints, and distributed lines are available at special quantity discounts for bulk purchases for sales promotion, premiums, fundraising, educational, or institutional use.

Special book excerpts or customized printings can also be created to fit specific needs. For details, write or phone the office of the Kensington Special Sales Manager: Attn. Special Sales Department. Kensington Publishing Corp., 119 West 40th Street, New York, NY 10018. Phone: 1-800-221-2647.

Zebra Books and the Z logo Reg. U.S. Pat. & TM Off.

First Printing: October 2003
ISBN-13: 978-1-4201-3290-8
ISBN-10: 1-4201-3290-3

First Electronic Edition: October 2003
eISBN-13: 978-1-4201-3415-5
eISBN-10: 1-4201-3415-9

10 9 8 7 6 5 4 3 2

Printed in the United States of America

Prologue
The Fog

September

There had been rain the entire time Finn Douglas skirted New York City. The Jersey Turnpike, never the easiest driving on the East Coast, was slowed to a torturous crawl, and with drivers becoming more impatient, fender benders lined the way. After crossing the Hudson, he nearly missed the sign that led to all of New England. Maine was still a hell of a long way away, and by this point, he was already exhausted.

He'd figured he might have at least made the state line that night, but it wasn't going to happen. By the time he crossed through Connecticut and followed the Mass Pike eastward, he realized he was becoming a hazard to himself, and everyone else on the road. At twenty, he could have stayed awake a solid forty-eight hours, and not felt a desperate need for sleep. That hadn't been all that long ago, and he taunted himself that at the ripe old age of twenty-eight, he should still be in decent enough shape. Strange. Once he crossed the line into Massachusetts, he didn't feel just tired—he felt as if he were being drawn to leave the road. By the time he neared the signs that told him he was coming up on the city of Boston, the urge had become a compulsion. He had to stop, and he had to stop there.

It was stupid to stop in Boston. The city lived in a constant state of "under construction." The roads all went one way. The congestion was terrible, and the motels, hotels, and restaurants would be higher here than anywhere north. But still . . .

Off. Get off now. It's imperative.

It was almost as if there were a voice inside his head. *That of a state trooper,* he thought wearily. One warning him that he would kill himself, and someone else, if he didn't rest a while.

He should have gotten off the highway in Connecticut, before hitting the Mass Pike and the highway in the city.

There was an exit ahead. He was somewhere in the north of the city, near the old turnoff for the airport.

He didn't know exactly where he was when he followed a ramp and naturally, found himself on a one-way street.

Boston. He'd never even find a parking space.

Ah, but Boston. A great city. Food.

A drink.

Those were of the essence. He had left Louisiana during the wee hours of the morning, and driven straight, allowing himself pit stops only when the car was nearly on empty. How the hell many hours had he been driving? He was simply a fool. An idiot for taking so long to come. After he had sat home so many nights, telling himself that she would come back, that he hadn't done anything wrong, Megan would know it, and come back to him.

But she hadn't done so.

And there had been a moment of startling clarity and panic when he had realized it didn't matter that he was right. He had allowed certain perceptions to grow because of his pride, and since he had furiously refused to deny any of those perceptions, he'd given her little choice. He lay in their bedroom, feeling the breeze from the balcony, hearing a muffled version of the cacophony that never really left the streets of New Orleans, and noting every little thing that was a piece of Megan. The beige drapes that fluttered in the night, the headboard and canopy of the large bed, the antique dressers, not yet refinished. One of her drawers remained open, and a trail of something made of silk and lace streamed from a corner of it. He could swear he smelled her perfume.

And if he were to rise, it would be to turn on the CD player, and listen to the sound of her voice.

He had almost called, but then, he hadn't. They had exchanged too many harsh words. He could see the fall of her long blond hair in a clear picture in his mind, the passion, and the tears, in the endless blue of her eyes. Calling wouldn't do it, not after the way he had shrugged when she had warned that she needed to leave, go home . . .

He was parked, he realized. He squinted. He thought he was somewhere near Little Italy, and thanked God that he somewhat knew Boston, since he had played it, though he knew almost nothing of the surrounding area—he had flown in and out before. There was a neon light blinking almost in front him. It was like a flipping miracle—he had gotten a parking space in the city of Boston right in front of a restaurant. Or a bar. Or something.

He couldn't make out the name. It wasn't just his exhaustion. There was a fog sitting over the city.

He stumbled out of the car and straightened, blinking. Wherever he was, it didn't matter. He needed something to eat, and something to drink. And no matter how desperate he had become to reach Megan in person, he was going to get some sleep, somewhere very near. Even if he paid too much for a hotel room.

He'd die on the road, for sure, and take someone else with him, if he didn't get some sleep.

But first . . . food.

And a cold beer.

Theresa Kavanaugh left the bar late, and, admittedly, a few sheets to the wind. However, she was deeply unhappy to realize that she would be walking home; George Roscoe was supposed to have given her a ride home, but that was before George hooked up with the pretty blond bartender. It hadn't mattered at the time, because Theresa had found the guy at the pool table to be totally fascinating, and she had been certain that he intended to give her a ride home. She had been rather careful *not* to introduce him to either Sandra Jennings or Penny Sanders, because though they were all coworkers at the office, they weren't really best friends, and even best friends, she had discovered, might hone in on a cute guy a girl met at a bar. She had seen him standing by the table first, chalking a cue stick. But he had no partner.

"I'm pretty good," she had told him. "Want to take me on?"

"What are the stakes?"

"We'll gamble a twenty."

"I had been hoping for something a little . . . more worth gambling on," he'd said, laughter in his eyes.

"Let's see how we play first," she had challenged, and he had agreed.

She'd taken the first game. He'd paid up immediately. They had laughed, they had talked—maybe she had talked more than she should have. Because after she returned from the ladies' room, he was gone.

And so was George.

And at closing time, she had realized she was alone. So, feeling somewhat irritated, she left alone. Naturally, she looked for a cab, usually available in abundance. But there was so much construction in the downtown area, the cabbies were avoiding the place, or they had already been taken, or, perhaps, because of the hour, they had given up and gone home. She could have tried calling, but when she returned to the bar to do so, the doors were locked and no one responded to her banging. She couldn't resort to her cell phone because she hadn't charged the battery. The whole thing had just gone bad.

Still . . . it was all right. There were plenty of lights in the downtown area. Her apartment wasn't that far.

And when she started out, it was fine.

But then . . .

. . . came the fog.

She thought she was imagining it at first. Even in Boston, it was rare for a fog to just begin on the ground and swirl to something as thick as pea soup in a matter of minutes. But that was what it did. She could see clearly when she left the bar, but she hadn't gone two blocks before it began to churn in puffy, blue-gray swirls around her feet.

She began to whistle, wondering why fog should make her so nervous. But it did.

She could hear the click of her three-inch heels on the pavement, and that made her wish she were wearing tennis shoes. But she was still dressed as she had been at work: smart business suit, with a great A-line shirt, and the tank that she liked so very much. Naturally, she had known they were going to dinner, and onward to party that night. Friday night. The workforce lived for Friday nights, or so it seemed in Boston. At least, it did at her company. They were a brokerage firm, still a Monday through Friday, nine-to-five kind of company. She was young, ambitious, good at her job, and still . . .

Well, young. And she liked to party. And since she

and Beau had broken up several months ago, now, she was beginning to feel a little lonely, and in need of the Friday night companionship. She wasn't ready to crash into anything with a man discovered at a bar, but by this Friday, when she had met the man playing pool . . . all right, so she would have invited him back to her apartment.

"Don't know what you missed, buddy!" she muttered aloud.

The fog had risen to her calves. It was the most bizarre color!

She kept whistling. She passed old buildings, many of which had been around for the birth of the country, along with new skyscrapers. As she passed one of the city's oldest cemeteries, she felt a little twitch in her spine. Now, there, the fog was downright creepy.

She decided not to look, but rather, concentrate on her memory of the man at the bar. She realized she couldn't remember his eye color, or his hair, or even what he had been wearing. Only that he'd had . . .

A magnetism.

Maybe he'd be there again. She might have been too talkative. But still . . . well, surely, he must have had some inclination that he'd get lucky. And she knew she was attractive, that the tailored suit accentuated her curves, and that she had a really nice head of long, natural blond hair, and a good face. One would think she'd meet someone at work, but in her department, it seemed that the men came in married, gay, or bald and potbellied.

She had plenty of time to meet the right guy.

Her eyes strayed to the cemetery. Ghostly stones rose just above the blue mist.

Something touched her foot, and she screamed out loud.

"Hey, lady . . . got a buck?"

She recoiled in horror from the bum who had touched her. He was just there—lying on the sidewalk.

"No!"

"Okay . . . got a twenty?"

"Get a job!" she shouted.

And she started to run.

A block . . .

Then her heel broke. She nearly fell to the pavement. Swearing, she steadied herself. Home wasn't that far! It seemed to be taking her forever to get there. She wasn't walking—or running—or so it seemed. Rather, it was like wading through the fog! It was up to her waist now. Soon, it would obliterate everything.

She passed the cemetery . . . the buildings. Soon . . . just two . . . three blocks to go.

The fog kept rising.

She stopped dead suddenly, seeing a form before her in the fog. She held her breath, praying it wasn't going to be another bum.

"Hey! There you are."

It was him. The guy from the bar. Charming, magnetic, seductive. He was standing at the end of the block, right in front of one of the few trees in the area. There was something strange about him, but she didn't quite know what . . .

"Hey!" she called back. Limping on her one heel, she started for him. A frown knit her brow as she studied him, and tried to figure out what was different about him. "I thought you left."

"I thought you had left!" he replied softly. His voice . . . it was like silk. He stood so still, and yet it seemed he emitted so much energy and power. "I had hoped to see you again," he told her.

She smiled, thinking that the cemetery, with its stones, eerie in the blue fog, was behind her now. Just as the bum was who had reached out and touched her.

And the night . . . it lay ahead with a sudden awesome and new mystery.

"Theresa . . . come on. Come to me, Theresa!"

Well, of course, I'm coming to you, gorgeous! she thought, smiling inwardly.

And she was.

Her one heel clicked on the pavement. A pathetic sound. The fog was to her chest, swirling madly. She was so close to him. Together, they could brave it.

She could see his smile. The flash of his teeth, she was so close.

She saw what was different about him. It was what he was wearing, on such a night . . . it was weird.

But on such a man, what did it matter?

She came closer, feeling more intoxicated than she ever had due to the influence of liquor. Maybe there were a few remnants of the cosmopolitans she had been drinking that stayed to warm her bloodstream, to make her feel as if her heart jumped with excitement with every movement that brought her closer.

It seemed that even the strange blue fog was a part of his magic . . .

She came to a halt, standing directly in front of him. "I can't believe I've found you again," she murmured.

"Fate," he said softly. "Destiny. Great things are to come."

The sound was still so seductive. As were his eyes.

She couldn't have moved if she wanted to. And yet . . .

There was something . . . off. Something not quite right.

Fate. Destiny. Oh, yes. And yet . . .

She didn't even know exactly why she knew, or what she knew, or what exactly it was that she saw . . . or felt . . . except that it was . . .

She struggled to understand.

"Come with me."

"Yes!"

"Serve me!"

"Oh, yes!"

He moved . . .

Ah, the seduction of it all. The danger. Something forbidden, and thus, ever so tempting, and still . . .

It seemed she was simply swallowed into the depth of the night.

And the blanket of the swirling blue fog.

"Hey!"

Someone nudged Finn, none too gently. Blinking, he opened his eyes.

"Hey, let's see some identification."

The police officer standing in front of him was reaching out. Finn automatically reached for his back pocket, so disoriented that he was moving by rote. Where the hell was he? Then he realized he was on the street, sleeping against a building.

For a moment he was afraid he wouldn't find his wallet in his pocket. He had no memory of how he had gotten here—wherever that was. The last thing he could recall was . . . ordering a beer and a hamburger.

To his relief, he found his wallet, in his back pocket, right where it should have been.

"New Orleans, huh?" the officer said.

"Yes."

"What did you do—pass out here on the sidewalk?"

Finn shook his head, standing, praying that he wasn't going to be arrested.

"I . . ." He hesitated, then decided to tell the truth. "I was trying to drive straight through to Maine. But when I saw the signs for Boston, I figured I had to stop and get something to eat. I think I was simply so tired that I came out, leaned against the wall . . . and nodded off. But I'm not drunk, nor was I drunk. I had one beer—hours ago, now, I think." He glanced at his watch. "Yes, hours ago. I'll take any blood test or breathalizer you want."

The officer was somewhere in his forties, Finn reckoned. Steady brown eyes, slightly graying hair, and a stocky build.

He handed Finn back his wallet. "You're on your way to Maine?"

"My wife is up there. Her family was originally from Massachusetts; they moved up to Maine her first year of college."

"How come you're in such a hurry?"

Finn hesitated again, then shrugged. "We had some misunderstandings. She left me. I'm going to get her back."

"Misunderstandings?"

He didn't really have to explain his marriage to a cop, but then, the cop had just awakened him from sleeping on the sidewalk. "Pride, maybe. She believed some things that weren't true. I was angry. You know, I didn't intend to be any pushover, and I was too damned self-righteous to give her any explanations."

"So you're rushing up to Maine . . . you're lucky you weren't hit by a pickpocket, but then . . . you're a pretty big guy, tall and wiry, and the way you tensed when I nudged you, I take it you've done some fighting yourself. Still, a badass with a gun can take down a black belt any day."

"I know. Look, I swear, when I decided I was going to get her back, come hell or high water, I really didn't think I needed to stop for sleep. Now, I know better."

The cop grinned.

"Maine and Louisiana are pretty damned far apart, and you bet your ass, you have to sleep. But, good for you. Go get your wife. You two work it out. Too many people call it quits these days at the first sign of trouble. Me and my wife Laura, we've been together twenty-five years. She left me once."

"What did you do?"

"I went after her. You got money on you?"

"Yes. And credit cards."

"Well, you didn't look like a vagrant from the start, even using the concrete as a mattress, and you sure as hell aren't dressed like a vagrant, and you sound honest. You've got a job?"

Finn hesitated again. "I'm a musician." The officer's brow went up and Finn said wearily. "A good musician, and yes, I do make money, a steady income, at my music."

The fellow grinned. "I wasn't going to jail you for being a musician. But you'd better get yourself to a hotel, huh?"

"Yes, I will."

"Head out of the city a bit; I don't need any of your blood. Hell, I've been at this way too long. I know a drunk when I see one, and you just look beat. I'm going to let you get on your way, but don't drive like a maniac. Maine is still a long way away."

"Thanks. Thanks, a lot. I've never done anything like this before in my life, I swear," Finn said. "I just shouldn't have been driving so hard."

"I'd better not hear that you've been in an accident."

"You won't," Finn swore.

"Go on, then. Drive carefully."

"Yes, I will. Thank you."

The officer gave him a little salute. Finn smiled and returned it, then turned to find his car. There was an awkward moment. He didn't know where the hell his car was.

"Parking is a bitch, huh?"

"Yeah, but I have a place right on the street, somewhere," Finn said.

"Want me to drive you around?"

"No, thanks again. It's got to be right around here."

"All right. A little walk in the crisp air will do you good."

Finn nodded, glad to see the officer stepping back into his car, which was double-parked in the street.

Finn started to walk, tense, afraid the cop would follow him all over the city.

But he hadn't really gone all that far. In ten minutes, he'd found his car. He slid into the driver's seat and headed for the highway. He wound up on US1 instead of I-95. A few minutes later, he saw a hotel on a little hill. Hell, it was almost morning. Checkout was noon. Still, he determined, waking on the street had been too damned scary. He was going to sleep.

He crashed into the bed, not bothering to take off his clothes. Within minutes, he was sound asleep again.

In the morning, the world was bright. He was glad of the hotel. Glad to shower and change. And glad, because Maine might still be something of a drive, but by the evening, he would reach Megan. Then, all he had to do was convince her of the truth. He loved her more than life itself. He needed her. And she needed him.

He knew she loved him, as well. Knew that she felt there was incredible passion in their lives, that there was a lot worth working for. The best way to get her back would be . . .

What the hell was he going to say?

He stopped along the way for lunch, mulling the question over all the while.

In fact, he practiced thoughts and words all the way up the coast.

He reached her folks' house, ready with his words. But Megan was on the lawn, sitting in the tree swing, and she wasn't able to move quickly enough when she realized it was him. She stood for a moment, blond hair shimmering in the moonlight that had risen, blue eyes like that of a doe caught by the sudden head beams of a car.

The words fled from him. He just strode toward

where she stood, still, that mesmerized deer. He took her into his arms. She was stiff for a long moment . . .

Then seemed to melt against him.

"You drove here? All the way? For me?"

"I came to get you," he said gruffly.

"What if I were to say no?"

"I don't intend to let you. Megan, I have a lot to say."

"Me, too, Finn . . . but . . . there's time to talk. Later." She moved even closer against him, a compact ball of tension and heat. The simple adjustment of her flesh against him was like being doused in liquid fire. The length of him quickened with a shudder. His voice barely rasped out.

"Your folks?"

"Gone for the weekend," she whispered back.

She was trembling. He swept her up, knowing the way to her wing of the house. It was hours and hours later when he finally talked.

Somehow, he said all the right words.

It had been a bright, outstanding day in Boston.

Crystal blue, beautiful.

A Saturday. Children played in the parks. Boccie games went on in Little Italy. Tourists thronged through Faneuil Hall and were lined up to enter the Paul Revere House. September and October brought a steady stream of people to New England, and to Bean Town, the North Shore, and beyond. The fall foliage was like a brilliant beacon, and provided a splendor that was a feast for the eyes.

Night fell softly, the weather cool, but not bitter, pleasant. Saturday night, and couples and singles partied and played. Families went to dinner. Clubs stayed open late.

Sunday came and went.

All in all, it was a quiet weekend in a big city where crime was inevitable.

It wasn't until Tuesday morning, when Theresa Kavanaugh failed to show up for work a second day in a row, that she was reported missing to police.

And though every possible lead was followed, no one had seen her since she had left the bar Friday night.

She had been flirting with a man at the pool table . . .

But oddly enough, no one could give a description of him.

There were no signs of her having returned to her apartment. And there were no signs of violence along the way from the bar to her home.

No sign of . . . anything.

It was as if she had just vanished into thin air.

Like hundreds, or even thousands, of young women across the country, Theresa Kavanaugh had simply disappeared.

She was well over twenty-one, an adult. She might have chosen to disappear. It would be her legal right to do so.

Her coworkers fantasized about what might have happened.

They could remember nothing about the man at the pool table, except that . . .

He'd been wicked good-looking. In fact . . .

Devilishly exciting.

Chapter 1

Megan was screaming.

In the terrible reality that *was* happening, she heard her own voice.

In the darkness, she knew the sense of a spiraling fear that threatened to become overwhelming, to smother her. She had a sense of fatality, and she saw the shadow figure, saw him entering the room. Adrenaline raced through her, desperation, the sense that she must move, must fight for survival.

The sound continued—it was all she heard and she screamed and screamed, knowing the deadly menace that had come to her. She knew, as well, that she had said something, done something, to precipitate what was happening. She knew each step as it occurred, the figure appearing, the fear, the terrible understanding of what was to come. She felt the violence as he came upon her, his touch upon her hair first, then her clothing, the blows against her as she resisted. The violation of her flesh, the hands around her throat . . .

Faceless, he was faceless, but she knew him, she had to know him.

Had to know his hands. Around her throat, then his

hands, pressing her down, and she knew she was going to die. She wasn't sure how . . . Would the hands so powerful against her flesh crush the life from her, or was this only to subdue her? Would there be a knife blade, a pressing against her throat, creating a rich spill of blood . . . ?

Whichever, it was coming, and she knew that it was coming, and she still couldn't see his face, only the darkness, and she was suddenly certain of a welling of sound, soft and low and underlying the chilling shrill of her screams, a sound of chanting, voices, many voices . . .

Whispers, laughter.

Eerie laughter, evil laugher . . .

She screamed louder, fought more wildly, desperate now not just to save her life, but to still the cackling sounds that seemed to enter her very soul, wrapping around it, crushing the life from it, as the hands upon her seemed to be doing with flesh.

She kicked, tried so hard to keep screaming, but she had no breath, no sound could come, no air could come . . .

Only the pulse, the thunder of her heart.

Fight, fight . . . even as a darkness deeper than night fell before her eyes. *Kick, scratch, fight . . . claw at the hands* . . .

The hands . . . that slipped as she dug her nails hard . . .

Screaming, still, the sound of screaming . . .

"Megan! Jesus, stop! Megan!"

Hands, again, on her shoulders, shaking her. She struck out, hard, desperately.

"Megan! Damn! Megan, wake up!"

She awoke, stunned, still hearing distant screams, but they were coming from her.

"Megan!"

Finn straddled over her then. His right hand was vised around her wrists; he was rubbing his jaw with his left. He stared down at her, his eyes as brilliant as twin knife blades, his face ashen.

"Megan! What the hell is the matter with you?"

Abruptly, her screaming stopped.

She was drawn from the incredible reality of the world she had entered in her sleep to the true reality of life. And in real life, she was in a quiet bed and breakfast in a quiet, historical town that only went a bit crazy during the month of October.

"Finn! Oh, my God, Finn!"

She tried to pull her arms free.

"Are you going to sock me in the jaw again?"

"I didn't!"

"You did."

"I'm so sorry . . . please!"

He eased his hold. She reached up, curled her arms around his neck, shaking, nearly sobbing.

A dream. It had been nothing but a dream.

He didn't push her away, but his shoulders were as stiff as boards. When she drew back, the look in his narrowed green eyes was wary, distant, and accusing.

"Megan, Jesus Christ, what the hell was that all about?"

"I had the most awful nightmare."

"A nightmare—and you had to scream like a thousand hounds were after you, here, now!"

He was interrupted by a hard banging on the door.

She bit her lower lip, wincing. Finn jumped up and reached for the terry bathrobe she had discarded before bed that lay upon the floor by their side.

He opened the door. From the darkness of the room, Megan could see the dimly lit hallway. Mr. Fallon, the groundskeeper and jack-of-all-trades at Huntington House, stood grimly in the doorway.

"What goes on here, Mr. Douglas?" he demanded sternly.

"I'm so sorry. It seems that Megan has had a nightmare," Finn explained.

Mr. Fallon gave Finn an up and down glare that implied he didn't believe a word of it. In fact, it looked as if he were about to call the police, and see that Finn was charged with some form of domestic violence.

"Sounded like a bloody murder!" Fallon said.

Megan couldn't just hop up and explain herself. She was naked. She called out weakly from the bed. "I'm fine, Mr. Fallon, really. I just had a horrible nightmare. I'm so, so sorry!"

"Well, then, it's a good thing you're in this wing of the house," Fallon said brusquely. "You'd be waking up the whole household, with such caterwaulin'! Do you have these nightmares often, young lady?"

"No, no . . . of course, not!" Megan called.

"As you can see," Finn told Fallon irritably, "everything is perfectly all right in here."

"Actually, young man, there's not all that much I can see—since it's so darned dark and all. But we don't take kindly to folks fighting around here—not in Huntington House. We're a fine establishment with a good reputation."

"Of course," Finn said.

"The Merrills have a reputation in these parts, too," he said, referring to Megan's family.

She wasn't sure if the reputation her family had garnered was good or bad.

"I'm honestly sorry, Mr. Fallon. There were too many tales filling my head when I fell asleep, I believe."

"Humph!"

"I had a nightmare," Megan said, her tone quiet but firm. She thought she resented Mr. Fallon. She was suddenly certain he didn't think much of the Merrill family at all.

"See that you keep it down," Fallon said. "There can be no more such outbursts—sir!" He had started speaking to Megan; he ended with a word of warning for Finn.

"Good night," Finn said.

Fallon nodded, and moved off. Reluctantly, so it seemed.

Finn closed the door. Darkness descended with the night-lights gone from the hall. But a second later the room was flooded with light as Finn hit the switch at the side of the door. He leaned against the door, crossing his arms over his chest, staring at Megan.

"He thinks I was beating you."

"Oh, Finn, surely not—"

"Everyone knows we've just gotten back together."

"Don't be ridiculous. Fallon doesn't know a thing about us."

"Well, he seems to know all about your family, and therefore, he probably knows we've just gotten together, and he surely thinks you made a major mistake and that I was about to slit your throat before he arrived."

"Finn, stop it. Surely, somewhere in his life, sometime before, someone has woken up from a nightmare, screaming."

"You think? I've never woken up before next to a woman screaming loudly enough to burst my eardrums."

"Dammit, Finn, I've said I'm sorry! I didn't do it on purpose! I had a dream, a really terrible nightmare. Someone was going to kill me!" she said, surprised to feel a hint of the fear rising within her again, as if it would choke off her speech. "In fact, a little sympathy would be in order."

He stood, still distant, staring at her for a long moment. Even the way he looked now, far too tall for the terry bathrobe, legs seeming impossibly long and honed beneath the white hem, she loved him so much. From his tousled dark hair to his bare feet. Things were so tenuous between them, now. Before . . . once, before, she would have flown from the bed and into his arms. But only a month had passed since they'd been back together, a month since he'd driven up the East Coast to Maine, come to her folks' house, and laid everything on the line.

"Finn!" she said, still shaky, and growing angry herself.

"Excuse me, you nearly dislocated my jaw, Megan."

"Why can't you understand? I was deeply sleeping. I had a nightmare. A really terrifying nightmare."

A muscle twitched in his cheek. Hair wild, arms folded over his chest, wearing the ridiculous robe, he was both imposing and appealing. He had a great face. Not too pretty. Classical, masculine structure, strong chin line, solid, defined cheekbones, fine, full mouth, dead straight, aristocratic nose. Not small, not too prominent. Deep green eyes set beneath a broad brow, rich dark hair. He was a natural athlete, thus in good shape no matter what his situation in life. Now, though, they were in the cool autumn of October in Massachusetts, they had just come from a week in the Florida Keys, and he was solidly bronzed and sleek, and ever more appealing.

She turned, lying back on her pillow, facing away from him.

A moment later, he was at her side.

She felt his fingers feather down her back. "All right, Megan, I'm sorry."

"I imagine it was the fireside tales," she murmured, still resentful, but not wanting the argument to go on.

Wrong thing to say. "You're from here!" he said with something that sounded like a snort. "You're the one with family around here. And you were frightened by stories about Salem?"

"They were different stories, not really about Salem, and certainly not in the historical sense," she said.

"Oh, right, let's see, All Hallow's Eve is coming, and

evil is something that grows, that feeds on the atmosphere, and clings to the places where man's cruelty to man has been strong? Get serious, Megan, consider history, and that would be almost anyplace on earth."

"Of course, you're right," she said stiffly.

"Ah, but then, a full moon will be rising. And the fog and the mist will swirl, and there are those living today who believe in the dark powers, who mean to raise the dead from their unhallowed graves, and set dark winds of evil free to haunt the world."

She sat up, suddenly feeling defensive. "Finn, contemporary Salem is a lovely place peopled by those who scoff at witchcraft, and those who believe in their pursuit of Wicca as a real religion, those who have darling shops and make a nice income off history, and those who run great restaurants and couldn't really care less. And yes, sadly, the victims of the persecution here were surely innocent of the crimes attributed to them, but do you know what? There always were—and perhaps still are—those who believed in witchcraft, or not witchcraft, Satanism, or whatever you want to call it, and they do bad things in their belief. Damn, Finn—think about it! Are there still bad people out there? Wow. Yeah, I think so. So I listened to stories about the evil in men's hearts, in their beliefs in the powers of darkness and things that go bump in the night, and I had a bad dream. That's not so bizarre, or unforgivable."

He laid back down, fingers laced behind his head. "And you have a cousin who operates a witchcraft shop."

"There's nothing evil about Morwenna."

"I didn't say there was."

"It isn't illegal to be a Wiccan now. It was illegal to practice any form of witchcraft in the sixteen hundreds."

"Right."

"Morwenna believes in earth and nature, and in

doing good things to and for people, especially because any evil thought or deed is supposed to come back at a Wiccan threefold."

"And her freaking tall, dark, and eerie palm-reading husband, Joseph, is a fucking pillar of the community?" he said sarcastically.

"Why are we fighting about my cousin and her husband?" she asked a little desperately.

"Because I'm starting to think it was a major mistake to come here," he said.

"You wanted to come," she reminded him curtly. "This was a good move for your career."

"I didn't think you'd come home and turn into a screaming harpy."

She turned her back on him once again, hurt more than she could begin to say. *A mistake? Had it all been a mistake?*

From the moment she had first seen Finn, her first day of college, she had begun falling for him. She'd never wanted someone so badly in her life. She had just about chased him shamelessly, but it had been all right, because he had returned her mad obsession. In a matter of days, she'd just about lost all thought of her classes, eager, anxious, desperate, to be with him at any given time. They'd eluded their friends time and time again to spend their precious hours together. At first, there had been no arguments—in truth, they hadn't talked enough to argue, they'd wanted nothing more than to touch, to be in one another's arms, naked, making love. The unfailing flame of simple chemistry had been so strong that they'd defied all advice and married one weekend, standing before friends and the priest in a small town in southern Georgia. For a few years, they had lived in the bliss of the young and innocent. Finn had graduated, and scholarships and student work programs had ended. Megan had another two years to go. Finances grew tight and music equipment was expensive. They'd begun to struggle. There were arguments about what made money, what didn't, what was good, what wasn't. The differences between them which had at first seemed so charming became points of friction. She had hunches and intuitions; he was entirely pragmatic. She was from Massachusetts, and other than her initial, abandoned adoration for him, she tended to a New Englander's reserve. Finn was from the Deep South, ready to plow into any situation and offer anything they had to anyone. She'd always been a good daughter and student, he'd been a bad boy at times, suspended for fighting now and then in high school, barely squeaking into college with a music scholarship just because he'd had such a natural talent. She was close to her parents; his were divorced and remarried. He made dutiful calls once a month, and sent cards and presents to his little half siblings, but they seldom visited either of his parents. Finn loathed his stepfather, barely tolerated his stepmother, and had been on his own from the day he had graduated from high school. Then his father died of a heart attack, and he was torn between resentment that he hadn't even been remembered in the will, and guilt that he hadn't made more of an effort to communicate despite his unease about his stepmother. He'd started spending long hours out when Megan thought he should have needed her most. He took more and more out of town work. Jealousy, doubt, mistrust . . . the little enemies that form together to tear down a relationship began to flourish and grow. Then, slowly, little shadows of doubt and anger began, and then, for Megan, the final, agonizing, hateful straw, the flutist Finn brought into the band they had formed when they weren't working together as a duo. She didn't leave right away; she was still too desperately in love. And arguments were too easily solved because anger was such a vivid emotion, and fights too easily solved by giving into the heat and adrenaline of the moment, falling back into bed, and rising later to discover that nothing had been solved. At last, the doubts moved in too deeply, and she had no intention of losing all self-respect for herself, or letting her own hopes for a fulfilling career become crushed by standing in the background, giving way completely. They'd had a fight in which she'd gotten mad and hit him in the head with a loaf of bread. They'd fought on the balcony; neighbors had seen them. The bread had become a wine bottle in the retelling, and in some stories, she'd beaten Finn, in others, he'd beaten her. Rumors had spread. He'd been furious with the things said about him, more concerned with rumor than with her, and so, she had left.

But there was really no way to leave Finn behind completely. She had always loved the look of him, the feel of him, the deep quality of his voice, the sound of his laughter. The scent of him. Her folks had been living in Maine at the time, and she'd gone home, and taken work with an old friend who was a guitarist, singing light rock and folk music at a coffee shop. The pay hadn't been great, but the hours and perks had been wonderful—great coffee, good food, and time to work on the songwriting that was her true love and passion in life—as far as her career went. Living with her parents wasn't difficult, their home in Maine was huge, and she had an entire wing of the place to herself—a carriage house that had been beautifully remodeled into an apartment.

She had been away for six months, wondering whether or not to sign the divorce papers, when he had shown up. And when they had come together then, he had been passionate, and honest, forgetting pride completely. There had never been anything between him and the flutist, any other musician, or any other woman, period. He couldn't live without her, and he wanted her back.

She could have melted on the spot, and in her way, she did, throwing herself into his arms, practically sobbing, ready to strip him then and there. And since then, they had talked, about everything, and she felt both secure and cherished. They'd gone back to New Orleans, and she had never been more certain about a decision in her life. She loved Finn; she would forever.

Still, she wished she hadn't screamed here, in Salem. Despite their deep commitment, the bread episode was still there, back burner. Forgiven by both of them, and yet, a memory that was not comfortable.

It was amazing that a rumor had come so far, all the way to Massachusetts. Here, where she was known, as well as her family.

She hadn't actually grown up in Salem, but in close-by Marblehead. And though she was able to see many members of her extended family, they hadn't come for that reason. Finn had come home one day to tell her he'd received a really top quality financial offer to entertain at a hotel in Salem for the entire week before Halloween. A man named Sam Tartan, head of entertainment and community relations for the new hotel, had read an article about them, and had thought they'd be perfect. Finn had been a little skeptical at first, wanting to make sure they hadn't received the offer because Megan's family had pulled strings.

They hadn't. Neither of her parents had ever heard of Sam Tartan. When she'd made an anonymous phone call, she'd learned that the hotel entertainment exec hailed from somewhere in the Midwest.

The money was truly impressive; the prestige of being offered such a solo gig was equally persuasive. With a fair amount of excitement, they had accepted the offer.

First, they were going on a vacation, taking the honeymoon they'd never had before, and spending time in Florida. Sunny Florida, and then spooky old Salem.

While they were gone, the workmen could do some of the necessary repairs on their home in the French Quarter, and it would all be perfect. Perhaps Finn hadn't realized just how far rumors had gone, and that her family members would all stare at him, wondering if he was a wife beater, if Megan shouldn't have stayed as far away from him as she could.

She turned, wanting then to make amends, wishing she'd never touched that loaf of bread.

To her surprise, he was no longer lying awake. His eyes were closed, lips slightly parted, and he was breathing deeply and evenly.

"Finn?"

He didn't answer.

Megan slipped out of bed, frowning, but he still didn't awaken. She walked over to the big, overstuffed antique chair by the fireplace and found her terry robe, wrapping it tightly around her. She pulled back the draperies to the balcony door, hesitated, then slipped out.

October in Massachusetts. A cool breeze was softly moving, but it wasn't uncomfortably cold outside. The sky was beautiful and strange, a deep blue, almost black in places, and light, almost ethereal in others. As she looked down at the street below, she saw a whirl of fog, and she found herself remembering the words of the crusty old storyteller who had been at the fireside tale-telling earlier in town.

Ah, but though those caught, hanged, and pressed to death, as old Giles Corey, were most probably true innocents, those earlier guardians of justice might not have been so foolish in their fears of evil, though they were daft in their methods of discovery. Think my friends, when there is goodness, there must be evil, and evil is rooted in the very history of mankind. Throughout the years there have been stories of man, and of beasts, and of those creatures who fall somewhere in between them. As there have been angels, there have been devils. There is the Good Book, and there are works of the greatest demonic frenzy, and there have always been, as there are now, those who seek the secrets of the Devil, of imps and demons from beyond, of the savage beings we remember only in the deepest, darkest, recesses of our hearts. It's said, you know, that All Hallow's Eve is the night when the dead may rise . . . especially if they are so bidden, if, perhaps, they are called from the fires of hell to walk upon the earth once again, and inhabit the lives and souls of man.

A log had fallen in the fire then; half the old man's audience had jumped and cried out, and then laughed. Megan had done so herself. She hadn't imagined that she would come back to their rented room, dream of evil, and scream in the night.

The fog below appeared to be blue. It seemed to spiral, puff, curl, and move like some living thing itself.

She wasn't afraid of fog . . .

She felt the lightest touch against her nape. Fingers, lifting her hair, softly, gently. She closed her eyes and smiled.

Finn had awakened. He was behind her.

That was his ritual. He would come to her. Stand in silence. Touch her hair, lift her hair, press his lips against the flesh of her nape. She felt him touch her, then. The hot moisture of his lips, the warm, arousing moisture of his breath. In seconds, his arms would come around her. He would tell her that he loved her. And being Finn, he would bring his hips hard against her while he held her, and probably whisper that if she was going to scream, he should see to it that she was screaming for all the right reasons, because the things he could do to her were just so good that she couldn't begin to help herself . . .

She felt his hands, sliding over terry cloth, beneath it, touching her flesh . . .

His touch fell away. She thought she heard him breathing . . . waiting. Waiting for her to turn into his arms, melt into them as she always did.

"Finn . . ."

She spun around, ready to do just that.

He wasn't there.

She was alone on the balcony.

The breeze suddenly turned colder. The eerie blue fog was rising from the street, moving quickly, coming higher, as if it were eager to engulf her.

Chapter 2

There were two other families staying at the bed and breakfast, a thirty-something mother and father with their children, a boy of about twelve and a girl around ten, and a younger couple, late twenties or early thirties, on their own as well. As Finn and Megan walked through the house to the dining room, where breakfast was served, Finn couldn't help but wonder if the others had heard Megan screaming in the night.

They had.

He knew, because as he approached, he heard them all talking. Then, as he and Megan came into the room, all six stared at them for a split second—they were like a tableau, frozen in time. Then—as if on cue—every single one of them stared down into their plates, as if suddenly finding an intense interest in toast, bacon, eggs, or cornflakes.

"They all think I'm a wife beater," he couldn't help whispering to Megan.

"Don't be silly," she said, but they had both frozen for a second as well, and she hadn't spoken with much assurance.

"Ah, well, let's brave it out!" he murmured, squeezing her hand, and giving her a slight wink. He didn't know why he had been so shaken up himself. She'd had a nightmare. His anger had been uncalled for, and today, he was determined to make it up to her. Part of the problem, he knew, was that he really loved Megan. Desperately. He'd thought once that he wasn't going to explain himself, or beg forgiveness for what he'd never done. But he knew differently now. Not that he didn't still believe she should have trusted him; he just understood that doubts and life without really talking could undermine a marriage, tear it apart. And he wasn't going to let it happen again.

"Good morning!" he said cheerfully, and with Megan's hand in his, he approached the large oblong table. Two seats had been left vacant for them, and he pulled out a chair for Megan. She sat, something of an awkward smile on her face.

"Morning," the thirty-something wife said. Finn thought that her husband nudged her leg beneath the table.

Susanna McCarthy, Fallon's female counterpart—as tall, skinny, and dour looking as the man himself—entered with a coffeepot and served them both without a word. "How did you want your eggs?" she asked them, eyeing them as if she were forced to feed escaped convicts.

"Scrambled, please," Megan said.

"Over easy, if you will," Finn told her, determined to smile no matter what. He was also going to break the ice at the table, let them think what they wanted, then. "I'm Finn, and this is my wife Megan," he announced to the table. "Weren't all of you at the hotel storytelling down at the square last night, too? Saw you all in the lobby here, briefly, but I think we're following a lot of the same events, as well."

There was a brief silence, then the twenty-something

man spoke up. "I'm John, and this is my wife, Sally, and yes, we were at the storytelling thing last night, too."

Sally, a pretty little thing with blond hair down her back, spoke up, "Yes, and was he something! I must have jumped cleanly out of my chair at one point."

"He was great!" the little boy said, speaking up. "Great! Some of the stuff is just hokey, like if you go to some of the haunted houses. But he was great."

"Very scary," Megan agreed, smiling at him. She had a nice way with kids. She really looked into their eyes, paid attention when they were speaking. Finn didn't doubt that, one day, when they had their own, she was going to be a wonderful parent. He wished he was as sure about himself.

"Hey!" the boy said. "I can tell you what to do and what not to do, if you don't want to hit the hokey stuff," he said.

"Joshua!" his mother said sternly. "Maybe they want to discover the places on their own." She looked at her son as she spoke, then looked over at Finn and Megan as if she had to, but wasn't necessarily happy about it.

"We'd certainly love to hear his suggestions," Megan said sincerely.

"But you're from here, aren't you?" the father said, looking at her.

"From the area, yes," Megan admitted. "But when I was young, most of this wasn't even here yet. A lot of them are fairly new businesses."

It was then that Joshua's little sister, a cute little redhead with a smattering of freckles, spoke up. "That's right! Mr. Fallon said that your family goes way back here! So, if you know all about the ghosts and stuff, why were you screaming last night?"

"Ellie!" her father said, aghast.

Megan laughed, and the sound was light and real and had the charm that her laughter always did. "Ellie, just because I know about some of the stories already doesn't mean that they can't still scare me. In fact, you and your brother were certainly very brave, because I came back here, went fast asleep, and then had the worst nightmare you could ever imagine!" She looked at the parents of the two with apology. "I'm so sorry, I guess I did wake everyone up." She shook her head. "I just had a terrible, terrible dream."

She must have been believed, because the father seemed to relent at last. "Hey, we were woken up by peacocks at the last place we stayed. I'm Brad Elgin."

"And I'm Mary," his wife said.

"And I'm—"

"You're Joshua, and you're Ellie," Megan finished. "And it's very nice to meet you, and please, even though I am from these parts, they change a bit every year. Finn and I are always up for suggestions. And my husband hasn't been here before. Ever! So, he may want to trust your judgment, just in case mine is a little tainted at times."

"Well, actually, I've been *through* here once," Finn said, glancing at Megan. "I got it into my head to drive up alone from New Orleans to Maine, and I'd never done it before. I wound up taking a few wrong turns off the highway, so I have had lunch in the center of town."

Megan grinned at him. Usually, he had a great sense of direction. She'd found it amusing that he'd gotten lost in New England, and sweet, as well, since he'd been on his way to find her.

Susanna came back in then, not saying a word as she set down their plates of eggs, bacon, and toast. She didn't even respond when Finn thanked her. She was halfway back out the door before she paused to say, "Cereal and such is on the buffet table."

There was silence for a moment again after she left.

"Well, you've just got to take your husband to the museum right by the Conant statue—that one is the best so far," Sally said, cheerfully taking up right where they had left off. "We were all just agreeing on that when you two came in."

"Right," John agreed, squeezing her fingers where they lay on the table. "And Brad, you were saying that the kids really enjoyed the Pilgrim village."

"Yeah, it was cool, too!" Joshua said. "And you know what? It's kind of easy, once you're here, to see why New Englanders are supposed to be so messed up."

"Joshua!" his mother moaned.

"No, no, sorry!" he said, realizing that, of course, Megan was a New Englander. "The Pilgrims . . . Puritans, they couldn't do anything! They couldn't sing or dance or have fun or act normal in any way at all! Look at the people who wound up dead because of some old stories told by that woman. I mean, really, a bunch of people got hanged because they were all so hung up and silly. It was more than four hundred years ago, but you're going to have people come out—what did you call it, Mom, *reserved?*—when they're ancestors were that messed up!"

"Joshua," Mary moaned. "The lady here is a New Englander."

"Yes, but she can't be all messed up and *reserved*, not if she had a nightmare like that and explained it to us!"

Mary looked mortified, red as a beet.

Finn's eggs had been pretty good, despite their dour server. They suddenly seemed cold.

"New Englanders can be very reserved," Megan said, smiling. "And, hey, by the way, Gallows Hill, where they believe the people convicted were executed, is here, and the judge, Hathorne, has his grave at the Burial Point, and there are a number of other locations as well, but the people involved weren't just from what we call Salem now. There was a Salem Town, and a Salem Village, but the area that used to be the village has different names now, such as Danvers. You can drive out there and see the Rebecca Nurse place, the home of one of the most pathetic victims of all. The writer, Nathaniel Hawthorne, put that W in his name to distance himself from his ancestor."

"You do know a lot about this place!" Joshua said, relishing his new discovery.

"Well, Marblehead is a little bit from here, too. My mom's sister lived here for a long time, and my cousin and a few others are still here. But I went to school in the South where I met my husband, and Finn and I live in New Orleans now, and trust me, we're not very reserved down there."

"No!" Ellie said, freckled face split in a big grin. "They're wild in New Orleans. Dad says so—we can't go there because it's a big den of . . . big den of iniq— iniq—"

"Iniquity?" Finn suggested, amused himself.

"For children!" Mary said quickly.

"Hey, the city has its reputation," Finn said. "But it's kind of like anywhere else—good things, and bad things. We have some of the finest music in the country. And granted, some entertainment that's only for adults, and certain adults, at that. There's a lot that's fine in New Orleans, too, and a lot of really great people. You learn in life, anywhere, to watch out for things that are bad."

"And people who are bad!" Ellie announced gravely.

"Exactly," Finn said, looking at the child, and wondering if her parents had already warned her that Finn might be a bad man—a wife beater.

"So—is this your first trip here?" Megan asked, glancing around the table so that her question was for anyone who chose to answer.

"First time, and I love it!" Sally said cheerfully.

"First time for us, too." Mary said.

"We're from Chicago," John told them. "Sally and I both."

"Great city," Finn commented, drawing a smile from them both.

"Brad is from Santa Fe," Mary said. "But I'm originally a Southerner, too. Montgomery, Alabama."

"Definitely a good Southern town, progressive these days," Megan said.

"So Megan is the only New Englander," Joshua said. "That's neat, really neat!"

A slow, rueful grin crept into Megan's lips. "And apparently, we can't be all that reserved, because someone told you that before we officially met, hmm?"

Even Joshua himself blushed at that.

"Naturally, we were all concerned about the screaming, and we had to ask," his father said, his tone somewhat stiff, and, it seemed to Finn, his eyes still carrying something of an accusation.

"And you've got lots of family here!" Ellie burst out. "You've got a witch for a cousin!"

"Wiccan," Megan murmured.

"You'll find all kinds of people here who are Wiccan," Finn said. He wondered why he was jumping in so defensively. He thought it was all kind of ridiculous himself. Not that he was a steadfast believer in organized religion himself, but his concept was in a traditional god, and he believed in most of the Christian tenets of life. He firmly believed that most of the practicing Wiccans were in it for the fun and money—hard to survive off a witch shop when you weren't a Wiccan.

"It's just a different way of believing," Megan explained. "You know that there are Christians, Jews, Muslims, Hindus and more in the world, right? Well, Wiccans are the same."

Ellie's father sniffed.

"You're one of them?" he asked Megan.

She shook her head. "Catholic," she told him.

For Megan, it was true. Finn went to church with her now and then, but she went far more often than he did.

He wasn't sure that Brad approved of Catholics any more than he did Wiccans, but it was his wife that broke in with, "That's one of the great things about our country, son. People are free to believe in whatever they choose."

"Even if it is all rather silly," Mary told her children.

"But the Wiccan religion isn't about evil," Megan said. "Honestly—it's more of a religion in which people honor the earth. I don't know all that much about it, but a true Wiccan would never do evil, their spells are only for good things. In their way of thinking, if you do evil to others, evil comes back to you."

"I want to have my palm read by a witch!" Joshua said.

"No!" his mother said sternly.

If it was all so silly in their minds, why such a vehement refusal? Finn wondered.

"Well, we're off," John said, rising. Sally stood along with her husband. "We're not doing the witch thing at all today—were off to the Mariner's Museum."

"And we're off to see the House of the Seven Gables today," Joshua told them.

Finn wiggled his brows. "We're off to see the Wiccan—Megan's family," he told him with a wink. "But don't worry—thanks to you, young man, we'll know to avoid the hokey stuff, right Megan?"

Brad and Mary were rising as well, and the kids stood along with their parents. "Well, have a good day," Mary said.

"Thanks, we will," Megan said. "You, too."

"We'll get to the House of the Seven Gables eventually, too," Finn told the kids. "There's a tremendous literary history here in Salem, too."

"Yeah . . . I guess we'll have to read," Joshua said a little remorsefully.

"When you read, you learn great stories," Finn said.

"Yeah, I guess."

Mary flashed him a smile, and filed out behind her husband and kids. With John and Sally gone as well, Finn and Megan were alone. She looked a little distressed.

He offered her his deepest smile. "All right, so they all think we're both weird. I'm a wife beater, and you're a witch by association. Hey, it's kind of fun."

She still appeared distraught, deep blue eyes dark, slender face, with it's perfectly chiseled beauty, drawn. "Finn, I'm so sorry—"

"Quit being sorry. I was the world's biggest asshole last night, and I'm going to make it up to you today. I'm going to be perfectly charming to Morwenna *and* her bizarre husband. I'm not going to crack a joke or sniff at the Wiccans in any way, shape, or form. I'm even going to have my palm read."

"Finn, you don't have to—"

He was surprised at the sudden tension that ripped into him—another feeling of absolute desperation. "I don't have to do anything. I *want* to make a great, fun day for both of us. And I want to get to know your family better, and . . . I love you, Megan. And I'm never going to let anything come between us again. Anything. Nightmares, my own stupid temper, anything. And as long as you love me, too, I don't give a damn what anyone thinks. Right?"

She smiled, slowly, leaned close, and kissed him. A perfect kiss, chaste, just right for the breakfast table. But Megan had the ability just to lightly press her lips against his, and make it the most sensual brush in the world. He felt a strange trembling, so stood awkwardly. "We should get going, too. Whoops, sorry. My eggs weren't so hot. Were you still eating? Didn't mean to rush you."

"No, no, I'm done. Let's get going."

It was as if they were both suddenly desperate to get out of the centuries-old house, and into the sunshine.

They left the breakfast room, which led straight into the main entry, the old foyer with its circular stairway to the floors above. Outside, in the crisp October sunlight, she stopped suddenly. "I love you, too, you know. So much that it scares me!" she said softly.

"Don't ever be afraid of loving me. You are my world," he told her, his words far more passionate than he had intended. He felt strangely awkward, as if he had said too much, even to his wife. "Hey, come on, my palm is just itching to be read. And I'm dressed appropriately, all in black. Hurry, while I'm in the mood to really suck up to your relatives!"

"Okay, I'm hurrying, but we're going to make a stop on the way."

"We're going to stop? Hey, I may run out of suck-up steam."

"No, you won't, because when you have a chance to talk more with Morwenna and Joseph than you did at our wedding, you're going to like both of them."

Finn didn't reply for a moment as he walked by her side. He didn't think she was right. He wasn't sure what color Morwenna's hair was supposed to be, but not the raven black she had it colored. And she continually wore black. Complete black. Joseph was the same. His hair was as long as his wife's; he wore it queued back. He wore black trousers and a black shirt, and a huge silver pentagram, at all times.

He wondered what the two would wear to the beach. If they ever went to a beach.

"Where did you want to stop?" he asked.

"The Salem Witch Museum. The boy, Joshua, was right. It takes about twenty minutes, and is the probably the best, most concise way, of getting an overview of what happened during the frenzy in 1692. You'll enjoy it, really."

"Lead on," he told her.

"There are more places we have to go, of course. The

Peabody Essex Museum is incredible. There's so much in there that's just about American lifestyles through the centuries. Lots of the historical buildings actually belong to the museum now. Sometime, we'll have to get to the House of the Seven Gables. It's a wonderful area, really, and a lot of what is historical is all within walking distance. Morwenna's shop is down a block or so and around the corner from the Salem Witch Museum, and it's just a block or so from the Peabody Essex Museum. And there are all kinds of little wonderful shops in between. And we can eat lunch at a little place on the water. Actually, I have to admit, I loved it all a lot more when I was growing up. Everything was a little spookier and more historical. Now, there's a fair amount of what's commercial going on."

"Then, of course, there has to be a bit of those who were just born here, have the good old New England reserve and stamina, and just grew up without finding the world spins on the history and witches—real and imagined—in Salem."

She glanced at him sharply.

"Hey! I'm just saying I'll bet there are a lot of normal people here just living their lives."

"Well, of course. It's just a town, a charming town."

"A beautiful town," he agreed.

And it was. October. A lot of the leaves had already fallen. No snow yet. The temperature was chill but not at all painfully cold. The colors of fall were everywhere, some of the leaves still on the trees, glorious in shades of orange and gold and amber. The town—whether they all believed in witchcraft or not—went all out with pumpkins, jack-o'-lanterns, scarecrows, and decorations. By day, they were light and airy—fun. But it seemed that every house they walked by had something going on—Wal-Mart ghosts hanging from their trees, a pumpkin patch by an old elm, skeletons flying from the porch eaves, bats . . . and at a few houses, the old green witches on broomsticks slammed against a tree, as if they'd run into it. Cute. Harmless.

"Morwenna hates those," Megan commented as they walked by one of the latter.

"Ah, come on, they're cute. Don't Wiccans have a sense of humor?"

"Well, sometimes. But I guess they feel that the old crone concept—warty noses, green flesh, broomsticks, all that—contributes to the idea of evil. And if you follow the concepts of Wicca—"

"Whether you follow the concepts or not, witchcraft is associated with Satanism, and Satanism has had a bunch of what you might want to call really, truly evil people over the centuries."

Megan shrugged. "There—that's the statue of Conant in front of us. The founder of Salem. And the museum is just ahead, on our right."

They had reached the center of the historic district. He'd noted the statue the night before, and remembered asking her something about the old Gothic building next to it and her saying that it was one of the area's best tableaus.

He thought that they were heading right in, but Megan suddenly placed a hand on his arm. "Look, Finn! Someone has a Great Dane at the park!"

Megan was a sucker for dogs—the bigger the better. But he suddenly felt as if a breath of fresh air rushed by them. Looking across the street at the common, he saw that a number of people were out, walking dogs. A few other kids were throwing a ball around; two young women were jogging together.

"Well, let's go see the Great Dane," he said lightly.

She flashed him a smile. They joined a throng of tourists crossing the street to the large, spacious common. People around them were laughing. A woman strolled a toddler in a cherry-pink carriage. The world seemed pleasant. And *normal.* It was a town, just a town, like any other. Taking revenge upon the evil of the past by making big bucks on tourism.

"Hey, is he friendly?" he called out as they reached the park, to the young man or older teen who was walking the animal.

"She's a total sweetheart!" the youth called back, grinning. Finn, with Megan at his side, approached. Despite the Dane's mammoth size, they both hunkered down. The huge dog immediately licked them both. She was so friendly that she knocked Megan over in her enthusiasm. The kid started to apologize, and Megan laughed, waving a hand in the air, accepting Finn's hand to come back to her knees to better get to know the dog.

"Lizzie doesn't know her own strength," the kid said. He extended a hand to Finn. "Hi. I'm Darren Menteith. And this, of course, is Lizzie."

"Nice to meet you. Finn Douglas. My wife, the incredible dog lover, Megan."

"Finn. And Megan. Are you playing here, at the hall?"

"Yes, that's us," Finn answered. Megan was busy telling the dog how beautiful she was.

"Wow! Wicked!" Darren said.

"Wicked?"

Megan, still cuddling the dog's massive head, laughed. "Wicked. It's an expression, Finn. It means good."

"Oh, yeah, exactly," Darren said. "You know, wicked. Like a girl can be wicked good-looking. You can have a wicked good time. You know?"

"Sorry, I'm from the South. Deep South. Haven't heard the expression before."

"Hey, man, come on, you must travel!"

"Oh, yeah, we travel, but sorry . . . just haven't heard it before."

"That's okay. Let me say then, wow, rad! I have some of your CDs."

Finn arched a brow. He had been getting something of a name, but still, his CDs were available through some of the major Internet chains, but he hadn't heard that he was garnering that much of a following. They did well with their music where they played, but so far, live appearances had been their major selling point.

"Well, thanks. That's great. I appreciate it."

"We've got a new one with us," Megan said, balancing back to her feet. "We'd be happy to give you one."

"Super. I've been planning to come to at least three of the nights you're playing. Starting tonight." He shrugged. "I'm in college here—didn't go too far out of the hometown after high school, I'm afraid. Thought I'd get the basic stuff out of the way, first."

"Sound plan," Finn said. That made Darren about nineteen or twenty, a little older than he had estimated. He had a pleasant face, bright green eyes, and a dead short haircut, almost a buzz. He was wearing a white sweatshirt with a surf logo and plain old blue jeans. Finn decided he liked him a lot.

"So—you're from here."

"Down the street," he admitted sheepishly.

"Megan's from Marblehead," Finn said.

"Hey, I know, I read up on the musicians I like," Darren said.

Megan grinned at him. "How old is Lizzie?"

"Seven."

"Ah."

"Yeah, I know. Danes don't usually have a very long life span. Seven is it for a lot of them. Their hearts can't take their size. But I'm willing to bet old Lizzie has a few more years. I take care of her. Give her the right stuff."

"I'm sure you do. And she is really beautiful," Megan said. She sighed. "I guess we'd better get going. We're not really here that long this trip . . . and I want to show Finn a number of places."

"Sure. Hey, don't let all the witchcraft stuff get to

you—it's Halloween, and you're going to be inundated," Darren advised Finn.

Finn nodded. Darren gave them a wave and started off with Lizzie. "Isn't she great!" Megan said.

He hugged her. "Magnificent. And we still can't get a dog yet. Not until we make enough to pay a good dog-sitter when we're traveling."

Her eyes were bright and beautiful. "That won't be long. Hey, can you believe it! A college kid in a small town has your CDs!"

"Our CDs. Okay, not a bad morning. Good for the ego. Let's see your museum."

It was a good morning. Tourists everywhere. The word *normal* fell back into his mind again.

The place was definitely jumping. They were the last two admitted to the next showing of the tableau, and as Megan had said, the production was excellent. The recorded voice of the narrator explained the medieval concept of the devil, and how people came to believe in the existence of the devil—and of witches. As he spoke, different tableaus were lighted. The events occurring in Salem in 1692 were then set out, with possible explanations being given. The darkness of the landscape, the depression of severe winter, and that of the lifestyle led by the Puritans were made tangible, and it was easy to see how children, desperate for some form of play, had begun to believe in the tales they were told by the Caribbean slave woman, Tituba. Then, the parents of the children, and others in the village, men of God, began to believe as well. The doctors could find no physical reason for the torment the girls truly seemed to be suffering. Therefore, by the beliefs of the day, it had to be witchcraft.

First, an old deaf woman, Rebecca Nurse, was accused, and nearly dismissed—she had been a good, churchgoing woman. But when she was nearly let free, the girls began to scream and howl in anguish again, and she found herself condemned. Others followed her to the wretched jails. A local man, John Proctor, protested. "The girls will make devils of us all!" he was reputed to have said. And soon, he was accused himself. A plateau of the gallows was later illuminated. A one-time minister said the Lord's Prayer perfectly—a sure sign of innocence, supposedly. But his words were ignored, and the murmuring crowd was shushed. The Devil had helped his henchman, and justice would be served. In all, nineteen were hanged, and old Giles Corey was pressed to death. Justice there, maybe, Finn thought, since Corey had stood as a witness against his own wife when she had been accused.

Years later, one of the girls recanted, her words read by a minister of the church. The craze was over. Witches had gone to trial before in the colonies, and they would go to trial again. But the insanity that had seized this little part of Massachusetts was over.

The lights came up. Finn realized that he'd been squeezing his wife's hand throughout the presentation.

She grinned up at him. "Good, huh? And sad, really sad."

"Very," he said softly.

They exited through the gift shop, pausing to look at a few books, T-shirts, and other memorabilia. As they studied some titles and Finn tried to decide what book to buy that would give him a good overview of the area, a man approached them.

"Megan?"

She turned around, frowning, apparently not recognizing the man who had tentatively spoken her name.

He was twenty-five to thirty, nicely dressed in a tailored suit and suede jacket. His sandy hair was a little shorter than Finn's, and had the look of being run through absently and often with his fingers. Good-looking face, all well-spaced angles, dark brown eyes. Medium tall.

"Mike?" Megan said cautiously.

The man smiled. Dimples creased in his cheeks, taking away the somewhat severe look of the academic the man had.

"Yeah, it's me." He caught both her hands, kissed her cheeks.

"It's great to see you," Megan said. "What are you doing here—well, obviously, you still live in the area."

"Grounded in the home haunting grounds, I'm afraid," he said ruefully. "But you—I haven't seen you in years! Have you moved back?"

"No, I'm living in New Orleans now." She turned then, looking at Finn. "I want you to meet an old friend, Mike Smith. Mike, this is my husband, Finn Douglas. We're back playing at the new hotel for Halloween week."

"So you kept up with the music!" Mike Smith said, turning what seemed to Finn to be a too adoring gaze from Megan to acknowledge her introduction. "Hello, Finn. Nice to meet you. And congratulations. You've married the girl of my dreams."

"Thanks," Finn said, shaking hands with the fellow. "Nice to meet you, too." Was it? He was disturbed by the sense of jealousy that took root inside him.

"So what are you doing these days?" Megan asked him.

"Working at the new museum." He glanced at Finn. "A really good museum. No hocus-pocus. This place is great—they do a really good job with the facts. Not all of the 'museums' here do. We're down the street, near the wharf, and cover the founding of the area, the Puritan tradition, and how it was possible for the craze to have gotten started. We also have a huge section on the seafaring days. Come by and see us."

"We definitely will," Megan said.

"We're a little booked for today," Finn reminded her.

Mike Smith waved a hand in the air. "I'll be there all week. I'll give you a behind-the-scenes tour when you come. Just ask for me at the window."

"Thanks," Megan said, and Finn nodded, acknowledging the invitation as well.

"Just stopped by to get a new book that they've gotten in and we haven't," he said with a grimace. "It's great to see you, Megan. And good to meet you, Finn. Congratulations on your marriage, and your music."

"Thanks," Finn murmured.

Mike Smith waved a hand in the air and walked off.

"Old beau?" Finn couldn't help but query.

Megan shook her head, smiling with a little wrinkle of her nose. "Way too academic for me, back then. I wanted to be a wild child. Of course, I wasn't very wild, either, but I suppose I was in my own mind. Mike was a few years older than me in school. Valedictorian and all that. Back then, he had huge, horn-rimmed glasses and his nose in a book all the time. I should have figured he'd wind up in a museum. Or teaching, or creating something in a laboratory, or the like."

The guy was gone. Megan had been so offhand.

Finn dismissed his absurd sense of jealousy.

When they came back out on the street, the beautiful bright blue sky that had graced the morning was gone.

A gray pallor had settled over the town.

"Want lunch now, or later?" Megan asked.

"Let's stop by Morwenna and Joseph's first," he said, wishing his grin didn't seem so forced now.

As they walked the short distance from the museum to the shop, he tried to tell himself again that the streets were still filled with tourists. Mothers, fathers. Children. Laughing. Some of them with costumes on already, though Halloween itself was still days away. Aliens, pirates, and princesses abounded, along with the more ghoulish. Movie theme characters were walking around as well—some sci-fi, others from horror flicks. Still, *normal*, he told himself.

They came down the street, heading for the centuries-old building with a large plaque that read "Spiritual Sustenance." Megan started right in.

Finn was amazed to feel as if a foreboding washed over him. No . . . as if a heaviness had come into the air, so strong that it was hard for him to put one foot in front of the other.

"Finn?" Megan paused, looking back at him.

He stared at his wife. She had never appeared more beautiful—or even angelic. Pure, filled with light, golden hair streaming softly around her shoulders, eyes like blue pools of the ocean.

She had worn black that day, too. A long black sweater-coat kind of a thing over black jeans and a scoop-neck long-sleeved black knit blouse. Both hugged her form. He wanted to keep her from the shop. From whatever evil lay within.

He gave himself a firm mental shake.

"Great window display," he said. He hadn't even looked at it.

"Yeah? Morwenna did major in art for a while," Megan said.

She didn't feel it. Didn't feel the miasma hanging over the shop.

Because it didn't exist. Once, he'd almost lost his wife. And after her nightmare last night, he was just being a horse's ass. He was afraid. He'd spent a few years thinking that he was just too hot, that he wasn't going to bow to what he considered ridiculous fears and suspicions.

And now . . .

He was damned afraid himself.

"Hey, maybe they have some really great gargoyle bookends in here," he forced himself to say cheerfully. Determined, he walked up the steps.

Bits of prayer flew into his mind.

Yeah though I walk through the valley of the shadow of death . . .

Ass! he charged himself. He was walking into a shop! And what the heck was the matter with him? He'd just watched a program on how feelings, suspicions, and spectral visions had sent more than a dozen innocent people to the gallows. *Get a grip, man, it's the twenty-first century, here. No such nonsense allowed.*

Hand in hand, he walked closer to the entry with his wife, a smile glued to his face.

Even from the sidewalk, they could see that the shop was crowded. There was a man—all in black, naturally—sitting on the stairs that led to the upper level of the old place. He was monitoring the amount of people heading in and out of the shop. He rose, about to stop them, then recognized Megan.

"Hey, Megan!" The fellow hugged her. Megan's hand was dragged from his own.

"Jamie!" Megan said, and turned. "Jamie, my husband, Finn. Finn, Jamie Gray. He's worked for Morwenna and Joseph for ages."

"Hey, there," Jamie said. "Good to meet you. Go on in. It's wild in there today. Getting close to Halloween. Tons of gawkers are out."

There was nothing evil or weird about the guy, Finn told himself. Lots of people wore black. He wore black a lot himself. Hell, they played a lot of Celtic music. Black jeans and loose-sleeved, medieval type shirts worked well on stage. That's what all this was, too, of course. Wiccan. They were performers. Living a lifestyle to sell their wares.

"Thanks, we won't stay long," Finn told Jamie.

"You're family—you stay as long as you want."

"Well, we're family, and so we shouldn't get in the way of the paying, tourist-season customers," Finn said. He sounded all right, he thought. Sincere.

He was sincere. He wanted out of the shop as fast as sanely possible.

There were far too many people in the main store area for the space. When they slipped in, Megan was immediately lost to him. He looked around the best he could while being jostled by those anxious to purchase the right little semiprecious gemstones, herbs, oils, books, and curios. The displays were excellent, a rational part of his mind told him. And Morwenna and Joseph knew how to buy for the store. They carried really beautiful pieces, glass and pewter dragons, fairies, and gargoyles. Excellent pieces of sculpture and art. Really fine jewelry, mostly in silver.

"Finn!" He heard Megan calling him from across the store.

He turned. She was trying on a black cloak. It was gorgeous on her. He hated it.

"What do you think?"

"She's incredible!" someone else by her side cried out. It was Joseph. Raven black hair queued back as usual. He was tall. Finn was a solid six-three, and Joseph might have been even taller than he was himself. Lean and hard. He didn't like the guy standing by his wife, admiring her.

For Christ's sake, he was getting paranoid! The guy was her cousin's husband!

Didn't matter. Weird guy. He might be into a ménage à trois. Hell, why not, weird good-looking guy with a weirder, voluptuous wife. And Megan. Beautiful blond Megan, a total contrast to all that black, except for the cloak she is wearing . . .

Don't be a complete asshole! he warned himself firmly before speaking.

"Megan is always gorgeous!" he called back. He excused himself to the woman at his side bemoaning the cost of a pair of earrings and reached his wife's side.

"Finn." Joseph shook his hand. "So—how are you enjoying Salem?"

"It's great," he lied.

Morwenna slipped from behind the counter to join them, despite the long line. Jamie had come in to man the cash register. She looked anxiously at both of them.

"Heard there was a commotion at the B and B," she said. Though she looked at her cousin, Finn was certain there was a note of accusation in her voice and that it was meant for him.

"My God, it is a small town!" Megan said with a sigh. "I had a nightmare and woke up screaming."

"Bizarre," Joseph said, and his single word seemed like an accusation to Finn as well.

"No more scary tales late at night for either of us," Finn forced himself to say lightly. He wasn't going to take offense—at least he wasn't going to let them know he was offended.

"I think I should read your palm," Morwenna told Megan seriously.

"You all are way too busy in here," Megan said, and Finn was glad.

"Jamie has the register, Joseph can watch the store, and hey! We've got a new girl working for us who is great. Actually, she's not so new, we went to high school together. Sara. She'll give Finn a reading while I do yours."

Megan laughed, shrugging, and looking at Finn. "You did say you were going to have a palm reading."

He wanted to protest. No. This was all silly. He had said he was going to do it. Be nice to her weird relatives no matter what. Have a palm reading.

"Sure."

"Call Sara," Morwenna told Joseph.

Sara didn't have to be called. Finn knew that she had to be the woman who emerged from the curtain at the back with another young woman—one with piercings in her brow, her lip, and her nose, who seemed to be mulling over whatever the palm reader had told her as if she had just immersed herself in a serious article in *Time* magazine.

Apparently, some people took their palm readings very seriously.

"See you next week," the pierced princess told Sara.

Then he was somewhat unnerved himself when Sara instantly turned to him, studying him with grave eyes. "You're my next reading?" she queried. She was a small woman, no more than five-foot one or two, with deep, dark, soulful eyes and long brown hair. Though small, she was shapely, like a compact dynamo, except that she didn't seem to move a lot, just to exude some kind of air that spoke of a leashed energy.

"Sara, this is Finn Douglas, my cousin Megan's husband," Morwenna said, in way of introduction. "And, of course, this is Megan. You two haven't met yet."

Sara turned to Megan first, smiling. "Hi. Morwenna talks about you all the time. Nice to meet you."

"A pleasure," Megan murmured.

"And Finn! Hm. Interesting. I must admit, I'll find this an intriguing reading," Sara said.

Finn looked at Megan, trying to control a rueful grimace. "Well, what the heck? I'm all for a reading."

Megan didn't reply with words. He could see the laughter and gratitude in her eyes.

"We're this way," Morwenna told Megan.

Megan wiggled a brow to Finn and followed her cousin through a beaded separator to the back, where, behind the wafting beads, he could see worktables, chairs, and to each side, doors to small little square rooms within the large rectangle of the shop's layout.

"That means we're behind the door to the right," Sara told Finn.

He had a strange feeling of being manipulated and overwhelmed again, but without being completely churlish, he couldn't back out now. And he was angry with himself; it was all ridiculous, and he wasn't going to take any of it seriously. They were in Salem for a week. He could be decent to Megan's relatives for that amount of time. He could listen to people extol the virtues of incense and gemstones. He could let a woman stare at his palm and pretend to see his past, future, and present.

"She's the best," Joseph said lightly, moving back toward the register to help Jamie, since the line of customers eager to pay for their wares was growing larger.

Finn followed Sara. The door to the left was already shut. Sara preceded him through the right doorway. The tiny room was what he had expected. Dark. There was a table, and a chair on either side of it. There was a crystal ball on the table, Tarot cards to the right of it, and a lamp. Sara turned on the lamp. It emitted a small pool of blue light.

"I'll need your palm," she told him.

"Oh. Sure." He extended his palm.

"Intriguing lifeline," she said immediately. He felt a featherlight touch as she ran her forefinger down the length of what must have been his "life" line. He was surely supposed to ask if he could expect a nice long life, but stubbornly, he refused to rise to any such bait.

"Very strange."

"Really? Does that mean long or short?"

"Disrupted," she said distractedly.

"That means I'm dying and coming back?" he queried skeptically.

"Not necessarily. It just means . . . that the regular tenor of what we call life may be disrupted."

"Sorry, I'm not really up on any of this. Now, I'm alive. One day, I'll be dead. There is no in between."

For a moment, she glanced up at him. The strange blue lamplight seemed to put an unearthly glow in her eyes.

"Really?" she said simply.

She shook her head, bending to study his palm again.

"There's a strange jag . . . and then lesser lines. Looks like children . . . but the lines are faded, as if they might just be dreams. There's . . . violence ahead for you. Danger."

"I'm in danger?"

"Maybe . . . or maybe you're the cause of the danger."

It was her words, the blue light, the darkness of the tiny space surrounding them, but he suddenly felt as if the temperature dropped by thirty degrees. He was icy cold. And the hand holding his . . . felt like nothing but a skeletal icicle. He was about to speak when Sara suddenly pushed back from the table. Her eyes rolled back, white orbs against her face, then white orbs washed with the uncanny blue light of the lamp.

"You'll hurt her . . . You'll hurt her. You're dangerous . . . Megan . . . Stay away from Megan. You'll hurt your wife. There's evil. It touches you. You are the evil . . ."

At first, he couldn't move. He just sat there, frozen and paralyzed, as the seer went into her weird, trance-like oracle.

Then he tried to move, and couldn't. He just kept hearing her, like a broken record,

"You . . . evil . . . you'll hurt her . . . I see blood . . . smell blood . . . evil . . . Finn Douglas . . . you're the evil . . . it's your touch . . . she'll die . . . evil, evil, evil, evil, evil . . ."

The words seemed to have a grip on him as powerful as the trance that seemed to have taken over the seer. He felt nothing but cold, and a seeping sense of raw terror.

He fought it.

And anger kicked in.

Fuck this whole place. It was a setup. These people knew that he and Megan had been split up. They'd heard about Megan screaming in the dead of night, and they weren't about to believe it had been a dream, no—they were all just convinced that he was one real bastard, beating his wife.

With a rush of fury and determination, he wrenched his hand free and stood.

The woman immediately seemed to snap out of it—maybe because he almost knocked the table over. She jumped up as well. Staring at him, her eyes rolled back into a normal position, she looked as if she was terrified herself.

"That's bullshit!" he swore.

"What?" Sara gave a good impression of being out of it.

"Look, I don't know what you've heard, or what you think, but I love my wife, and I'd shoot myself in the head before I hurt her."

"I said that you'd hurt your wife?" She sounded truly baffled.

He fought to control his temper. They weren't going to get the best of him.

"You know what you said."

"I don't, but . . . hey, whatever. Yes . . . of course, whatever I said . . . it's just a tale, a story, what might be . . . bullshit!" she said herself. She shook her head strenuously, looking from where he stood to the two inches to the door, as if she wished desperately that he weren't there, blocking it. "Morwenna should give you a reading, not me . . . not me. I'm sorry. I suck, really, I'm new . . . I . . . Let's go out, shall we?"

He turned, nearly slamming open the door.

The scent of incense wafted over him again. There was an Enya CD playing. There was light, pouring in then from the work area.

The cold fell from his shoulders like a discarded cloak. He felt like a fool. He had been scared in that room, really scared. He was an adult male in his prime, in pretty damned good shape, and he'd been scared by the silly words of a little five-foot-two woman in a blue-lit closet.

He turned to her. "Sorry—but you shouldn't do that to clients. No matter what you might have been told."

She gazed at him, then carefully stepped a distance past him. "You know, I'm new here. I don't know anything about you, or Megan, except that she and Morwenna are cousins. I told you, I'm sorry. I'm not . . . never mind. You should go to someone else."

She was irritatingly believable, and he was appearing like a royal idiot. He gritted his teeth, determined to calm down, or else he'd have her thinking the whole Shakespearean thing—*Methinks thou doth protest too much.*

"I don't believe in readings," he said flatly.

"Well, that's good. Good for you."

The door opposite from them opened then. Megan stepped out, laughing at something her cousin had said.

"Perfect timing!" Morwenna said. She smiled deeply. "So how was it, Finn?"

"Great. Just great," Finn said. "And thanks, thanks so much. We can see how busy you are, so we'll get out of your way for now. Please, come tonight, we'll get to spend some time together during the breaks. Meg, you ready? I'm starving, too, you know. My palm has had too much of a workout."

"Absolutely. Morwenna, thanks, and we'll see you all later," Megan agreed. She looked relieved, her eyes thankful as they met Finn's. Great. He'd earned his wife's approval—for being told that he was evil and going to hurt her.

Kill her . . .

He'd die first. It was bullshit. All bullshit.

He caught Megan's hand, lifted his free one in a good-bye salute, and made his way through the milling customers in the shop to the door.

All the way, despite the warmth of his wife's hand,

he felt as if he were touched by a blade of ice. And he knew . . .

The palm reader was watching him. Watching him all the way out of the store.

And beyond.

Chapter 3

Finn held her hand comfortably at her side, and whistled.

"What's wrong?" she asked him.

He glanced down at her as if he were surprised by the question. "Wrong? Nothing."

She shook her head. "You're too cheerful, you know."

"Not at all." He had one of the world's best smiles. Devastating.

"The reading went badly?"

"Megan, you know I don't believe in any of this stuff."

"Well, not many people do believe completely in a reading of any kind. They're just fun."

"I had fun. Barrels of it," Finn said.

He was walking quickly. He was tall and long-legged. She wasn't short herself, but keeping up with him wasn't easy.

"Are we in a hurry?"

"What?"

"You're running."

"I'm just walking . . . Hey, well, we're not here that long, and there's a lot to see, right?"

"We don't have to see it all," she said.

He was silent. She had the feeling he was thinking he should see it all now—because he wasn't coming back.

"What's the pirate museum?"

"A cute place. There's some great maritime history. It only takes a few minutes and it is fun."

"Let's do it."

The pirate museum took about twenty minutes, and it was fun. A figure that appeared to be that of a mannequin jumped out from behind a barrel, startling Megan into a little yelp, and bringing gales of laughter from a number of the children around them. Megan held on to him, laughing, while they went through the rest of the museum, stopped in the gift shop, and took off back onto the street.

It was still just after noon, but the sky was growing suddenly dark with a cast that hinted of the oncoming winter.

"Want to go by and see the new place where Mike is the curator?" Megan asked Finn.

He hesitated. "Let's save that for tomorrow."

"Sure."

"Hungry yet?" Finn asked.

"Getting there," she said agreeably. He had changed again since they had done the pirate museum. He was more like his usual self. He wasn't holding her hand, his arm was draped warmly around her shoulders.

"Want to see the memorial and the Old Burial Point, and then head down by the water for lunch?" she suggested.

"Sure. Nothing like a graveyard on a dark autumn afternoon."

"Hey, I love old graveyards; you know that. There are great sayings on the tombstones."

"True. Let's head that way."

They did, stopping first at the memorial to those caught up in the hysteria of 1692; walking around the small area, they read the names of those who had been hanged as witches, and then found the stone for Giles Corey, the old man who had been pressed to death. The memorial, dedicated in 1992, the four-hundred-year anniversary of the events, was a peaceful place. Trees shaded the stones, set in their space adjacent to the Old Burial Point.

Then they entered into the graveyard. There would always be something a little eerie about a graveyard that was so old. The trees, casting off their autumn colors, cast down branches that appeared like skeletal fingers. The sky was gray; the breeze was chilly and seemed to encompass the visitor. The day was dark.

Fascinating. Megan loved it.

Finn seemed distant again, despite the fact that he was talking, joking, staying with her . . . touching her with his usual affection. But he seemed to be distracted, as if he were making a deliberate point of behaving normally, curling his fingers around hers, or casting his arm about her shoulders.

"It's really a great old place," she said softly.

"Absolutely," he agreed.

"Come on—I'll show you the hot spots," she teased. She knew the graveyard well, and didn't need to refer to a guide to find the stone for the man who had been a Pilgrim on the Mayflower, or the Hathorne grave—she showed Finn the spelling, telling him that Nathaniel Hawthorne had changed the spelling of his name, probably for a bit of disassociation. There were other intriguing graves, that of a man with a number of his wives buried nearby, and sad stones with skeletons and old funerary art that indicated the graves of babes. They read sayings to one another, and at one point, Megan laughed, and lay down before a stone with a very peculiar design in it, tossing up a handful of autumn leaves. Finn seemed uneasy then, his features taut, as he came to her, pulling her to her feet.

"Megan, you shouldn't lie there like that."

"Why?" she asked, startled, laughing as she shook fallen leaves from her hair. "What—do you think that I'm going to get sucked into a grave, or something?"

He shook his head. It was exactly what he'd been feeling, even if he hadn't given the thought full form. He wasn't going to laugh and tell her that of course he wouldn't be thinking anything so ridiculous.

"Sky is getting really dark," he told her. "Does it snow this early here?"

She shrugged. "It can snow. I don't think it will. The darkness too much for you?" she teased.

He glanced at her, a curious look in his eyes. "Scared? This is hallowed ground, right? No suicides or hanged criminals in here, I'm willing to bet."

She angled her head, studying him. "None that I know about."

He nodded kind of absently, running his fingers through his dark hair. "Hey, should we head into either of the museums on this street?"

"I don't know about you, but I'm starving now."

"Lunch, um. Yep, sounds good to me."

His arm around her, they left the cemetery, heading down to the waterfront. There was a new place just opened and Morwenna had given it a good recommendation. She didn't mention to Finn that her cousin had suggested it.

She was relieved to see that the restaurant had been decorated in a way that emphasized Salem's maritime history. There was charming, shiny wood everywhere. Ships bells and trophy fish adorned the walls. The curtains were beige with soft blue crustaceans abounding upon them. There was enough light in the place to read the menus, and they had been led to a pleasant table with a window that looked out on the water.

"Terrific so far," Finn said. He leaned closer to her. "Now, if only the food is good!"

"Clam chowder and scrod," she said.

"Scrod."

"With butter and bread crumbs. Delicious. You'll love it. It isn't as good anywhere in the world as it is in Salem."

"You know, New Orleans does offer some darned good seafood."

"Not scrod the way you can get it in New England."

He closed his menu. "Scrod it is!"

Their waitress came to the table and took their order. Megan saw that Finn's eyes fell upon the pentagram the young woman was wearing.

He noted Megan watching him and smiled.

"You're sorry you took this gig, aren't you?" she said softly.

He shook his head.

"I wish I believed you."

He shook his head again, reaching out across the table, curling his fingers over hers. "In all seriousness, I think that Salem is wonderful. The first museum was really well done—it made the history concise, and touched upon the incredible sadness of what happened. The memorial is exceptionally well done, too. It's a great town."

"Then . . . ?"

She was hoping that he would somehow convince her that nothing was really wrong at all. But he hesitated. "It isn't Salem, honestly. Or New England. I think it's beautiful. Even with autumn passing us by a bit—the colors are still fantastic. I love the old buildings and the shops."

"And you think Wiccans are silly."

He sighed. "Megan, you know that I'm not a big believer in organized religion. I believe in God . . . and mostly, being decent to your fellow man. So . . . Wiccans don't do any evil. They believe in an earth goddess—or whatever, I don't have any of it down exactly. There's just something . . . personal going on here that makes me a little uncomfortable. All right—I don't think your folks are happy that we're back together."

"Of course they are! Mom told me that all young couples have problems, but if they believe in marriage, they work them out. My father told me once that I'd only ever be happy with another musician, because it's a language of its own, and someone who loves music the way I do can only be happy with someone else who speaks the language."

"Your father really thinks that we both need nine to five jobs."

She laughed at the wry twist of his lips.

"Fathers the world over tend to worry about the future for their offspring. Honestly, Dad likes you."

"Except that now, he'll really think that I beat you, or that I'm an abuser."

He didn't sound angry. Or as though he thought it was her fault. It was as if he had really gotten past the dream. But he was bothered by something.

"What went on in your reading?"

"Ah, the reading."

She'd hit pay dirt. She could tell by the pulse ticking in the vein at his throat.

"Well," he said with a shrug. "Seems that Sara thinks I'm really bad for you."

"Sara doesn't know either of us."

"Yes, but she's a seer, right?"

He had ordered a draft beer. It arrived as he spoke offhandedly, lifting it to her.

Megan stirred her iced tea, staring down at it. Morwenna's reading had been disturbing as well. She didn't intend to tell Finn about it.

"Finn, I'm really sorry. I guess they can't help but be concerned."

"Sure. Your family." He managed another rueful smile.

"So . . . just how many people here are you related to?"

She sat back, laughing at the sound of his voice. He was managing to joke. "Well, there's Aunt Martha. I think I've told you about her."

"The old lady?"

"You'll love her. She's totally straightlaced. Thinks Morwenna is an idiot—or a commercial opportunist. She couldn't come to the wedding because she was ill, remember I told you at the time? But I sent her a copy of the pictures, so she'll feel as if she knows you already."

"But she's not really your aunt?"

"She was my grandmother's half cousin, or something like that. There's a blood tie, but not a strong one."

"But she means a lot to you, right?"

"Oh, yes, she's a sweetheart."

"We'll stop by quickly this afternoon, right before heading for the hotel and the hall to set up."

"We should do that by six."

"I don't think we need to start so early," Finn said. "This is Salem, Halloween week. They're not opening the doors until nine."

Megan studied her tea glass, a slow smile curling into her lips. He was really trying to make her happy. "Fine. We'll set up by seven, then. How's that?"

"Seven is plenty of time. Thank God for electronic music, huh?"

"Um. Are you sure that's time enough to set up?"

"Sure. The hotel has their own guys on duty to help, should we need some manual labor. But I'm accustomed to carting stuff around. It's not a problem."

He was trying so hard. Megan was grateful for his effort—and yet worried that being here was such an effort for him. Actually, it had all been going well enough—

until last night. Then this morning, he had been determined. And he was still determined, just different since they had left Morwenna's shop.

Thank God he hadn't asked about her Tarot reading, she thought uncomfortably. Morwenna had been seriously shaken by something she had seen. Deeply concerned. And—incredibly hesitantly—she had suggested that Megan shouldn't be with Finn. At least, not here, not now, with Halloween at the end of the week.

The scrod arrived. Finn bit into his and praised it lavishly. "You're right. The best scrod in the entire world."

She grinned ruefully. "You'd say that no matter what."

"It's good. Really good."

She thought she smiled, but she must have looked perplexed because he stared at her, fork in midair, and asked, "What's wrong?"

"With me? Nothing. Nothing at all. I just wish . . . well, I wish that you honestly liked this place."

He set his fork down, his eyes not wavering from hers. "Megan, I swear to you, I do like this place. Salem is beautiful. People—tourists and locals—are as nice as can be. I think the whole witchcraft thing—at least the way you've explained it to me—is great. A respect for nature. Spells that can only do good. And the pumpkins and decorations are charming. The respect for the tragedies of the past that is shown is tremendous."

"But . . . ?" she prompted.

"But?"

"There's just something more. As if you think that some kind of evil lingers on here."

"Absolutely not," he said firmly. "I don't believe that a place can be evil. I do believe that people can be evil. Living ones."

She frowned. "And you think that I know evil people here?"

"Of course not," he denied.

She didn't believe him. A little surge of resentment sprang forth in her soul. *Morwenna and Joseph.* He did think that her cousin and Joseph were evil.

Her scrod was suddenly tasteless. She smoothed the paper place mat beneath her plate. "The Wicca that Morwenna practices is based on ancient Celtic paganism. And the celebration of Halloween has nothing to do with evil. Originally, it marked the end of one year, or the death of that year, and the beginning of a new one. It was 'Samhain,' as the Celts called it. The people believed it was a time of the year when the spirits could visit their loved ones, walk the earth for one last time. They honored their dead; they didn't fear them. Especially in early Ireland, I know, the people believed that the worlds of the living and the dead were separated by something like a veil, and the veil became thin, and could disappear on Halloween night."

"Megan, I'm not related to any witches, but guess what? The modern-day practice of Wicca may be entirely harmless, but those pagan religions were often led by the Druids, and guess what else? Historically, Druids did believe in blood sacrifices."

She sighed with exasperation. "And the Catholics created the Inquisition!"

He gritted his teeth—absolutely determined on patience. "True," he said evenly. "Look, I'm just trying to tell you that it's really kind of a two-pronged thing. I absolutely believe that there are people practicing witchcraft today who do honor the earth, believe in the power of goodness, and may be among the finest, most giving people in the entire world. But you've got to admit that—whether twisted or not!—people have used the practice of magic in other ways. Whether there really is such a thing as magic—white or black—I sure as hell don't know. But it gets back to the main point. The tenets of most religions are very good. They teach us respect, peace, and kindness. But any idiot out there today knows that any religion can be twisted to create terror. I meant what I said. I think Salem is wonderful, just as all the charming towns are that surround it. It's an incredible place to visit, and Halloween here is . . . enchanting. I swear to you that I'm not speaking about anyone in particular—especially not your relatives—when I make the simple statement that places are not evil, only people can be evil. Okay?"

Had she been that defensive? Still staring at him somewhat perplexed, she nodded.

Then, as she sat there, a flare of panic seized her.

They had to get out.

They had to get away.

If they didn't . . .

"Want dessert?"

"What?"

"Did you want dessert? Or should I get the check?"

"We never eat dessert."

"We can never afford dessert," he said, jiggling his eyebrows. "But we're making a fortune for very little effort in this incredibly charming place! So . . . ?"

"Let's split something."

"What?"

"Whatever you'd like."

"Nope, this is your neck of the woods. You choose dessert."

Oddly, she still felt defensive. As if she didn't want to be the cause of being here. "Un-huh. We're here because you got the gig. You choose dessert."

"All right, then. Something gooey and decadent. Chocolate and gooey and decadent. Covered with whipped cream. Slathered in it. Richly. All over."

She laughed. He'd made every word entirely sensual.

"Did you want dessert? Or sex?"

He leaned back, shrugging. She was surprised that her words seemed to bring out something defensive in him. "Sex—with Fallon monitoring the halls? After last night? The old buzzard would probably be at the keyhole."

She sighed, folding her arms on the table, looking down at them. It was going to be a long time before she lived down last night.

She looked up at him again, forcing her jaw to unclench. "Great. Well, here's to a mini working vacation. Sexless," she added, lifting her water glass toward him.

"Hey, don't be silly. There are all kinds of dark nooks and crannies around the town," he said lightly. Except that his words weren't light. They were dark, with an underlying anger as well.

"I don't think I want dessert," she said abruptly, rising. "Ask for the check; I'll be right outside."

She noticed her own wrist as she spoke, since her hand rested on the table. She frowned, deeply dismayed to note that her bracelet was gone.

"I lost it!" she murmured.

"What?" Finn asked.

"The claddagh bracelet my dad gave me."

"You're sure you were wearing it?"

She nodded glumly. "It's Irish good luck, you know. And a gift from Dad. I don't know why—it seemed important to wear it today."

"All right, well, don't panic yet. We'll retrace our steps. Hopefully, somebody found it. Maybe it fell off at the museum, or at Morwenna's, or even in the park."

"If someone found it, it's probably gone," she said mournfully. "It was light and delicate, but eighteen-carat gold, and a really beautiful piece."

"Hey, there's hope. Don't give up yet." He motioned to the waitress and paid her, then caught Megan's hand and headed out with long strides.

She was startled to realize that she was almost glad about the bracelet. The tension between them had dropped like a hot potato. He knew what the bracelet meant to her.

They returned first to the witch museum, but no one had found or turned in such an item. Finn pointed out that they needed to look around the park, since they had been playing with the dog. The catch might have come undone when she was playing with the Great Dane.

But though they tracked the park over and over again, there was no sign of the bracelet.

"It's not here. It's just gone, Finn," Megan said, dejected. "And I suppose it's silly to think that I will find it now. I shouldn't have been so careless. I mean, if I did lose it here, and someone found it, they'd keep it, surely—I mean, even if they hoped to give it back to a rightful owner, where do you turn something in when it was lost at a park?"

"We can still try Morwenna's," Finn said. He looked up at the sky. Nearly winter in New England. It was already growing dark. He shrugged, offering her a hopeful smile. "Well, we did this right, anyway. Searching the park before total darkness. Morwenna's has light—a little, at least."

"Um," she murmured.

He frowned, seeing something on the ground, reaching down. "What is it?" she asked.

Hunkered down, he shook his head. "Sorry, just a bottle cap. And . . . fall!" As he stood, he tossed up a pile of leaves. In muted but still beautiful colors, they fell around her, a few landing in her hair.

She was startled at first, then laughed, reaching down to scoop up a pile of the leaves herself, tossing them out in turn. "Fall, is that what it is? Fall?"

He grabbed more leaves and she reached down again herself, this time determined to stuff a few down his shirt.

"Hey! That's the way we're going to play?" he countered. He had a handful of leaves and a wicked gleam in his eyes.

"Finn . . . now wait. You can just shake them out of

your shirt . . ." There would be no mercy, she saw. With a yelp, she started running, heading for the street. He caught up with her far too quickly. She stumbled when he spun her around; they both wound up on the ground in a pile of leaves. She squirmed, trying to keep him from getting the leaves down her clothing. By then, she was protesting and laughing at the same time.

"Stop!" Finn said suddenly.

"Stop—so you can fill my shirt with the remnants of an entire oak?" she demanded.

"No! Seriously, lie still!"

"Broken glass?" she asked.

"No—"

"Then . . . ?" She started to squirm again.

"No!"

"What?"

"Poop!" he exclaimed.

She lay still, staring at him.

"Great Dane poop, I think," he said seriously. "A really big pile. Don't move to your left."

She turned her head. He wasn't lying. She started to laugh. "Boy, you'd have thought we'd have smelled it, huh?"

He grinned. "Careful, careful—with your every move," he said in his best undercover spy voice. "I'll get you out of this."

He started to move. She pulled him back for a moment, suddenly dazzled by his smile, the one dimple, the feel of his warmth, and the knowledge of just how much she loved him. And just how feeling him like this, the length of his body hard against her own, could make her realize the many layers of just how much she wanted him.

"Poop," he repeated, frowning.

She nodded. "I know. And I'll be careful. I was just thinking that . . . we're not really going to let Mr. Fallon influence our nights, are we?"

He watched her gravely for a long moment. "Well . . . just so long as you think you're capable of keeping the ecstacy down. We'll have him in bed with us—and that's a damned scary thought!—if he hears you screaming again. That old geezer would never know the difference between pain and pleasure. Ugh. Okay, no matter how incredible I am, you have to keep it down."

She punched him in the shoulder. "You could elicit utter silence, you know."

"Nah—never," he teased.

"Hm. Well, we'll see. Poop. We should get up now."

But he didn't move. He laced his fingers through hers, drew them to the ground, and kissed her. They were married. They'd kissed a million times. But there was something erotic about this. And something a little painful and desperate as well. And yet she found herself thinking that he was right, if they were to continue from this point in a hotel room, she might well be screaming . . .

Yet, as she was thinking of the pure sensuality of his simple gesture, he was suddenly rising. He pulled her up with him, and started dusting off his clothing. "Public park," he said ruefully. "Or common, or whatever you call it."

She nodded. "Finn," she said softly.

"What?"

"I love you."

She thought he would say something like, "I love you, too." Or, "You know I love you, too." Perhaps, "Ditto, kid," or something like that.

Instead he was silent for a long moment. And when he spoke, his voice was deep. There was almost a tremor in it.

"I'd die for you," he told her.

The wind picked up around them. His eyes were emerald in the coming darkness. Leaves seemed to rise and fall, as if the elements garnered in on their private conversation. Despite his words, she was suddenly cold.

"Well—let's hope it never comes to that!" she said lightly. "Hey, we need to head to Morwenna's. We'll have to skip Aunt Martha's for today—we'll see her tomorrow. We should look for the bracelet, then head back to the B and B and get ready for tonight. You think?"

He nodded. He reached out. Not taking her hand, the way he usually did. He reached out, and waited for her to accept his hand.

They started out of the park.

It had been empty. The streets were not. Once again, they joined various groups of people on the sidewalks. Couples here and there, parents with kids. Young people. Some decked out in costume apparel, some in the hip clothes of the younger generation. People talking. Laughing. Even arguing. Mostly enjoying one another.

It took only a matter of minutes to reach Morwenna's. The store was still crawling with both the curious and paying customers. Sara was on guard duty at the door.

Sara was startled when Finn pulled back at the sight of her, almost as if he were a dog or a horse that sensed extreme danger in the path.

"Hey!" she called to them.

Was she getting paranoid? Megan wondered. Or did Sara seem uneasy at the sight of Finn as well?

"Super busy in there, huh?" Megan said.

"There's always room for family," Sara said. "Sorry!" she said to a group of people waiting for the shop to clear out before they entered. "Morwenna's cousin."

Apologetically, Megan and Finn slipped through the door, past the waiting group. Inside, it was wall-to-wall people. Megan reached her cousin, telling her about the bracelet, asking if it had been found.

"No, I'm so sorry. Or not yet, at least," Morwenna told her. "But, don't despair—once we close, I'll really look around the place and see if it's fallen on the floor, or behind something. Wow, something your dad gave

you. I can ask around town as well—maybe someone
did find it in the street and turn it in. I doubt it, but . . ."
She broke off and laughed suddenly. "If a really good
Wiccan found it, they would have turned it in somewhere. Doing a good deed like that is bound to bring
back good luck triplefold."

Joseph, who had apparently been listening from behind Megan's shoulder, moved up, startling her. "We
can hope," he said. "But if a not-so-good Wiccan or
someone else found it, they'd probably go, 'Hey, what a
great Celtic bracelet, must be mine now.' Sorry, Megan,
there is the chance that it will turn up."

"I know it's probably lost for good," Megan said.
"But . . . I had to try to find it."

"Like your cousin said, we'll keep looking."

Megan turned around, searching the shop. Finn was
no longer at her side. He was standing by a shelf that
held all kinds of beautiful little curios and art pieces.

"I need to collect my husband and get going," Megan
said. "Thanks, both of you."

"Sure thing—and hey, we'll get there late tonight,
but we'll be there."

"That's terrific."

Megan excused herself to a heavy-set woman, making her way toward Finn. He was reaching for one of the
pieces on the shelf, a really beautifully carved wooden
dragon. He picked up the piece, swore suddenly, nearly
dropped it—then caught it right before it hit the floor.

When she reached him, he had the dragon, but was
wearing a severe scowl.

"Finn?"

He looked at her, eyes still dark, brow knit tightly, jaw
clenched.

"What's wrong?" she demanded.

"I've been gouged."

"What?"

He balanced the weight of the dragon into his right

hand and raised his left. She was startled to see a major stream of blood trickling down his palm.

"Finn! How deep is it?" she demanded with concern, reaching for his hand.

Once again, Joseph was right behind her.

"Wow, sorry!" Joseph said, voice tinged with what sounded like real concern. "We have a first-aid kit in the back. Sara!" he raised his voice. "Grab the kit in back, will you? Come on back through the curtain. We'll get some peroxide on it and see how deep it is."

"It's really all right," Finn said impatiently. "I didn't mean to make a big deal out of it. Meg and I have to get going."

"Finn, you need a bandage or something!" Megan protested.

Joseph had a hand on Finn's shoulder and was leading him toward the back. "Absolutely, a bandage at the least. I hadn't realized there was anything so sharp on that piece. It's dangerous, and I'm getting it off the display."

"Look, it's no big deal," Finn repeated.

"Hey, it could have been a huge deal. Thank God you're family. You won't try to sue us. At least, I don't think you'll try to sue us."

Finn was growing impatient. "It's a scratch, Joseph. No big deal."

They'd reached the back. Sara was already at the business desk, the first-aid kit out, a bottle of peroxide in her hand.

Aware that for some reason Finn seemed to have a real aversion to Sara, Megan smiled and reached out to Sara, taking the first aid supplies from her.

She poured peroxide onto a cotton swab and dabbed at Finn's hand. He had gotten a real gouge, right in the palm. Her brow knitted with concern. Finn balled the cotton swab into his hand, his eyes meeting hers. "Meg, it's all right."

She nodded. "Just let me bandage it."

She did so. The bloody cotton swab lay on the desk. She reached for it, but Sara was already picking things up.

"You're sure you're all right? You going to be able to play tonight?"

"Oh, yeah. Nothing would stop me," Finn said.

Megan noticed Sara walking away with the kit and the garbage.

"I'll get that dragon right off the shelf."

"At least I didn't break it," Finn joked.

Joseph shrugged, returning a rueful smile. "I may go break the damn thing myself. That could have been a kid. Not that you're not just as important. I don't mean that, but . . ."

"Like I said, no big deal," Finn insisted. "Meg, we do have to start to make tracks now."

"Right," she agreed. She took his good hand, suddenly, within the shop, feeling the need to be as close to him as possible.

"We'll be there tonight!" Morwenna called encouragingly.

"Thanks!" Finn called back.

When they returned to the street, darkness had fallen completely. Only the lights from the shops still open poured out with their false illumination.

"That's so deep," Megan said with dismay.

"It's all right," Finn said. But though they had already walked half a block away, he turned back, studying Morwenna's shop with a dark and brooding expression.

"Finn . . . ?"

He turned back to her. He smiled. And yet his look was as a false as the illumination that fell upon the streets.

"It's all right," he said firmly.

He took her hand, forgetting the wound, and wincing when he squeezed right at the point of his wound.

"Sorry," he said lightly.

"Oh, Finn!"

"Can we just forget it, please!" he said sharply.

But he still had her hand.

And she could feel where his blood was soaking through the bandage.

Chapter 4

The hotel was new, and on the outskirts of town. It did, however, have aesthetic appeal, having been built in a colonial style popular in New England. To compete with the many bed and breakfast places in and around town that oozed history, charm, and ghost tales, it offered its own brand of enticing atmosphere. Gardens adorned the surrounding lawns, balconies and porches circled around the structure. The room where they were playing was customarily a supper club, and the set-up hadn't been changed much—except to add seasonal enhancement. The room abounded with nylon spiderwebs and little plastic arachnids. A kettle that emitted fog had been set up in one corner, with an attendant who wielded a huge dipper—ready to pour out the spiked and seasonal punch—two bucks a shot. Creatures swung from the ceiling, both grotesque and comical, and all in all, it had been decorated for one great Halloween party.

Meals were served until eleven; snacks and drinks after that hour. They were to begin their first set at nine each night, and play until one, with breaks in between. Finn had been surprised at the thousand a night they had been offered to play, and when setting up the equipment with the help of Adam Spade, the muscle-bound bouncer, he wondered if they'd actually make it back to the establishment.

Spade had a clean-shaven head, and though a few inches shorter than Finn, he had the huge bulk of a body builder. He looked as if he had been born to be a bouncer, but he was a decent enough guy, even if he grunted more than actually talked. He wasn't from the area; he had worked for the hotel chain at another location. To him, Halloween meant money and good business, nothing more.

Sam Tartan, the man who had hired Finn long distance, was Spade's exact opposite—skinny in a suit, lanky as Ichabod Crane. He had a nervous way about him when he greeted Finn and Megan, telling them it was a supper club, but a hotel, and now and then, a late night guest could be young. The lyrics had to be clean.

Finn told him not to worry.

But by the end of their first set—a mixture of their own music and pop covers—he was elated to see that the place was packed. Sam Tartan's pinched face had somewhat broadened with a smile.

Strange crowd.

A number of the local Wiccans—those with a touch of humor, willing to accept the fact that other citizens would arrive in costume—chose to dance the night away in what might be called seasonal dress, but was, however, the same attire they might wear out on any evening.

Black.

It was definitely the color of the night here.

Those who weren't Wiccan and weren't in costume were often in black anyway. Black suits, black cocktail gowns, black flowing gowns, black jeans and sweaters . . . black.

Then there were those who were in full tilt with the

commercial fun of dressing up. A Frankenstein monster arrived with his bride—exceptional costumes. Finn personally thought they deserved the prize given out each night for best dress-up attire. Another group that deserved special notice were the four collegians who had come as the members of the rock group Kiss. Great makeup—though he feared that one of the young men just might break an ankle trying to balance on the boots all night.

Some young women had come as the Pink Ladies, straight out of *Grease*.

There were three Elvis Presleys.

Some people wore complete face masks, many as horned demons, some as creatures from horror movies. As he played a cover song by rote, Finn found himself thinking that they could be anyone, anyone at all. But then again, that was half the fun of dress up. It was a way to be someone else. You could ask anyone to dance, listen in on any conversation, do all kinds of things and be completely unknown.

He chimed in on the harmony for the old Fleetwood Mac song they were doing, and found himself listening to Megan. She didn't just have a good voice; she had a beautiful voice. An ungodly range, and a quality of sound that was totally beguiling. Nothing was ever forced; elegance and ease simply seemed to pour from her lips. He could carry a tune well enough himself, but his talents were more in arrangements, and he did have a way with a number of instruments, and a true gift for synchronization. In fact, Megan had no concept of just how good she was. In her mind, she was an extension of his creations. He wasn't a fool, nor so egotistical that he would ever purposely allow her such an illusion, but when it came to work, she always respected his opinions.

Her voice faded on a perfect, enticing trail; he played

the last bars of the song, and was then glad to close his eyes and take a moment to find pleasure and relief in the sounds of applause that greeted him. Megan, in front of him on the stage area, turned around with a pleased smile as well, then made a motion with her hand to her lips, showing him that she was going for something to drink. He nodded, and when she arched a brow, a clear query that she was asking if he wanted something as well, he nodded. She stepped out into the crowd where people immediately began to come up to her. He lowered his head, smiling to himself, and went over to change a string on his acoustic guitar.

As he sat on the edge of the stage to work, he too, found himself barraged—mostly with monsters. Partyers in full face masks or bizarre makeup. A nice crowd, all telling him how they were enjoying the music, a few asking for more slow numbers, others asking for disco, and some wondering if they knew anything at all from the Big Band era. He assured them all that they'd try to oblige them.

Megan hadn't gotten very far. He glanced through the crowd and noticed that she was stopped beneath one of the oversize decorations—some kind of a gargoyle-type monster with huge, branch-like fingers dipping down as if they were about to attack.

And actually, they had attacked. He could see that Megan had walked too close and the fingers had tangled into her hair, almost as if they were real. He started to rise to come to her assistance as she grimaced and tried to untangle herself.

He didn't need to rush to her rescue; a tall fellow—or a short fellow in a tall costume—stopped. He was almost as grotesque as the creature holding her. He wore a brown robe with a cowl, and beneath, a blood red demon mask with crimson horns, huge hooked nose, and obscenely large lips. He had nimble enough fingers—despite the bloodred and crimson latex gloves he was wearing. He spoke to Megan, who laughed as he disentangled her.

Despite the fact that Megan needed no knight in armor, he was almost compelled to rush forward. A strange sense of jealousy washed over him as if he had been doused with buckets of anger. He clenched his teeth and realized that the guitar string he held had almost gouged through his finger, his grip had gotten so tight. He gave his head a shake, wondering what had possessed him. Megan had walked beneath a prop; she had been entangled. A passerby had politely paused to come to her assistance. And yet . . .

Something was racing through his bloodstream. Anger. Jealousy. But more. The two had been speared by a sudden and ridiculous flash of stark, cold—*fear.* A tremendous unease.

He gave himself a firm mental shake, demanding that he get a grip on himself.

First, he'd been jealous because a fellow Megan had gone to school with had stopped to talk to her. Now, a casual passerby, helping her out of a predicament, was making his temper soar and his libido take over. Ridiculously.

"Finn? Finn Douglas?"

He turned. An older woman with bright blue eyes and a cherubic face was smiling at him. She wasn't in costume, or in a Wiccan's cape. She wasn't even wearing black, but rather a lovely sparkling silver dress and shawl.

"Yes?"

"I'm Martha. Martha Scott. Aunt Martha, to you, young man."

"Well, hello!" Finn said. "How are you, and what a pleasure to meet you. I know how much you mean to Megan. We were coming by today, but—"

"Yes, I heard. Poor Meg, losing that bracelet. She's not a material girl at all, but she loved that piece when her dad gave it to her. He was great for telling her all the old Irish stories, and it meant a great deal to her. Oh, well, it may turn up! Anyway, I wanted to say a quick hello. I'm afraid this night life is a little too much for an old lady like me. I saw the first set—lovely. Absolutely lovely. But I'm on my way out, so give me a quick kiss on the cheek and we'll get to know one another later."

Finn stepped forward, delighted by the woman. She was quick spoken, matter-of-fact, and charming with her twinkling blue eyes. She made him forget his discomfort.

He kissed her on the cheek. "We will be by to see you tomorrow."

"Indeed, you will, young man. You've married our little songbird. You will have to abide the family, and actually, I'm a marvelous storyteller—and an excellent cook. I'll see you for lunch, and that's that."

"Absolutely. We run a little late here."

"Two o'clock will be lovely."

"We'll be there."

Martha turned and walked away. She was a small woman, trim and compact for her age, and walked as she spoke with a quick, no-nonsense strut.

"Finn!"

He turned. Joseph was calling him from the other direction. He hadn't changed for the party. He was dressed as he had been earlier, long black cape over black trousers and black shirt. He grinned, ready to compliment Finn on the music. "You two are great together—I've got to hand you that. Morwenna always said that Megan was a little nightingale, and that's true, but I've never seen her better. You do something special for one another."

"Thanks, thanks a lot," Finn said. Had he misjudged

Joseph? Or was he simply so ready to have his ego stroked that he didn't realize he was being nose-butted, tasted, by some kind of a shark?

"I saw that you met Aunt Martha."

"Yes. Lovely woman."

Joseph shrugged. "Opinionated as all hell—and not at all averse to expressing those opinions, I guarantee you. But that's okay. I think she means well—but she's hell on me, and Morwenna. We love her anyway."

"Well, I'm forewarned. I'm going to have lunch with her and be the best I can be—Megan loves her a lot."

"That's true. Hey, need any help?"

"What? No, I, sorry—all set. I was just replacing a string when I met Martha. We do a couple of things without the sound boxes. Guitar and voice, that's it. Had a bad string. It's all set now."

"How long do you break?"

"Twenty minutes."

"Why don't you come to our table? Get something to eat."

"We're already down to about thirteen minutes left, no time, but thanks."

"Come over to the table, order for Megan and yourself, and your food will be there for your next break."

Finn hesitated. Joseph's invitation made sense. Meeting Martha had made him feel more comfortable. But now that she was gone, he felt the touch of a lingering sense of unease. He wanted Megan away from all these people.

Stupid. People were being great. They were playing terrifically. It wasn't even an old place, it was brand new. No ghosts. Just ribs, fries, steaks, drinks, dancing, laughing, a good old time. They were making great money. It's what he had wanted. The college student working the register, Corey Vale, wearing a black cape over his white tailored shirt and jacket—the former looking like a garment required for his position at night during the

Halloween season—had stopped by to tell him that he'd already sold a number of *boxes* of their CDs. He couldn't have asked for better. Finn thanked him, and told him he was more than welcome to one himself.

He wished to hell he wasn't here.

"Finn, you okay?"

"Yeah, Joseph, I'm fine, just thinking. Sure, I guess your invitation is a great one. Just don't let them put our meals on your check—dinner for the two of us is part of the gig."

"Don't worry. Morwenna has a talent for barely glancing at a dinner bill as if she couldn't possibly conceive of a server making a mistake. But trust me—she reads it like a hawk in the two seconds she glances it over."

"Terrific," Finn murmured. He stood, then hesitated again and tried to sound casual. "Who else is with you two tonight?"

"No one. Just Morwenna and I. We left the place with others tonight. They're closing down and trying to set the shop to rights after so many people have been going through it handling everything. And hey—how's the hand?"

The hand hurt. Like hell. But Finn shrugged. "It'll heal."

"You playing okay with it? Dumb question—you sound great."

"It's just the palm. It's all right."

"I'll buy you a beer—unless alcohol is part of the gig?"

Finn shrugged with a rueful grin. "Nope. You can buy me a beer."

"We're right over there."

"Megan's on her way back here with something liquid at the moment. I'll come as soon as she returns."

"She can't miss us—we're on the way back to the stage."

"All right, then I'll join you now."

Finn set down his guitar. He followed Joseph toward the table, then found himself suddenly pulled back as if a giant hand had reached down to grasp him by the hair at the top of his head. He winced, pulling back, then swore softly as he saw that he had been accosted by the same stupid prop that had snagged Megan.

Joseph must have heard his quick, startled curse. He turned back. "Dumb thing—I've seen people caught up by that monster all night. Here, I'll give you a hand."

Finn didn't want a hand. He was feeling irate again, unreasonably so, and less than gracious. "It's all right, I got it," he said, curbing his temper, and stupidly ripping out a good handful of hair in his haste to prove that he was free from the thing.

"Poor baby!" Morwenna cooed as he reached the table. She halfway stood, rubbing the top of his head. That irritated him even more. Somehow, he kept his cool. He was sure he ground through half the enamel on his teeth.

"It's all right."

"The steaks are great," Joseph said.

"So Wiccans aren't vegetarian?" Finn said.

"Some are," Joseph said with a shrug.

"Great, then," he said, determined that come hell or high water—or every stupid prop or piece of scenery in the place—he was going to get along here. Megan was his wife; he loved her. No asinine Tarot reader was going to make him blow this in any way. "Steaks sound good. I guess I'll go ahead and order for Megan, too. She likes a good steak."

"We'll see to it that they arrive for your next break," Morwenna assured him.

"Thanks." He peered through the room. Fog machines were keeping a constant, low mist going. At first, he couldn't see her. Then, through a sudden clearing gust of air from an overhead vent, he caught sight of her through a milling group of friends in all forms of bizarre fashion. She was standing dead still, listening to someone. A frown knit her brow.

Finn shifted around, trying to see the person who had her so engrossed in conversation.

"It's just old Andy Markham," Joseph said.

"Markham?" He looked at his cousin-in-law sharply. "Isn't that the old geezer who was telling the 'haunted' stories the other night?"

"Andy is harmless. Once upon a time, way back, he ventured to Boston and did some Shakespeare on stage. You know, good enough actor to get a few jobs, not good enough to make a real living. So he tells tales really well." Morwenna said. She inclined her head. "You know that I don't personally approve of any of the hokum they do around Halloween. Even for those really dedicated to concepts of organized religion, it's supposed to be a holy day. But we have all kinds of ghoulish creatures—pulling peoples' hair out!—and stories about the spirit world and evil that seeps through time and such rot. But hey—they make a living out of it here."

Finn hadn't quite realized that he'd stood until he saw that Morwenna was then frowning up at him. "Honestly, Finn, Andy is harmless."

"Sure," Finn said. He wanted badly for his tone to be light. "It's just that the last time Megan listened to him, she had the worst nightmares I've ever seen. I think I'll just go rescue her."

"Nightmares, of course," he heard Morwenna murmur as he started from the table. Once again he gritted his teeth. Hard.

There was just something in her tone.

She pretended to sympathize.

But her words came out as a far different shriek of accusation in his head.

Wife beater.

He was going to hurt Megan . . .

He was bad for Megan. So said Sara, the palm reader.

Before he could reach Megan, he paused, fighting again to control the waves of fury that came crashing over him.

He could make it. They were in Salem for a week. He was paranoid because their being back together now was still so fragile.

Hell or high water, he reminded himself.

Or every demon in the place.

He was going to be decent. A good guy.

The perfect husband.

"Smoke!" Andy Markham was saying. Maybe the simple word sounded so sinister coming from his lips because he was just so darned . . . ancient. Even his wrinkles had wrinkles, Megan thought, and wished she could smile inwardly at least at the observation. His eyes—so pale a blue they seemed colorless—were all but sunk into the deep caverns of their sockets. Only a few wisps of snow-white hair remained on the top of his head. He resembled a living, breathing crypt keeper, the great puppet on the television show. His skin was almost translucent. He was more than skinny, he was a pile of bones with not nearly enough flesh stretched over them.

He wasn't in costume. He didn't need to be.

"Smoke," she said politely in reply. She wasn't at all sure what he'd been talking about so far, only that he'd seemed desperate, and then, strangely hypnotic. He'd said something about nightmares, and nightmares being projections of the past, and of the future. She'd thought at first that he'd heard about her dreams and come to apologize because he'd done his job so well that he'd scared her half out of her wits.

But he hadn't come to apologize.

He stopped her, in the middle of the floor, to warn her.

"Don't you understand? Always, where there's smoke, there's fire beneath. Subtle. But smoke is a warning. Oh, there are so many stories, of course. But myth and legend always have root in fact. You're not one of them. Doesn't matter."

"Andy, I'm not one of who?"

He shook his head. "Not a Wiccan, not a pagan, girl. But your roots are from here."

"Andy, I was born nearby, grew up nearby, but I've actually been gone a long time. My folks moved up to Maine. I went through college. It's been years since I've really been around. I guess I was just susceptible to stories again."

The old man shook his head. "I feel it. I feel it! Take time, take a breath, feel it. Like I said, there's something to the old stories and legends. There are more stories, tales I don't tell folks 'cause they are just too close to . . . real. To life. There's a veil, don't you understand, a thin veil between life as we know it . . . and what lies beyond."

She smiled, still confused, and still surprised that she didn't seem to be able to make up some excuse and walk away. She'd gone to get water for herself and Finn ages ago, or so it seemed now, and she hadn't even reached one of the service stations.

"Andy, my folks were both from Irish ancestry. I've heard lots of stories. About banshees, leprechauns, pixies, fairies . . . and the old ways of Halloween. Actually, it's just darned decent, remembering those who have gone before with a lot of love. Respect for the dead, and—"

"No, the veil lies thin on All Hallow's Eve," Andy said firmly. "Too thin. And usually, that's just fine. Someone who lost a mother gets to feel as if they know her tender touch upon a shoulder again. A wife who has lost a husband may feel as if he whispered an assurance in her ear. But there are those who were not good in life, who wanted to touch the other side. There are those who are evil. And they're used by evil. Usually, they don't know that they're selling their souls. They are too beguiled by false promises. The world is ancient. You don't understand what came before man."

"I think there was something called the Big Bang," Megan murmured, a touch of humor and dryness surging forth. Still, she didn't seem to be able to walk away.

The old man suddenly seemed to see something behind her. His voice lowered to a raspy whisper, like wind blowing through fallen, brittle leaves.

"I *need* to talk to you." His emphasis had a desperate edge. "I must talk with you, make you understand that something is happening, you're in danger, you're—"

He broke off abruptly.

"Hey, so what's going on here?"

Finn. He was at her shoulder, standing right behind her. His arm came protectively around her, drawing her back against his frame. "Mr. Markham. You've got to watch it with your tall tales of terror. Have you heard? Sure, you've heard. The whole town has heard. Megan woke up screaming her head off the other night."

Andy Markham stared at Finn, as if assessing him—and sizing up an enemy.

"Tall tales. Right. Tall tales." For a moment, Megan thought that he would dive in, and start telling Finn that something was going on, that evil walked, or try to convince him that his tall tales were not so tall at all. Smoke. Where there was smoke there was fire. Where there was a myth or a legend, there was a fact somewhere lying beneath.

Smoldering.

"As you say, young man, as you say. I'll be watching it with the tales. Taking care. Well, good evening to the both of you. Lovely music. You've got the young crowd hopping and the old timers like me entertained as well. Enjoy the rest of your night. By the way, the steaks here are excellent."

He seemed straighter as he turned and walked away. Still ancient, but straight and proud.

Finn's arm tightened around her. Actually, it seemed to jerk, as if he had been riddled with a spasm.

"So what's the old creep been telling you now?" he demanded rather harshly.

She turned and looked at him. His appearance was bizarre. Finn was a really handsome man, with his strong facial bone structure and contrasting coloring. He was angry, though, and trying to smile through it. The effort gave him a very strange look. As if he were a satyr. Something macabre. Evil . . . and still, as alluring as evil could be.

"Meg? No more horror stories, right? You're not going to wake up screaming again?"

She shook her head. "No—no." She didn't know why, but she lied glibly. "No, he just wanted to say hello, and tell me how much he liked the music." Now that he was gone, she felt as if the the poor old fellow was absurd. She managed a brilliant smile, and then a show of real enthusiasm as she threw her arms around his neck.

"Finn! It's really going incredibly well, isn't it?"

He grinned back, the touch of evil gone.

"Really well," he agreed, brushing her lips quickly with a kiss. "Really, really, well. Hey, I got to meet your Aunt Martha."

"She's a doll, isn't she?"

"Did you see her first, and send her to say hello?"

She shook her head, a small smile twitching. "She gave me a two-second hug and said she was tired and leaving, and was going to go and inspect you up close with the five minutes during which she could still stay awake. I promised that we'd see her—"

"Tomorrow, lunch at two," Finn finished for her.

"Lunch, she didn't tell me the time," Megan agreed.

"Two o'clock, and she promised she was a good cook. Our break time is up, we've got to get back up there. Hey, Morwenna and Joseph are ordering our food—we'll join them at the next break, um?"

His words touched her. She knew it was difficult for him to pretend a real friendship and liking for Morwenna and Joseph.

"Perfect. Hey—have you seen the kid we met in the park yet? Remember, I promised him one of the new CDs."

"I may have seen him, and not known it was him," he said ruefully. "Some of these costumes are absolute disguises. But don't worry about it. I asked the fellow at the register to make sure that if he sees a Darren Menteith, he gives him a CD."

"What if he doesn't ask?"

"He'll ask. Maybe he isn't here tonight. I'm willing to bet he'll come up to the stage at some point."

Megan nodded. He took her hand, leading her back to the stage. When they were there, he picked up the hand microphone, switched it on, and reintroduced them. Megan went to retrieve her own mike. She listened as Finn welcomed them, and thanked them. He was a natural. A totally natural front man. Speaking to a crowd came as easily to him as buttering a piece of bread. He had a pleasant sense of confidence that was still somehow self-deprecating, a deep, smooth voice that was sexy as all hell. She was amazed that despite the many things that had come between them at times, there had never been once when it hadn't been the most natural thing in the world to work with him.

He introduced one of their own songs, a duet, a love ballad about a highwayman, the lady with whom he fell in love, and the hangman with whom he finally met. He did it with the acoustic guitar only. The melody was haunting, the lyrics a complete and tragic story. She wondered if it would work with this crowd, with people wanting to dance, with waiters and waitresses delivering food, glass clinking, forks and knives hitting plates.

But Finn went into the number with a grin and a shrug and his customary devil-may-care confidence and so she shrugged as well and they went through the number, eyes touching across the stage as they picked up on their different cues.

He strummed the last chord on his guitar. Megan was stunned to realize that the room was in absolute silence. She looked around. Even servers had stopped in their tracks. At various tables, half the people had been given their plates while others remained on trays.

There was a sudden spate of applause. People stood and clapped. Someone shouted out a glowing, "Bravo! Wow!" Then the applause sounded again.

Finn winked and shrugged at her. He spoke into the mike, thanking them all. She realized that half his charm was his ability to make everyone out there think that he was speaking to them personally.

Nor did he allow their moment of glimmering triumph to drift into anything less. He walked around to the keyboard and sound system, nodded her way, and cued her with, "We've had a request for the Big Band era. Megan can't be all the Andrews Sisters in one, but she still does a great 'Boogie Woogie Bugle Boy.'"

They went from the Big Band era to the latest on the pop charts, did another of their own songs, and ended with another duet, "I Can't Help Falling in Love with You." Then Finn announced their break, and that they'd return, and thanked everyone for coming.

He caught her hand quickly, once he had turned off the mike and set it down. "I'm not letting you get away again. Andy Markham might grab you again and your meat will be as cold as ice."

"I won't move," she said.

"You have to move. They'll all think I'm doing something evil if I have to pick you up to carry you to the table." His tone was light. He was honestly joking. She felt a strange relief, and was glad that they had been received so well in Salem. She knew that his parents had seriously discouraged him from being a musician. It was important to him that he make his living at his work.

She brought her hand up, stroked his cheek. "You're incredible."

"Of course," he teased, then added seriously, "but only when I have you."

"That's sweet," she murmured, then turned quickly, seeing that Morwenna was waving wildly to her from her chair.

They hurried to the table. Morwenna had definitely worked some kind of magic because the moment they sat down, plates appeared in front of them. Good old American cuisine. Two sizzling steaks, baked potatoes, green beans.

"Terrific, thanks so much, what timing!" Megan complimented.

"And the steaks do look great," Finn said. He cut into his meat. "And rare. Very rare. Bloody rare, my favorite."

He didn't like his meat all that bloody, Megan thought, and wondered if he was being sarcastic. But when she glanced at him, he was looking at Joseph, really appreciating the order that had been put in for them.

"Yes, they're just great," Megan said.

"Good, I'm glad. Now, the two of you don't worry about talking—just eat! Of course, chew slowly, we don't want you choking or anything," Morwenna said.

"Look, here comes a goblin or some other wretchedly costumed thing," Joseph muttered. "You'd think they'd let you eat."

"It's all right," Megan said, jumping up. She wasn't sure how she recognized the person in the shredded dark robes and zombie mask, but she did. It was Darren Menteith.

"Darren! It's great to see you," she said, reaching out a hand as he came forward.

He stopped in his tracks. "You know it's me?" he said, tremendously disappointed.

"Yeah. Sorry."

Finn had risen as well.

"They are trying to have dinner," Joseph muttered.

"Sit, Megan, finish. I'll take Darren over for a CD. And be right back."

Megan sat back down. "Finn, I can go—"

"I can wolf down a rare steak in two seconds," Finn told her. "You take your time."

"Hey, I am sorry, I should have waited to say hello," Darren said.

"No problem, we're just glad to see you," Finn told him. "Come on, let me give you a disc."

As the two walked away, Megan noted uneasily that both Joseph and Morwenna watched them go.

"I didn't realize that you knew Darren," Morwenna said, realizing that Megan was staring at her.

"We don't really know him. We met him today in the park. I didn't know that you knew him," Megan said.

She shrugged. "Small town, that's all. Hey, come on, eat up. By the way, honey, that one number you two did—dynamite."

"Thanks."

"It's just too bad that . . ." Morwenna began, then broke off with a shrug, looking at Joseph.

Joseph cleared his throat. "Great number," he muttered.

Megan set her fork down. "Both of you! Pay attention. I respect everything about you. I love you both. But I don't believe that Finn is dangerous to me. I do not believe that he is evil in any way. Get this straight— I had a nightmare the other night. A dream. And woke up screaming. And I made him look really, really, bad— especially with the way rumor seems to travel around here. And he's taken it really, really well. So don't go acting as if we're not a steady thing, as if our marriage isn't going to work. Got it?"

Morwenna looked down at the table.

"I didn't say a thing, Megan. I know you love him."

"Right," Joseph agreed.

She wanted to hit them both. There was pity in their voices. They both believed there was something wrong with Finn, that it would come out—that she would see there was evil in him, or that he couldn't really be decent, and that in a matter of time—he would be gone.

Maybe it wasn't just pity. It might have been more.

Pity laced with . . .

Fear?

He'll be gone, or . . .

You'll be dead.

Neither of them said such a thing. Neither was speaking. They were just looking at her. And yet she felt as if someone had shouted the words in her head.

An uncomfortable silence fell between the three of them. It became unbearable. Megan cut her meat, but was afraid she wouldn't be able to chew.

"Hey, it's gone," Joseph said.

He was frowning, looking toward the stage.

"What's gone?"

"That stupid monster thing that was catching everyone's hair."

Megan looked around. It was true. Someone had removed the monster with the branch-like fingers.

"Good riddance," Morwenna said.

"I'll have to agree," Megan said, glad that the silence had been broken. "I think I have a bald patch on the back of my head."

Morwenna laughed softy. "I don't see any bald spots, but I'm glad they got rid of the thing. It really was dangerous. You got caught in it, and Finn got caught in it.

Better check him out tonight—he may have a bald spot."

"The man has no patience," Joseph told her. "He didn't wait for any detangling assistance, just ripped right away."

"I'll check him out tonight," Megan said. She could chew and swallow. The world was seeming normal again.

Finn came back to the table and sat. "Steaks are delicious," she said.

"And here's my beer," Finn said, sliding one around her at the table, and lifting the bottle of Michelob in front him in the air toward Joseph. "Thanks."

"My pleasure," Joseph acknowledged.

"You'd better eat—we've only got a few minutes left," Megan warned him.

"I'll be chewing away in two seconds, I promise," he said, setting the beer down and starting to cut his meat as well. He could eat quickly—he had learned that trick while waiting tables himself. A bad habit, actually. Megan had always heard that it was best to eat slowly. But Finn was usually a little too impatient to eat slowly.

Joseph pointed out the fact that the dangerous, hair-pulling monster was gone.

"Probably a good thing," Finn said, washing down his food with another swig of beer. "The hotel probably saw a few hairless customers walking by and got frightened of a lawsuit."

"Could be," Morwenna agreed cheerfully.

Break time was up. Finn thanked Morwenna and Joseph as he drew Megan from her chair. They both nodded happily.

On stage, Finn slid into another of their own songs, a dance number, and their last set of the evening, then proceeded to pack up quickly. Most of the tables were still filled when they finished. Finn gave Megan a thumbs-up sign as he immediately started to cover their equipment for the night and following day.

She was going to help him but Morwenna and Joseph came over to say good night.

Morwenna whispered to her, "You know . . . your husband really is quite incredible." Despite her words, she sounded hesitant.

She whispered back, though Finn was at some distance. "That's not what you said when you did the reading."

Morwenna stared at Finn, and looked uneasy. "I know . . . I don't understand. He's wicked good-looking. Sexy, talented . . . and he dotes on you. But according to the Tarot, he's . . . I don't know, cards can be interpreted differently. It looked as if he offered you some terrible danger, but then . . . maybe it's just that you're so in love with him, your heart or soul is at risk, or something. I should do another reading."

"No! Thank you. I do adore him, and our marriage is going to work. Your cards would have me offing him in the middle of the night or something!"

"Never!" Morwenna protested.

There was a tap on her shoulder. She jumped and turned around. But it wasn't Finn, only Darren, minus most of his costume's headgear. He had come to thank her for the CD and offer his enthusiasm for the evening's entertainment. She thanked him for his support.

When she finished speaking with him, she saw that Morwenna and Joseph had gone on out, heading home, she assumed.

Finn was almost done with the equipment, and the room was clearing out. When she would have stepped forward to give token assistance, he smiled and waved a hand, telling her to relax, he'd be ready in a minute.

She stood at the foot of the stage, waiting. Something drew her eyes to one of the balcony exits.

Andy Markham was there.

Staring at her.

His gaze was unnerving. Not because he looked at her in any manner that might be construed as dangerous.

But because he seemed to be watching her with pity, as if a great danger was headed her way, and he was powerless to stop it.

As if he knew that she was . . .

Doomed.

A cold trembling seized her. Ice raced through her veins. She might have been standing atop a ragged tor in the October wind, naked, entirely vulnerable, with the wind bringing shadows of whipping, screaming, darkness closer and closer . . .

He nodded to her gravely and turned, disappearing out the balcony door.

Chapter 5

"Ready?"

She nearly jumped a mile when Finn's hand landed on her shoulder.

"Ready," she assured him, forcing a smile.

Finn frowned. "What's wrong?"

"Nothing," she said quickly, and knew how false she sounded. She shrugged. "I don't know. Something silly. I just had shivers, you know, like the expression—someone walking over your grave. But I'm fine. Really."

"You sure?" He seemed skeptical.

"Yep. Just tired." It was late. Nearly two in the morning.

She must have assured him at last. He offered her a slow smile, and his suggestive whisper caressed her earlobe. "How tired?"

An honest grin replaced her forced smile.

"Tired enough to get out of here—and into a closed room. Alone. Well, alone with you, of course."

With an arm around her shoulder, he led her toward the main exit, thanking the fellow who had manned the cashier's station for selling their CDs. A few minutes later, they were in the car, and heading out.

Despite the shift between them, Megan moved close and rested her head against his shoulder. "It was a really great night, huh?" she said.

"Fantastic. Everything went well," he agreed.

"So it was smart to come here," she said, and wondered if she was trying to convince him, or herself.

"Well, great until now," he murmured.

"What's the matter?"

"No parking spaces," he said.

"That is a problem, once you get into town. You know, Huntington House is a big place. They should have spots right on the property, and not make their 'guests' have to park out on the street."

"Right—especially if they're going to have a Mr. Fallon on the property," Finn said lightly.

"We should have stayed at the hotel—they offered us a decent rate," Megan murmured.

"Ah, but Huntington House sounded so much more intriguing," Finn said.

"There's a lot around the corner with extra parking. Mr. Fallon did tell me about it. I'd forgotten. It says that it's a tow-away zone, but that's because the property belongs to Huntington House."

"Sounds good. It won't be much of a walk back."

Finn rounded the corner. The lot wasn't really that convenient. It was small and behind a row of colonial houses that had been altered in the Victorian period so that they were adorned with "gingerbread" latticework that had been so popular at the time. They parked and exited the car. The night seemed eerily silent. It had been clear when they'd been driving.

Now, a thick fog was rising.

Pea soup thick. Megan felt as if she were stepping into a swamp as she crawled out of the car.

"Wow, will you look at that? All of a sudden," Finn said.

"Hey, it's New England. Like they say, if you don't

like the weather, it will change in a few hours. Unfortunately, it doesn't change for the better all that often."

"Come here while I can still see you," Finn told her.

He walked toward her and she hurried for his outstretched arm.

"Creepy, hm?" she murmured.

"But it's keeping you nice and close."

"You can barely see the street lamps."

"True. Let's just hope we're walking in the right direction."

Megan looked up to the sky. Through the haze, she could see the moon. Not quite full, but it appeared that it was. The full moon this year was projected, aptly, for Halloween.

"'By the light of the silvery moon!'" she quoted from the song.

"Um. Well, so far, that is sidewalk beneath us."

"Right. And we're not even a block away."

"I can see the sign ahead."

Megan was glad. She couldn't explain the terror that seemed to be seeping through her, just like the dampness of the fog. And then, she thought she heard something coming from behind them.

It wasn't the sound of footsteps.

It seemed to be a strange whispering sound. As if something flew, or floated just above the ground. Something like a cold, dark wind with a scratchy human voice. She swallowed hard and started walking faster.

"Hey, what's the matter?" Finn demanded. "You don't want to trip on anything."

"Yeah, sorry. I just don't like it out here tonight."

"I'm with you."

She was silent, guiltily feeling as if his presence might not be enough to ward off the danger coming toward them.

"It's just . . . a mugger could pop up from anywhere."

"I did take some classes in martial arts," he reminded her.

"Muggers carry guns. And knives."

"I haven't heard that Salem has a huge violent crime rate."

"You never know."

"Hey, a mugger would have to be as blinded as we are."

She didn't think that this particular "mugger," the one becoming more and more real in her mind with every second that passed, was blinded by the fog. Rather, he saw better in the fog. Darkness was his forte.

And his weapons weren't conventional. No knives, no guns.

And Finn, for all his determination and prowess, didn't have the power to fight him.

Terror was becoming panic. She felt her breath coming more quickly each time she inhaled and exhaled. Her flesh was beginning to creep. That feeling was coming over her again. She was naked against a cold, dark wind that whispered . . .

"There's the sign for Huntington House," Finn said.

"Beat you there!" she told him.

And she started to run.

"Megan, you're going to kill yourself!" he cried.

She didn't care. She ran. She heard him pounding after her. A few moments later, she was on the porch. He was there behind her. "Meg, you could have tripped over that step, and broken your neck."

"Get your key out, please, quick—it's freezing out here," she said.

He slipped his key into the door, and in her mind, entered too slowly behind her. Once he was in, she pushed past him, closing and locking the main entry door with the speed of light.

"What on earth is the matter with you?" he queried, looking both concerned and impatient.

"Nothing—I'm just cold." She brought a finger to her lips. "Sh. Don't want Fallon coming out to tell us that we're disturbing the entire place again. Let's get to our room, okay?"

He nodded, his gaze still curious and skeptical.

To Megan's annoyance and unease, it seemed as if some of the fog had crept into the house. Of course, only night-lights were on to guide the guests through the house to their respective rooms. The night-lights were muted and an eerie yellow.

They passed from the entry through the dining room and down the hall to their own quarters, opposite from the rest of the guest rooms. Their own wing. Private, special.

She wished that they were surrounded by tourists. By kids. People. Even crusty old Fallon would be good now.

They entered their own room. Finn switched on the light. It blazed, and she felt better. Actually, she suddenly felt as if her fear had been ridiculous. It fell from her as if she had doffed a cape from her shoulders.

Megan didn't want Finn reading the relief she felt from her face. "Running into the shower," she murmured briefly.

In the bathroom, she turned the shower on hot and lingered beneath the spray, letting the warmth and confidence seep into her, just as the cold and fear had seemed to do earlier. She scrubbed herself studiously, as if she could wash away the remnants of any unease. At last, she turned off the spray, and wrapped herself in one of the B and B's heavy terry towels.

When she emerged, she saw that the drapes to the balcony were open and fluttering inward on a gentle breeze. She walked over to the open French doors and slipped on out. Finn was at the short, Victorian-intricate railing, looking out at the night.

"Look," he said.

She stared out. She saw the sloping lawn and the street beyond. Trees, becoming denuded of their brilliant autumn covering. Buildings at a small distance, cloaked in the gentle shadows of night.

"What am I looking at?" she asked.

"The fog is gone," he said briefly.

"Yeah, well . . . New England," she murmured.

He turned and gave her a brief kiss. "I'm hopping in the shower. Be right out."

He was gone. She stood on the balcony alone, looking out.

The fog was gone. Completely.

And yet, as she stood there . . .

She felt as if she were being watched. The moon, so nearly full, rode overhead. With the fog gone, it, combined with the muted glow of street lamps, gave the area a surreal look. As if the houses weren't really solid, as if the ground didn't really lie still.

The breeze shifted, wafted, soft, and gentle . . .

She thought she heard her name whispered. The wind, nothing but the wind, air moving through dry and brittle leaves.

Her fingers tightened around the railing.

They were there, somewhere. The eyes that watched her. They came out of the shadow, they watched her every movement, knew her fear, knew . . .

"Megan?"

Once again, she nearly jumped a mile. And yet, she knew it was Finn. He was hot, still emanating a shower-warmth from beneath his bathrobe. His hands rested on her shoulders. And then, she felt that brush of his fingers against her nape, sweeping her hair aside, a touch that was so totally Finn. He set his lips against the skin bared by the movement of her hair, and they were warmer still, a touch that seemed to send the slow heat, a liquid shimmer, down the length of her spine. His fingers were long, instinctive and practiced, moving over her shoulder blades, kneading and brushing, pulling her back tautly against the length of his body.

"Tired?" he murmured.

"Um."

"How tired?"

She turned into the circle of his arms. "I suppose I could be persuaded to stay awake a little longer."

He touched her face. She loved the simple feel. Thumb caressing her chin, long forefinger stroking over her cheek. He gazed at her for a long moment, rueful grin sliding into place as he pressed closer against her, a subtle movement that was endearing and erotic, locking them more intimately together, and allowing the tension of his length to seep into hers, along with the more obvious intrusion of the hard rise of his sex. His mouth covered hers then, encompassing, molding first, then the tease of the tip of his tongue, and something more forceful as it slipped between her lips, invasive, hungry, awakening whatever desire might not have been evident in the simple magic of his hold. Megan clung to him, still awed by the explosive sweep of longing he could create, the surge in her blood, the simmer, then the surge of sheer physical urgency he had the power to create. It had been like this from the beginning . . . the touch, and everything that was known was new; she was shaky and trembling, hot and breathless . . . as desperate as ever.

He drew back for a moment. "Think I can keep you awake a few minutes?" he asked softly.

She pushed away from him, doing her best to offer a casual shrug. She cast her head back with a pretend yawn, and went walking slowly back into the bedroom. But once there, she kept her back to him, letting the robe slip from her shoulders to puddle to the floor. And there she waited.

And he came. A subtle, sensual assault from such a position, once again, his fingers at her nape, and then his lips, and then just the touch of his kiss, the brush of his tongue, slowly down the length of her spine. Mercilessly slow, far too quickly . . . but then his hands, upon her hips, and the sudden shift of her body, him on his knees, hair soft against the tender flesh of her abdomen, and then his lips, tongue . . . caressing all over again . . . until her fingers were entangled in his hair, and the world seemed to spin. Any fog was silver, any thought was purely carnal, and her words were whimpers and pleas, then warnings that she would fall.

He was up, and ever the romantic, sweeping her up into his hold, and carrying her the few steps to the bed. There was a brief touch of laughter as he nearly tripped flat over his own shoes in his effort to kill the light, but then they were falling, and the sheer heat, rippled power, length and breadth of his body blanketed her, and a moment later, they were entangled as one, and she knew what she had missed when they were apart, and she didn't think she could ever bear to think they could stay apart, that he might not be hers forever, that *this* might not be hers . . .

She cried out, and tried to twist into the pillow to silence her own sound.

"Fallon!" she whispered with alarm.

But Finn, arms braced, hair tousled, features taut, had a quick reply.

"Damn Fallon!" he swore, voice low and ragged, a sound that swept into her, and ignited even more excitement.

She half smiled, until she was swept up into the urgency of another wet, sloppy, liquid kiss, and the sear of his body within her own, and . . .

The hunger.

He stood on the street, a figure as dark as the night, one with shadow and fog. He lifted his head toward the night sky, and then his arms, feeling the power that was his now, savoring it. The time was coming, and he would be rewarded even more richly for the service he had done.

Ah . . . the mind.

And all that lay beneath the sunlight of the day, the charade of logic and learning!

The fog swirled around his feet, blue in color, beneath the uncanny glow of the moon, so nearly at its radiant peak. The time was coming . . .

And there would be no stopping what was about to be.

He turned his gaze from the sky to the centuries-old house, there, in the midst of so many others, and yet on its own little hillock.

They hadn't thought to close the balcony door. And though he couldn't see, he could see, and so, he closed his eyes, and thought again of the power that was his. As He had promised, all would be fulfilled. Pieces fell into place, and all that was needed would be obtained.

The time was coming . . .

For a moment, he was disturbed, feeling again the surge of power, thinking of what that might mean for himself. The things that he could do . . . the things he longed to do.

The things he now felt, saw in his mind's eye.

But he served a greater power. He could not falter. He could not allow the greed, the lust, and all that might be go beyond the state of wonder.

For he served a greater power.

And he was smart enough to know both the tremendous gifts that came with all he had been given, along with the . . .

Fear.

He would serve, and thereby, know reward.

He lifted his eyes to the sky once again. To the moon, glowing blue like the fog that swirled at his feet. He raised his arms to the deep, roiling sky, and began to say the words.

* * *

In his dream, he knew first that he was walking. He felt the pads of his feet fall upon the earth, and the feel was good. Dirt, rich, ever so slightly damp, no grass, no stones, no sticks, just the feel of his bare feet and earth, and it was strangely erotic.

More so when he felt the cool breeze that touched him, that seemed to wrap around him. And he realized that the sensation was so powerful because he was walking naked, and every moment in that strange breeze, on the barren earth, was sensual.

There was sound. At first, he thought it was the air, the sound of it whirling around him, touching him. But then he knew. The soft, melodic chants were real. They came from the group who awaited him, and he knew it was he that they awaited, that they adored him, and were ready to fall on their knees before him. It was exhilarating. He felt the play of his every muscle as he walked, and he felt stronger, more powerful than ever before. He could feel his blood rushing through his veins, the even sound of his breath, rising and falling with his movement.

They were ahead. Chanting still, and the words they chanted were lauds to him. He came closer, and still, they were elusive, for they were shrouded in the soft blue mesh of the fog that stirred so thickly around the ground. It was beautiful. Deep, rich, soft . . . and yet simmering. Enticing, yet promising something volatile and exciting beyond belief.

He kept walking. There were two at his feet. He couldn't see them clearly. Women. Flesh blue-tinged, hair long and wild. They kissed his feet, stroked his calves as he moved. They were not the ones that he wanted, and he shook off the hold they had upon him. He kept moving, for there was something far ahead, an altar in the woods, and it offered . . .

The answer. The release for the tension winding within him. Something he had wanted for eternity.

His rational mind fought such an image, for there was nothing he wanted. He knew he had all he wanted . . .

No. A voice whispered at the back of his head that there was more. So much more. He kept moving, and even through the fog, he saw that the world had gone bizarre. There were still people. Chanting. Some half clad in strange robes, and half naked. There was a goat ahead. No . . . not a goat, a man, a creature, half goat, half man. The head of a man, but horned, with a long, strange chin that added to the look of a satyr. The creature had cloven hooves for hands at the end of long, furry arms. He wondered if the creature was the one whispering to him, bringing the thoughts to hover beyond his conscious thought. He came closer to the goat, then started to turn away, for the goat was busy fornicating. A hideous creature, but the woman before him was laid out in extreme ecstacy, her moans rising above the sound of the chants.

Closer . . .

The invitation beckoned him. And he kept walking, past the goat, and all the people, men and women now, all of them in different stages of copulation. Yet, as he passed, they followed, whispering words of adoration, begging for his word, his command. They ran at his side, they touched him, stroked him with oil as he moved.

Again, he was embarrassed, for they ran their fingers down his back, his arms, his chest, his buttocks, then cradled his penis, anointing it with the oil.

And he kept hearing words, silent, shrieking, part of the breeze, the chants . . .

What you have waited for . . .

Centuries . . .

The hunger has grown and grown . . .

She *will be there.*

They followed, they chanted, they threw flowers. They hissed words in his ears, then, words of what he should do, how he should take his prize. And at last, with the host of demons and humans at his side, brushing him, stroking still, he came upon the altar in the midst of the forest.

And there . . . what had awaited him.

The woman. He knew her, did not know her. She was tied, yet surely knew she was the sacrifice, surely she gave herself up to the ecstacy and power that awaited, after all these years. Closer . . .

She was shrouded, in blue-black veils. Glimpses of flesh teased his senses. The gauze draped over her midriff, but bared her breasts. Drifted over kneecaps, but allowed glimpses of thigh, evocative in the blue light.

Their whispers were coming at him, harder, harder, making every step then urgent.

He reached the altar . . .

The gauze covered her face. It didn't matter. His blood was pulsing. His muscles were tightening and contracting, filled with violence and tension. He knew what he was to do, knew the sense of force and violence.

A cry came, for he was upon her, and naked nymphs were at his backside, touching, stroking, urging him on. He was the king of this strange copse, all powerful, force, the force of nature, of the wind, of . . .

Evil.

He reached out, and grabbed the woman around the middle, and he leered at her, hands rough as he touched, as he brutally forced himself into her, touching her breasts . . .

He saw himself, where he stretched to touch her so callously. His arms were richly furred. His fingers had convulsed into something cloven.

His head . . .

If he reached up to touch, he would feel that horns had grown from his temples, and that he had done all that was wrong that had been bidden, and that he had become . . .

* * *

He awoke with a violent start, unable to catch his breath, terror holding his heart at a dead standstill.

He breathed.

His heart thumped.

And still, for a moment, the dream had been so real that he was afraid to look around the room. He forced himself to do so.

Night still, but maybe, just barely. He could clearly see outside, for they had left the balcony doors open. Stupidly. It was freezing in the room, he realized.

And still, he was covered in a sheen of sweat.

Megan!

Terror for his wife seized him.

But she was there, turned away from him, curled into her pillow, long blond hair spilled upon it. He reached out to touch her, then nearly recoiled. Her hair was damp. Damp, as it often was after making love . . .

He kicked off the covers and stood, reaching for his robe. He walked around to the side of the bed, almost afraid to touch Megan. But she was sleeping. Soundly. Her breath came in an even, slow rhythm. He studied her face. Her beautiful face. And he was afraid.

Ridiculous. He'd had a bizarre dream.

Just as she'd had a bizarre dream.

It was this place. All this talk about witches.

Witches. Wiccans. But they were good, so Megan swore. They did no evil to others, because it would come back upon them threefold.

He was losing his mind. He was so afraid of losing Megan that he was losing his mind.

He gave himself a mental shake and walked out to the balcony. Sunrise was coming. The air was very cool. Yet he was glad to stand there shivering.

Trees rustled softly.

The moon shone down, benignly.

The coming day would be beautiful, he thought. Almost a touch of Indian summer.

He stepped back into the bedroom, hesitating just a second to look around. But there was no movement anywhere. The world might have stalled.

Suddenly, a noise. He jumped, then laughed at himself. It was just a car backfiring.

He walked into the bedroom, and carefully closed and locked the balcony doors. As he did so, he hesitated, having the strangest feeling that it was too late.

And so, he walked around the room. Looked in the closet, in the bathroom, in the shower. When he came out, he even looked beneath the bed.

They were alone, as they had been.

And still . . .

He had the strangest feeling he had let something enter. Something had come into their bedroom as they had slept. He was furious with himself for having left the doors open.

And yet . . .

He didn't think the doors would have stopped whatever it was from entering.

He groaned aloud, and spoke clearly to himself in the darkness as well.

"Dickhead! Ass!"

He gave his head a shake. More light seemed to be drifting in. He glanced at the bedside clock. There was a small coffeemaker on the dresser. He filled the pot with water from the sink and threw in a filter. The four-cup machine took only seconds.

While the coffee brewed, he dug into his belongings. He didn't smoke often; this morning, he wanted a cigarette.

He found a half-crushed pack of Marlboro Lights. He got his cup of coffee and his cigarette and headed for the balcony.

He hesitated, then forced himself to open the doors, walk out, and take a seat on one of the little patio chairs there.

The sun was rising. It was beautiful.

He lit his cigarette, sipped his coffee. The sun kept rising. It wasn't like a Southern sunrise. The brilliant crimsons and golds didn't streak across the sky. But still, day came magnificently. Soft grays became violets, and that color became softer still, an incredible powder blue.

He closed his eyes. There were noises now, too. Car doors, shouts here and there, conversations . . .

The world was awakening. Day-to-day. Usual. He heard a mother remind a child to grab a lunch bag.

He crushed out his cigarette, drained his coffee, and went back inside, ready to go back to sleep, despite the coffee. The dream had, at long last, left him. Only vague, scattered remnants remained.

Still . . .

He paused as he closed and locked the balcony doors again.

He had forgotten so much.

And still, that vague feeling remained.

Too late, too late, far too late . . .

There was no way to lock out . . .

Evil.

He swore, set the cup down, and crawled back in next to Megan. Oddly, he hesitated again, as if he had wronged her somehow.

Tentatively, he pulled her into his arms.

She came, not really awakening, just readjusting into his embrace.

I love you. I will protect you against any evil! he swore silently.

But then another thought plagued his mind.

What if I truly am the evil?

He slept at last with one very logical, disdainful, and determined notion.

Bull!

Chapter 6

Megan awoke around ten. Finn, a rather restless spirit at the best of times, was usually up before her.

Not that morning. He was out like a dead fish. In fact, he seemed so still that she found herself besieged by a moment of panic, checking to make sure he was breathing. He was.

She hesitated a moment, then touched his injured hand. Somewhere along the line, he'd lost the bandage. But the bleeding had stopped, and the injury didn't appear to be too bad. It would be annoying on his hand, but there was already a scab forming on the slash.

She started for the coffee machine and was surprised to see there was about an inch or two of cold coffee in the pot. He'd apparently awakened, and gone back to bed. Caffeine never had an effect on Finn. She thought it was because so many of his waking moments were so intense.

And getting strange, she thought ruefully.

Like last night.

Newly disturbed, she rinsed the coffeepot, and grimaced when she saw that the only little package left was decaf. That wasn't going to help her a lot. She'd have to get dressed and make her way out to the dining room. Breakfast would be over, but coffee and tea were available throughout the day. And she didn't need anything to eat. They were going to Aunt Martha's for lunch.

That thought gave her a smile. Martha was so wonderfully pragmatic. Down to earth, *and* a sensational cook. The concept of going to see Martha was a cheery one, banishing some of the discomforts that began to plague her more and more.

She started the coffee, then stepped into the shower while it brewed. The water crashed down on her hard and she let out a little cry, realizing for the first time that there actually were bruises on her arms and hips.

What the hell had gotten into him?

Part of Finn's sexual charisma was his ability to be subtle. The slightest brush could seem to awaken every erogenous zone in her body. He could go from a touch softer than a whisper to a tumult of fever, electricity, and passion with a finesse that was breathtaking and so seductive she never knew sometimes how she wound up in such mindless frenzy. He could be gentle, and then rugged and forceful, in his lovemaking.

But never hurtful. Until . . .

Last night.

They'd have to talk, she decided. He'd been so . . . weird.

Yes . . .

But exciting.

Like a stranger.

Being with a stranger would not be exciting, she thought ruefully, and honestly. He was incredible; even when she had been determined she couldn't live with him, she'd never wanted anyone else, and she'd been certain she would never find anyone who attracted her again, not after Finn. So . . .

She shook her head, then rinsed quickly, frowning at the bruises once again. They were definitely young and in love with healthy sexual appetites, but even living in a city like New Orleans, they'd never been . . . weird. Sadistic, or masochistic. She vaguely remembered that there had been moments of pain.

But still, she'd been so enwrapped in the frenetic rise to climax that she hadn't realized just how he had held her . . . pinioned her, actually.

She dismissed the uneasy notion that Finn was changing as she stepped from the shower. And she didn't want to think that being here, close to her home, among her family members and old friends, was bad for them. That it was causing them both to be different.

The decaf had gone through. She poured a cup while she quickly dressed in jeans, T-shirt, and a sweater. As she tied on her sneakers, she saw that Finn was still sound asleep.

She left him, heading out to the breakfast room for real coffee. The dining room was empty. In fact, it seemed that the entire house was as silent as a tomb.

She was standing still, looking out the bay window in the dining room, when she was startled by a voice behind her.

"Ms. Douglas!"

Coffee slopped over the rim of her mug as she spun around. Susanna McCarthy was behind her. She hadn't heard the woman walk into the room. In fact, the housekeeper's movements seemed downright creepy.

"Yes, good morning, Ms. McCarthy," she answered in kind.

"There's a telephone call for you."

She frowned, instantly worried that something might have happened with her parents. But her emergency number, which she insisted both her folks keep on them at all times, was her cell phone number.

She didn't have to worry long. Not about her folks.

"It's old Andy Markham," Susanna said with a sniff. "Do you wish to speak with him?"

The question implied she shouldn't. Perhaps because of that, she decided to take the call, even though she wasn't sure she wanted to be talking to old Andy.

"Of course, Ms. McCarthy, thank you," she said sweetly.

"You can use the phone in the salon, right on through there," Susanna said, indicating the very formal living room.

"Thank you."

Megan walked on into the adjoining room and sat in the elegant Victorian chair next to the phone. "Hello," she murmured into the receiver. Looking back into the dining room, she saw that Susanna McCarthy was gone.

She was probably listening in on another extension in the house, Megan couldn't help but feel.

"Megan. Megan Douglas?"

It was definitely the old man. He had a way of sounding like an old Maine fisherman.

"Yes, it's me. How are you Mr. Markham?"

"Andy, it's Andy, I've told you to call me Andy."

"I'm sorry. Andy. What can I do for you?"

"Something very important," he said seriously. He sounded very sane. And determined. "You can listen to me. Really listen to me. Then you can call me crazy, if you still wish."

She hesitated, aware that she didn't want to listen to anything that he had to say. He did sound crazy. And it was all the crazy talk that seemed to be getting to everyone.

"Please."

He knew she was hesitating. And his entreaty was so earnest.

"I swear before God Almighty, I am trying to help you, woman!" the old man insisted.

Again, he sounded so sincere.

"All right, Andy. I'm listening."

"No. You've got to meet me."

She hesitated again. Meet him? Finn would go through the roof.

"Where? When? I'm afraid I have a number of appointments during the day."

"Now. It's a ten minute drive. Just on the outskirts of town, not far from the hotel where you're playing. And now."

"Now? What if—"

"Your husband is still sleeping, isn't he?"

She was startled by that.

"Give me the address. I'll come—if I can."

He didn't give her an address, but explained the route. Andy hung up.

She sat in the chair a long moment, the receiver in her hand—certain that she heard a second click. *Susanna McCarthy,* she thought. *Listening in.*

She exhaled on a long sigh. All right, if Finn was still sleeping, she'd go. And if he had wakened . . . well, she'd said that she'd come if she could.

If Susanna had been listening in, she would tell Finn where Megan had gone once he started prowling around, looking for her.

But then again, she didn't intend to be gone long.

She rose with a strange determination, dreading the idea of meeting the man, and wondering why she was even contemplating doing so when the idea was so loathsome to her.

It had been his voice. The pleading in it.

She hurried back to her room. Finn was still sound asleep.

"Finn?" she spoke his name.

He didn't stir.

She walked to the dresser and picked up the car keys. They jangled. He still didn't make a move.

Shaking her head, she grabbed her handbag and walked out of the room.

By daylight, the car was just a stone's throw away. Bizarre how last night the walk from their auto to the B and B had seemed so ridiculously long. And scary. By the sun's light, it was a pretty walk, even with the dead and dying leaves of autumn scattering the paths. Some—a few—remained on the trees. It seemed a gentle day.

She followed the easy directions he had given her, leaving the center of town behind in a matter of minutes. Soon she was passing the new hotel where they were playing. Just about sixty seconds after the hotel turn-in, she found the trail he had indicated she take, a narrow, winding road into what looked like a forest area.

Foolish. Down the trail, the trees were thick. Despite the coming winter, there were enough branches and leaves on the trees to block out a great deal of sunlight. She began to think that Andy Markham was really crazy; the trail seemed to go nowhere.

Then, she reached a large copse at the end of the trail, and parked, looking around.

There were trails leading through the woods, but none big enough for a car. Whoever ventured down those trails did so on foot. But to either side of the central clearing in the woods were other pockets of cleared areas. They were overgrown with grass and underbrush, but the trees had been cleared, probably ages ago. As she sat, staring out the window, she noted that there were bits of stone among the long grasses, weeds, and bits of bush here and there. The place was eerie. She noted that some of the stones were larger than others, weather worn. She squinted, trying to see better from her distance. One of them looked like it had been an angel or something of the like at one time.

A chill seized her. She thought she had come upon some time-forgotten cemetery.

A tap on her window nearly sent her flying right through it.

She turned to the passenger's side of the car and saw that Andy Markham was standing just outside the car.

For a moment, she hesitated again. Maybe the old man was crazy. He had lured her here to murder her.

The thought was not without value, and yet, she suddenly doubted that the skeletal old man could take her in any kind of a fight.

He could have a gun.

But he didn't. His clothes hung off his body in a way that allowed for no hiding of any kind of a weapon.

She had come this far. And obviously, it was just she and Andy in the godforsaken, eerie clearing.

She stepped out of the car.

"Hi, Andy."

He walked around to her, his eyes anxious on her. "Thank you for coming. I swear, I am trying to help you."

"That's great," she said lightly, "but—"

"But you don't believe in tall tales or hauntings, the spirits of the dead, or anything like that."

"Right," she said softly.

"But hear me out. Do you know where we are?"

"It looks like some kind of a cemetery. I see what was an angel over there."

"Yes, it's some kind of a cemetery."

"So . . . we're on hallowed ground. Nice and safe," she murmured cheerfully.

He shook his head so gravely that she felt as if one of the dead branches on the distant trees had reached out to scrape her spine.

"Andy—"

"It's unhallowed ground. Centuries ago, it was where those who died outside the sanction of the church were buried."

"Oh!" she murmured. "How sad! You mean like Rebecca Nurse, or others prosecuted in the witch trials—"

Andy snorted. "History and research show us that Rebecca Nurse was a fine old woman who was simply not appreciated by her neighbors. She had a loving family, and they got hold of her body. I'm talking about the truly evil."

"I see," Megan said evenly, wishing she hadn't come. What the hell was this creepy old man up to?

He continued to stare at her earnestly. "You must believe that there is evil in the world."

"Andy, I have a cousin who is a Wiccan, and I know—"

"Not Wiccans!" he interrupted with a snort, then gave her a deep sigh. "It should be evident that if there is good in the world, there is evil. There is a benign god, and, even in the Old Testament, a god of wrath. Say you believe in the general tenets of the day. God is good, and sits above in Heaven. But those who believe in that God believe in his nemesis as well. Lucifer, the fallen angel. And just as the great God of our fathers is good, his nemesis is evil. They believed, once, that Satan had come to New England. Satan is a busy fellow. But just as the great God rests among the angels and what spirits surround him are those of good, Satan has his imps and demons, and creatures of pure, malignant evil."

Megan just stared.

"Walk with me."

She didn't know why she did, but when he turned, walking toward the stones in the underbrush, she followed.

They reached what she had thought to have been a marble angel. Seeing it up close, even in its state of aged decay, she saw that it was no angel. It was a demon. Horned, tailed, with a lean jutting jaw that gave it a terrible impression of pure carnal amusement and . . . evil.

"Andy, this thing is awful!"

"And too true," Andy said softly. He scratched the day's growth of stubble on his chin, looking at Megan, then added flatly, "He's trying to come back."

Chills snaked through her, but she said firmly, " I'm sorry, but marble creatures are the artistry of men."

"Aye, girl, and you need men, the living, to bring about the return of the dead."

"Andy, you're creeping me out here," she said honestly.

"You've got to understand. I have to make you understand."

She inhaled on a deep breath. "Andy, I'm trying to understand. You think that a man is trying to bring a demon to life. A demon—a broken-down old statue—back to life."

"He came before," Andy said, and his words were barely a breath.

The wind shifted. A cold breeze rippled past her face, lifted her hair, and seemed to caress her throat.

"Andy, I understand that this is a graveyard. For people who might have been bad news. But surely, if there were such a thing as a demon, he wouldn't allow himself to be buried among humble men."

"You don't understand. He came before."

"Before what?" She was getting frightened, and therefore, impatient. She didn't believe any demon was coming after her, but she was beginning to fear the old man out in the middle of nowhere with only skeletal trees, the caw of crows, and a chill in the air as company for them.

"After the witch trials. During a phase you won't hear about in any old history books. People were ashamed. Very ashamed of all the innocents who suffered. Oh, not just those who died. Those who were incarcerated for years. Who died in prison because they couldn't pay the debts for the cold hovels and chains that held them. No one wanted anything to do with such persecutions. So the time was ripe, just right, for those who were truly evil. Not Wiccans. True Satanists. Devil worshipers. *Demon* worshipers. There was one such man. Convinced he was the chosen one to bring back to a human incarnation an ancient demon, Bac-Dal, first seen in Persia, eons before the time of Christ. That man came here. Right at the time when both men and women were deeply sorry for all the death and destruction that the hysteria had caused. When they were least likely to watch what their neighbors were doing. When they were quick to turn blind eyes to whispers of sorcery. His name was Cabal Thorne. He wreaked havoc among men and women, created a life of true debauchery, and committed many murders for his blood lust."

"Andy, surely if there were any truth behind such a story, the history books or legends would have some hint of what had occurred."

"The Elders allowed no word of it, once they believed. Men came here from elsewhere, and were closeted with some of the most learned men of the area. There could be no arrest for Cabal Thorne. No trial. No record of him, or what was to happen to him. And no one knows exactly what did happen. They grouped together one night, and what they did remains secret to this day, what power they used, no one knows. But Thorne was killed. And brought here."

"Surely, an anthropologist would have dug him up by now!" she said, trying once again to speak lightly.

"At the turn of the century, unbeknownst to history, someone did try to dig him up. A man known as Aleistair Crowley. Ever heard of him?"

Megan gritted her teeth. "A very famous necromancer, Satanist, into the occult, a debaucher, all that, yes, I've heard of him."

"He tried to dig up the remains. It was claimed that he found nothing."

"There was probably nothing to find. Look, Crowley was known to be one of the most hedonistic—if not evil—men of the past two centuries. If he didn't stay—"

"The history books won't even say that he was here."

"Andy, did it ever occur to you that all this might be . . . tall tales?"

He cocked his head strangely. "I'm an old, old man. I've seen a great deal. Aye-uh, girl. It's men create evil most often. But there are forces in the world. And I've lived so long that I know when those forces are at work. Look at the things done! In the name of God? Don't you think that sometimes, something not so godly slips in? Haven't you felt it when there's a touch of evil, just a touch, at the base of your spine, creeping along, setting ice at your neck? There's evil out there. And some men who can manipulate it better than others."

The trees rustled in a chill breeze. Somewhere, there was sunshine. It didn't enter through the canopy here. *God, yes, she felt a chill!*

"All right, Andy. Say a really evil man lived in the very early 1700s. And he thought he could become one with this demon, Bac-Dal, or whatever. He was hunted down and killed. Probably for murder and rape and other crimes—far too well known to normal men. What can that really have to do with now?"

There was a sudden sizzle in the sky, a flash of light, and then, a crack of thunder that caused Megan to jump.

Andy was staring at her sagely.

"Weather!" she sniffed, though those icy fingers he was talking about had a really heavy grip around her neck by now. "Rain, thunder, lightning. Natural phenomena!" she said.

He nodded. "Aye-uh, girl. Natural phenomena. Don't you see? The time is right. The full moon is coming for All Hallow's Eve. And even that goes back . . . so far back. The night of the dead. When the souls of the departed are allowed to converse with the living. Don't you sense it? This is a playground for those who would twist what is good . . . and turn it to evil. The time is right for Bac-Dal."

"Andy, I have to go. Finn will be up by now."

"You haven't understood me."

"What is there to understand?"

"That there are forces in the world. Forces of good and evil."

"Andy," she said very gently, "think about it, please. People cause the evil in the world."

He shook his head stubbornly and stared at her. That stare that could make her so uneasy. So aware that there was no one else near them.

She very well might be alone in the secluded woods with a man who had truly gone a little bit mad.

"The time is coming," he said stubbornly. "And you must be aware." He gripped her wrists suddenly, a grip that was as tight as any vise she had ever known before.

"Andy, you're hurting me."

He released her instantly. But even so, she was aware of the leaves, rustling, as if they watched the two of them, creating shadow, chattering softly, whispering.

"What time is coming? Halloween? Andy, it's a holiday, it comes every year."

"All Hallow's Eve. When spirits and demons can walk the earth."

"Andy—"

"Bac-Dal is coming. And I'm afraid."

"Afraid of what?"

"You must be afraid, too."

"Why, Andy. Why must I be afraid?"

"Bac-Dal wants you."

Finn was sitting on the balcony when she returned. The day wasn't that bright, but he was wearing his sunglasses. He'd made more coffee—the maid must have brought him more of the regular packs, Finn never bothered with decaf. And he was smoking. Usually, he just smoked on occasion. She could see that he'd gone through half a pack of cigarettes.

She hadn't a clue of what he was thinking, not with

the sunglasses covering his eyes. He looked tense, though, drawn and tired. Not a good sign, when they'd only just gone through their first night of work here. And he didn't appear to be in a good mood.

Now that she'd left Andy and the eerie graveyard, she was beginning to feel silly for having let him get to her so. The whole thing was so entirely ridiculous. When she'd asked Andy why he was so convinced that the demon was after her, he hadn't known. When she'd wanted to know what he meant—and exactly *whom* he was talking about who might want to resurrect a long dead man or a demon, he didn't know. Her impatience, along with her fear, had soared.

Somehow, she had forced herself to remember that he was a very old man, with only his tales left to him. She had told him she would be very careful, and that she would consider his words. She had also told him he mustn't say any of it to Finn, that she would not do so herself. He hadn't seemed happy, but rather resigned.

"I have, at the least, warned you," he told her gravely.

He hadn't brought a car. He had come through one of the footpaths through the trees and foliage, and though she'd offered to drop him somewhere, he had refused, remaining in the eerie little place when she had left.

And oddly, the glowering sky, the lightning, the threat of rain, had passed. It was an almost absurdly beautiful day for late October.

"Where have you been?" Finn asked as she joined him on the balcony. She couldn't even tell if his voice was ringed with any kind of anger. The sunglasses seemed to hide all. Despite his almost haggard look, there was something very appealing, almost rawly sexy, about the way he slouched in the patio chair, long legs stretched out on the wrought iron rail, hair falling over his eyes, the length of his body in a languid stretch, almost like that of a cat.

"Out and about," she said. "Just taking in a few sights. When did you wake up? I've never seen you sleep like that."

He shrugged. "Had a bad time waking up."

"Well, you must have been up early and gone back to bed. No wonder you feel dragged out."

He frowned. She could see that much, despite the glasses.

"I wasn't up before."

"Yes, you were. You made coffee in the middle of the night, or first thing in the morning, or sometime."

He stared at her as if she were crazy.

"No."

"Finn! When I woke up, there was cold coffee in the pot."

"There was cold decaf when I woke up," he said with a sniff.

"Honestly, you had to have been awake. Unless some little gremlin came in while we were sleeping, made coffee, smoked a cigarette, and left," she said, amazed that she had to force a smile.

He was still frowning. "There's a bruise on your arm."

"Yeah, there is. You need to cool it a little."

"What?"

"Finn! You gave me that bruise."

"I did not!" he said indignantly.

She leaned against the railing, staring at him. "Finn, I swear, you woke up in the middle of the night."

"And made coffee, so you say. What did I do? Come over and slug you before plugging in the pot?"

"Finn, you gave me the bruise before you made the coffee. I don't believe this! You don't remember waking in the night, like a man who'd been in prison for decades or something like that, and made love like an SST?"

"Megan, I remember coming out to the porch after a shower, and having a lovely and passionate time—but I never bruised you!"

"Not the first time."

"There was a second time?" he demanded incredulously.

"One of us is losing it," she murmured. She eyed him cautiously. "How much did you drink last night?"

"One beer that Joseph bought me," he said irritably. She was silent. "Finn, I didn't bruise myself."

"I can't believe I would do that to you."

He suddenly seemed distant—and resentful. She had the bruise, *bruises!* And he seemed resentful.

But she needed to be near him. Even growing angry now, he still had that long, lean look of a lounging cat. The hair, his face . . . freshly shaven, shampooed, a little wild . . . built like brick, incredibly sensual. And attractive. She didn't want to jump back into bed at the moment; she just wanted to be held. Assured.

She came over and sat on his lap, stroking his chin. The subtle sandalwood scent of his aftershave was pleasant, elusive, evocative. Like his warmth, and the feel of his arms, instinctively coming around her.

"I didn't say you weren't incredibly exciting," she whispered, nuzzling his ear. "Just a bit too . . . forceful." She didn't want to use the word "violent."

"Great. I was exciting and forceful, and I don't even remember it."

"And you had coffee."

"Man, I must be really tired."

"You're sure it was just one beer?"

"Megan, what's the matter with you? It sounds as if some darned scary Puritan roots are coming out here."

"Only my dad's family goes back to way back when. My mom was an immigrant, you know. Of course, she was a baby when her family came over. And I'm not a Puritan. You're not a drug addict, or a drunk, and I know it. And we both like to have a few drinks now and then. I'm just trying to get to the bottom of this."

His smoothed his hand over her hair, studying her

eyes. "Megan, I'm horrified that I could have hurt you in any way—and especially horrified that I don't remember it. Are you sure you weren't dreaming again?"

"I dreamed up a bruise. Actually, a few of them," she added ruefully.

He frowned. "Maybe you were tossing and turning, banged into the nightstand, or something. Or maybe even got up and banged into the furniture."

"Without waking you?"

He shook his head, staring out at the lawn reflectively. "I was sure out of it last night. Exhausted. And sleeping like the dead."

"Ah, well, you were sure great in the dream. Just tone it down a little next time, huh?" She didn't believe that she'd been dreaming for a single second. But she didn't want this to turn into a knock-down-drag-'em-out argument.

And she didn't want him blaming it on her family, Huntington House, or the whole Wiccan thing going on with her relatives. Better to let it lie. Maybe he deserved a night of dead-out sleep, even if he moved in it as if he were far more than wide awake.

"So, hey! Where did you go this morning?" he asked her.

At this point, she was definitely not going to tell him anything whatsoever about Andy Markham and his bizarre theories about demons and Satanists.

"I took a ride, looked at old sights, that's all. Why didn't you call me on the cell phone?"

"I did."

"Really? I never heard it ring."

"Maybe you weren't paying attention. Too busy seeing the sights."

"Honestly, I just didn't hear it."

"I would have seen those sights with you, you know."

"I didn't want to wake you."

He nuzzled her neck. "You can wake me anytime," he murmured suggestively.

Apparently, she thought, she didn't need to wake him. She refrained from saying so.

"You needed the sleep."

"I don't need sleep now."

She smiled, thinking in a brief moment of pure bliss that she loved the sound of her husband's voice. Just his words, his whispers, could slip beneath her skin. She could hop up, right then, and happily drag him back into the bedroom.

But, of course, she couldn't. Not at this time.

"We're due at Aunt Martha's in . . ." she paused, looking at her watch, "thirty minutes."

His lips moved with playful eroticism over her throat, to her ear. "Won't Aunt Martha wait?"

"Aren't you hungry?"

"You bet, my love."

She laughed. "For Aunt Martha's incredible meat loaf and mashed potatoes?"

"Sure . . . later."

"She's furious when you're late for a meal."

He laughed. "Give me fifteen minutes."

"Fifteen minutes?"

"Hey, you got the long ones, and the short ones. When I get old, you know, we may be down to five minutes."

She laughed. "We have to be there on time!" she said firmly.

He rose, setting her on her feet.

"I'll think old right now. We won't be late for lunch."

She needed to be with him. Wide awake, teasing, laughing . . .

Tender.

"It's seriously a fifteen-minute ride."

"And we won't be sixty seconds late. I swear it."

They weren't late. They arrived at exactly two. Aunt Martha had come to the porch in a timely fashion, and was there to greet them.

"Punctual! I love my guests to be punctual!" she said cheerfully.

"Yes, ma'am. We wouldn't have dreamed of being late, under any circumstance whatsoever!" Finn lied, with a very straight face. Megan was tempted to punch him, but he grinned at her like the cat who had eaten the canary and she was tempted to laugh out loud.

He would have gladly skipped the afternoon all together.

"Come in, come in, then! Lunch is ready, we've just got to take it from the oven to the table," Aunt Martha said, preceding them into the house, and leaving Finn, at the end, to close the door behind them all.

The home was a masterpiece of antique and Victorian charm. Some pieces were colonial, some Edwardian, and some Victorian. The lace doilies here and there added a touch of both the old, and the charming. Oddly out of place on a desk in a little room just off the grand dining room with its heavy, richly carved, mahogany table, was a state-of-the-art computer.

Aunt Martha herself was a bit of a strange amalgamation. Megan's mom had always told her that Martha had been old as long as she could remember, but despite her age, her blue eyes remained sharp and twinkling. She had a slender, straight body without a touch of arthritis or even the hint of a stooping at the back. Her mind was like a razor.

"So, young man! My fine young musician!" Martha said, setting down the last of the food and taking her place at the table. "I hope you like meat loaf."

"Love it."

The food was passed around the table.

"And how about the community here? All the goings-on? Pass the peas, please, Megan, dear."

Dutifully, Megan did so. Martha still had her keen gaze on Finn.

He shrugged. "Interesting. The past, of course, is extremely sad. Apparently, it serves an excellent opportunity for twenty-first-century capitalism."

"Aha! Exactly," Martha said. "Finn Douglas, take more potatoes than that! They're hand mashed and delicious, I promise."

"They are exquisite," Finn assured her politely.

Martha waved a hand in the air as she cornered a few peas. "Morwenna and this Wiccan thing! She drives me crazy, though I am certain it's just a stage."

"She's happy, Aunt Martha. And there's really nothing wrong with the tenets of her craft. 'Blessed be.' That's the greeting. I don't think it hurts for anyone to believe in a bit of superstition, or that herbs can help you through a crisis—or even that a mixture of oils can be a love potion," Megan intervened quickly.

Martha arched a brow to her, then shook her head. "It's all just silly, I'm afraid." Her eyes narrowed at both of them. "Heard you had a terrible dream the other night and woke up half the town, Megan."

Megan sighed deeply. "I had a nightmare, and woke up Mr. Fallon."

"It's all ridiculous hocus-pocus, and that's why the whole thing has it's negative side," Martha said, waving her free hand in the air once again. She looked at Finn and grinned. "Don't go letting any of it get to you. It's Halloween, and all the crazies are out."

"We're fine," Finn said, reaching for the salt. "I'm from New Orleans, and we've the whole voodoo thing down there, so don't worry, this kind of thing really doesn't get to me."

Martha once again shook her head. "Back in my day . . . well, it wasn't so commercial. And every silly college dropout in the world wasn't pretending to be a Wiccan or a fortune-teller. You were right when you said that the whole thing was a form of capitalism, Finn."

"Aunt Martha, Morwenna is not a college dropout, you know. She went through and got her degree in business. Same as Joseph."

"Joseph!" Aunt Martha said with a rise of impatience and ire. "With his silly dyed hair, and his capes. He should know better."

"Aunt Martha, they're happy," Megan reminded her gently.

"Yes, of course. And harmless. I believe. It's just that . . . well, you know, the history itself should be enough! So much harm done, so much cruelty, to so many people. The town needs to remember all that with more gravity," she said firmly. She smiled then. "Ah, well. My darlings, I have to tell you, I was so impressed. Megan, you really are a little songbird. And Finn. You too! That voice. Well, I am a very old woman, but I can tell you, young man, when you come in with some of those husky tones, my old heart does go into a few palpitations!"

Finn laughed. "Thanks. I'll take that as a great compliment."

"As it was meant," Martha said briefly. "And that playing machine thing you've got going! Terrific. It allows the two of you to be a major band all by yourselves."

"Well, not exactly, but we can churn up some good dance music and effects," Finn said.

"It was all quite wonderful," Martha said. "Finn, you need more greens."

"Yes, ma'am."

"So, tell me more about life in New Orleans," Martha insisted.

Megan glanced at Finn. "It's wonderful," she told Martha, describing their little house, small terrace—and the proximity of their neighbors. "But it's a wonderful city, despite the crime, of course. It's like everywhere else, you know where to go, and where not to go. But I do love it. Despite the fact that it's a major tourist mecca, we go to Café du Monde a lot, read the paper, sip coffee, eat beignets . . . and the jazz at the corner spots is incredible."

"Lots of strip joints," Martha murmured, disapprovingly.

Megan laughed. "That doesn't mean we go to them."

"Aunt Martha, strip joints are alive and well across the entire country, you know. Even in New England," Finn reminded her with gentle amusement.

"Of course, dear, of course. I guess I am a prude, an old New Englander. Merged in our old history. But then, you mustn't mind us, and you mustn't think that everyone here back then was exceptionally evil or cruel. The belief of the day—a very European belief at that!—was that Satan, like God, existed, and that he could force people to make pacts with him. Far more women were accused—here as well as across Europe—but then, enough men died in the fires and all as well. And do you want to know one of the reasons why? Women were not considered to be as bright as men; therefore, they were more easily led astray by Satan. Also—they were supposed to be far more carnal, more prey to the devil's seduction. Then again, merely dancing naked in the moonlight was often a crime punishable by death. To do such an evil thing meant that you were prone to do much more. People believed in the evil eye and all that rot. They didn't know any better. Science hadn't come very far. When you consider what went on in Europe over several centuries, we were incredibly slow and careful here in the colonies. Ancient history, I say." She looked directly and sternly at Megan then. "You've listened to me now and know how ridiculous such rot is—and was—back then. So don't go listening to any of Andy Markham's baloney," she finished firmly. She rose, picking up the remaining meat loaf. "We'll have coffee on the porch."

When she was gone, Megan leaned over to touch Finn's hand. "Sorry. She is a bit of a bossy old matriarch."

He ran his thumb lightly over her hand, smiling. "I like her. She's down to earth. No bullshit."

Megan grinned, wondering if Martha would be pleased to hear herself described as a "no bullshit" woman.

Megan realized that she wasn't helping, and jumped up to help clear the table. Finn joined her, but Martha shooed them out of the kitchen, assuring them that she'd pick up later, she wanted to enjoy their company for the time. Finn carried the coffee carafe and Megan picked up the plate of delicate little tea cookies Martha had made and they went out on the porch.

It was already growing dark, but it was pretty on the porch. The falling sun set the world into gentle shades of lavender.

"I hadn't realized it was so late," Finn said.

"It's not late, it's just October in New England. It's not even four," Martha told him.

Finn sighed, sipping his coffee, looking very comfortable. As if he didn't want to leave, which made Megan feel very happy.

"We will have to get going soon," he murmured.

"Of course." Martha said, staring at him. Then she gave a happy sigh as well and looked proudly at Megan. "He's quite something, your young man. Gorgeous— oh, I don't mean that you're not a manly fellow, Finn, you're quite that. Most musicians these days are scraggly, unkempt, skinny, scrawny little things. You make a fine match for my beautiful Megan. Why, almost like Barbie and Ken! Except you're not so effeminate, Finn. You've got some muscle there, as well."

Finn laughed. "Thanks. I liked martial arts when I was a kid. Took karate, and some other forms of Eastern defense."

"Rugged, I like that," Martha approved. "Perfect form . . . and that voice. You do complement Megan. Not that looks matter much in life, mind you," she said firmly. "But you seem as good and decent a human being as my Meg, and she is just as beautiful at heart as she is in body. So—not that you're asking me!—but you sure do have my approval." She sat straight suddenly. "Now, I must admit, I heard there was some trouble between you. Don't you go letting anyone break you up for any silly reason. And if any silly Halloween malarky starts getting to you around here, you just come back to Aunt Martha's warm kitchen, and I'll set you both straight. Got it?"

Finn laughed loudly, his eyes flashing toward Megan. "Absolutely, Aunt Martha. And thank you. We'll depend on you in times of trouble, for sure."

Martha nodded firmly. "Well, you've both finished your coffee. Get going. Take care of the things you need to do. See more of the town. I'm here, whenever you need me."

Finn gave her a very warm hug as they departed.

Megan hugged her as well, giving her an extra squeeze. When they pulled apart, Martha searched out her eyes.

"You know, you are a true beauty, baby. You keep good care of yourself, you understand?"

"Of course, Aunt Martha."

By the time they reached the car, darkness had fallen in earnest. The moon was shining down, and the light still seemed to be an eerie blue.

Megan didn't care. Martha had made the world right. Andy Markham was a ridiculous, desperate old man, bordering on senility.

And Finn was beside her, his arm around her shoulder as he drove.

Fear was a thing of the mind. . . .

Martha had cleared her mind, and the world was a beautiful place.

Then, suddenly, Finn slammed on the brakes. There had been something in front of them. Something like a huge dark shadow flying across the front of the car.

"What the hell was that?" Finn said tensely. He had the car under control. He was a good driver, despite the fact that they spent many days walking where they had to go in the French Quarter.

"I don't know . . . something . . . black?" Megan said uneasily. "It looked like a giant, flying, low-swooping shadow. Finn, we didn't hit it, did we?" she asked worriedly. "Whatever it was."

"No . . . no, there it goes." Finn started to laugh with relief. "It's all right. I didn't hit it."

"What was it? Where is it?"

"What else? A black cat. And there it goes, slinking away into the brush."

"A *black cat.* That was it?"

She loved cats. Especially black cats. But as he put the car into gear again, she felt a strange sweeping of unease come over her again.

A black cat.

"Yeah, look, you can just see his eyes. There, glowing in the reflection of the car's lights."

She could see the eyes as he pointed them out. Pinpricks of fire, glowing at them from the bushes.

Megan shivered. Just a cat. A black cat. She didn't understand her feelings.

The world had become beautiful, but now . . .

A black cat. An omen.

A foreboding of all that was dark and . . .

Evil?

To come.

Chapter 7

Finn felt good. Visiting Martha had been like a return to normalcy. The cat in the road hadn't bothered him; he had swerved and slammed on his brakes carefully. Tough call for any driver anytime—avoid killing an animal and cause a wreck that might kill a person, or run over the creature. His reflexes were sharp; he'd avoided the creature after making certain there was no one following right on his tail.

Megan, however, had gone strangely silent.

"I really like Martha," he told her.

She flashed him a quick smile via the mirror. "She's adorable, isn't she?"

"Blunt, certainly. When she wants you to leave, she tells you so."

Megan laughed. "She knows we're playing tonight."

"I have to do sound checks, of course, but we're pretty set for tonight."

"I doubt if she understands anything about amps, sound checks, or equipment," Megan said.

"Still, we have some time before going in," he reminded her. "What do you want to do?"

She hesitated. He had the feeling she wanted to tell

him that she wanted to crawl beneath a rock or something of the like.

"Megan, there was an animal in the road. We missed it. That was good. So what's the matter?"

"Nothing," she said quickly. Too quickly.

"Meg?"

"Okay—it was a black cat."

He laughed. "Lots of cats are black!"

"Right."

"Hey, where's my girl who gives to the Humane Society on a monthly basis?"

"I'm glad you missed the cat. It's just, you know . . . the whole Halloween thing here. Witches and black cats and all that."

"You're the mighty defender of the Wiccans. Please, if I were to walk into the room with a broomstick, you'd think I meant to sweep, not fly, right?"

She laughed, and her tension eased somewhat. She suddenly sat straight up. "Let's go to Mike's museum."

"What?"

"My friend, Mike. Let's go to that new place where he's curator."

Finn glanced at his watch. "Those places close between five and five-thirty," he reminded her.

"So, we kill the next hour."

"Whatever you wish."

Finding parking wasn't easy. More and more people seemed to be milling into the small city as Halloween approached. Twice around the common, though, and they found a space. Finn warned her that the museum would probably close just as they walked up to it, but Megan kept up a quick pace and they reached the museum in a matter of minutes. "New" described only the fact that the facility within the building had just opened; the museum was housed in an old building, freshly painted, certainly refurbished inside, but the plaque on the door indicated that the structure itself had been built in 1678, that it was on the historic register, and had originally been built by a man named Stevens whose father had come over on the Mayflower.

"Impressive, huh?" Megan said as they approached the ticket counter.

"I'm sorry, we stop selling tickets at four-thirty," the young woman told them. She had short, very dark hair. *Dyed dark,* Finn thought. It seemed a number of the Wiccans liked pitch-black hair. Of course, there was nothing about her to indicate that she was a Wiccan, but Finn was willing to bet his bottom dollar that he had her pigeonholed just right. She had a cute, gamine's face, and had to be in her early twenties, if that. Tiny holes on her face indicated that, when she wasn't working, she had a piercing in each brow, one in the lip, and one in the nose. She was sincerely apologetic about not selling them tickets, however.

"I didn't think we'd make it," Finn told Megan. He was sorry himself. She'd seemed so anxious to get in. He was, for some reason, relieved. He didn't know what was wrong with him. After the fiasco they had nearly made of their marriage because of their different jealousies, they had both determined to learn a lot about trust. A good thing, because, when they played, they were both often besieged by members of the opposite sex.

His feelings, he determined, had nothing to do with trust. He trusted Megan.

He didn't trust her friend Mike. He hadn't a reason in the world to feel that way. Except that he'd known Megan before Finn. And . . .

All right, it was strange to be here. Megan's old haunting grounds. Megan's family, Megan's friends, and he was too often plagued by feelings of insecurity. He'd just gotten his wife back. And he was afraid that she could too easily be wrested from his fingers, here, where she seemed to know everyone, and he was a total outsider.

"Okay," Megan said with a shrug, and turned back to the window. "Can you do me a favor, though? Will you tell Mike that Megan and Finn came by?"

The girl's eyes widened. "Hey . . . Megan. You're Mike's old friend, and the two of you are playing at the new place. Hang on!" she said cheerfully. "I'll go get Mike." She started to rise from her swivel chair behind the little counter. "You don't recognize me, of course. I'm Gayle Sawyer. I was there last night. You two were wonderful. We need entertainment like you two around here so much more! I mean, of course, the place is small, but to see anything hip or popular, we usually have to go all the way into Boston. Don't go anywhere, I'll get Mike."

Finn was startled when she paused a moment, looking directly at him. Her eyes traveled from the tip of his head down, loitering in the crotch area, going on to his feet.

Then she disappeared.

"You've got a fan," Megan told him. She didn't sound angry, just amused.

"I am beloved by all pincushions," he whispered back.

"She does have a lot of piercings, huh?"

He pulled her against him, resting his chin on the top of her head. "I like my women without holes, except of course, those charming little punctures in your ears."

"I've been thinking about a belly button ring," she said.

"On you, I'll love it," he swore solemnly.

"Glib," she told him, "very glib. How about I get a great big tatoo on my back."

"One that says 'Mother' or a giant snake wrapped around a Harley?"

"I think I'd go for the snake and the Harley."

He angled his head so that he could whisper in her ear. "Are you forgetting that little rose you already have on your ankle?"

"But that's so small!" She laughed suddenly. "I thought my father was going to have a heart attack when I got that!"

He didn't have a chance to reply. Mike Smith, in dockers and a black sweater, was coming into the foyer area where the ticket sales were done. He had a broad smile on his face—dimples showing—and looked confident, assured, and pleased to see them.

"Hey, you made it!"

He came forward and Megan stepped toward him, accepting his warm hug and placing a kiss on his cheek. The act made Finn sizzle inside, despite the innocence of it. Smith looked equally glad to see him, though he offered a handshake rather than a hug.

Finn found himself pulling Megan back against him, resting his arm around her shoulder. "Looks like a great place," he told Mike.

"It is. Come on in, I'll show you."

"Oh, hey, you know, you're trying to close down for the day and all. We can come back," Finn told him.

"I'm thrilled to give you two a personal tour," Mike assured him. "I never get out of here until late, anyway. At least tonight, I'll be staying for a pleasurable occasion."

He spoke bluntly and casually. Finn mocked himself for finding offense at the word *pleasurable*.

"There are three branches of the museum . . . we start with the founding of Salem up through the end of the witch trials that way, maritime is to our left, and Salem today is upstairs," Mike told them.

"Maritime," Megan said.

He swept an arm out. "This way, then."

"Hey, I'll be seeing you again tonight!" Gayle called to them.

"Terrific, thanks," Megan said. They were a few steps behind Mike as they walked. "I think she means that she'll see *you* tonight!" she whispered lightly.

"Strange little thing," he replied softly.

"She knew right where to hone in," Megan murmured.

He was startled. Megan seemed to be feeling little bits of jealousy now as well.

"Not my type!" he assured her. He was annoyed to realize, however, that he was thinking of the girl, still picturing her in his mind's eye. Little bits of character and build that he hadn't noted at first were filling his thoughts. She was small, compact, with a tiny waist, emphasized by the belted, dark wool dress she'd been wearing. Plentiful chest. Exceptionally well shaped legs; she worked out, evidently. Huge lips—Angelina Jolie lips. He remembered the way she had zeroed in on him, intimately. He wondered about her mouth. What it would feel like . . .

"Can you even begin to imagine, Finn?"

Megan was talking.

He hadn't even realized that they had come to a room. There was a model of a three masted ship in the center of the room. Display cases were filled with harpoons, from very old ones to newer, mechanized designs.

"Pardon?"

"Can you imagine? Being out on a ship for years— the whalers were sometimes gone for up to three years at a time!" she said.

"It wouldn't be my line of work."

"For a lot of New Englanders, it was a way to riches," Mike said. "And naturally, there were many disasters as well. That's why you'll see so many of the coastal houses with their 'widow's walks.' Wives, children, lovers, used to pace those walks, waiting for the ships to return."

They moved on to a display that explained the many uses for whale oil. He forced himself to concentrate.

Another case was filled with tiny models of ships, showing changes in design from the sixteenth century through present day. Another case was filled with little miniatures that the sailors had whittled from whalebone. He kept walking, glad of the total normalcy of the tour, wondering why he wanted to escape so badly. Smith really seemed to be a decent sort—the total academic, just as Megan had described him.

"Actually, you should see the part of the museum dedicated to the witch trials," Smith said, pausing, running his fingers through his sandy hair. "We've really done an incredible job."

"Sure," Finn said.

They exited the maritime section down a back stairway, but Mike walked them around to the entry so that they could view the exhibit in the proper order.

The exhibit began with a picture of Roger Conant, the founder of Salem, with a tribute to his steadfastness when he began the new plantation at "this place called Naumkeake." It was 1626, right after the failure of the English settlement at St. Ann.

The following displays began with the Puritan ideology, and continued on to the determination that the Pilgrims would leave England. The hardships of settling in New England came next, and then, an overview of the concept of "witchcraft" and the terrible events going on in Europe at the time. Finn found that he was intrigued, especially after a display on the beginnings of the craze in New England, with scientific theories on what might have caused the accusing girls to have gone into such hysteria. Life-size tableaus followed, with the one of the hanging scenes so well done that it might have brought tears to the eyes. Both the incredible tragedy was brought fully to light, along with an understanding of how the suppressed citizens of the time might have believed with their whole hearts that the devil had come to Massachusetts, and that they were in danger of losing not only their lives, but their souls. He was intrigued to realize that a "confessed" witch was not hanged; only those who believed so deeply in the tenets of their faith that they refused to admit—for fear that their immortal souls would be damned for such a lie—to such a travesty went to the gallows, as it turned out. There was a scene, labeled as having taken place in Germany, that showed the executions of thousands on a single day, to demonstrate what a real fear witchcraft had been in the different cultures of the so-called civilized world.

"Oh, Lord!" Megan exclaimed suddenly. "Finn—it's seven o'clock!"

"It's all right," he said easily. "We're really set for the evening." He looked at Mike Smith who had given them such a down-to-earth, matter-of-fact tour that even he had become completely absorbed—forgetting what nonsense had plagued him, he had a new respect for the man. Something about being here had seemed to put darkness, shadow, myth, legend, and even dreams in retrospect. He shook the man's hand. "I'm only sorry that we forced you to stay so long."

Smith grinned. "That's all right. That's all right. I'm never forced to stay here; I love the place. It's my baby. And my only plans for the evening were coming to watch you two tonight."

"Oh, well, great, then."

He stood awkwardly for a moment, not sure where to go from there.

Megan solved it. "Want to grab some coffee or something with us and head over?" she asked Mike Smith.

"Thanks for the invitation. I've a few things to catch up on, though. I'm happy to take a rain check on that offer, though."

"Terrific," Finn said. "We'll get going then."

Switching off lights as they went, Smith led them out. Past the tableaus. Finn found himself looking into the eyes of poor, deaf, old Rebecca Nurse as the noose was set around her neck. In the half light that then illuminated the museum, the scene was hauntingly real. He felt as if the mannequin could come to life, and perhaps turn and damn them all for what they had done to her.

At his side, Megan shivered.

He was startled to hear himself reassure her. "She was, if I've understood this all, almost a sainted old woman in truth. She wouldn't wish evil on anyone."

"Rebecca?" Smith said affectionately, almost as if he'd had a personal acquaintance with the victim. "She was possibly the saddest case in the debacle. She was judged innocent at first. But the girls put up such a hew and cry that the judges went back and deemed her guilty."

They reached the front, and Mike locked them out. Megan looked at Finn, smiling. "Great place, huh?"

"I agree. Let's get that coffee, and head on to work."

"Sounds good to me. No ordinary coffee, though. I want some kind of a wickedly rich mocha latte, with whipped cream."

"*Wickedly* rich?" he teased.

"I'm picking up my New England mannerisms, huh?" she murmured.

"We both seem to be picking up a little local atmosphere," he agreed. "Come on. We'll find you a *wicked* good mocha latte."

The book lay open before her. The great and ancient book of wisdom. It wasn't one that she kept out for any casual visitor to see. It was kept locked away. She wore the key around her neck at all times.

As she read, she smiled. She had managed to obey all the instructions with incredible precision.

She looked out the window. Night.

Almost all was done. Even the one who served her, about whom she had to admit to great trepidation, had served well. He knew what reward lay in obedience—and what punishment might lie in failure.

She looked out the window and saw the darkness of night. The moon was shining down with its strange and eerie blue cast. The fog would come again tonight.

Just a little more to do . . .

And then the night would come.

All Hallow's Eve . . .

And the world, and the future, would be hers . . .

They found a great place that advertised coffee in almost every shape and form. It was pleasant. With 'Salem's Haunted Happenings' going on, the streets were still busy. They were able to find an intimate little table at one of the coffeehouses anyway, and for a few minutes, they discussed the virtues of the museum, across from one another, but with their heads bent close together. An intimate little tête-à-tête. Finn felt good. He loved his wife. She loved him.

"Strange, isn't it?" she murmured suddenly.

"What?"

She laughed ruefully before explaining. "We live in New Orleans. We're surrounded by ghost and vampire tours—we walk home through them all constantly. Horrible things went on there at times. And yet . . . I don't know. I'm from here—from near here, at any rate!—and it all seems so creepy. I mean, we live in the 'zombie' capital of the States, for heaven's sake!"

He found that he could laugh as well. "It's Halloween season, that's all," he assured her. He ran a finger over her hand where it rested on the table before him. "We started out our first night with some major fanciful tales. But all we have to do is look around. In the street right now, see? They have a kids' table right there, and they're all busy making jack-o'-lanterns. We've just been suckered in by stories, huh?"

She nodded. When they rose, she walked in the arc of his arm. They meandered to the car, and once in it, Finn started to head straight out to the hotel.

"Ah, hell," he murmured. He glanced at her. "We need to change clothes!"

"We're just supposed to appear kind of Gothic, right?"

"Yes."

"We'll just run by Morwenna's. She has black shirts and capes—that will do, won't it?"

"I suppose. We could just go back to Huntington House—"

"And you won't have a chance to do a sound check. We're right by Morwenna's. We'll just stop there."

He wanted to argue with her. He felt uncomfortable in the witch shop. Except that what she was saying made perfect sense.

"All right," he conceded grudgingly.

He found a place for the car and they hurried through the busy streets to Morwenna's. Joseph was sitting guard at the door, monitoring the number of people in and out of the shop.

"Hey, you two, wasn't expecting to see you when you're due on the stage so soon."

"We need to borrow some clothing," Megan explained.

Joseph nodded. "Morwenna is inside. She'll set you up. Hey, she'll set you up good. And if you get a chance, mention that your clothing came from our place."

"Absolutely," Megan promised.

"Wait, I've got the perfect outfit for you, Finn. Bought it for myself, actually, for fun. May not fit, you've got some broad shoulders on you, but . . . we'll give it a go." He opened the door to the shop, calling for Sara to come out and change places with him.

Sara came. She greeted both Megan and Finn, but stared at Finn. Hard. She tried to smile, and looked a little sick—as if she didn't want to be anywhere near him.

Ditto, you bitch! he thought.

She stepped back, almost as if he had spoken the words aloud.

"Come on in, I guess we need to hurry," Joseph said.

They followed him into the store. Sara gave Finn a wide berth, stepping out of the way of the door.

Megan didn't seem to notice.

Joseph didn't intend to give Finn just a cape, he really had an entire outfit. Sleek black pants, ruffled black shirt with a medieval look, and a huge, sweeping black velvet cloak. When he was dressed and came out of the small, curtained, changing room, Morwenna let out a whistle and Megan's raised brow and pursed smile assured him that he wore the costume well.

"You are absolutely gorgeous. In the studliest way possible, of course," Morwenna assured him.

He looked to his wife. "I have to agree."

A teenager—probably a visitor, since she wasn't dressed in black—gave out a little wolf whistle and set down the incense burner she had been studying.

"That's it, for sure," Morwenna said.

"I don't like to take something that Joseph ordered for himself," he said, wondering why he wanted to protest the outfit.

"It's perfect, and he doesn't care in the least," Morwenna said. "If he did, he wouldn't have offered. Now, Megan . . . as to you . . . hm. Follow me," she commanded.

Megan shrugged and followed her, leaving Finn standing by the changing room.

As he stood, waiting, watching the customers jostle around in the outer room, an uneasy feeling swept over him. He was being watched.

Sara had come into the room.

"Well, the outfit is quite . . . fitting," she murmured.

He didn't reply. He felt as if a strange animosity created a static in the air between them.

But Sara kept talking.

"You're beginning to look the part."

She took a number of steps toward him. A pounding began in his ears. His heartbeat, he thought. The closer she came, the worse the pounding. Harder, faster. He felt it pulse through his limbs, down through his extremities. She was a little bit of a thing. But she kept coming, as if she dared him, as if there were some confidence within her that allowed her to taunt him, as if she pulled a tiger's tail, knowing that she could whip out a .38 Special at any moment.

Small . . . but powerful. The pounding continued. It created a whirl of thoughts in his mind.

Pounce.

Break her neck.

But first . . .

Grab her, threaten her, touch her. She wore her customary black, but not in any conservative style. Her black silk shirt was unbuttoned way down, so far down that her bare breasts were nearly fully visible. She moved with a sway of her hips that was purposely provocative. He narrowed his eyes, realizing, dimly, beneath the sound that roared in his ears, that she was coming on to him. She emitted hostility as if it were tangible, but she was coming on to him as well.

To his amazement, he felt the pounding surge into his groin.

And his feelings of violence . . . and more . . . skyrocketed. His fingers were twitching. He was ready to reach out, draw her against him with fury and force, use her, degrade her, touch her with every depravity known to man, and then . . . wind his fingers around her throat.

And she came closer still. Her eyes were on his. Dark,

taunting, full of some kind of strange knowledge, urging him to reach out to touch her.

The pounding was a ragged pain. He gritted his teeth, willing himself to move, to step around her. He couldn't move. He managed to keep himself from reaching out, but he couldn't force his feet to action, to step around her. A warning sounded from deep within his mind. *She wanted him to lose control, to give in to lust, violence, and insanity. She wanted to scream then, and have everyone in the store see him for the monster that he was, beneath.*

"Finn, what do you think?" Morwenna called, with a note of pure pride and pleasure in her voice.

He felt as if he literally ripped his eyes from their absurd lock with Sara's.

The pounding ceased, instantly.

Blood seemed to drain from his temples, back into his veins, where it belonged.

Morwenna was sweeping into the area between the fitting rooms and the worktables and desks. She had an arm linked with Megan's.

His wife was more than beautiful, and far beyond sexy. Black lace hugged her breasts. The long sleeves of the garment were belled toward the wrists. The bodice hugged her waist, and silk, velvet, and lace combined in the long skirt that swept around her limbs with an exotic appeal. Her hair, so long and light, created a stunning contrast against the ebony of the costume, like her eyes, which seemed to glimmer with a gemlike quality deeper than sapphire.

"Whoa!" he applauded softly.

And he could walk. He swept past Sara, as if she weren't there at all, and even brushing her person as he moved meant nothing. In fact, he might have imagined the entire interlude.

Megan looked up, delighted by his approval. Morwenna seemed as proud as a peahen.

"Perfect, right?"

"I can't find the words," Finn said.

"Well, you don't need words right now. You need music. It's after eight. Get going. We'll see you there later. We will be late, though. We're keeping the shop open until ten, and I still have all kinds of preparations to make for the actual holy day. Get going!"

He was startled to find himself planting a quick kiss on Morwenna's cheek, and thanking her. He still wasn't looking at her. He and Megan gazed at one another with both amusement and appreciation, and they were still doing so as they left the shop, walking through admiring customers, and at the end, thanking Joseph, giving him a wave, and then continuing on.

There were demons everywhere.

As Megan looked out on the crowd that night, she thought that whole city had gone movie crazy. Someone had come as the monster from *Pumpkinhead*. There were at least five "Pinheads" from Clive Barker novels, three or four "Freddies" from the *Nightmare on Elm Street* films, and several "Jasons" from the *Friday the 13th* series of flicks. A few Frankenstein monsters were roaming around, along with several incredibly well done mummies. Some people were more inventive, creating their own form of monsters, such as stone creatures, tree creatures, goblins, orgres, and more. For certain, with the bizarre lighting, the ever rolling fog machine, and the room's decor—silly and obvious by day—this night in the ballroom was creepy.

They were doing incredibly well. The hotel's entertainment manager had told them that when word had gotten around about their success of the previous evening, they had been inundated with calls. They were having to turn people away at the door. The clerk had sold more than two hundred of their CDs, and people had already been asking to make sure that they could be purchased again that night.

It was more than they could have imagined.

They had been highlighted on a newscast from Boston. A review had been picked up on syndication that had aired across the country. They couldn't be flying higher.

And amazingly, she was almost sorry.

Though they'd had a good day, basically, she was still disturbed by her encounter with Andy Markham. And then the black cat. Silly. But she was almost wishing that they could just drop everything, leave, and go back to New Orleans. A normal place—despite its reputation for zombies, voodoo, and vampires.

A round of applause and catcalls sounded as Finn finished the last chords of one of his own pieces on his acoustic guitar. He announced their next number, his voice deep, husky, and casual. She turned her gaze from the audience to her husband. It was true that the black fit him well. The pants hugged his hips, the silk emphasized the muscle structure of his shoulders and chest. More. The Gothic appearance of the clothing, combined with his chiseled facial bone structure, added an element of danger and mystique to his appearance. Highly sensual. She wasn't the only one who had noted it; some of the *surely* younger, college-age girls—when close to the stage—had voiced some almost obscene approval. He'd had one invitation to crawl through a dorm window and pounce, and another to meet a young woman in a dark alley. He had the look of a fantasy creature that might be purely evil, might suck out your blood and your life, but be so erotic in the process it wouldn't matter.

She'd felt a few little twinges of jealousy, but then he'd met her eyes each time, rolling his own with impatience. Maybe part of his charm was a certain easy confidence in knowing that he'd go where he wanted to, but being immune, or even unaware, of the extent of his magnetism.

He was staring at her then, a flicker of irritation in his eyes. She realized that he'd strummed a few chords: her opening. She was supposed to be singing.

She turned back to the audience and began the number by rote.

They played through the set, and Finn announced their break. She didn't wait for him to tell her that she had missed a cue. She hurried from the stage, and headed for the bar, suddenly determined that she needed a drink to get through the night.

At the bar, a kid in a skeleton outfit hit on her. She could have managed by herself, and was startled when the boy whipped around because a hand had fallen on his shoulder.

Finn. He towered over the kid. In the black, he seemed a real menace.

She opened her mouth to protest; she moved to set a hand on her husband's chest, to reassure him that she could take care of the boy. There seemed to be such a leashed violence about her husband lately, she realized that she felt like she was walking on eggshells, worried that he would explode.

"Finn—"

"Hey, friend. The lady is my wife."

Finn spoke softly.

The kid backed off. "Hey, sorry, should have realized . . . I'm outta here!"

As good as his words, he spun around and disappeared into the crowd. "You know, I was okay, I could have handled him."

Finn leaned against the bar, looking out over the crowd. "Who can tell in this group?" The words should have been light, offhand. There was an underlying grate and menace. He seemed fierce, larger than life, with that same, strange, dangerous appeal.

Yes, go for it, rage, take that prowess and tear them apart . . .

The thought was shocking to Megan. She took a huge swallow of her beer.

He turned dangerous eyes on her. She felt something like an absurd jungle pleasure. Yes, the beast was hers. A beast indeed, but that was okay, as long as he was her beast.

"Did you order me one?"

"One what?"

"A beer?"

"No, here, take this, I'll get another."

"Thanks, there's something off on one of the speakers. Hey, Joseph and Morwenna are here. They've ordered food again for after our next set."

"Great!"

He disappeared. She ordered another beer. She felt as if she were being watched.

She was.

The man in costume who had helped her detangle her hair from the prop monster the night before was at the end of the bar. He lifted a glass to her. She smiled uneasily, lifted the bottle of beer she had just received, and slipped from her bar stool.

People stopped her—none she'd ever recognize again—as she headed back to the stage. She chatted, thanked them, acknowledged their compliments, and hurried back to Finn.

Later, they ate with Morwenna and Joseph. Conversation was casual.

The night came to an end.

They didn't linger. Finn was in a hurry to get back to Huntington House. They found a parking spot with near miraculous ease. She lay down while he hit the shower. She'd meant to take one herself when he came out.

She fell fast asleep almost as soon as her head touched the pillow.

It began with the darkness, and the strange blue light that began to penetrate through it. There was fog, and for a moment, she thought she'd had a blackout, and that she was still on the stage. It was cold, icy cold, but she shouldn't have felt the chill so deeply, not when she was wearing one of the black capes over the gown with its draping sleeves. But, she realized, she had shed the gown, and that was why she was so cold, the breeze and the blue fog were slipping between the fold, wrapping around her.

She was embarrassed, as if she had walked into one of her own worst nightmares. The fear of the performer, being on stage, and realizing that she had forgotten her clothing. But it was all right. She wondered if they had agreed that night to perform for a nudist colony, because she could vaguely see the audience. They were hazy forms, indistinguishable in the blue fog, faceless, with only bits and pieces of their visages visible. Now and then, she could see floating, toothy, blood red smiles; she could see eyes here and there, staring at her. They all seemed to be red as well, rimmed with fire, and yet, of course, they couldn't be. Eyes were blue, or brown, green, even hazel. Sometimes they had exceptional color, and could even be described as azure, turquoise, or gold. But they never really burned, as if they were red . . .

What she could see was that they were all wearing cloaks or capes as well. All were cowled, but the breeze would come now and then, lifting a hem, shifting an opening, and she could see the flesh. So, of course, it was all right, because they were all the same.

She struggled, thinking she must be dreaming, because it wasn't all right at all; she would never appear anywhere without being fully clothed. They didn't even dress suggestively. She thought she was supposed to be singing; she could

*vaguely hear music, but it didn't sound like anything Finn
had written, nor any of the cover songs that they did. He
would be angry, looking at her the way that he had earlier, but
she still stood there in silence, because no matter how she tried, she
couldn't recognize the music. Someone was singing for her, she
thought, because it was as if she could vaguely hear words.*

*Maybe it was the crowd, trying to get her started; they
seemed to be pushing closer and closer to the stage. There was
something low-lying and ominous in the music; she didn't like
it, didn't like the feeling of discomfort . . . unease . . . and then
the fear that it began to create within her. Nothing sudden, just
a feeling that seemed to sweep through her limbs. The crowd
was pushing too close. They weren't singing; they were chanting. Something like a church song, only it wasn't really church
music at all, not with the haunting menace that seemed to be
at its base . . .*

*She started to back away. She would knock into the equip-
ment, she thought. Finn would think she was mad, having
stage fright at this point. He would have to understand.*

*He hadn't understood about the nightmare. He had pre-
tended to, but . . .*

*She turned, desperate to reach him, to get behind him, be-
cause the black-cowled spectators were coming too close, they
were grasping at her, trying to touch her . . .*

*She screamed as fingers reached out, wrenching away her
cloak.*

*"Perfect," someone said, not a compliment, but a cool, dis-
affected assessment.*

"A few bruises," came another intonation.

"Chant!" came a firm voice.

*The noise level grew. How she could have ever thought that
it was music was beyond her then. The words were rising in a
singsong, but there was a harshness to them. She couldn't recognize any of the sounds.*

"The time is coming . . ."

"Now!"

"*No!*" she cried out loud herself, and she turned at last. She had to get behind Finn.

But Finn wasn't there. She wasn't on a stage at all; she was in the woods.

The crowd began to part, leaving way for someone to break through.

She felt the breeze, a shadow of darkness. There was grass around her . . .

And little protruding stones.

Then she saw him . . . it . . . the reason the crowd had parted. Walking toward her, not walking . . . sliding toward her. And she saw that it was the creature, the marble creature from the cemetery. The face was horrible, terrifying . . . a satyr's face, long and lean, pointed chin, horned head . . . and yet, it was familiar. It was leering, ogling, laughing . . . so amused. There was something about it, about the eyes . . . that were hypnotic. She'd been so cold. Those eyes touched her, raked over her, seemed to burn her flesh. She had never been more frightened in her life . . . or more lured. She wanted to run, to flee . . . and she wanted to be touched.

It moved on cloven hoofs, not feet at all. That was why the strange gait as it came. It breathed something like fire, and that was why the sudden warmth. But she stood, aware that her cloak was gone, and she lifted her chin, because she could feel its heat, its gaze, brushing over her flesh, and the warmth within her grew until she was ready to fall upon her knees, accept whatever odious dictates the creature gave, as long as it touched her in truth. She could feel it more and more, and her thighs burned, liquid rushed through her, just knowing that the creature was coming was making her feel a raw excitement, a longing, a desire to lie before it, parted, naked . . .

The face, the face, so familiar!

Then, it was upon her, and the hands or hooves that touched her flesh were brutal, painful. There was a scent of death and decay around the creature. She started to scream, but too late, it was on her, and she was pinned to the ground, *and it was in her, and she was fighting, but to no avail, for his power was tremendous, his invasion complete, ripping, tearing, and then she knew what she recognized in the face . . .*

"Finn!"

She awakened abruptly, only to find out that all of it hadn't been a dream, or a nightmare.

He was over her, teeth gritted, features strained, body convulsed.

His eyes . . .

For a moment, it seemed that his eyes gleamed like fire.

She screamed.

Chapter 8

A second later, a hand clamped over her mouth. She heard Finn's voice, quite normal, and incredibly annoyed.

"Megan!"

There was a moment in which it didn't matter in the least, in which she lay enshrouded between a world of wakefulness and sleep, lost somewhere between the conscious and real and the tricks of darkness and subconscious.

"Megan!"

He repeated her name. She started; a trembling swept through her. She felt the bed, her husband's form. She knew where she was, exactly, and that once again, she'd experienced a nightmare so real and terrifying that she'd been desperate to wake . . .

To escape.

Shaken, but released from the tentacles of fear the dream had wrapped around her, she gasped out a sigh of relief. She was still trembling. For a moment, he was still with her, at her side, holding her tensely. Thoughts ripped through her mind at lightning speed.

She had just been dreaming!

Part of the dream had been grounded in fact. They'd been making love. They were both bathed in a damp sheen of sweat. She was shaking; he was as rigid as a steel pipe.

"I had another awful dream! What a nightmare," she breathed.

"Well, hold tight," he muttered irritably. "The nightmare may be just beginning. Fallon could come knocking at the door any second now."

Finn rose. She needed to curl into him; it seemed that he needed to be far away from her.

The room was dark except for the thin trail of light beaming out from the bathroom. She could see the agility and sleekness of his form as he moved about, going for a robe, impatiently shrugging into it.

He dug through his things, then stepped out on the balcony.

Megan waited several seconds. She saw the flare of his lighter. Finn was resorting to cigarettes frequently now, when he had cut down to smoking only on occasion. She held very still for a minute, trying to recall each phase of the dream, but once she had awakened, it had all slipped away. In the dream, though . . .

Something evil had been after her. It was because she had listened to Andy Markham. She had gone out to the strange "unhallowed" cemetery to meet him, which she never should have done, and she had listened to him again, and had nightmares. A psychologist would sniff at her, and point-blankly explain the reasons for her absurd dreams.

So now Finn was out on the balcony, disgusted with her again, smoking.

She gnawed on her lower lip, feeling a flare of her own temper. It was his fault just as much as her own. She didn't understand what was with him lately. He was so rough . . . and still, she had to admit, that no matter what . . . he was still exciting.

Megan rose as well and slipped into a robe. She walked out on the balcony. Finn was standing by the rail, looking out over it.

"Look, I'm sorry I screamed."

"Hey," he murmured with a shrug, not looking at her. "You had a dream."

"Horrible. I can't even remember it now. But there was this awful thing attacking me."

"Great. You're *dreaming* while we're making love. I hadn't a clue you were even asleep. You looked straight at me half a dozen times."

"I couldn't have," she protested.

"Megan, you did."

"Then I've started sleeping with my eyes wide open."

"And imagining that I'm an 'awful thing' attacking you." He looked at her at last. His eyes were distant. *He* was distant. Cool, aloof. "What a surprise. Fallon hasn't shown up yet."

"Apparently, I didn't scream that loudly."

"Either that, or he's decided that you're a hopeless, abused woman."

"Finn, stop it."

She could see that his jaw was locked. It took him a minute to speak again, then his words surprised her. "We should leave."

"Leave? We're a huge success. We've sold hundreds of CDs in two days. We've had national news coverage."

"Right. But look what's happening to us."

She frowned, feeling a little ripple of fear, but it was all so absurd. They'd be idiots to give in to it. "We can't leave. You don't just walk out on a job like that."

"If it's costing us our marriage, yes, we do."

"Working here isn't costing us our marriage!" she protested. She shook her head vehemently. "We're the only ones who can cost us our marriage. It would help if you didn't suddenly consider yourself to be the Marquis de Sade."

"What?" The word was sharp, fast, and furious.

"Finn, you're . . . you're just getting too rough! Like a conquering barbarian or something. I told you—"

"Wait, wait, wait, wait, wait!" he said angrily. "You dream that you're being attacked by 'an awful thing'— your words, not mine—but it's me, I'm being too rough."

"You don't even remember the other night—"

"Yeah, and you were asleep through it all tonight."

She fell silent, then turned sharply and walked back into the bedroom. He followed her. "Megan, we should leave."

She stood still for a long moment. She couldn't help but recall how old Andy Markham had terrified her in the woods. *Bac-Dal wants you.*

And then there had been Morwenna's concern, when she'd done her "reading." *There's something . . . I don't know, something bad. Did . . . Finn ever hurt you? I mean, really. There were the rumors of violence . . . it looks like something terrible in the future. A horrible danger, and it's as if it comes from . . . Finn.*

She'd been irritated with her cousin. Rumor. All rumor, and everyone playing into it.

They should leave. Yes. They should leave!

Right. Ruin their careers over old myths and legends and a crazy old man who liked to tell stories.

She spun on Finn. "You're saying we should leave. You don't believe in ghosts. The whole thing with Wiccans or witches or ghosts, spooks, goblins, whatever, is pure rot. But despite that, you think that we should take a chance on *never* getting work again—or getting really decent work again—because I, sorry—and I am sorry!— have had a few nightmares?" She was amazed at the scorn in her voice.

"Whatever, Megan. I agree, it would suck to walk out. But it might be the best thing. When we're here . . . you're very strange."

She was strange?

She bit her lip, startled by the sudden flash of tears that threatened to spill from her eyes.

"Megan . . . this is all very strange, don't you think?"

"Yeah. And maybe it's . . ."

"Maybe it's what?"

She hesitated. "Maybe it has to do with our breakup," she said quietly. "We could go home . . . and find out that nothing was any better."

She saw the flash of anger in his eyes. "I never hurt you, Megan. I never would."

"I didn't say that you did. At least, not physically. Maybe . . . I don't know, maybe beneath the words we say to one another, we're still lacking trust or something. The point is, I'm not acting any more strangely than you are!"

"I don't remember acting strangely at home, or in the Keys," he said. "And I haven't been acting strangely. You're the one waking up screaming."

"That's right. You don't bother to wake up," she murmured.

"What?"

"Finn, we're going to see this gig out," she said quietly. "If we were to walk out . . . well, what we did would surely make the news. We wouldn't be taken seriously. Maybe really big names could get away with it. Or people without any kind of a track record at all. But walking out would hurt our reputation badly. And in time, you'd really resent me. So . . . if I walk out on anything, it will be you . . . for the time that we're here."

She was startled by her own words. She hadn't really meant them that way, but as she listened to her own voice, she didn't know how to stop. Or explain.

And when she finished speaking, he was dead still. Straight, tense as a bowstring, features in a deadlock. He turned his back on her and walked out on the balcony.

She stood still for a long moment, then fled after

him, determined to explain herself. To suggest that, since she seemed plagued by the ridiculous nightmares, she should sleep at Morwenna's or something, and therefore, no one could ever accuse him of hurting her in the night.

But when she reached the balcony, he was gone. She stood staring out at the moonlit night. It was crazy. He had jumped the little wrought iron fence in the chilly darkness, and gone walking around with bare feet and nothing but a bathrobe.

"Finn?" she called his name softly, but there was no answer. "Finn!" she called more loudly, and still no answer.

"You didn't understand!" she murmured miserably out loud. But still, there was no one to hear, and no one to reply.

She stood on the balcony for a long, long time, until the chill of the night seemed to seep into her bones, and she was shivering so violently she had to go back in.

There, she paced by the bed. She alternated between being terribly hurt, and then angry. At last, she gave out, and wrapped in the bathrobe and the blankets, she lay back down. The tears that had earlier stung her eyes must have flooded over because her cheeks were damp.

How long had he been gone? How could he be out there in nothing but a bathrobe?

As last, still alternating between a growing fury and a deep, knifing pain, she drifted to sleep.

And did not dream again.

Megan was gone.

She had been there when he had come back in at last, cursing himself for having been the biggest idiot in the world. But now . . . peering at the bedside clock he could see that it was nearly eleven. And Megan was up.

He rolled out of bed and walked toward the bathroom. "Meg?" He hadn't really needed to call out; the room had felt empty. He knew, as well, that she wasn't out on the balcony, and he doubted that she was in Huntington House at all.

Last night had been a maneuver of sheer stupidity. And yet . . .

Walking away—even crawling over the iron railing and scraping the family package—had seemed right. He'd needed to get away. Into the cold night air, barefoot, barely dressed. He'd felt an unreasoning sense of anger growing. Albeit, a lot of it was due to the fact that *she* hadn't been awake. Impossible. Or worse. She couldn't have fallen asleep *in the middle* of their lovemaking. That would surely be one of the worst affronts to man, ever. And then, imagining, or dreaming, that he was some kind of a *terrible thing*.

His walk had taken him out to a large rock at the front of the property where he had sat, convinced that he'd be alone—it was past even the "wee" hours of the night, and Salem, even with all its happenings, wasn't Vegas or even New Orleans. It did close down. But hell, leave it to his luck, he'd been sitting on the rock, smoking another of the cigarettes he stashed into his robe pocket, when a young couple had sauntered by. She had screamed—he seemed to have that effect on women lately—and the guy had said hello, but they walked around him as if they'd come upon dog poop. But then the girl had looked back. She'd recognized him, and despite the man, she'd turned back, startling Finn at first, causing him to rise. Then she'd gushed about his music, and kept touching him, on the shoulder, the arm . . . and he'd found himself saying that he couldn't sleep, so he was sitting on the rock. In a robe. In forty degree weather. Well, hell, that would probably be all over town by now.

He showered and dressed, hoping that Megan would return while he was so occupied. She didn't.

He came through the house and found that, despite the fact that breakfast time had long passed, John and Sally, the picture-perfect young American couple they had met at breakfast their first day, were enjoying coffee by the fire.

"Hey!" Sally called in greeting.

"We caught your act the other night," John said.

Finn paused. "You did? Great. Thanks for coming."

"Well, it was strange," John admitted. "We were just heading out to dinner, and we'd heard they had a decent meal out there, and usually, some kind of entertainment. We'd just happened to pick up the national paper and there was an article in it about you and your wife, and it mentioned you were playing. It was great. We'd just met you—and there you were. In color in the paper, and in person on stage."

"I hoped you enjoyed it," Finn said. "What paper?"

"I still have the article in my purse," Sally said, setting down her cup and rummaging through her bag. "Here!"

She produced a folded sheet. "Some girl wrote it in New Orleans, it seems, but the article was picked up and syndicated along with some other suggestions for Halloween."

He should have been jumping up and down at the national exposure. Instead, he found himself nearly surprised. They'd been interviewed for the article weeks ago—before leaving for their quickie Florida vacation. The woman had arrived when they'd been playing a local jazz club. Jade Deveau. She and her husband had been in the audience and he and Megan hadn't even known anything about the interview. They'd been pleased—and cautious, as well. Articles could become skewed.

Reviewers could do some major harm as well.

And her husband—not a writer, he had assured them—had still asked plenty of questions, especially when it had come to their playing for the week in Salem.

Neither of them had looked like reporters, but he'd checked the woman out the next day and, apparently, she was well known in New Orleans. She had her own little publishing company, and put out respected travel articles along with a number of guides to the Crescent City. She was exceptionally attractive, and well dressed, and her husband had been a tall guy, dark, with some of the strangest eyes Finn had ever seen, red, gold, ever changing, but never seeming to be the color eyes were supposed to be.

Contacts, he'd thought.

Megan had been impressed with him.

They'd both been nice.

And he'd seen a good review on their act at the jazz club the next day, so he'd thanked his lucky stars, and forgotten the pair.

But now . . .

"Wicked!" he murmured.

"What?" Sally said, frowning.

He laughed. "New England expression, so I've been told. I hadn't seen this."

Hadn't imagined that it might have existed. There was a large, clear picture of Megan and him on stage. There was information about their performance, and more information about the wonderful time to be had in Salem.

Then . . .

At the bottom of the article was a strange little notation where the author was given credit: *Jade McGregor Deveau is a frequent contributor.* Her E-mail address was down, and there was an invitation for anyone to write to her—*especially if they knew of the bizarre, unusual, or downright scary and dangerous.* A number of her books were listed—they all seemed to deal with the paranormal, rather than simple travel.

"Great article!" John complimented.

"And you were great," Sally said. "You know, we didn't

get a chance to buy the CD, and I'm not sure if we're going to be able to get back—"

"I'll be happy to get you one."

"We can pay you?"

He had the feeling she was expecting his response, but that was all right. He'd been taught in his business classes that there was nothing like putting giveaways into the right hands to promote talent.

"It will be my sincere pleasure to give you a CD," he told her. He started to hand the article back to her.

"You can keep it—just in case you can't get a copy of the paper."

"Hey, thanks."

He brought the couple a CD, hoping then that he didn't run into anyone else. It was growing late.

Susanna had a habit of always looking dour and ruining a good mood if you happened to be in one.

And Fallon . . .

Fallon always looked at him as if he were surely an ex-con in disguise.

But exiting quickly through the front of the house then, he saw no one else.

Megan hadn't taken the car, so he assumed she was walking around town somewhere. He'd do the same, he thought, until he found her. He was anxious to show her the article, but once he was down the street, he realized he'd left it in the room.

He didn't want to go back. He wanted to find his wife.

Everywhere, pumpkins, skeletons, and ghosts decorated yards and buildings. Boys playing kickball in the street apologized when they knocked their ball at his legs. He waved a hand and gave the ball a solid thrust back. They grinned and waved in return. He kept walking.

When he reached the common, he saw that Darren Menteith was out with Lizzie. Darren waved, and Finn walked over to the young man and the dog. Lizzie wagged her tail with delight, a friendly creature, despite her massive size.

"Caught your act again last night," Darren told him cheerfully. "Man, I wish we had more like you around."

"Thanks. I didn't see you."

"I didn't want to bother you."

"Don't worry about bothering us," Finn said. "Trust me, there have been those times when I've thought we were playing to the walking dead."

Darren grinned. "Well, hey, you know, it's Halloween around here. You might be playing to a few walking dead—dope-outs and lushes. But, hey, what the hell. As long as they move and put their hands together, huh? This whole Halloween thing here gets so crazy. Cute, too, though. I've seen some great art projects for kids going on in the streets."

"It is the ultimate Halloween destination," Finn said.

"Well, you must have expected it. Your wife coming from here, and all."

"I don't think I was completely prepared," Finn said wryly.

"Where is Megan?" Darren asked.

"Up and about somewhere. I slept late. In fact, I'm looking for her."

"Haven't seen her. But tell her Lizzie and I said hello."

"Sure thing."

Finn moved on. He realized that he was heading straight for Morwenna's, and his footsteps slowed, but then he knew he was being stupid. If Megan was around here somewhere, she'd surely stop at her cousin's place.

There was no one at the door at the moment; he entered through a full shop, but one that wasn't as insanely busy as he'd seen it at times. Morwenna was behind the counter. She gave Finn a beaming smile when she saw him across the store. A few minutes later, she came around the counter, leaving the cash register to the young man they'd met on the first night.

She gave him a kiss on the cheek. "Hey, handsome. You're off on your own? Where's my cousin?"

"I'm not sure. I thought she might be here."

Morwenna shook her head, frowning. "Are you two having an argument?"

His muscles quickened, and he willed himself not to appear tense, or take immediate offense. "Nope. I just slept late."

"Well, you two work hard, and late, poor darling," Morwenna said, studying his eyes. "I haven't seen her today, though, I'm sorry. I wish I would. Finn! You wouldn't believe it. Since you two appeared costumed from my shop last night, I've filled out more order forms than you can imagine. And we make the capes right here, you know, so it's incredibly wonderful for local business. I can't thank you enough."

"Hey, you bailed us out. We owe you the gratitude."

"Well, I hope you sincerely feel that way. I'd like you both to pick out something new for tonight."

He hesitated, then shrugged. He still felt so uneasy—on guard—every time he was around Morwenna and Joseph. Foolish. They were trying hard. "I hate to keep taking your things, Morwenna. There's surely some wear and tear on them by the time we return them."

"I swear! You're doing us the favor."

"Well, then, sure."

"Do you want to find something now?"

Again, he hesitated. Absurd. He didn't want to change clothing in that store. Not without Megan around. Great. He was a grown man afraid to take off his clothes.

"I think I'll find Meg, and come back, if that's okay? We can choose things that complement one another."

"Great. If you want, though, take a quick look at some of the new things that just came in. Back room, by the reading area and dressing rooms. We received a massive shipment, today, can you imagine? Clothing and books, mainly. But take a quick look."

What he wanted was to get out of the shop. Still, it was a fight to maintain a really friendly relationship with Morwenna and Joseph. He had sworn to himself that he would do so.

"All right."

He walked into the back room, thinking he should feel privileged. Regular customers didn't get past the beaded curtain that separated the front from the back unless they were being led back for readings, or to use the fitting rooms.

The curtains fell around his shoulders with a little tinkling sound. He paused for a moment, then saw a rack where a number of shirts hung, having been just unpacked. There was a large, commercial steamer standing by the rack, since the clothing arrived folded and wrinkled.

He walked over to the shirts, and as he absently looked through them, he felt that strange sensation that warned him of another presence. He turned.

Not ten feet from him, Sara was on the floor with a stack of boxes. These contained books. She was pulling them out, discarding the packing material, and sorting them. But she had paused, her eyes on Finn.

"Sorry. I didn't mean to disturb you," he murmured awkwardly. "Morwenna said I should look through the new things."

"You're not disturbing me," she said.

But she hadn't moved, and didn't still. She sat, legs—clad in black tights—sprawled at her sides. For a minute, she looked like an innocent little urchin.

"The books are a pain in the butt," she muttered then, lifting up the one she was holding. "I don't know why on earth Morwenna ordered this thing in. It's by some travel writer with a little publishing house in the south and it's a look into the absurd. One of those things that makes a mockery out of the true practice of Wicca." She glanced at the back cover, shaking her head with irritation.

He caught a glimpse of the back cover of the book and a little jolt of recognition shot through him. "May I see it?"

She shrugged. "Why not? You put on a good facade in the shop, but you really think we're a bunch of idiotic pagans anyway."

"I just don't believe in casting spells or any of that mumbo-jumbo," he said. "It's a free country, and freedom of religion is guaranteed. I am a big believer in the Constitution. May I see the book?"

She handed it to him. He turned it over. There was a picture of a very attractive woman on the back. The author photo was a casual shot, taken in Jackson Square, right in New Orleans. Naturally, he recognized Jackson Square. But he realized that he recognized the woman as well.

"Jade Deveau," he murmured.

"An old girlfriend?" Sara asked.

He shot her an irritated glance, and decided not to reply. He didn't know why he was surprised that a book written by the woman might be in a Salem store. The author acknowledgment had stated that she was . . . what? Into the occult? Or intrigued by stories about things that went bump in the night?

It just seemed strange that a woman he'd met recently should—in a roundabout way—reenter his life twice within a few hours.

"You wouldn't like the book," Sara said. "Trust me, you'd think it was a bunch of bunk!"

"Have you read it?"

Sara shrugged. "She has some strange ideas, certainly." She sighed. "All right, maybe you would actually like the book. She feels that anything out of the ordinary needs to be inspected more deeply. In other words, she isn't of the opinion that all witchcraft is benign. By the way—where's your wife today?"

"Seeing some sights," he muttered.

"So . . . did you let her out on her own, or did she trust you on the prowl?"

"Sara, being married doesn't mean that you're glued together."

"No, it doesn't, does it?" she said huskily. Then added a quick, "So where do you think she is? And with whom?"

"I think she's shopping, and maybe saying hello to a few friends."

Sara nodded. He wanted to walk right by her, but he kept staring at her. He could feel his jaw tightening, his teeth clenching. At the same time, he found himself noticing that she'd left a number of the buttons on her sweater undone and that she was almost spilling over the wool.

"You should leave, you know," she said.

"I'm going."

She shook her head. "Not the shop. Massachusetts."

"Why? You go into some silly trance and tell me that I'm going to hurt my wife. I love my wife. You tell me I'm dangerous, but you also seem to have your claws out, as if you'd jump me if you could. What the hell is it with you, and what do you think I'm going to do? Or would breaking up a marriage just make you happy as hell?"

He was startled to see her look distraught, and somewhat ashamed. She looked down for a moment, as if confused herself.

"No, I don't intend to be a home wrecker. And as to what you're going to do . . . I don't know . . . exactly. But you should leave. There's just something about you . . . I don't . . . there's some *thing* over the two of you. There you are, nice and tall, broad shouldered, sleek and wiry, exuding that he-man, masculine aura! And there's your perfect blond Barbie-doll wife." She cleared her throat, losing her air of confusion. "Isn't it scary sometimes, being so fucking perfect?"

"We're far from perfect—"

"Have you hurt her yet? Is that why she's away from you?"

He started past her, not willing to listen to any more. She caught his calf as he tried to walk by. "If you realize that you do need help, I'll be around." The fingers curled around his calf suddenly stroked up his thigh. She jerked her hands away, as if she hadn't touched him on purpose. "You're an asshole. You should leave."

He felt a strange prickling at the back of his neck. It was exactly what he wanted to do, no matter how sanity and logic fought against it.

But enough was enough. So much for being eternally polite just to get along with everyone for Megan's sake.

"Sara, leave me the fuck alone, will you?"

"I wish I could," she murmured, her words almost incoherent. Then she stared at him hard. "Sure, you should stay. Like I said, when you realize you're in way over your tough, inflated, macho head, come see me."

He stepped over and walked out of the back, listening as the beaded curtain crashed around him. Morwenna was behind the counter. He lifted his hand, waving good-bye.

He couldn't get out to the street fast enough.

It wasn't until he had walked far down the street that he realized he still had the book in his hand.

Chapter 9

"So what do you think of him?" Mike Smith asked, a certain wry amusement in his voice.

"He's certainly . . . evil enough looking," Megan replied.

She wasn't sure what had brought her back to the new museum where Smith was curator. She had avoided Morwenna's shop because she didn't want to start telling her cousin any of her problems. So she had wandered, seen the museum, and found herself hesitating in front of it. Then the same young girl who had been at the ticket counter the day before had spied her, and greeted her with tremendous enthusiasm, telling her that her own dream was to become a professional singer. Soon, Mike had come out, and told her that she had to see the new exhibit they were preparing.

The next thing she knew, she was walking through a door that said "Museum Staff Only," and viewing their new display on the seventh-century vision of the devil and witchcraft.

The "devil" was big. About eight feet tall. Blood red with black markings. A forked tongue was just visible, and a long, arrow-shaped tail was fully evident. The eyes were truly creepy, seeming to follow the observer, and naturally, the creature came complete with horns in the temple.

It gave her a little jolt, reminding her of something very uncomfortable. She knew it had something to do with the nightmare that had so violently disturbed her in her sleep, but for the life of her, she could no longer remember much about the dream.

"I wouldn't want to be locked in here with him, that's for sure," Megan added, grinning.

Mike studied the larger-than-life creature with a grin, then looked at Megan. "Can you believe that people really thought this guy came down and forced people to sign pacts? We've come a long, long way, thank God!"

"Right. Thank God."

"A great deal of the problem in the colonies, of course, stemmed from the European background. This was really serious. And, whether legal or not, torture was widespread. You should read some of the confessions from the cases in Europe. But then again, you torture someone long enough, and they don't just confess, they get garrulous and creative. Once one person had confessed and given his or her tormenters a story, others were sucked in. But people did confess to relationships with the devil. They confessed to wild parties, kissing the buttocks of such a creature, dancing naked in the moonlight—and much worse, of course. Now, to our educated senses, it's easy to realize that someone being racked, burned, or broken would admit to almost anything to stop the pain. But back then . . . they just believed that they were forcing the truth from their pathetic victims."

"The power of suggestion is very strong," Megan murmured.

Mike looked at her, frowning. "Are you all right?"

"Oh, yes, of course," she said quickly. "I've just noticed that during the last few days . . . well, people talk about monsters, and then you dream about them. You know, you see a particularly eerie jack-o'-lantern, or some such thing, and then you put it into dreams."

Mike laughed. "Well, that's true. Mine are usually a bit different. I was watching a game show before I went to sleep one night, and I had the greatest dream in the world. I'd won millions of dollars. The dream was incredibly real. I was heartbroken when I woke up and finally had to force myself to realize that I wasn't rich."

Megan laughed. "Well, dreaming that you're rich isn't a nightmare, anyway."

"Right. Waking up and realizing that you're not rich is the nightmare. But, hey, I love what I do, so I don't need to be rich."

"That's the real payoff, isn't it?" Megan agreed.

"So we're both lucky."

"Very," she murmured.

"Hey, I'm due a break. Want to get some coffee or something?"

"Sounds great," Megan agreed.

They left the museum, walking onto the main strip in the center of the old-town tourist section. They tossed a coin to choose between two coffeehouses, and laughed, since they both called heads, but forgot which side of the street was "heads." One of them boasted the best hot mocha in the world, so they decided on it.

Once seated with two large mochas topped with whipped cream, they talked casually, Megan telling him how sorry she was when he shrugged and told her that his mom had died of cancer soon after he'd graduated high school, and he'd lost his father just two years ago to heart failure. "I think he missed her too much," Mike said. "Anyway, they're together. What about your folks?"

"Alive and well in Maine," she told him.

"Good for them. Of course, I see your Aunt Martha all the time, and she's still just as ornery as ever."

"Ornery?" Megan protested.

Mike laughed. "Okay. Opinionated. Actually, I like her a lot. She's a no-nonsense kind of lady, all down to earth and practical. You should see some of the town meetings around here. The Wiccans are all up in arms about the trashy display of green women riding on broomsticks in certain advertisements, and Martha is always there to remind them that there is a percentage of the population that likes to have fun with Halloween and all. This remains a small community. Of all types. And she's like the voice of stern sanity at all times."

"Good for her."

"I thought she and Morwenna were going to come to blows, once."

"What happened?"

"It was a silly argument over a decal someone wanted to sell. And bless her, Morwenna backed down rather than punch out Aunt Martha. Who knows—Martha might have been the one to deck her, she is one feisty lady."

Megan laughed and moved her stirrer through her mocha. "What's the story with Andy Markham?"

Mike lifted a brow. "The story? Well, he tells stories. That's how he survives."

"He seems to believe them."

"Hey, you know what? People around here can convince you of almost anything. It's how they make a living. Megan!" he murmured suddenly, setting his hand upon hers. "It really does sound as if you're letting some of this get to you. Kid—you come from these parts! This stuff has been going on all your life, and you should remember it, even if you moved away for a while. You've got to remember that this place can be great—there's nothing as beautiful as autumn in New England. It's great that you're here, and I've never seen such a total community success as you and Finn have been, playing at the hotel. Relish the triumph! Savor it. Don't let the creepy-crawlies get into your dreams.

Watch game shows before you go to sleep—even Huntington House offers dozens of cable channels these days. Cartoons—whoops, maybe not. Once, I dreamed I was the Road Runner and Wily E. Coyote was after me."

Megan laughed again, remembering how she had always liked Mike, even in his ultraserious and academic moods. He had a nice, wry way of looking at the world, and could find humor in almost any situation.

She hesitated, then admitted, "Mike, I'm telling you, I've had such bad nightmares that Finn has suggested we just up and leave."

He digested her words, watching her, and answering carefully, "Megan, it's really a small, tight area, like I said. And we do remember the old families, and the past. You're basically a native child. To some people, your husband is still a Confederate, a Rebel—certainly not good old Yankee stock. You're loved—he's under suspicion. But you two are a great pair. Don't let other people dictate your lives, or ruin something that is going great for you both. You spoke earlier about the power of suggestion. I'm dead serious. Make sure that any power of suggestion that's around you before you go to sleep is totally good, and then you'll have nice, sweet, dreams. You could wake up ruing the fact that your life is great but you're still broke, but that will be better than waking up in cold sweats and terror."

"You're right. I told Finn that I wasn't going to give in to any kind of idiotic suggestion and run. And still . . ."

"He's not the one having the nightmares, huh?"

"He doesn't wake up screaming. But . . . I think we're both sleeping . . . weirdly."

"Weirdly?"

She didn't want to explain that her husband didn't even remember intimacy when he woke up in the morning. That was too personal—as much as she did like Mike, and feel really comfortable about being with an old friend.

"Restlessly, I guess."

"A different bed," Mike said sagely, wiggling his brows.

She smiled. "Maybe. Except that we're both pretty good on the road. You have to get accustomed to different beds when you're musicians."

"Listen, everyone knows that you two had split, and gotten back together not all that long ago. So here you are—your hometown. Naturally, you're both going to be uneasy. Even though you're the loved one here, you're worried about his reactions to your hometown. He's worried about what people think of him, because he knows they all love you. I had to take a fair amount of psychology to get out of school with my doctorate, you know."

Megan leaned back, smiling. Mike had a nice, neat ability to put the world into perspective. Yet, as she sat back, she glanced out the window, and found herself frowning.

Finn was there.

Just outside, staring in. She could see his face over the glass where a large cup of steaming coffee had been painted on it.

She froze for a moment.

It didn't look like Finn. It *was* Finn, but . . .

She suppressed a little shiver, aware that his eyes were on her, and for a fleeting moment, they appeared to be red again.

Fiery red, like those eyes she had seen in her dream . . .

And his features . . . they were taut, so strained that he appeared almost skeletal. And the look he was giving her was filled with rage, menace, and . . .

Evil.

Evil. The word kept coming to her mind, in so many ways now, so very often.

She blinked, and swallowed. She'd imagined it all . . .

No, she hadn't. Finn was indeed there. But his eyes were their customary color, and his face wasn't pinched or taut at all. He'd donned one of his favorite coats, a black leather railroad jacket, and it fell nicely from his shoulders to his ankles, somehow very nicely emphasizing his height and the breadth of his shoulders and the clean lean lines of his waist, hips, and long legs. His hair was clean, a little shaggy, giving him an ever so slight rough-around-the-edges quality that was very appealing. He wasn't smiling; he looked a little grim, but not at all evil. In fact, she felt a little chill of excitement at the sight of him. Finn was, beyond a doubt, sexy.

He walked in.

"Finn!" she acknowledged.

He bent from behind, kissed her cheek, stood tall again, and nodded to Mike. "Hi, there. Nice to see you."

The words were spoken with even civility. It was still clearly evident, to Megan at least, that Finn wasn't in the least pleased to see Mike.

Mike rose, offering Finn a hand. Finn took it—then let go of it quickly, drawing over an empty chair from the table beside theirs, and straddling it. "Break time from the museum?" Finn queried.

"I take a break when I choose," Mike said pleasantly, as if he didn't notice in the least the note of hostility in Finn's voice. "Hell, I put in about eighty hours a week. That buys me the right to take a break whenever I choose. Hey, you guys were great last night."

"Thanks. I didn't see you there," Finn said.

"Oh, well, what the hell. When in Rome, you know. I wore a costume. And I'm not big on makeup, or fussing around in a way that takes a lot of time. Masks are the way to go for me."

"Still!" Megan said. "You need to come up to the stage and say hi!"

"Next time, I will," Mike promised.

"Do," Finn said. His fingers had curled around Megan's empty cup. She thought that if it hadn't been made of thick ceramic, it would have crushed beneath

the tension in his fingers. "Did you two run into one another in the street?"

"No," Mike said.

"Yes," Megan began. Finn arched his brows. "In a way,"
Megan continued. "I was just out walking, one of the
young museum employees saw me, Mike saw us . . . we
went in to see a new exhibit going up, and came out for
coffee then."

"New exhibit?" Finn said.

His voice was bass deep. Hard.

"I planned it, and I really think it's one of my best,"
Mike said, still being friendly and polite. How could he
not hear the menace in Finn's voice? Megan wondered.
She longed to kick Finn under the table, but oddly, she
was afraid if she did so, he'd go straight for Mike's
throat.

Or her own.

"What people don't grasp today about the situation
in 1692 is just how serious the majority of the people
considered the crime of witchcraft to be—and what
they believed witchcraft to be. Remember, this is the
same general time when young boys could be hanged
for stealing loaves of bread—and before we hanged
horse thieves in the American West with little thought
of due process of law. So—"

"I'm sure it's a great exhibit," Finn said.

Mike was perplexed by the interruption, but he still
didn't seem to realize that while he was being friendly,
Finn had suddenly decided to act like a horse's ass.

"Is it all set up?" Finn asked pointedly.

"Still in the process."

"I can't imagine how you're tearing yourself away
from it."

"Good point." Mike laughed a little awkwardly and
rose. "I should get back. Please, both of you, stop by anytime. And if I can help in any way—clearing up any

local hogwash or the like!—please don't hesitate to come by. I'm more than happy to help if I can."

Finn's brow was seared by a deep furrow as he stared at Megan. "Did we need help clearing up any local hogwash?"

"I did," she snapped, and rose as well. For a moment, she was almost afraid to tell Mike good-bye with a kiss on the cheek.

But Finn was being a total ass, and he'd surely realize it.

"Mike, we'll see you soon," she said firmly.

Finn rose as well. "Good afternoon," he managed to murmur. Mike had a hand out. Finn pretended not to see it.

"Have a great night then," Mike said, and offering a smile to Megan that assured her everything was all right, he made his way through the tables and exited.

Megan sank back into her chair and stared furiously at her husband. "What the hell was that all about?"

"You tell me," he said coolly.

"What are you talking about?"

"What did you do, come running to your old friend for help? 'My husband has become a monster! What do I do? I have nightmares, and he's in them all!' "

For a moment she was so startled that she didn't reply. Then she leaned toward him, heedless of the darkness in his eyes. "You are truly being a jerk, and surely, you must see that yourself!"

He stared back at her. There was still a fury so intense in his features that she again felt a second's fear that he would leap; there was also something disturbingly seductive about the hot tension that radiated from him.

She was losing her sanity, that was for sure. Maybe he was right—they should screw everything else and leave.

But . . .

What if nothing changed? What if the problems were between them, and had nothing to do with time and place, or even All Hallow's Eve?

Finn leaned back suddenly. He lowered his head, and looked at her again. "You know what?" he said softly, a husky sound that was as much caress as apology, "You're right. And I'm sorry. I was acting like a jealous jackass. It's just that I woke up, and you were gone." He hesitated, his jaw twisting. "After last night. When you said that you'd leave me before you'd leave Salem."

"I didn't mean that the way it came out, Finn," she said earnestly. "I just thought that if . . . if I were going to have these nightmares and wake up screaming . . . and I wasn't with you, well, then, no one could accuse you of doing anything."

"Megan, they can accuse away." He hesitated, features still tense, pained. "Megan, I'm still one insecure asshole. And I don't think I could bear it if you left me again."

A slow smile curved into her lips. A damp hint threatened behind her lids. He was her life, everything she wanted in life.

But she didn't intend to burst into tears in the coffee shop, or even get more carried away with letting him see just how completely she was in love with everything about him, how desperately she needed and wanted him, always, in her life.

"How on earth could you ever be insecure?" she asked lightly, leaning back some and studying him as if she did so objectively. "You walk into a room, and all eyes turn on you. Women drool in your wake, you know," she finished, and she was only halfway teasing.

His fingers brushed over hers. "Because there's only one woman I want drooling in my wake."

There was still that something about him . . . he just had it all. The size, the smile, the eyes . . . the way he moved. Even the music. She wondered if she'd be this desperately attracted to him all her life.

"You could have denied women drool in your wake, you know."

"Well, I would have, but I've been taught that perception is nine-tenths of the law. Therefore, if that's your perception . . . hell, I wouldn't want to change it."

"Um, I see," she murmured, then frowned, realizing that his arms were still taut, and held close to his body. And beneath one of them, something was sticking out. "Hey, what are you holding?"

"What?"

"What do you have clutched to your chest?"

He frowned, then seemed to realized that he was holding a book. "Shit!" he muttered.

"What?"

"I just stole a book. From your cousin's shop," he said sheepishly.

"You stole a book from Morwenna?" she inquired skeptically.

"By accident. Hey, I forgot to tell you—we were written up, *nationally*, yesterday. Remember the reporter who came to the jazz club? Seems she wrote more—a little Halloween entertainment-across-the-country article, and we—and Salem, of course—were the main focus."

"What does that have to do with the book?"

"Well, that's what's weird—and why I walked out with the book by accident. It's by the same woman." He handed Megan the book, backside up, and tapped on the author photo. "See?"

Megan, looking at him, halfway grinning, slowly arched a brow. "This woman gave us great national exposure, and so you stole her book?"

"I took it by accident, I told you. Sara was there—making me feel all creepy—and I kind of hurried out."

"Ah. Sara was making you feel *creepy*? Strange. I get

the feeling Sara would like to make you feel something else."

"Hey—who is being jealous now?"

She wanted to smile. She couldn't. "Me. But oddly enough . . . I think I'm right. I didn't say that you would respond, only that I think Sara . . . is just strange. It's as if she can't keep away from you."

"It's my charm."

"Of course."

"I can eat garlic, or wear a cross, to keep her away from me."

"I don't think that crosses do anything against horny Wiccans."

He laughed, leaning back, threading his fingers lightly through her hair. "Probably not. Can I suffice it to say that I really, truly, find her creepy?"

"That will do pretty well. But it's strange, isn't it? Mike's girl acted that way about you, too. That Gayle Sawyer. She stared at you as if you were Michelangelo's *David*."

He leaned close to her. "Maybe we're not that different."

"Hm. I forgot to check out just how well hung that statue was."

"Megan, I promise you, I'd sure as hell never let Sara get that close. You've just become too accustomed to my aura of raw sexuality."

A shiver seized her suddenly. *No, that's certainly not it at all,* she thought, but had no intention of bringing up the strange volatility of their nights. Not now.

"Don't worry any," she assured him. "If Sara gets too . . . too . . . close, I'll deck her for you."

"You?"

"I preach nonviolence, and I believe in it. But I'll still deck her," she assured him.

"I think I can manage."

"Hey, you like to protect me at a bar!"

"Right, and you get mad when I do."

"Because drunks can be handled."

"They can be handled better when they see a six-foot-something bigger guy at your side."

"And Sara will be handled if I deck her—only if she wants to get too close."

"If she's smart, she'll keep her distance," he said gravely.

Megan smiled, but was startled to feel a moment's sheer possessiveness. It wasn't like her. Maybe it was the banter, which was dangerous, because the trust was so important between them now. And maybe it was just the light, quick conversation as well, but she also felt . . .

Like crawling over her husband, then and there. Doing what Sara wasn't at all allowed to do.

"You know what?" she said, whispering close to his ear. "It's early. Actually, for people with a nighttime work schedule, it's very early. The afternoon and early evening stretch ahead."

"You're in the mood for some drooling, are you?"

"Perhaps I could be convinced."

He stood, stretching out his hand. She curled her fingers into his.

A pleasant smell of coffee filled the air around them. Children were laughing at one of the nearby tables. A waitress impatiently called out an order.

Her husband was grinning, the curl of his lips a bit wicked.

Good wicked.

She felt a surge of longing kick in as if she were being touched already, intimately.

The world was right.

He came around the table and pulled her against him. "I think you are a bit of a witch yourself," he whispered softly.

She felt the oddest desire to protest.

Instead, she stroked his cheek, came on her toes, and

murmured suggestively against his earlobe. "Let's go fool around. I'm just dying to see how well, how deeply and completely, you can apologize."

"Watch that tone of voice," he murmured, "or I'll be apologizing far too deeply and completely right here, right now."

Laughing, she caught his hand and hurried ahead of him.

As they left the coffee shop, a little shiver shot through her. She paused for a minute, that odd feeling of being watched searing into her. She paused, turning, looking for the eyes that were surely boring into her back.

Finn was directly behind her, his hands on her shoulders. They warmed her. They seemed to give her a certain strength against whatever tugged at her. Insanity maybe, because the streets were busy, filled with activity, and if someone was standing somewhere, staring at her, she sure as hell couldn't see him—or her.

"Let's—" she began, looking up at Finn, and breaking off. He, too, was searching out the crowd.

"What's wrong?" she asked.

He shook his head, as if shaking off a feeling as well. His eyes touched down on hers. "I love you. I really love you, you know. And I would die before I ever let anyone hurt you."

She smiled.

The breeze was gentle. The sun was still visible in an autumn sky that was still somehow soft blue, and wonderfully gentle, almost bright.

"I love you . . . so come on, please, let's hurry. I do hate to drool in the street."

Chapter 10

Darkness came so quickly in October in New England.

Of course, as Megan explained, while they lay curled together, watching the daylight fade through the crack in the curtains, it was even worse in December.

It was the best time they'd had together since they had come here. No dreams had plagued either of them. Megan had been playful, sensual; there had been moments of barely breathing urgency, muscle-knotted soaring, and mind-shattering climax. Intimacy so complete that it seemed no outside force could be noticed, much less intrusive. Their bond, combining hearts and senses, had never seemed so solid, and Finn was loathe for the afternoon to wane, and so, even as the darkness came, they lay together, spent, disheveled, limbs entangled, just watching as that darkness came.

Still entangled, though, the mundane had come into what at first was idle conversation, choices of music for the night, what they didn't want to do again, and what, though they'd done it already, was signature and popular, and therefore, good for the agenda once again. Megan turned to him suddenly, smiling, skimming a damp lock of hair from his forehead, and murmured, "It's almost like being back home again, isn't it?"

He smiled, catching her fingers, languidly teasing them with the tip of his tongue.

"Finn, for real, there's something special this afternoon . . . and you owe it all to Mike."

He had just been feeling the slow, simmering rise of a renewed erection. Her words deflated him like a popped balloon.

"Mike? Wow. Was he in bed with us?"

She kicked his calf. "No, and if you're going to act like a jealous ass again, I'm going to get up."

"You might want to explain what you're talking about, then."

"He's just so wonderfully logical and pragmatic. I was really starting to worry about the dreams. I confess, when you said you wanted to leave, I wanted to run away from here more than anything in the world. But he was talking about his psychology classes, about the power of suggestion . . . and I realized, I was having nightmares because I was allowing myself to have them. Listening to old loons like Andy Markham, and whatever else. And, though you don't want to admit it, Mr. Tough Guy, you are subject to the same force of suggestion. So . . . before going to sleep from now on, we're going to watch game shows. Or old sitcom reruns. Like *Gilligan's Island.* Or *The Cosby Show.* Or Lucy!"

"I see," he murmured.

"You're going to insist that you haven't had weird dreams? I'm the one who might have awakened screaming, but the other night . . . you don't even remember making love."

Finn stared at the ceiling. "At least I didn't imagine you as some kind of wicked beast or awful, hideous creature."

"The power of suggestion. I'd seen a statue of a beast of some kind, and therefore I dreamed it up. So . . . I'm not even going to take a good look at a well-carved jack-o'-lantern from here on out. Lucy and Desi, *Family Ties,* *Cheers!* That's it from now on."

Finn tried to tell himself that maybe he should be grateful to Mike Smith.

If not grateful, he should at least manage to be decent around the guy. Trust had been a big issue between him and Megan, helping to break them apart before. If he had half a brain in his head, he'd quell the temper and jealousy that kept rising in him.

"Want me to write Mike Smith a thank-you note?" he queried.

"No." Megan's toe moved over his calf.

"So . . ."

"When you see him, I just want you to be polite."

Her toe moved up to his thigh. Her fingers crawled down his chest.

Hallelujah. What had died seemed to be rising again.

"I can be very polite," he assured her huskily.

Megan was agile. Her toe and fingers collided.

"There are times to be polite . . ." she purred, her whisper heating his ear, "and times, you know, when you should just be downright friendly."

"Very friendly," he agreed, and decided they had talked enough.

He could be incredibly agile as well.

Darkness fell in deep soft blues. They were immune to the slow spiraling ground fog and the strange mist that surrounded the rising moon.

It was a deep blue orb as it rose high over the old cemetery.

There was no form of communication that could be trusted, except that of meeting alone. And so the two came together.

The woman arrived first, and as she waited, she ran

her fingers over the weathered marble of her idol, knowing every angle and curve of the structure. She touched it lovingly, as tenderly as if it were flesh.

In time, her protégé arrived. She was not pleased with the tardiness of his arrival, and of course, he was aware of that fact when he saw the way she gazed at him. Once, he would have felt a sense of shame, that he had served badly, and a sense of fear as well.

But in the days past, he had tasted his own power. And he knew that she was just a servant of the master, no greater than himself.

Except that . . . well, she would be greater.

"You should fall to your knees in the presence of the Master!" she said angrily.

He knew how to pay homage, and did not need her tell him how. He kissed cold marble, and felt a trembling in the coldness of the stone, and a surge of strength and vigor within himself.

"You didn't need to summon me," he said coldly. "I know my business, and I have been about it well."

"Not well enough," she said sharply. "You have obtained much of what we need . . . but you know that there is more. You can delay no longer. What is necessary must be acquired now. We have but days left. And at the proper moment, the chalices must be full."

"I told you, I know what I'm about," he said. "You!" He pointed a finger at her. "You see to it that all is in readiness when the moment arrives. There can be no one there who lacks faith in His power, no one who will falter. The number must be complete."

"I have known what I'm about for a very long time," she said quietly. "You mustn't hesitate any longer. You must move. Not soon—now."

He nodded curtly to the woman; as he had surely told her quite plainly, he knew the business he was about, knew his responsibility. He acknowledged the idol again, lips hot against stone, and closed his eyes and savored the strength and power that seemed to rip and tear into his center and his limbs, like bolts of lightning, electric and shattering.

Without another word, he turned and left.

Below the moonlight, she watched him leave, and she closed her own eyes, envisioning the majesty of what was to come. She stretched her hand before her, beneath the deep blue cast of the night sky, and smiled. She stared at her arms, and dreamed of what would be. The differences that would change the world, *her* world.

She had planned so carefully. For so very long.

The Time of Darkness was coming.

Coming so soon.

Above her, blue clouds roiled, and she luxuriated in the feel of the misty ground fog that was slowly spiraling as if kissed by a strange wind, rising . . . soon to encompass the night.

And create a new day.

They were two sets into the night, and everything was still going wonderfully when Megan had the run-in with the man at the bar.

Like usual, Morwenna and Joseph were there, clapping enthusiastically after every number, supporting them completely. Darren Menteith had come, minus Lizzie, and with a number of friends from the college.

Megan hadn't felt so good since they had arrived in New England. But tonight . . . Finn, again, looked incredible, clad in another outfit from Morwenna's shop. She liked her own outfit as well, with the delicate, slit silk sleeves, tight bodice, and flowing skirt. Finn had really seemed to be getting along with Joseph. He hadn't hedged his conversation, as if afraid that every word would somehow relate to witchcraft. They had talked soccer and beer. She and Morwenna had laughed about incidents during their childhood. They had talked about friends from school.

She wished that Mike Smith would have approached them. Finn would have been as easy with her old friend, she was certain. But if Mike was there—which he very well could be—he was in costume, and not about to let himself be known.

Well, Finn had acted like an ass.

"Hey, honey, let me buy you a drink."

She turned. The man in question was medium tall, in a brown cape, with brown makeup. He had on prosthetic makeup as well, giving him an enlarged forehead and a huge nose. If she were to run into him again on the street, she'd surely never recognize him again. Except for maybe his voice. It had a high, whining quality to it.

Of course, that might be due to the amount of alcohol he had already consumed. Or he might have even been putting on the voice.

"Thanks," she said lightly. "But I'm just drinking water with lemon, and I have a new one here. Right in front of me."

He edged closer.

"One drink won't kill you, honey. It could be *wicked* good for you."

She felt Finn come up behind her. "Hey, I think the lady said that she was fine. Thanks for the offer, but no thanks."

He spoke pleasantly enough, just an edge of warning in his voice.

"Think you're a big shot, huh, buddy, just because you're up on that stage with her."

Finn still held his temper. "I think that the lady is with me, because she's my wife."

For a moment, it looked as if the man was going to challenge Finn anyway. Then he shrugged and backed off. Finn took the seat next to her, grinning. "Was I okay? Assertive, but not aggressive, firm, but not impolite?"

She laughed, setting a hand on his arm.

"You were quite perfect. Although, you know, I can defend myself against a drunk."

"Probably true," he said philosophically. "But did you really want to have to deck the asshole?"

"You've a point. Might have ruined the costume."

"His, or yours?"

"Mine, of course. It's borrowed finery."

Finn sat back, frowning. Megan's attention was drawn down the bar. The drunk was now hitting on another woman. It was the pretty young woman who worked at Mike's new museum, manning the ticket booth. She had introduced herself as Gayle Sawyer.

She wasn't wearing a costume—at least, Megan didn't *think* it was a costume. She was in a black knit dress that hugged her compact but well-shaped body. Tonight, there were a number of studs and rings in her ears, a silver stud above her left eyebrow, and a tiny diamond in her nose. She was nursing an amber-colored cocktail, and had been talking with another girl, very slim and blond, also in black, at her side.

The drunk had come between them. Gayle was obviously his target.

"Swallow it down, and I'll buy you another," the man encouraged her.

"I'm good with this," Gayle said, impatient that her conversation had been interrupted.

"I'm really good-looking beneath this makeup. And rich," the drunk said.

"Look! Fuck off—I don't want another drink!" Gayle told him, completely irritated then.

The drunk gripped her by the arm, dragging her off the bar stool. She fell against him, and struggled to straighten herself. The drunk slipped his arm around her, holding her close.

"So you wanna dance!" he laughed gleefully.

"Let me go!"

The man wasn't listening. He started to pull her out onto the floor.

"Hey!"

Finn stepped forward at that, striding toward the pair. He set his arm on the drunk's shoulder. "Buddy, she wants to be left alone."

The man looked around—his putty nose starting to descend a bit. "Hey, what are you, the dating police?" he growled to Finn.

"You need to go home," Finn said.

"This ain't your wife, your girl, or your concern," the man said angrily.

"Common courtesy. She doesn't want to be with you. Let her alone."

At that, the drunk dropped hold of Gayle Sawyer. He'd been holding her so tightly that she staggered back. Finn went to support her, and the drunk swung violently at Finn.

Finn ducked the blow with a second to spare. When he straightened, the drunk swung again. Finn blocked the blow, but lost patience and control. He swung back, catching the fellow dead square on the jaw, and the drunk fell like an axed oak.

"Oh, man, thank you!" Gayle Sawyer gushed out, flinging herself at Finn, hugging him tightly around the neck.

"Hey, it's all right," Finn murmured awkwardly, trying to disentangle himself and get down on the floor to check on the offender. By then, Sam Tartan was heading through the crowd. He didn't look so thankful. He stared at Finn as if he had hired a pariah to play at his club.

"What the hell?" he demanded crossly.

"Your 'guest' was attacking the young woman," Megan said sharply, before Finn could even begin to move his lips. She'd spoken with such a contemptuous air, that even Tartan stood dead silent for a minute.

"We employ people to handle this kind of problem!" he stuttered out after a moment.

"Well, your employees were apparently not available and I was practically being raped on the dance floor!" Gayle Sawyer said, looking crossly at Sam Tartan, and then adoringly at Finn.

"I hope you haven't broken his jaw," Tartan said.

"I hope he has!" Gayle muttered.

Someone else—in a two-foot blond wig and velvet Victorian costume had come through the crowd and stooped down by the drunk.

"Hey!" Tartan said.

The "woman" in the velvet dress growled up at him in a deep voice. "I'm a doctor. He's fine, won't even have a bruise on his chin. He's just drunk as a skunk. Anyone here know the guy?"

A startled little cry sounded and a tiny woman came rushing through them, falling to her knees. "It's Marty!" she cried. And she stared at all of them as if she were surveying a circle of vultures. "What have you done to my husband?"

"Your *husband?*" Gayle repeated disbelievingly. "You're here with . . . *him?*"

"Of course! He's my husband, and what did you do to him?"

"Lady, he was being totally obnoxious at the bar."

"Marty? Never!" she protested angrily.

"Ma'am, really," Megan said. "I'm sorry, but he was being really obnoxious."

The woman wasn't about to take it. She glared at the occupants of the bar. "I'm sure he turned all you prostitutes down, and so—"

"Prostitutes!" Gayle cried.

"This is getting out of hand," Tartan said, his lips twitching. "Doctor—" he began, then shuddered, looking at his "guest" in his drag-queen apparel—"can we move him?"

"Of course. He's just drunk."

"Drunk. Marty never drinks too much!" his wife argued.

"Lady, smell him," the doctor said.

"But you!" Mrs. Marty rose, pointing a finger at Finn. "How dare you! What did you do?"

"Excuse me," Finn said firmly. "Perhaps your husband is allergic to alcohol, I don't know. He was rude and obnoxious to my wife, and then to the young lady there—"

"Young lady!" the woman sniffed. "My ass!" she exclaimed.

"I'll lay you wicked flat in two seconds, lady," Gayle warned.

"Please!" Sam Tartan said. By then, Adam Spade had pushed through. He looked at the drunk on the floor, the wife, the crowd at the bar, and seemed to have a handle on the situation. "I'll get him up," he said briefly. Spade even seemed to know that the figure in the Victorian dress was a doctor. "I can move him."

The doctor nodded. "You have a room here?" he said to the wife.

"Yes. And we'll take Marty up to it, but I promise you, there will be a lawsuit. I have witnesses."

"Ma'am, the witnesses will all say that your husband was drunk and obnoxious," Megan heard herself say, her own voice rising.

She was startled to hear Finn speaking, calmly. "Why don't we call the cops right now, just so that there are no questions or hesitations later?"

Sam hesitated, as if the last thing he wanted was cops. But Megan could see that Finn was still angry, and not about to be accused of undue force against the man.

"Hey! I'm a cop," a man, dressed in a Freddy costume, said. He came forward, pulling off his mask. "I'm not on duty, but I did witness what happened." He looked at Marty's wife, a little sadly. "Ma'am, I'm sorry, but your husband was drunk and obnoxious."

"Marty barely even drinks!" she said, and the sound of her voice was definitely pathetic.

"Maybe that's what happened," the Freddy-cop said gently. "Maybe he had a drink, and it just all went wrong in him. Marty is probably a great guy who would never bother the ladies, especially when he's got a nice little wife like you. Do you want me to call out a man who is on duty? Do you want to file this? Marty could be charged with being drunk and disorderly—"

"No!" the woman protested. She looked at Tartan. "Just take him up to the room. Please."

Adam Spade, the huge bouncer, concealed a grin as he gave the Freddy-cop a grateful smile and bent down to pick up Marty. He lifted him as if he were no more than a few pounds.

Tartan started to follow Spade and his burden and Marty's wife. He glanced back at Finn. "Can you play?" He hesitated a moment. "Please? I don't want everyone in the place over here!"

"Sure," Finn said.

But he turned to the Freddie-cop first. "Thanks. You really defused a situation there."

The man shrugged, also intent on concealing the depth of his amusement. "Hey, he could have charged you with assault, but the young lady there"—he indicated Gayle—"could have charged him with assault as well. Dumb incident. Can't believe the wife let him get in that kind of condition and could still insist to herself that her husband was a good guy who didn't drink—and wouldn't think of bothering a woman at a bar."

"Who knows? Maybe Marty can't drink," Finn said with a shrug.

Megan tugged at his arm a little nervously. "We need to get on stage. Officer, thank you."

"My pleasure. I'm Theo Martin, by the way. Officer Martin, by day. Nice to meet you."

"Our pleasure, sincerely," Megan said.

They started to walk toward the stage. Finn had Megan's hand. She was almost wrenched away when Gayle came rushing up between them, throwing herself at Finn, giving him a choker hug. "Thank you! All those other folks—including a cop, so it seems!—did nothing. And you saved me."

"I don't think you were really in danger," Finn told her, trying to politely disentangle himself from her arms.

"And you're fine now," Megan said. She clenched her teeth. What was it around here? Gayle hadn't wanted a drunk fondling her—but she didn't seem to mind becoming a drape over Finn's body—while Finn's wife watched.

"You've got balls! You're the only guy here with real balls!" Gayle insisted.

"He has to get his balls on stage to play now," Megan said, firmly, but nicely.

"Oh! Sorry. But thank you; thank you so much!"

She slipped from Finn at last. He looked at Megan and shrugged. "It must be that power of suggestion thing you had going on today. About women drooling." He was serious suddenly. "Megan, I didn't set out to start a fight. He went swinging for me hard, twice."

"I know, Finn."

"I know how you feel about street brawls—"

"Hey, I was there. I saw what happened. You did what you had to do. Let's get on the stage before Tartan comes back in."

Finn dead stopped for a minute, turning to her. He didn't glance at it, but flexed and relaxed the hand that had been gouged at Morwenna's shop almost absently as he stared at her.

"What? He'll fire us?"

"Maybe."

"If he does, it was meant to be."

"You don't believe in destiny and all that, Finn!" she reminded him.

He muttered something and turned away. They walked up on stage. Finn picked up his guitar and took a seat on the stool. Before he even leaned toward the mike, a thunderous applause suddenly filled the room.

Speechless, he gazed at Megan. She shrugged. It was his ball game. She felt a strange pounding in her heart, and was annoyed with herself. Finn had gotten in trouble at school when he was young for fighting. Usually, because someone had decided to come after him. After nearly being suspended once, he'd made a point of taking classes in the Asian arts, which, along with self-defense, taught discipline. They had talked about it several times in college, because she'd seen her husband square his shoulders, turn and walk away, many times when a situation might have become explosive. Not tonight.

And to her amazement, she was glad. That Finn had stepped in. There was something archaic and medieval about the pride she was feeling. The word *pagan* suddenly popped into her mind. As if she had the most powerful caveman in the tribe, or the like.

She shook off the feeling. The incident was regrettable and strange. Mrs. Marty had really appeared to be stunned and brokenhearted that her husband had behaved so badly. She had been so stunned that she had been unwilling to believe the situation. Megan didn't get the feeling that she was the kind of woman who threatened to sue all the time. Her words had been in self-defense because it had been a situation she had been unwilling to accept.

"Hey, guys," Finn said, stilling the applause. "I guess we all kind of have to be careful, this much partying and all. Especially all of you out there who are driving. We have to drink responsibly, no matter how wild the nights may get. Okay . . . this one is a takeoff on a medieval love ballad, very romantic and sad. Hope you enjoy it."

He stared at Megan. He'd changed the lineup for the second set. She shrugged again. It was slow and sad, with a beautiful melody, and a calming influence. She nodded imperceptibly, but found that she couldn't quite tear her eyes away from his. The green seemed to be catching the light strangely. It looked as if his eyes had turned gold. Very strange eyes . . .

Like those of the black cat, reflecting off the lights, as it had stared at them from the brush when they had left Aunt Martha's the other day.

The lights in the room were bizarre. Black lights, strobe lights. It might be natural that a strange reflection was occurring. But the color, or the glare of it, was oddly hypnotic and seductive. At last, she felt as if she ripped her gaze from his, and turned back to the audience.

Finn had to play the intro twice.

But then it was all right. She slipped into the melody, and as they went through the ballad, the room became quieter. Waiters stopped by tables. Glasses and silverware ceased to click.

A pretty song, and Finn's arrangement made it even more so.

As they finished, his music cues warned her that they weren't going to stop for applause, but that they would slip right into the next number, a dance tune.

His choices were good. By the time they finished the set, the night had worn on in a way that had pushed the incident at the bar to the back of peoples' minds.

It didn't matter. For Megan, the rest of the evening was a nightmare. Gayle Sawyer had become an attachment. It turned out that she knew Morwenna and Joseph, not surprising, since it was a small establishment. Mike Smith was there as well, and during the breaks, Morwenna made arrangements for a larger table. A bizarrely dressed small woman in a green flower costume and makeup turned out to be Sara, and she, too, joined the table. More of Morewenna's employees were there, including Jamie, with whom Megan usually felt very comfortable as she had known him a long time. That night, he was dressed in a strange brown cape and cowl and carried a plastic executioner's ax, which somehow seemed far too real. When she excused herself to go to the ladies' room, she was stopped at a table where it turned out that Brad and Mary—her co-guests at Huntington House—were sitting. They'd arranged for baby-sitters for the kids, since Sally and John had told them how much fun an evening at the hotel could be. She chatted with them, promised them a free CD, and managed to leave them. When she returned to the table, she found that Darren Menteith had joined the table as well. Her chair, next to Finn, had been taken. Sara was now on his one side, while the adoring Gayle was on the other. She couldn't hear any of the conversation. Everyone was drinking—except for her. She'd been sticking with water and a twist of lemon all night. The conversation was loud, and annoying, and Finn, though he looked tense and uncomfortable, seemed to be listening to something that Sara was saying, as if she were giving him world-shattering information. Sara's green "forest goddess" costume was skintight. Her cleavage spilled over. Finn wasn't usually an ogler. Megan felt that his eyes, that night, were glued to Sara's breasts.

She wondered at her growing irritation. To everyone here, Finn had behaved admirably—almost heroically—trying to avoid violence, but proving his prowess with a single moment when he was no longer able to do so. She didn't resent the attention given him—at least she didn't think so. She loved him, she was proud of him . . . and felt that strange almost gluelike attachment to him as well. She didn't want to behave like a jealous idiot. She believed that he loved her.

Didn't she?

She glanced at her watch. They were due back on stage. Finn was always so careful about their breaks. He didn't appear to have a care in the world. Other than Sara's breasts.

The cop stopped by their table, and started up a conversation with Finn. Megan was ready to hop to her feet and say that they had to be back on stage. But Sam Tartan himself came by then, and apologized to Finn, telling him he did what he had to do, and the hotel was grateful, since they prided themselves on the fact that single female guests were never harassed there. With a machismo wink—odd in a man who looked like Ichabod Crane—he noted that there was an exception, of course. Sometimes, they wanted to be harassed.

Finn listened to Tartan, his expression controlled, but then his eyes touched Megan's, and his easy grin half filtered into his lips. He didn't need to speak to her. She knew what he was thinking. *What an asshole!*

She returned the grin with a shrug. He was the asshole who was paying them.

Finn rose on his own then, saying they needed to get back on the stage. Gayle had tried to stop him to say something when he had risen. Her hand lingered on his arm. He seemed not to notice, but extended his arm across the table to Megan.

It was all right.

The night went by quickly after that. Megan thanked God that most of Finn's new fan club had departed by the time they left the stage again.

Adam Spade helped them cover the equipment, and they were on the road back toward Huntington House by one-fifteen.

"What a bizarre night," Finn murmured as he drove.

Megan was silent for a minute. "Very."

"I just thought it was odd . . . I mean, you know, both ways, sometimes husbands and wives don't really know one another. But that guy—Marty—his wife was really appalled, and I think, in both her heart and mind, she couldn't begin to believe that her husband would have walked off, gotten tanked, and attacked women at a bar."

"I got that impression, too. But who knows? Maybe Marty has been living a secret little life, and she just hasn't known anything about it."

"I guess." He hesitated. "Megan, really—"

"He swung at you twice, Finn. I was there. You don't need to keep giving me apologies or explanations."

She felt him nod after a moment.

"And I'm seriously thinking of violence myself."

"You?"

"Your fans are getting up close and personal."

He laughed. "Go to it, then."

She grinned as well, settling against him. "Does Sam Tartan look like Ichabod Crane or what?"

He laughed. "The cartoon character—or Johnny Depp?"

"He's no Johnny Depp."

His arm nestled more tightly around her. His eyes were on the road. "Do you believe this shit again?"

"What? Do you mean Gayle Sawyer?"

"No, silly. The fog. You'd think it was San Francisco or something."

She hadn't been giving the road all that much attention, but when she looked out the front window, she could see that once again, ground fog was rising. And beneath the moon, once again, it was cast in an eerie blue glow.

"It's New England," she said, as if that explained it all. To residents and natives, it did.

"And once again, no parking," he said.

"It's not that far a walk."

It wasn't. Still, the minute they got out of the car, Megan felt uneasy.

"What's the matter?" Finn said, coming around to her side.

"It's just . . . eerie."

"Hey, it's New England."

"Touché."

She wanted to be light, to feel a sense of security. As she well knew, Finn was no pushover. She also believed that he'd die for her.

She still felt as if they were watched through the fog. And, for a moment, she remembered the way Finn's eyes had looked . . . a few times now. When she had awakened from her dream, and even tonight, while they had played and looked at one another.

She glanced up at him cautiously, alarmed by the feeling of something akin to terror that tugged at her heart while she forced her eyes to raise to his, got him to look down at her. For a moment her heart stood still. They would be gold, red-gold, orangish red-gold, like the eyes of a cat in the night. She didn't need to be afraid of the fog, because the horror that was after her was walking along at her side.

She expelled her breath as Finn looked down, giving her an encouraging grin. His eyes were green. Just as they had always been.

But then, assured that her husband was her husband, just that and nothing more, she felt again as if the blue fog was hiding a multitude of . . . eyes. Demon eyes. Eyes, perhaps, belonging to a creature with a forked tongue, a horned head, a long, evil tail with a strange extremity that could reach out and touch . . . like a hand.

She quickened her pace.

"Careful, we'll trip over something. Why are you shivering?"

"Cold," she lied.

He stopped, ready to pull off his own black cape.

"No, I'd rather just get there. Finn, come on, hurry."

He shook his head, then shrugged. Megan felt the breeze pick up. Branches with dead leaves seemed to whisper and chatter at the onslaught. She had said that she was cold. Now, it was as if waves of icy sleet were washing over her.

There was something in the fog.

And it was after them.

She heard Andy Markham's words ricochet in her mind.

Bac-Dal wants you.

Despite Finn's presence, she started to run.

"Megan! What the hell is the matter with you?"

He ran behind her. Long-legged, he easily caught up, catching her by the arm. Irrationally, she struggled against him. "Finn, we have to get in!"

"Megan, please, I'm with you!" he said sternly.

Looking past his shoulder, she could see a huge old oak. There was something in it. Tall, big . . . small. She didn't know.

But it had eyes. Eyes that glowed red and gold.

She broke free from Finn and raced for Huntington House. As fast and long-limbed as he was, he didn't catch her until she sped her way up the steps, and was struggling with the key at the door.

Finn's hand fell on her arm. She started violently, swinging around to stare at him.

"Megan—"

"Finn, there was something out there. There is something out there."

He took the key from her, fitting it into the lock. He was stiff and angry. "Great, Megan. A pack of weird, pierced, Wiccan women think I'm the next best thing to Arnold Schwartzenegger, but I can't even protect you from a fog."

He pushed the door open. She preceded him in. He locked the door behind them. Once it was closed, Megan began to feel relieved, and a little bit silly. Finn remained uptight, walking ahead of her through the foyer and dining area to their room in the solitary right wing of the house. She followed behind him.

He slipped the room key into their door, and once again, walked ahead of her. She followed him in. Finn walked straight into the bathroom. She heard the fall of the shower as he turned it on. Locking their door, she eased on into the room and sat at the foot of the bed, wondering herself what had gotten into her. It was the power of suggestion, Mike had said. She needed to turn on a ridiculous sitcom.

She turned on the television, pressing the button to get into the main channels.

One of the *Friday the 13th* movies was on. She flicked channels, coming to a Dracula movie, the Lon Chaney *Werewolf,* and then, on to the one of the offerings from the *Nightmare on Elm Street* series. She changed the channel again—no good. Mike Myers was busy chasing the Jamie Lee Curtis character in one of the *Halloween* offerings.

"Surely, there's a cartoon channel!" she murmured aloud.

She found it. No good. A cartoon duck had been bitten by an evil, demon dog.

She looked for a rerun of the local eleven o'clock news.

There could be no horror movies on the news channel!

But in fact, the news was no better. The grisly remains of a girl who had been missing from Boston for several weeks had at last been discovered—washed up on a cold North Shore beach. The family had been notified, but the coroner, as yet, was not giving out any information as to the cause of death. Detectives were dismayed at the condition of the body, because the seawater, time, and elements would have destroyed so much evidence that might have been recovered.

She turned the channel again.

Another news channel. The dead girl's name had been Theresa Kavanaugh. Once again, the newscaster announced that the coroner's office had refused to speculate on cause of death until the autopsy had been performed.

She turned back to Lon Chaney's *Werewolf*.

There were the trees . . .

Mist rising.

She turned off the television. The bathroom door opened and Finn emerged in a cloud of steam, wrapped in a towel. His flesh seemed extremely bronzed against the white terry. Muscles rippled. Hair damp, freshly washed, slicked back. He barely glanced her way, still impatient with her, or more—obviously still angry. He walked on by her, opening the drapes. Steam continued to waft from the bathroom.

Like the strange fog, it, too, seemed blue.

Finn, just wrapped in the towel, stood by the balcony doors, and opened them. He looked like Atlas standing there, naked back oddly evocative. She wanted to walk up and touch him, lean against him. She wasn't about to do so, not when it appeared that he would shake off her touch.

She walked into the shower herself.

That night, the dream was ever more vivid.

And incredibly . . . gratifying.

He was walking, walking, walking. Striding . . . no, almost strutting, with confidence. Almost floating on air. He could hear the chanting, see blurred imagines of those who were applauding him. More, worshiping him, bowing down before him as he came, leading him onward, though he knew where he was going. Instinct kept him moving. Excitement riddled his body, enhanced and increased by the chants, the cries, the applause, and the wonder. Women touched him as he

*moved, stroked him, eager to do anything, please him in any
way. Whispers caressed his ears, tongues laved over him with
hot liquid homage. They fell to the wayside, because there was
only one he wanted, one worthy of all the power and wonder
that was* him.

*He felt the bare earth beneath his feet, and even it enhanced
the raw, elemental sense of rough, carnal pleasure that was en-
veloping him. All lay ahead . . . He was there . . .*

*Filled with strength, bursting with prowess, falling upon
the sheer splendor of the perfection cast before him, his due.
Taking what he would with ragged fury, knowing that all
must fall down before him, that any decadence, any desire,
must be met. He strained, blood pulsed through him with a
bursting fury, his muscles tensed with power, the world, and
anything he wanted, was his. He soared higher, burning with
that explosive power, none would deny him, for he was a
god . . .*

No!

*He struggled inwardly. There was something very wrong . . .
He was not a god; there was something that wasn't pleasure,
that was pain. Beneath the chanting, there was a screaming, a
protest. He heard his name being cried out.*

"Finn, no Finn, no Finn . . ."

"Stop, stop, stop . . ."

*What the hell was he doing? He had a greater strength than
this, and there was a voice within him, telling him that it was
so.*

Never hurt . . .

Never hurt . . .

*The lure, the enticement, of flesh and blood were powerful,
surging, a force that swept away archaic beliefs of right and
wrong.*

"No."

"Finn." *His name. Her voice.*

*Drenched, sated, floating back to earth, with the chanting
going on and on, he was stroked again and again, adored,
and applauded . . .*

* * *

Finn woke, groggy and miserable, only strange remnants of the dream remaining, a terrible headache plaguing him from the second he realized he was awake. He couldn't open his eyes, but rather ground them more tightly shut. He groaned aloud and turned over, longing to draw Megan against him. He wanted to hold her, and tell her he was sorry, it was just that she had rather shattered his ego, being afraid of *fog* when he was with her, when he did love her so much, and would die to defend her.

She wasn't close. She was probably still angry. He moved his hand farther across the sheet. It was cold . . .

He opened his eyes. Megan wasn't there.

"Meg?"

He cast the sheets off, sliding his legs off the side of the bed and coming up. He had to sit again, his head pounded so fiercely.

He managed to rise and walk to the bathroom.

"Meg?"

She wasn't there. He walked back to the bed, holding his pounding temples.

At last, he looked around the room.

And then he realized.

Not only was Megan gone, but . . .

Her things . . . purse . . . makeup . . . clothing . . . luggage . . . all was gone.

His jaw dropped.

His wife had left him again.

Chapter 11

Her cell phone was ringing. It was Finn, and Megan knew it. She didn't answer.

She sat on Aunt Martha's porch, sipping tea Martha had made, special tea, guaranteed to soothe, she had been assured.

Martha was great.

She hadn't asked any questions, assuming that Megan would talk when she was ready. Naturally, she realized that Megan was upset. Beyond upset. Scared, dismayed, disconsolate, and still . . . *what? Was she an idiot? She loved him so much; she didn't understand, couldn't understand, it was all too bizarre, strange.*

The phone stopped ringing. The sound began again. Every strident note seemed to tear into her.

She didn't intend *not* to talk to him—just not yet.

Aunt Martha came out with her own cup of tea and sat quietly at Megan's side.

Megan glanced at her. "Whatever you do, please don't mention any of this to my parents."

"Dear, I can hardly mention anything to your parents because I wouldn't know what I was saying," Martha told her. "Besides, you know us. We're all family . . . but it's not as if we chat on a weekly basis or anything. Since your folks have been in Maine . . . it's Christmas cards, birthday cards, that kind of thing. So don't worry."

"Thanks," Megan murmured.

"I'm sure you'll work things out," Martha said.

Megan remained silent. Martha commented on the fact that almost all the leaves had fallen. "Another winter. I don't know why I live here, sometimes," Martha said. "The cold can be so fierce up here!"

"Winter can be pretty, too," Megan murmured.

"Well, we're just chatting here, when you've much more serious things on your mind," Martha said. She cleared her throat. "Megan, you're welcome to stay here as long as you want, of course, and you know that. And I have no idea of what happened that brought you here, and I'm not asking; if and when you choose to tell me, you will. But let me just say that I think your young man loves you very much. And let's face it, you have some strange relatives here. I don't approve of Morwenna's 'religion' and you know it. She and her coven can be downright, wicked weird! So if things are strained between you and Finn, you've got to admit that you might have thrown a lot at him, bringing him here."

"Aunt Martha, I didn't bring him here. The offer from Sam Tartan brought us both here. I didn't push it in the least. And if my relatives were Hindu, Buddhist, or something else not quite so well known in the States, anyone out there would have said that they had the right to worship however they pleased. I'm supposed to stay away from Morwenna and Joseph because their doctrine might be considered weird?"

"Of course not, dear! But to other people, Wiccans might be . . . There's so much that's suggestive here, that's all. Ghouls and goblins, Halloween nonsense! Then there's all that's real in history, the poor victims of the witchcraft craze, the beliefs in the devil and all that rot that went on. You are two nice sane young people with a grip on the world. You shouldn't be letting all this hogwash get to you!"

It was more or less what Mike had told her, Megan thought. But they didn't understand what was happening, and she didn't want to explain, because she wasn't sure that she was really seeing what she was seeing, that she *could* be seeing what she was seeing, or experiencing. And she didn't want to find out that she should be locked up herself, that she was half mad, so susceptible to suggestion that she was losing her mind.

And Finn, because of it.

But there *was* something happening with Finn. It seemed he was falling prey to the power of suggestion, though exactly what *suggestion* she didn't know. He had simply changed, and it was in the middle of the night, between the world of sleep and wakefulness, dreams and the conscious mind, that the changes took place. And she wasn't sure if they were her dreams, his dreams . . .

Or if it was real. If he became someone . . . something . . . else. A demon with red-glowing eyes, hands that forced rather than caressed, a touch that was cruel, rather than seductive.

Or had Andy Markham planted seeds within her mind that had made her waken to the belief that her husband was a monster? Was she the crazy one? All she knew for certain was that in what *seemed* like reality, she had wakened before the light had come, and had believed that she was living her nightmare of the first evening, that Finn was there, the threatened menace, ready to wind his fingers around her throat when he had used her up, and was ready to cast her aside. She had seen it in his eyes, when it seemed there was no green, only the burning reds and yellows of hell's own fires.

Crazy. Certainly. But her fear of him was now real.

"Megan, you love that young man. It's my suggestion that you do whatever you have to do workwise, and get yourselves home, and to a marriage counselor," Martha said. "I mean . . . this work is important to both of you, right?"

"Absolutely!" Megan said. "Oh, Aunt Martha, I have no intention of not showing up for work. It's just . . ." She didn't want to tell Martha that it was really just at night when things became so very weird. "I need a little distance during our off hours."

"Um. Well, you be careful coming and going from that hotel alone at those wee hours, Megan. Unfortunately, the world has its share of maniacs. Did you read about that poor girl they found the other day? Missing almost a month . . . then her body shows up. The killer disposed of her in water, a good way to hide a lot of evidence." She made a face. "I like to watch forensic shows when I'm knitting. HBO does some great stuff on autopsies."

Megan arched a brow trying to imagine Martha intently staring at the screen during human dissections. She lowered her head, hiding a small smile.

"I promise, I'll be careful. You're sure you don't mind me taking your car? I can rent one, you know."

"Good heavens, there's still the old truck in the barn if I need transportation. You're more than welcome to the car. But, honey, be careful with what you're doing. Morwenna's Tarot cards are a bunch of—do excuse the language—pure crap. Don't go ruining your life with a man who is just perfect for you because of a bunch of would-be magicians!"

"Thanks, Aunt Martha."

"The house phone is ringing," Martha murmured. She stared at Megan. "Now, I'll let him know that he's not welcome here at the moment, but if he wants to know that you're alive and well, I intend to tell him, and if he feels the need to speak with me, well, I want you to know that I'll listen to him."

Megan smiled. "Of course. I love him, Aunt Martha. I just don't know what's happening."

Martha rose to answer the phone.

She returned a moment later. Megan arched a brow to her.

"No, dear, it wasn't Finn."

"Oh."

Aunt Martha chuckled softly. "It was just a telemarketer, trying to sell one of those publishers series of books."

"On what?"

"What else? It's Halloween season. The history of witchcraft!"

Finn hesitated on the street for a long time, staring at the shop window.

At last, he determined to go in.

Sara was on guard duty at the doorstep. She looked at Finn warily.

"Is it busy in there?" he asked

"What do you think? But you can go on in. You're family." She said the last as if she were mimicking Morwenna.

"Thanks." He walked by her. Joseph was behind the counter. Morwenna was showing someone capes. Jamie Gray was busy adjusting the store logo T-shirts on the shelves.

Morwenna saw him from her position near the beaded partition to the back. She smiled and waved enthusiastically. He realized as she did so that Megan hadn't come to her shop.

He looked at a display shelf full of dragons, but this time, refrained from touching. A minute later, Morwenna came up to him, giving him a hug and a kiss on the cheek.

"Where's my cousin?" she asked.

"I was hoping you would know," he said honestly.

Morwenna frowned. If nothing else, she was a good

actress. "You've lost her? In Salem? It's not that big a place," she teased.

"She hasn't been here, I take it."

Morwenna shook her head. "Is something wrong?"

He didn't mean to hesitate, but he did. "No, nothing."

Morwenna studied him gravely. "Finn . . . I have a good friend here who owns a really great bookstore, and . . . he thinks that something is going on. And that you're the key to it."

"Something is going on, and I'm the key to it?" he repeated.

Morwenna sighed. "I can hear it in your voice, you're not about to believe anything that I say. Finn . . . haven't you felt . . . strange, at times? Joseph and I were commenting on the nights lately. We have fog here a lot, but . . . not like the fog we've had lately."

"I agree, weird fog, a weather phenomena," he said.

Morwenna studied him for a minute, then rushed in, "Wiccans are good, Finn. I swear. And intuitive, and . . . there's a feeling that something that isn't good is going on. Eddie started telling me about an old story he found in a diary, about a group—*not of Wiccans!*—but of Satanists who were at it here once, years and years ago, a few centuries ago, actually—"

"And they weren't burned at the stake?"

"No one was burned at the stake here, Finn. They were hanged; Giles Corey was pressed to death. Of course, others accused of witchcraft were also executed in the colonies, but the 'hysteria' always refers to that one time—"

"I know all that, Morwenna. My point is, how would Satanists rise in a place where the populace was being arrested right and left for 'spectral' evidence and any other flimsy excuse?"

"That was the perfect time, right after, don't you see? The people were horrified about what had happened within the past decade. No one at that time would have thought of openly accusing someone of witchcraft again. The community was embarrassed. Many were appalled. So if something came up . . . well, according to Eddie, the people who knew about it simply took care of it all on their own. And that's why it's not in most history books."

He was startled when someone spoke softly behind him. "She left you, didn't she?"

He spun around. Sara, who else?

"My relationship with my wife isn't really your concern, is it?"

"People are trying to help you. Though I don't know why."

"I don't think it's your help that I need. What I need is for people to quit telling Megan stories that give her terrible dreams."

"Finn, I know you don't believe . . . well, in us," Morwenna said. "You won't allow yourself to believe that there is anything in the world that you can't touch, and understand."

Angrily, he took two steps toward the display of herbs. "Keep this in my pocket—and money will come? Light some kind of incense, and my love life will improve? No, I'm sorry. Worship a tree? You know what I do believe? That there is one God, a supreme power. And—"

"If there is a god, one God, a supreme power, then what else may be true, Finn? A God, angels, and perhaps an angel that was cast from Heaven. Forces of good, and evil. Have you ever read the Old Testament, actually read it? Did an angel come down and speak to Mary? If you believe in any of these things, Finn, then you must understand that there can be forces of good as well as evil."

"Why don't we just run out on the street and start arresting people again—since there can be those forces of good and evil?" he countered.

"He can't be helped," Sara said.

Finn hesitated. The women were both staring at him so seriously. But there was Sara again, with that strange tension about her, as if she despised him, but could barely keep her hands off him. And God help him, there was that tension in him in return. He gritted his teeth. Every muscle in his body was painfully constricted. He needed to run out of the shop, to get as far away from her as he could.

He looked at Morwenna, who was staring at him so intently. *Forces of good and evil. So, do you really want to help me, or seal the lid on my coffin? Are you doing your best to make sure that Megan stays as far away from me as possible?*

"Finn, you should come with me to see Eddie. Just come with me, and look at some of the books he has."

He had to get out of the shop. He couldn't seem to tear his eyes away from Sara's cleavage. If they were alone together . . .

He would want to pounce, drag her down, and everything would be rough; he wanted to taste her mouth with its bizarrely red lipstick, rip off her clothing, ground into her against the hard floor, the walls . . .

And all at the same time, he wanted his wife back.

He had to get out. Had to. He was a fool. There was no way to trust Morwenna.

He fought every bizarre urge that seemed to have possessed him, so tense he could barely speak or move. "Morwenna, thank you. I'll call you later. Maybe we'll see this friend of yours, Eddie."

"Anytime, Finn. I don't care how busy the place is. I'll go with you. Please . . . open your mind Finn. For yourself, and for Megan."

"I'll try, Morwenna. Hey, all right . . . sometime. We'll go see this guy. I like books, any books. Can't hurt, right?"

He turned and started out. Joseph was behind the counter, without any customers at the moment. He had spread out the morning paper, and was reading intensely. He looked up as Finn started out.

"Hey, Joseph."

Joseph didn't reply. He was staring at him, as if he could look beneath Finn's skin, and see something inside him. An answer he was seeking.

"Finn . . . you went through Boston, didn't you?"

"Yeah, we flew in through Boston, why?"

Joseph shook his head. "No . . . before. When you went to see Megan's folks in Maine when she was staying with them. Last month. You drove up the coast, right?"

"Yeah," he said slowly, wondering what Joseph was getting at."

"Ever go to a bar called the Lobster's Tale?"

"The Lobster's Tale?" Finn shrugged. He was tempted to tell Joseph that it was none of his business. He might have wondered why Joseph knew his every move when he had driven up to Maine to find his wife and repair his marriage, but that would have been ridiculous. Megan's parents knew every move he had made. Her father had seemed happy that the two had settled their differences, and he imagined that Megan's mother had told her sister, her sister had told Morwenna, her daughter, and Morwenna had told Joseph.

Families were just great.

"Did you?" Joseph persisted.

Finn shrugged his shoulders, irritated with the question. What the hell did it matter to Joseph? "Not that I recall. I drove up I-95 from the Washington area . . . wound up on US1 out of the city, and hate to admit it, but took a few wrong roads from there, when the path should have been pretty evident."

"Did you sleep in Boston then?"

"Did I sleep in Boston?"

"Spend the night there when you were driving up."

"I . . . yeah, I think I did. Or some little place right outside of the city. It was near a steakhouse with a bunch of cows in front."

"Ah."

"Why?"

"You don't remember the Lobster's Tale?"

"No, I don't remember any place called the Lobster's Tale? Why?"

"Oh, just curious."

"Joseph, no one is that persistent when they're just curious."

"We're trying to help you, Finn."

"Joseph, do me a big favor. *Don't* help me," Finn said angrily.

As he passed by the counter, he caught the headlines on the paper Joseph was reading. "Slain Girl Last Seen at Lobster's Tale, Boston Bar."

His anger was suddenly explosive. He had to get the hell out of the shop. If he didn't, he was going to grab Joseph by the black collar and strangle him.

The temptation was so great he could feel his fingers itching. He fought the urge desperately.

A second later, he burst out of the door, and out of the shop.

As soon as he hit the street, the tension left him. Joseph was an irritating, self-important asshole, and that was all. And the thing with Sara . . . hell, Sara was a short, annoying little creature who was not in the least appealing.

It was cold, and he was covered in sweat. He needed to get away from the throngs of people.

He needed to find his wife.

He bit into his lower lip, plagued by doubts, uncertainty, and a new anger.

With long strides, he started walking toward the new museum.

And a showdown with Mike Smith.

* * *

Megan did laundry, a mundane task that didn't do a thing to keep her mind off her marriage.

Walking back through the parlor with a pile of clothing, she found Martha going through scrapbooks.

She looked up at Megan and grinned. "Come and look. I wonder if you've seen these in a while!"

Megan set her clothing on the end of the sofa and curled next to Martha. She assumed that Martha had dragged out a lot of old pictures from when she had been a child. They weren't those pictures at all.

They were Megan's wedding. Martha hadn't been there. Megan and Finn, broke college students who hadn't wanted her parents laying out a fortune, had decided on a quick ceremony with only their closest friends and immediate families.

But Martha had all the pictures. Megan assumed her mother had sent Martha a set, naturally.

They had chosen one of the oldest churches in the city. Finn had been incredibly elegant in tails with his own little quirks of design. She had opted for a medieval style wedding gown in a pearl color. A close friend with a small design shop on Bourbon Street had cut and sewn the gown from something she had seen in a magazine.

There were pictures of the two of them at the altar, getting into the carriage, dancing at the reception, cutting the cake. Megan looked through them slowly, feeling a dull ache in her heart. The best picture was one of the two of them at the carriage, Finn reaching up to help her down. So much that she had always loved about him seemed apparent in the picture. Not just the way he looked in the tails, dark hair enhanced by the ebony of the tails and the white, medieval shirt, impossibly tall, lithe, and indomitable, but the way that he looked at her hair. She wanted to touch the picture, as she so often touched his face. She loved every angle of it.

Loved the deep set of his eyes, the arch of his brows, the line of his jaw, even with his ability to set it so stubbornly when he was determined or angry. She had never been attracted to anyone from the onset as she had been to Finn. The first time she had seen him, she had known.

"You two cannot throw it all away," Martha said gently.

"I'm not throwing anything away."

"But then—"

"I'm afraid of him," Megan said honestly.

Martha hesitated a long time. "So . . . he was violent with you. And that's why you left him the first time and went to your folks in Maine."

"No. He's just strange since . . . since we've been here."

Martha sighed. "Megan, I know I keep repeating this, but honestly! You are two intelligent young people. And you're simply listening to too much hogwash!"

"Probably." Megan smoothed the page absently. "He suggested we should just leave. Maybe I should have agreed with him. It's just that . . . well, I believe he loves me. But he loves his music, too. And if we just took off on this job . . . You know how it goes. I mean—look how a silly little family rumor spreads! You and Morwenna know as much about my life as I do, so it seems, without ever having talked to me."

"Families do talk, dear. And, of course, we care about you. With the greatest pride and concern! And . . . well, things do go around. When I received these pictures from your mom, for example, I showed them to everyone I came across. You two are just so very beautiful together."

Megan laughed ruefully. "Did you happen to tell Mr. Fallon over at Huntington House that Finn and I had a fight with a loaf of bread?"

"Good heavens, no! I don't air laundry." Martha looked disgruntled. "If anything of that ilk got anywhere . . . well, never mind."

"You were about to say that Morwenna had been talking."

Martha shrugged. "I wasn't really about to say anything," she said, clearly lying. "But . . . you're right. You must stay, and finish your commitment at the hotel. Tonight, when you see your husband, make sure he understands that you love him, that you haven't really left him, that you believe you've done the best thing possible for the moment, keeping some distance from him. But it means nothing. You'll finish your stint at the hotel, go home, and see a counselor. Because you're going to find out just what is causing your problems, solve them, and stay together for the rest of your lives!"

Megan smiled.

"Sounds like a plan," she said softly. "One problem."

"What?"

"What if he's just so angry that he doesn't care about the music—or me."

Martha shook her head firmly. "Finn Douglas came after you once. I don't believe that he'll leave you. He's going to be just as determined to keep you now—even if he has to bow down to your wishes for the time being."

"I hope you're right," Megan said softly. She rose, picking up her clean clothes and heading for the guest room.

She put her belongings away, then walked back out to the front porch. Already, night was falling.

She stared at the dusk coming on, and then wondered if she hadn't done the most stupid thing in the world, leaving Finn now.

There were too many other women in Salem who seemed to feel the same instant, deep, carnal attraction to her husband.

He wouldn't!

Or would he? She didn't seem to know him at all anymore.

As luck would have it, Mike Smith wasn't in when he went to the museum. Gayle Sawyer was working, though, and he thanked God that she was working because she used what few minutes she could to go on and on about how he had saved her the night before. He was glad of the counter between them as well, because he had never felt so convinced that she'd simply jump him were she on the other side.

Restless, irritated, he wandered into a few shops. Many had the same T-shirts. Some had great silver jewelry. Many had extensive book sections. He idly picked up a few titles. Most were on the Wiccan way of life. Some dealt with herbs, meditation, the power of different metals, and so on.

He came back out on the street. He hadn't attempted to dial Megan's cell phone again; she wasn't picking up. She didn't intend to do so. He wondered if she intended to show up at the hotel to play, but since she had been the one so determined not to wreck their careers, he had a feeling that she would do so. There was no sense in dialing her repeatedly for nothing.

He was studying some interestingly shaped incense burners when he realized that someone was standing in back of him. Someone who made his spine run cold. He swirled around.

Sara.

He frowned, keeping a safe distance. "Did you . . . hunt me down here?" he asked.

"Yes."

He arched a brow, and Sara shrugged. "Morwenna would have come after you, but she's busy. There's not just the store, but to us, Halloween is a high holy day. And you may scoff, but it's important to us."

"I'm not scoffing at anything, Sara," he said wearily.

"Is that true? I hope so. Because Morwenna is very afraid for you."

"She's afraid for me? I thought the fear was for Megan—and that I'm the one who is to hurt her."

"Morwenna doesn't believe you would ever hurt Megan intentionally."

"That's—good of her."

"You're being used."

"By . . . ?" he demanded skeptically.

"A demon."

He shook his head and turned his back on her. Sara came around the shop, facing him over the display. "Finn, you scare the hell out of me. Because there's something . . . some kind of a strange power in you already. I don't personally know how any of this stuff works—"

"I thought you were a steadfast Wiccan, Sara," he murmured.

"Wiccan, Finn. Wiccan. Not Satanist."

"Satanists, Wiccans, Christians, Jews, Hindus—they're all men, Sara. Just men. And women, of course, forgive me. That wasn't a slight, just a manner of speech."

She waved a hand in the air. "There are powers in the world, Finn. You've got to realize that, and see it."

"So . . . you believe that demons run around walking the earth?"

"If you believe in God—"

"Yes, yes, I know, then why not Satan—and of course, then, there would be demons."

She stared at him hard. "Can you explain everything that happens, Finn?"

"I'm not a scientist."

"Your wife has left you, and you don't even know why—except that it had to be something you did last night."

"My marital problems are my own business."

"Do you want help, or not?"

"No," he said, and turned away, but he stopped, his back stiff. He couldn't explain anything. And he didn't understand his own dreams.

He turned back. "Look, Sara, I don't mean to be so rude and hostile."

"I'm sure you don't. But, listen to me, Finn, please. That was no act I put on in Morwenna's store when I read your palm. There is a terrible, frightening aura of evil hanging over you."

"I'm not an evil person, Sara."

"Maybe you're not; but maybe, just maybe, there are powers around you. And they are using you."

"I can't accept that. I won't accept that I could be used by some . . . some . . . demon!"

Sara cast her hands on her hips. "Not even one with hundreds—no, thousands!—of years to get to know human psychology, the human mind, and the power of suggestion."

"I don't care what anyone—Satan, or God himself—told me to do, I'd never hurt Megan."

"I know that you mean that," Sara said earnestly.

"Okay, Sara, what is this help you're going to give me?"

"Knowledge."

"Knowledge? That's it? No spell, no incantations?"

"You should be blessed, and learn a few incantations—it certainly wouldn't hurt. But for now . . . Morwenna and Joseph just want you to meet Eddie."

Finn hesitated, head cocked, hands on his hips as he studied her a long time. Morwenna and Joseph. Were they really trying to help him—or seal the lid on his coffin?

"What is this knowledge?"

"Come on down the street. There are just books in here, same old, same old. Eddie has bound books that are centuries old, true collector's pieces."

"Then he'd want a mint for them."

"When he sells one of his historical volumes, he does sell it for a small fortune. He has a number, though, that he won't part with."

"All right. Lead the way," Finn said.

* * *

Morwenna stood in the basement, a place where only those closest to her, those who shared her beliefs, were ever allowed to come.

The altar was to the rear. Herbs, far superior to any she sold in the shop, lined the walls in various bottles. Her own wand, an exquisite piece with a crystal handle, lay near the altar. Her best ceremonial robe was around her shoulders.

She approached the altar, and said the words, earnestly, from the heart. She made the proper motions, then moved to the centuries-old fireplace. She had burned ash, the proper wood, throughout the afternoon. The potion within the cauldron bubbled and brewed. She added the last of the ingredients, her lips moving as she did so.

She had become so involved that, at first, she didn't realize that Joseph stood in the rear. He had come down the steps, slipped through the false wall, and waited.

When he spoke, his words were terse.

"You're certain you know what you're doing?" he demanded.

"I'm certain that I can read, and follow directions," she snapped. "And you mustn't come in like that again. You might have interrupted me in the midst of a chant."

He turned away, ready to depart, but then he paused. He spoke without turning back to her. "You mustn't make any mistakes. Any mistakes at all. If we're right . . ."

"We are right. And we won't make any mistakes."

"It is happening. It has all truly begun."

He started to slide the door.

"Joseph," she said, calling him back.

He paused again.

"Blessed be," she said.

He inclined his head. "Blessed be."

* * *

Eddie's book shop was just that—a book shop. He didn't sell incense burners, herbs, T-shirts, capes, or anything else. The space was narrow, and there was barely room for two people to pass one another in the aisles between the bookshelves.

There was a new section, a used section, and a "collectibles" section. Sara led Finn by them all, calling out to the young man working the cash register that she was on her way to see Eddie.

The tall, lanky, college-age kid nodded his shaved head, waving her on by.

Beaded curtains seemed to be big in Salem that year. They passed through one on their way to the back of the shop.

There was a desk there, with the typical computer. Nothing in the back was surprising except for Eddie himself.

Finn started. He was certain he had met the man before. Except that his name hadn't been Eddie, and he hadn't said that he ran a bookshop.

The man behind the desk looked exactly like the cop he had met in the bar the night before—albeit he had been in costume. The man who had introduced himself as Theo Martin. *Officer* Theo Martin.

"Eddie, this is Finn Douglas," Sara said. "Morwenna called you about him."

"Hi, Finn." The man rose, extending a hand.

Finn stared at him, automatically accepting the handshake. "Eddie?" he said.

"Yeah." The man frowned for a minute, then grinned quickly. "I take it you've met my brother."

"The cop?" Finn said. "You're twins?"

"Identical," Eddie said.

"I believe it."

Eddie grinned. "I hear you want to see some of my books."

"Well, I've been told I should see a few of your books."

Eddie nodded. "The old ones are under glass. Hang on a minute. Hey, have a seat. There are chairs under the coats there."

Sara didn't mind dumping the coats on a stack of book boxes on the other side of the desk. She indicated to Finn that he should take a chair. Awkwardly, he did so. He'd followed Sara here; he still had a strange urge to keep his distance from her.

Eddie returned a minute later, having gone downstairs in the back, presumably to a basement area. Finn didn't know a lot about books, but he knew that the volume Eddie was bringing was *not* an ancient text.

He glanced at Sara. "A firsthand account of an ancient Babylonian demon?" he mocked.

She shot him a warning glare.

"Actually, I have some very ancient pieces," Eddie said, taking a seat now on the edge of the desk, facing Finn and Sara. "But they wouldn't do you any good— unless you can read ancient and archaic languages. Hell, even English is hard in some of the old stuff."

"You speak ancient and archaic languages?" Finn asked him.

Eddie shrugged. "I can read Arabic, Hebrew, have a sound understanding of hieroglyphics, and majored in Latin."

"Wow," Finn said, acknowledging his admiration.

"But this . . ." he indicated the book he held, "was written by a man named Cabal Thorne in the early seventeen hundreds. Thorne was convinced that he had properly translated an ancient text. He belonged to a number of secret organizations—very secret at the time, of course. And he had been careful to get the hell out of Europe—witch crazes went on for several more years there than they did here, in the States—or colonies, as they were, at the time. Anyway, Thorne was born in

England, had a very rich father, and an absurd hatred for traditional religion of any kind. He traveled extensively in Africa, India, and the Middle East. Somewhere along the way, he became convinced that, if circumstances were just right, and he had the correct number of followers, and performed the rites exactly as they were prescribed, he could bring a demon to life. Bac-Dal was the creature's name, and was an intimate of the Devil himself. Bac-Dal, of course, as Satan's minion, was a true menace to all who were 'good,' obeying the basic tenets of behavior found in almost any known religion— you know, like refraining from murder, adultery, stealing, mauling little children, rape, ravishment, looting, what have you. Power went to those who most deserved it through their ability to seize it, survival of the fittest, and any lechery and decadence as well. Do you follow me?"

"I'm following your story. I don't believe in demons."

Eddie shrugged. "Bac-Dal needs servants on earth, naturally, to bring him to life. Those who intend to bring him back begin by forming a coven—"

"Not a *Wiccan* coven," Sara said firmly. "A coven of devil worshipers."

"Right," Eddie acknowledged.

His hair was neatly trimmed, a little long. He was wearing jeans and a blue denim tailored shirt. Finn had no idea if he was a Wiccan, Christian, Buddhist, or maybe even an atheist.

"Once Bac-Dal was properly titled and summoned by the followers, a certain power was to come to the one who orchestrated his return. That power would help him or her gain strength over others in the pursuit of preparing the circumstances just as they must be for the return of Bac-Dal, or his ability to take on human form."

"A certain power?" Finn queried.

"What the power is, exactly, I don't know. ESP,

telekinesis—the ability to make dogs bark, I'm not sure; it doesn't say exactly. However, Thorne does talk about the fact that he murdered a young woman. He claims that he walked into her home, with her family present, abducted her, and they didn't even know."

"Ah," Finn murmured. "Well . . . he wrote the book. He could claim what he wanted, right?"

"True enough," Eddie said.

"Show him the passage that Morwenna found," Sara said impatiently.

Eddie opened the book, offering it to Finn.

Finn, frowning, accepted the volume. It was large, and the cover was leather. The pages were fragile.

"I shouldn't be handling this," he murmured.

"Just read," Sara said.

But he frowned again. The pages were handwritten. The language was indeed archaic.

"I can't understand this. It seems to be about . . . items needed for a strange stew or something. In fact . . . it almost reads like a kid's Halloween book. 'Eye of newt' and all that."

"There's no eye of newt in there," Sara said impatiently. She pointed down the lines, and read aloud. "'Thou shalt take the greatest care; the blood of the anointed must be mixed with that of the sacrifice; and the hair that is taken must not be cut, but torn from the head. Of all that is needed, these three are of the greatest and utmost importance—the blood of the sacrifice, the blood of the anointed, the hair of the anointed. And as these come together, as there has been life, there will be death, and where there has been the sleep of the dormant like dead, there will be life. And to all who would honor He who is the God of Darkness, remember that All Hallow's Eve, that which falls upon a full moon, is a night when the elements of the spirits and those who roam the nether world are strongest, and therefore, it can be as well, the Time of The Coming.' "

Finn looked at Sara, and then at Eddie. "I'm sorry. I don't see where any of this means anything. This man, Cabal Thorne, was a devil worshiper who came to Massachusetts at a time when he was . . . what? Left alone, because people were still ricocheting from all the horror that the craze had created. But . . . lots of people have written things. That doesn't make them real."

"Hey, Morwenna found this text, and she wanted you to see it," Eddie said with a shrug.

"Well, thank you," Finn said, still lost. He rose, "I appreciate the time—and your faith in me even holding something so old, and surely rare."

"Finn!" Sara said, rising.

"I've got to go," he told her. "Thanks. Thanks for the concern." He was feeling that strange sense of friction within himself again, looking at Sara. An urge to reach for her . . . and God knew just what exactly he wanted to do to her. He needed distance right now. Real distance. Away from Sara, and this bookstore, and even normal-looking, guy-next-door Eddie.

"I have to do some things before tonight," he rushed out. "Sound check," he lied. He started out. "But thanks . . . thanks, both of you."

He made it back to the street. Kids in costume were in abundance. He wanted to shout at them all. One little kid crashed into him, and he fought the urge to pick him up, and throw him far from himself.

He made it back to Huntington House, giving a quick wave and ignoring the fact that Sally and John were in the parlor, sipping tea, and wanting him to join them.

He made it to his and Megan's room. His room now; Megan was gone. And everyone around them was crazy.

He threw himself on the bed, grating his teeth. Damn, he could use a drink. That would be just great. He could play drunk—and confront Megan in the same shape.

He reached for the pillow at his side, needing something to punch.

He touched something else.

It was the book he had inadvertently stolen from Morwenna's shop. The one written by the woman in New Orleans who had gotten both local and national coverage.

He halfway sat up, grabbing it to draw it closer. He pushed it off the bed instead. Swearing, he rolled over and stuck his head over the edge of the bed to see just where it had fallen.

Right in front of him. It had fallen open. On the left side was an old etching of a horrible, fire-breathing, horned creature and the chapter title "The Known Demons."

On the right, the chapter began. He read the heading and jerked up, throwing the book from him.

He laid back on the pillow, breathing hard.

He'd imagined it. Power of suggestion.

He forced himself to rise and go for the book. It still lay open, on the same page. He looked at the heading again.

Bac-Dal.

Chapter 12

In New Orleans, a Thursday night poker game was growing tense, despite the fact that it was hardly a high stakes game and was a weekly game as it had been for over a year, since the DeVeaus had moved to New Orleans from Charleston to be nearer their close friends, the Canadys. There were sometimes others involved in the game, good friends all, but tonight, it was just the DeVeaus and the Canadys.

"I'll see your quarter, and bump you fifty cents," Lucian DeVeau said, tossing the money into the pot. He leaned forward, dark-haired, menacing, dark eyes holding a touch of a fiery sizzle over the kill he was certain he was about to make.

Sean Canady, blue eyes equally as hard and bright, leaned inward to the table as well, ready to meet the challenge. He ran his fingers through dark hair with just a touch of silver, and offered his nemesis a grim smile. "I'll just see your fifty cents, and bump you another fifty cents," he announced.

"Let's see 'em!" Lucian said.

"Excuse me, want to wait a minute? Jade and I are in this game as well."

Both men paused, looking to the end of the table. Maggie Canady, even in jeans and a T-shirt, had the ability to appear elegant with her sweep of dark auburn hair and riveting hazel eyes. She spoke imperatively, reproachful and chastising as she demanded attention.

Jade DeVeau, at the other end of the table, burst into laughter and reminded her husband and Sean, "She's right you know. You two seem to have this game down to some kind of a macho thing."

"Don't be ridiculous," Sean argued. "We would never get macho over a friendly poker game, right?"

"Or take it too seriously," Maggie mused lightly.

"Never," Lucian said dryly. "So. Sorry, we forget to let you follow. What is it, Maggie, are you in?" Lucian asked.

"No, I fold."

"There, you see," Sean said, shaking his head. "Maggie folds."

"She folds, but I don't," Jade told him.

"Throw your money in," Lucian told her. Jade did so. "What've you got?" Lucian demanded of Sean.

"Full house," Sean said, laying them out.

Lucian grinned with relish. "Four fours." He started to rake in the pot.

"Excuse me!" Jade said.

The men paused and looked at her. "Four tens."

"Two four-of-a-kinds!" Sean said with disgust. "Who dealt that mess?"

"You did, my love," Maggie said complacently.

"Oh."

Jade started to rake in her haul of quarters. As she did so, two-month-old Gwyneth, the newest edition to the Canady household, began to cry, the sound coming to them from the little speaker box on the kitchen counter. And as Maggie rose, Jade's cell phone went off.

Lucian leaned back in his chair, his eyes on his wife's. "This is going to be him," he said.

Jade looked at him a little skeptically. "One time, you may be wrong," she said softly.

"Yes, one time I may be," he said flatly, "but this isn't going to be it."

Jade rose, going to her purse to rummage through it for her cell phone. "I'll be right back," Maggie murmured.

"Will you check on Aidan while you're up there?" Jade asked, referring to her adopted son, nearly two years old now, and going through the hell-on-two-feet stage when awake, but an angel baby at night. He always slept a solid twelve hours, but nevertheless, Jade looked in on him constantly. As she spoke, she gave half her attention to her search, and half to Maggie.

"Naturally—and if you intend to leave him with me for a few days, you're going to have to trust in the fact that I will look in on him!" Maggie reminded her.

"I can go check on them both," Sean said, obviously still disgusted over the loss of what he had considered an incredible hand, and still, equally curious as to the phone conversation.

Maggie shook her head.

"Hello?" Jade said, staring at Lucian. He arched a dark brow.

"Yes, it's Jade DeVeau," she said. She glanced across the table at Lucian. "Of course, I remember you." She listened for another few minutes, then said softly, "If you don't mind, I think you need to speak with my husband."

She turned the phone over to Lucian, who switched to speaker phone so that they could all hear what the man on the other end was saying. He had a deep, resonant voice, with just a hint of his Southern upbringing. Easy to remember, he was tall, on a par with Lucian's six feet, three inches, deceptively long and lean in appearance, as his height somewhat hid the breadth of his shoulders. She'd been impressed with his talent, drive, and professionalism; Lucian had been disturbed by something about the man, tense since they had met, certain that something was lurking behind the fellow's strong chiseled features and direct gaze. While Jade had felt that his love and admiration for his wife had been evident and charming, Lucian had again felt something else. Something that was brewing . . . smoldering, there, just beneath the surface. To Jade, they had been almost picture perfect. Megan Douglas was blond, feminine, beautiful, and had a voice that bordered on the heavenly. They were Barbie and Ken in a nutshell, almost too perfect to be believed.

"Actually, I'm not sure exactly why I'm calling you. I've just been hearing some of the most absurd stories, and I happened upon your wife's book, and since we had just met recently . . . this is ridiculous. I mean, it's not as if I can call 'Ghost Busters,' right? And I haven't been seeing ghosts or anything like that. But the book mentioned that you like to know about the unusual. There are some . . . unusual things happening here."

"Really? Well, you're in Salem, Mass, and it is approaching Halloween," Lucian said. He stared across the room at Jade, then Sean. "But what a coincidence. My wife and I were considering a trip to Salem for the weekend. She'd like to do an after-the-event piece. And naturally, we'd like to meet with you. Find out whatever we can on just exactly whatever it is that's bothering you."

"I wish I knew exactly." They could all hear the caller hesitate. Then he cleared his throat and spoke clearly and directly. "I'm a musician. I don't know what . . . well, what you charge for assistance or whatever in . . . well, whatever. I suppose that what I really need is information. I don't believe in the occult . . . things that go bump in the night. But I do believe that bad things can happen, brought on by people with motives of their own. Everyone up here swears that Wiccans can't wish harm upon others, but . . . hey, like I said—bad things happen. I don't understand what's going on. Maybe we're being drugged somehow. You can't imagine the dreams, and what's worse, I don't even know just whose dreams they are at times. God, I'm not making a lot of sense. And as I was saying . . . I'm afraid that we're not wealthy."

"I told you, we were thinking about coming up anyway. We never charge for . . ." Lucian paused himself, staring at the other two. "We never charge for investigating the strange, weird, downright frightening, or bizarre. Jade is a writer. You know the old saying—it's all grist for the mill. But maybe you'd like to explain just a bit more about what is going on?"

"I don't know, really. Maybe nothing. Maybe it's all imagined. Mostly, at the moment, no matter how bizarre this sounds . . . it's dreams. Both my wife and I . . . her cousin is a Wiccan, and we started out here listening to some wild tales about murder and mayhem in colonial New England. There's the standard concept, of course, that dreams and fear are all brought on by the power of suggestion. And since it's Halloween season here, any manner of creature in the street is acceptable, so the power of suggestion is surely strong. But still . . . there's a weird fog out around here all the time. A blue fog. And there are more strange things . . . hard to explain over the phone. And it's impossible, you see, to really trust anyone here, not that I believe in spells and things like that, but . . . and of course, Wiccans aren't supposed to be evil. Actually, I can't believe I'm calling people who are practically strangers . . . but it was just so odd, too, having met you, seeing the article in the national paper . . . and then the book."

"Was there something particular in the book?" Lucian asked, looking at the others once again while he waited for the answer.

"Again, I'm sure all this has to do with the power of suggestion, of course. I mean, none of this can be real.

But even my wife's family . . . supposed friends . . . are suggesting that I . . . well, they're reminding me that I was in Boston, and, I'll bet, making sure that she knows I was in Boston . . . never mind. There was a murder in Boston. Almost a month ago . . . on the last full moon. I realize I'm not making any sense. It's difficult to suddenly confide in and explain things to people who are . . . well, really strangers. But then . . . if I had to trust in having friends here . . . I think I'd be in a fair amount of trouble. If you're really coming here, I would appreciate the chance to talk with you again."

"Oh, we're really coming," Lucian murmured. "We'll see you by tomorrow afternoon."

"Tomorrow afternoon? You're coming so soon?"

"It's the day before Halloween," Lucian reminded the caller.

"Right, of course. You know, I was really ready just to walk away. Screw our careers. But Megan was afraid I'd wind up resenting the fact that we had to leave a great job and experience because she was having nightmares. Now I'm afraid she's convinced that I'm a monster myself."

Maggie was back in the room, holding the baby. She spoke very softly, looking at Lucian. "She's left him," she said.

Lucian nodded. "Finn, whatever the problem, don't let your wife walk anywhere alone in the dark."

"What?"

"Just keep an eye on her, no matter what the circumstances."

There was a long, drawn out pause from the other end. "Did I mention that there were . . . circumstances."

"Is your wife with you right now?"

"No."

"Watch out for her," Lucian said.

"At night. In the darkness . . . he needs to beware of the fog," Maggie whispered.

Lucian nodded. "The dark hours are when . . . well, you know, when most bad things happen. Don't let her be alone in the dark—or the fog. Take care tonight."

A sniff sounded over the phone. "I told you that I was ready to throw it all in. Get the hell out of here. Megan thought I'd resent her for what it would do to our careers. And now . . . now, I'm not even sure that I could get her out of here."

Maggie stared at Sean. "Tell him that it wouldn't have mattered. He'd have wound up back there, one way or the other."

Lucian repeated Maggie's words. "If something really odd is going on, it probably wouldn't make any difference, whether you were there, or if you'd tried to leave. Circumstances might have conspired to get you back. But don't worry. We'll be there by morning. We're going to check into the old place right off the common. If you don't find us by early afternoon, we'll find you. Jade will have this cell. And, of course, yours is now with our caller ID."

"Right."

"We'll see you."

They rang off. Maggie took her seat again at the end of the table, cradling her now sleeping child. "This guy gets on the phone, and I'm immediately getting some really weird vibes." She paused, glancing quickly at Jade. "By the way, Aidan is just fine, sleeping soundly." She turned her attention back to Lucian. "I don't know whether to be afraid of him—or for him. I admit to being totally confused. I knew when you showed up with the luggage that it wasn't going to be an ordinary night playing cards—but neither did you suggest that you were aware something was going to happen—or is happening. You knew this guy was going to call; as soon as he did, I felt something very strange, and I haven't even got the intuition I once had. Still . . . it's so strange. I don't understand what's going on at all," she said. She hesitated. "There's a conflict there . . . in the man himself, I believe."

"Yes, there's something there. And yes, a tremendous conflict. But in what way . . . I don't know. It was the same. I knew it the moment I first saw him."

Lucian rose, and began idly pacing around the table. Maggie stared across the room at Jade, and Jade shrugged, shaking her head in a way that meant that she didn't really understand the situation at all either. Jade felt a prickling at her nape; Lucian and Maggie had known one another a very long time. Jade knew that Maggie loved her husband, just as she believed with her whole heart that Lucian loved her. But there were times when Maggie and Lucian shared those strange instincts and Jade couldn't help but feel a little stab of jealousy. She would never have exactly the same little spark of knowledge that the two shared.

And yet, she loved Maggie as well. She was her best friend.

They were frequently visitors here, as were a number of their other close friends and associates, drawn together despite a few tremendous differences in their lives. It was a wonderful place for friends to get together—an old plantation on the way out from the city. The place had been in Maggie's family for years, just as a neighboring place had belonged to Sean's. It was delightfully big, and far from the bustle and populace of New Orleans. Not that anything odd was really taken note of in New Orleans, but the plantation still offered them all distance and a certain privacy that might not be guaranteed elsewhere.

"What's bothering me is that I can't quite touch it!" Lucian said, coming to a dead standstill and staring at the three of them as if they should understand. "I know . . . I know that something really horrible is about to occur . . . and I'm absolutely convinced that Finn Douglas is a major part of it, and I'm actually surprised that it took him so long to call. He's dealing with a lot of pride, and, of course, he's worried about his sense of sanity, maybe."

"Now I'm really lost," Maggie said, staring at Jade again, then at Lucian. "You're wired like a cat, know something is up, but have no idea what—yet, like me, you knew the minute you came into contact with this man there was something strange about him. You haven't really explained any of this, and it isn't like you. Let's begin with this—who is this Finn Douglas? The name sounds familiar."

"He's a local musician. He and his wife have done a number of the clubs around here. They're very good," Lucian said.

"I was interviewing them not long ago, and Lucian came along with me; we went to the club where they were playing," Jade explained.

"As I said, the minute I met the guy, I knew something was wrong," Lucian said. "But not *what*."

Maggie was quiet a long moment, staring at him. "Is he one of us . . . *you*, I mean?" Maggie asked, staring at Sean.

"No."

"You're certain?"

Lucian looked at her with irritation and reproach. "Of course, I'm certain."

"Sorry!" Maggie said quickly. She glanced at her husband with a wry smile.

Sean told them, "His adult record is as clean as a whistle. He had some trouble in high school, but nothing major. The guy is gifted, went through the university with a full scholarship in music. He and Megan Merrill were married while still studying. Megan writes music as well, but Finn is responsible for arrangements and their technical work. They were split up not long ago, and just got back together last month."

"How do you know all this?" Maggie asked her husband.

Sean shrugged. "Lucian asked me to check him out."

"And you didn't tell me?"

"There wasn't any reason at the time."

"Do you have anything on that murder in Boston?" Lucian asked Sean.

Being a cop offered Sean a great deal of information that might not be so available were he not. "The police have nothing as yet. They've interviewed family and friends. They know her movement up to the time when she left the bar she was at that evening, but after she left the bar . . . she simply vanished. Until she was discovered in the water. The amount of time she was submerged has certainly taken its toll; what trace evidence the crime scene detectives might have found has literally been washed away. I haven't been able to access the exact cause of death yet because the autopsy report hasn't been released to law enforcement yet."

"And you know all of this, too?" Maggie said, still staring at Sean.

"Hey!" Sean said softly. "I hadn't even put the two together until now. As far as I knew, Douglas was in New Orleans. The murder took place in Boston."

"Lucian—" Maggie began.

Lucian lifted a hand in a gesture of self-defense. "Maggie, I was going on pure intuition."

"Right, but you knew this guy was going to call, and amazingly, you already have airline tickets—and you've got me watching Aidan!"

"Maggie, I swear to you, I was groping in the dark on this one."

"This is frighteningly like the poker game—you're trying to keep me on the outskirts—"

"Maggie, you have children."

"You have a son now, as well!"

"And you have a two-month-old baby," Lucian said quietly.

Maggie stared hard at Jade. "You've known that something is going on."

"All I know is that Lucian has been uneasy since we met Finn Douglas, and that we're going to Salem to talk to him—and that Lucian did somehow know that he'd call by tonight."

"Maggie, if there were something I could really tell you, I would. And if there were something you could do . . . I'm afraid I'd feel compelled to let you do it. But I don't understand what is happening yet. Honestly." Lucian sat again, drumming his fingers on the table. He glanced at Jade. "How much time do we have?"

"We need to be at the airport in about two hours," Jade said.

"I really should come with you," Maggie said stubbornly

"Maggie," Sean said impatiently.

"No," Lucian said.

"You may need me."

Lucian looked at Sean. "She isn't listening to me. Tell her that you two have a family. That she has a baby daughter, only two months old."

Sean and Maggie exchanged a long gaze. Sean stood, folding his arms over his chest and looking at his wife with both reproach and amusement. "*I* should go. Hm. I am the one who is a cop, you know."

"Of course, Sean, but once . . . well, once I was different!" Maggie murmured.

Sean shook his head and sighed with a feigned display of great largesse and patience. He smiled slowly, turning to Lucian. "We'll see, Lucian. We'll see." He turned back to his wife. "If we decide we just can't live without a trip to New England, we'll come together. Hey, it might prove to be a good idea—like I said, *I am the cop.* Never hurts to have a cop around, even if he's a Southern boy in the far North."

"Sean is right—it's always good to have a cop around," Lucian said.

"But I do still have a certain sixth sense," Maggie protested. "I can tell what you're trying to do right now. You all want to go, and you want to leave Maggie safe at home. It can't work that way and you know it."

"We'll see," Sean and Lucian said simultaneously.

Maggie exploded with an impatient sigh.

"We should get to the airport," Jade said uncomfortably. She stood up. "By the way, Ragnor and Jordan are arriving in New York tonight, and I've put through an E-mail to Tara and Brent."

"And what did you tell them?" Maggie demanded.

"To stand by," Jade said.

"Ten," Lucian murmured.

"What?" Maggie said.

Lucian looked around at them. "There are ten of us—if need be." He paused, smiling. "Ten of us, including you, Maggie! Yet, I have a feeling we may need a few more."

"A few—as in twelve?" Jade said, puzzled.

"A coven of twelve," Sean murmured, looking at Lucian.

"No . . . thirteen," Lucian said.

"A coven? Because it's *Salem?* Oh, come on, please!" Maggie protested. "I've known numerous Wiccans in my day! They really don't believe in evil—"

"And in your day, you've known a lot more than *Wiccans!*" Lucian said flatly, standing as well.

"But Lucian," Jade murmured. "Surely . . . we can just put a stop to this?"

He shook his head. "If it were a simple matter of silly men and women playing at parlor games, *I* could easily put a stop to it. But . . . I think that certain forces have already been unleashed. If I'm right . . . we're dealing with a tremendous power. For now . . . well, let's catch that plane, huh?"

* * *

Megan was sleeping. A peaceful, dreamless sleep.

Martha watched her from the doorway, smiling. She was such a beautiful girl. Such a kind spirit, a gentle soul.

Ah . . . well, life changed things like that.

But still . . .

Megan breathed in easily, exhaled softly. Hair draped over her face, lovely long fingers splayed out over the pillow.

Martha felt fiercely protective of the stunning young beauty on the bed.

"I will never let one speck of injury come to that perfect young body, my dear!" she whispered softly from the doorway. She closed the door. Megan would sleep peacefully for a few hours, thanks to Martha's simple herbal tea. She would have the rest that she needed. In Martha's home, all of her sweet youthfulness and beauty would be guarded—Martha felt like an old bulldog herself, but that was that. She smiled, glad that the girl had come to her.

She headed for her kitchen, then snorted out loud. "Wiccans!"

That Morwenna and her silly husband, Joseph, with his ridiculous, dyed black hair!

And Megan's husband. That man might well be proving more of a menace than Martha had imagined, causing all kinds of trouble.

Not he, not anyone, was getting to young Ms. Megan. No one, Martha determined. Thus determined, she went on with her chores.

Not long after he'd hung up the phone, Finn began to question his own sanity.

By chance, surely, the book had fallen open to *Bac-Dal.*

And so, he had gone off the deep end.

Great. He'd made a writer and her husband think he was crazy. Grist for the mill. He hoped he wouldn't give her too much to write about.

He'd already showered, but he decided to shower again, hoping the hot water would ease the tension in his muscles and help clear his mind.

As it sluiced over him, he felt a sense of calm. Megan had gone to Martha's, and she would be all right there. Whether they thought he was crazy or not, he had a feeling that the couple from New Orleans might have the ability to clear away some of the nonsense—make all that was bizarre become rational.

He determined that he was going to be completely calm himself. He would greet her that evening in an entirely businesslike fashion. He wouldn't even ask her for an explanation.

But as he lathered in a fury, he had to fight to maintain a sense of sanity and determination. He'd been told to watch out for her. In the dark. Beware the fog.

Well, that was just great, and hard to do. You never knew when the stinking fog was coming, and she wasn't staying with him, she'd left him, so it was going to be rather hard to watch out for her.

Drying in an equal fury, he thought again that they should just get the hell out. Maybe he could talk to her that night. *Megan, don't you just hate it in those stupid horror films when teenagers stay in the woods, fooling around, when the killer comes into the woods, and hacks up teenagers who are in the woods, fooling around? I think we're in the woods. It's time to get the hell out, and screw our careers. Let's just opt for our lives.*

But Lucian DeVeau had just told him that it wouldn't have mattered at all if he had tried to run. He would have wound up back there.

That had to be bull. And he had to have been nuts, calling those people. They were probably just as crazy into an imaginary psychic power as the Wiccans. And still . . .

He dressed, then determined to head into the parlor area of Huntington House for a cup of coffee. Something good and strong that would keep him awake—and thinking sanely.

Dressed for the night, he strode into the parlor, wondering if he would run into anyone or not. Fallon—who might know that Megan had left and would stare at him like the wife-beating monster he assumed Finn to be.

Susanna, dour, nasty—there to serve the guests, but doing so with a reserve and superiority that would make many would-be bed and breakfast managers cringe.

But neither Fallon nor Susanna was around. The only occupants of the parlor were the children, little Ellie, and her big brother Joshua. They were playing a board game on the table. Despite his mood, he greeted the two with a cheerful hello, and said that he hoped they were having fun.

"Sure," Joshua said with a shrug. "How did you like the museum I told you about?"

"You were right, I liked it a lot."

"I like the place Mr. Smith has!" Ellie piped in.

"Dr. Smith," Joshua corrected her. "He has all kinds of school degrees, that's what Mom said. But he's cool."

"Yeah, I guess so," Finn agreed, gritting his teeth. Why? The guy was bright and rational. It wasn't his fault that he was an old friend of Megan's—and bright and rational.

Ellie stood and came over to where Finn was pouring his coffee. "It's scary here," she said.

He smiled, setting his cup down, and hunkering down by her. "Ellie," he said, though he had known the touch of fear himself, "it's just Halloween. Dress up. You know that even in those monster museums, the monsters are either mechanical, or plain old dummies, or people in costumes, right?"

"Monsters are just people in costumes," she repeated. "What about when they're not in costumes?"

Finn arched a brow, looking over at Joshua.

Joshua grimaced, looking uncomfortable. "I think Mr. Fallon is a monster, and maybe Susanna, too."

"Oh? Why is that?" Finn winked at Ellie. "Susanna is kind of like an old scarecrow—sh! Never tell anyone I said that! But she's just a cranky old lady, really."

"They were doing things."

"Things?" Finn said, wondering at the child's revulsion. He wondered if the two old crankpots—Susanna and Fallon—had been getting it on together. The idea sure was repulsive, and he could see how it might scare a child.

Hell, the two might never want to have sex as adults, were they to witness such a coupling!

"I woke up in the middle of the night," Ellie said. "And I thought I'd run to Mommy's and Daddy's room . . . but I heard a noise and I called for Joshua . . . and we came down. And they had a big pot hanging over the fire in the kitchen. They were throwing things into it."

"Maybe they were making mulled wine," Finn said.

"They were talking funny!" Ellie told him.

"Chanting," Joshua corrected sagely.

"Oh, and what were they saying?"

Joshua looked troubled. "I don't know. I couldn't understand them."

"Hm. You don't think that they were maybe just talking to one another?"

Joshua firmly shook his head.

"Did you tell your parents?" Finn asked.

Ellie sighed. "They were mad."

"Why?"

"Because we left our room and went running around in the house. And they said the same thing—that Susanna and Mr. Fallon were just making something—wine, or food, or something—and that we should mind our own business. Just because it's almost Halloween, we shouldn't think that everyone is a monster."

"I see. Well, hmm. I'll tell you what. I'll check it out tonight myself, how's that? You two stay in your beds in your room. You're safe there, all right?"

Joshua had joined Ellie before him. Both of them looked at him with wide, solemn eyes.

"You'll really wake up and go see what they're doing?" he asked.

"Solemn promise," Finn told them.

Joshua let out a little sigh of relief. "I will feel better."

"Me, too. I'm scared, even in bed."

"Halloween can be very scary," Finn said. "Don't worry, monsters can make me feel a little uneasy, too, but I could swear that if you just stay in your room through the night, you'll be just fine. And, of course, say your prayers before you go to bed."

"Every night!" Ellie said.

Finn wondered what had caused him to say the last. Monsters were just evil people. He had to believe that. It was all that was rational. And rationally, it didn't mean that something wasn't happening. Evil people might very well be around, thinking they had the power to do something awful, whether it was real or not.

Half the heinous murderers throughout history had been psychotics, thinking that dogs talked to them or the devil demanded that they do it.

He smiled firmly at Joshua and tousled Ellie's hair. "You two go ahead and sleep tight tonight. I gave you my solemn vow to check it out, and I will."

After I watch over Megan! he thought.

Ellie slipped her hand into Finn's and squeezed it. "Thanks, Mr. Douglas. I don't know why adults just never want to believe children!"

The seriousness of her voice made him smile, along with the wisdom of the words.

"Sometimes adults can believe that they really know

better; they don't usually intend to be mean or dismissive," Finn told her. "Joshua, remember—you two stay locked snug and tight in your room. I have to work now, but I won't forget."

Joshua nodded seriously. "I know you won't."

He left the children, meaning every word he said. He would take a good walk around Huntington House tonight.

After he watched over Megan. Carefully.

He couldn't . . . he couldn't try to talk to her tonight, give explanations—or even beg an apology for whatever it was that he supposedly did.

He would be strictly business. Distant from her.

But watching. Because he felt as if he'd been warned by someone who somehow knew something, however illogical it might be.

Don't let her walk through the dark . . .

Or the fog . . .

Alone.

As he left Huntington House, he was suddenly angry and determined, and he knew that he'd be damned if he'd let anyone hurt her.

Anyone, or . . .

Anything.

Chapter 13

Megan came to work with a fair amount of trepidation and unease.

She had left without an explanation, and she had the feeling that Finn was going to have no idea why. And when she told him she had left because she'd been certain that he'd intended to strangle her, he wasn't going to believe her. He was going to be disdainful, certain that she was having more dreams, that she was listening to Morwenna's stories and palm readers who suggested he was bad for her, that she needed to get away from him, that he was such a violent human being she could wind up dead.

In his own mind, he probably had a right to feel that way. He truly seemed to have no idea that his eyes could glow like those of a wolf in the night, or that he could pin her down as if she were the victim of an assault, wind his fingers so tightly around her flesh.

What if she were the one losing her mind? No, she had known that she had been fully awake. She had been awake enough to pack.

Whatever power of suggestion had come into either

of their minds, she didn't intend to ruin the rest of their lives.

She just wanted to make sure that they had lives, she reasoned with herself.

But if so, it was important she show up for work.

Halloween was now just two nights away and the parking lot was crowded. She was dismayed to find herself far from the hotel when she at last found a spot. The wind seemed exceptionally chill as she locked Aunt Martha's old Chevy and made her way to the entrance. Hotel staff greeted her pleasantly, and she returned their hellos. When she came to the Conant Room, as the dinner and dancing spot was called, waiters and waitresses were setting up, and serving the few early diners who had arrived.

Finn was at work already, doing sound checks.

He glanced up, acknowledging her presence with a nod, then went back to the task at hand. A moment later, he rose from the squat he'd been in to test the wires, and told her, "We're closing in on the actual holiday. I was planning a lot of cover songs for tonight. Four of our own each set, and I have a list of what we'll cover as well. We'll do some Concrete Blond from the *Bloodletting* CD, and a lot of real Halloweeny stuff, 'Monster Mash,' 'Time Warp,' 'Hey There, Little Red Riding Hood,' 'Be My Frankenstein' . . . I've written it all out; you'll find the list on the podium over there. If there's anything you don't like, let me know. I'm going to get some coffee."

He stepped off the stage and started by her. A breath away. He didn't touch her. She was still startled by his completely businesslike greeting.

What had she expected? Greater anger, dismay. A determination that he would get her back.

Maybe not. Finn had his pride.

She could feel the warmth of him, smell his scent. Her heart ached suddenly.

"Finn."

He stopped and turned back.

"That's it? That's all? Read the list?"

His hands fell to his hips, his jaw twisted. Naturally, he was angry. "Let me see, you left me because I've turned into a maniac in the middle of the night, and you're afraid I'm going to hurt you. You didn't bother to tell me where you went, or even call and say, 'Hey, Finn, I'm okay, just having a few problems.' Or even, 'Finn, you're having severe problems, you asshole, and I need some distance.' But, hey, you were the one who didn't want to leave Salem, work ethic and all, so I figured you would be here tonight."

She stared at him. He kind of had it in a nutshell, so she wasn't sure what to say.

"What, Megan? I was supposed to have dropped everything in life and come chasing after you again? I called and you know it. Somehow, it seems to me that we should try to get to the bottom of this together, but, what the hell. I've had a few strange dreams of my own and you weren't trying to kill me in them, so . . . check over the list. If you've any problems, let me know."

He walked on over to the bar. They were getting to know the bartender fairly well. The bearded guy greeted Finn, and had apparently known that he'd come for coffee, because a large cup was in front of him in a matter of minutes.

Megan walked up on the stage, found the list, and looked it over. Horror classics for the most part. She had no problems with any of the songs he had chosen. She'd go to the bar and let him know, and try to make him understand a little better what she was going through. It hurt that he had implied she wasn't worth coming after again. *Had* she wanted him to tear the city apart, looking for her? No. She had left because she was afraid. Really afraid.

She glanced at the bar and was startled to see that

though it was near empty, there was a woman sitting right next to Finn. It was Sara, from Morwenna's shop. She hesitated, then walked up and took a seat beside her, asking the bartender for a water with lemon. Sara said hello to her and Megan smiled. "I would have thought you'd still be at the shop. It must be as busy as a hive in there now, so close to Halloween."

"It is busy, but Morwenna brought in some of the part-time help. She'll be here herself in a while. When they close the shop, she, Joseph, and Jamie are all coming by."

"That's nice," Megan said. She glanced around Sara to Finn. He was busy turning a stirrer in his coffee. "I wish Morwenna wouldn't feel as if she had to be so supportive that she came every night. She must be getting tired."

"Morwenna doesn't get tired. Not around Halloween time."

"Well, that's good," she murmured.

Sara looked at her, studying her features. "Morwenna draws energy at Halloween. For us, you know, it's really like a high holy day."

"Yes, I know."

Sara smiled. "Um. You know, you just don't believe." For some reason, the girl's grin reminded Megan of that given by the Cheshire Cat. It made her feel uniquely uncomfortable.

Or maybe it was just the way that Finn and Sara seemed to have gotten over their differences and were suddenly so chummy.

"It's about time to get started," Finn said abruptly, rising. "Thanks for coming, Sara."

Megan thought that the two exchanged a strange glance, as if they were sharing some secret information. A trickle of jealousy snaked through her. She wasn't imagining any of this. Finn . . . he had seemed to dislike Sara before. Now he was talking to her in a way that seemed to intimate that they had become best friends.

Finn didn't wait for her, but headed for the stage. She shrugged to Sara, determined that she wasn't going to allow either of them to note that she had realized the sudden change, and followed Finn. Before she had reached her position, Finn had picked up his mike, and went through his spiel, introducing the two of them, welcoming the guests to the Conant Room, and telling them that they were headed into some real Halloween funk.

He started right off with "Monster Mash," and they segued into one of their own songs, "Angel of Darkness," and then straight into an Ozzy Osbourne piece.

Finn watched the light play on Megan's hair.

He wished he could reach out and touch it.

He could not.

She wanted distance, and he intended to give her that. He meant to be simply businesslike, cool, collected.

Mostly, he thought, he was succeeding.

Then, there were those moments . . .

His fingers moved over the keyboard synthesizer by rote. He found himself looking out at the crowd, in shadow to him because of the lights on stage. It did appear as if they were in a den of monsters. But they were normal monsters. All the sickles held by grim reapers were plastic, as were the knives carried by the Jasons, Freddies, and others. Some costumes were cheap, some were good. They kind of merged in the shadowy recesses of the club.

Monsters, in life, didn't look all that different, he reminded himself. Ted Bundy had been a monster. A good-looking man, capable of engaging charm. That was where sanity came in, and that was what he had to remember. He was still amazed himself that he had called the couple in New Orleans, and that he was giving any credence at all to a book on entities and demons. But he was glad that he had called. It all came back to *people*. Old crazies like Fallon, cooking up potions in the kitchen. The *people* here were not trustworthy. Whether they were in actuality strangers or not, he had a lot more faith in the folk from New Orleans than he did in anyone here. Even if it seemed that he and Sara were now on something of the same wavelength, he didn't trust her. He definitely didn't trust Morwenna or Joseph. He'd go ahead and shoot himself before he ever risked a word to Fallon or Susanna. Mike Smith was after his wife. The folks at the hotel seemed decent enough, but they were definitely and essentially strangers. The cop and his twin the bookseller seemed all right, but the bookseller had some strange reading habits. Theo Martin seemed on the up and up, but . . .

Megan turned slightly, and he could see her profile. Bands seemed to constrict in his heart. She was truly perfection. Her face, so well etched, bone structure so cleanly designed. She was lithe, she was graceful. Perfect skin, beautiful eyes, full, generous mouth, white teeth, flashing smile, high breasts, slim waist, long, sculpted legs. Maybe someone here wanted him out of the way. Because he, too, saw Megan as perfect.

It didn't make sense. How could someone else make him have *dreams*?

Make him want to take her, seize her . . . hurt her.

He looked at the sea of faces in their various forms of masquerade before him. An eerie sensation filled him.

Someone did want him out of the way. Whoever, it seemed, was succeeding. Megan had split from him.

She was with Aunt Martha. Safe.

And he had to keep his distance. Watch after her, but keep his distance. Tomorrow . . .

Hell if knew why. Tomorrow was going to be better. He knew how to fight.

And he intended to do so.

* * *

During the first break, Finn excused himself and disappeared entirely. Megan, chatting with diners at the bar, was disturbed to realize that she didn't see Sara either.

"Who are you looking for? Maybe I can help you."

Megan swung around. The question had been asked by the Frankenstein monster at her side. Good costume and makeup. He appeared to be entirely green.

"No one," she replied, forcing a smile. "Just observing all the costumes. They're great. Yours is great."

"Thanks!"

If nothing else, she had made one monster very happy.

He complimented her appearance, and she thanked him, still watching for Finn and Sara. At last, she saw Finn heading for the stage. She excused herself to the monster, and headed on up to join him.

During the second break, Finn had a beer with a man in a brown monk's cowl and half mask. Morwenna and Joseph arrived during the third set. Her cousin waved to her, indicating that she'd ordered dinner for her. Megan smiled back, nodding. She thought Finn would have joined them for dinner. He didn't. But Morwenna and Joseph obviously knew just what was going on.

"You could have called me," Morwenna said reproachfully.

"I knew Finn would think I had gone to you."

"Well, Megan, my dear, it would have been rather decent of you to have told him that it was all right. And you should have come to me."

"Morwenna, no offense intended, but he already thinks your Wiccan beliefs might have something to do with me losing my mind and having nightmares. Aunt Martha is such a neutral, she seemed the right person to go to."

Morwenna shrugged, studying her over a cosmopolitan. "Whatever is going on here has nothing to do with Wiccans. But I do believe with my whole heart that there is something going on here!"

Megan remembered old Andy Markham's words. *Bac-Dal wants you.*

Ridiculous. Other than that, with words like that said to her in a spooky old cemetery filled with *unhallowed* graves, she was made to feel a certain superstitious fear.

But what about Finn? He hadn't been with Andy in the woods; he hadn't heard the words. And she had never told him she'd gone out to meet with Andy, never told him any of the things Andy had said. She'd been afraid that he'd be too furious with the story the old man had told her, and more. He'd have been too angry with her for going out to such a godforsaken place to meet with the fellow.

He'd heard different stories, she reminded herself impatiently. There were ghosts and skeletons and monsters everywhere.

"There is something going on," she said, forcing herself to sound impatient and incredulous. "Like what, Morwenna? What on earth could possibly cause you to have bad dreams—except for the things you experience during the day? Maybe it's me, maybe it's Finn, maybe it's both of us. Halloween is almost here and gone. I just want to keep a distance for both our sakes until . . . until we leave here. Go home. And if we keep having weird dreams, we'll find a reputable psychologist in our own area who can give us some help."

Joseph leaned across the table. "Listen to me, Megan. You can't continue to be such a skeptic when . . . you both need help!" he said firmly.

Not surprised by his words, but definitely taken aback by his strange tone, Megan frowned at Jamie Gray, hoping he would offer a line of sanity. But Jamie shrugged.

"Who the hell would any of us be to say that strange things *don't* go on in the world."

"The murder in Boston is really distressing," Morwenna said.

Frowning, Megan stared at Morwenna. "Murder is always horrible. I saw the news. A young woman was apparently raped, murdered, and thrown in the river. Yes, that's very distressing. Unfortunately, it happens far too often. Why is that particular murder so distressing?"

Morwenna stared at her hard. "Meg! Come on. Boston. She was apparently killed a month ago. In Boston."

"So, what does that have to do with us? All right, sorry, we're not an hour out, so someone who committed a heinous murder did so not very far away. We have a high murder rate in New Orleans. It doesn't stop us from going out."

"Megan—" Morwenna began.

"Don't," Joseph said suddenly, firmly.

"Don't what?"

"Don't get her going on things you know nothing about!" Joseph said firmly.

Megan stared at Joseph, then at her cousin. "What? You think that this guy is in Salem now? Do you think he's a serial killer? From what I've seen, the police don't really know anything yet. It might have been a horrible crime committed because of jealousy and anger. I'm sure they're checking out any ex-boyfriends, her family, and coworkers. I don't remember the exact percentages, but most violence against women comes from their immediate family or social circle. Although random killings happen as well, when there is a psychopath on the loose."

All three of them were just staring at her. Almost as if she were a naive child, and Joseph had been right, there was no real need to make her open her eyes to real terror in the world.

She glanced toward the stage and saw that Finn was back. Time to go play. As she rose, aware that the three of them were still watching her covertly, she felt a chill seep into her.

Boston. A month ago. Right. Finn had come through Boston a month ago.

Was that what they were trying to say to her?

Lord, that was the most ridiculous thought that had passed through her mind yet. What? On his urgent trek to reach her, he had stopped off in Boston to murder a girl? That was beyond absurd. She knew Finn.

She had known him once.

He played through the intro to a Sam the Sham and the Pharaohs' hit twice. She picked up on her next cue.

Their last break came. Finn left the stage first and went by Morwenna and Joseph's table, smiled, gave Morwenna a kiss on the cheek, then moved on. This time, he didn't disappear. As Megan wandered over to the bar for a fresh water with lemon, she saw him talking to Sam Tartan, who seemed pleased with the busy turnout, and then, once again, he had a beer with the fellow in the monk's cape and half mask.

As she sat at the bar, she felt a tap on her shoulder and quickly turned around. She didn't recognize the person in the executioner's mask and black cowl.

"You all right?"

"Mike?" she said, hearing the voice.

He gave her a broad smile. "Okay, so I gave in to the concept of dress-up. You look stunning, by the way. Great show, lots of fun. I love the music you're choosing."

"Finn chose it."

"Hey, I'd compliment him, but I don't think that he'd appreciate it. He doesn't like me very much."

"That's not true. He's just . . . tense . . . here."

She could sense that Mike was smiling. "I don't know, Megan. I'm getting vibes."

She had to laugh. "You're getting vibes? Mike, you're the academic. You can't be getting vibes."

"Okay, then maybe it's the way he looks at me. Or when he shakes my hand. Powerful grip your fellow has there. I feel like he's ready to crush my bones."

"We should all go to lunch together. I know that you two would actually get along very well, if you just had a chance to really talk."

"Maybe, somewhere along the line," Mike said. "Can I get you something?"

"No, thanks, I just stick with water and lemon during the evening."

Mike nodded, then inclined his cowled head toward the stage. "I think you're being beckoned."

"And so I am."

She grinned at him and headed toward the stage. Now, Finn was staring at her very coldly. Had he recognized Mike? How?

She neared the stage and started when it appeared that she was touched by the skeletal branches of a tree. She started, then heard laughter. "Wild costume, huh?"

She turned. Another green face, entirely green. Surrounded by plastic, vinyl, and latex in an incredible green forest costume. It was Darren Menteith—despite the green makeup, she recognized him immediately. But the costume was really great. Standing still, he might very well look exactly like a tree.

"Darren!"

"In the flesh—and all," he told her.

"It's stupendous."

"I have outdone myself," Darren said, grinning. "Didn't mean to hold you up. I just wanted you to know that I'm an even more avid fan, and here to support you whenever I can be!"

She paused, seeing the earnestness in his eyes. She caught him by the green latex shoulders and kissed him on the cheek. "Thanks!"

"Take my hand, and I'll make sure you don't trip on that divine black skirt on your way up on the stage."

His hand was so well done. His fingers were gloved in the vinyl, and other little protrusions in heartier material added to the appearance of the twigs and leaves at the end of a branch.

"Thanks."

She came up on the stage. Finn was still staring at her. She met his gaze, then turned to face the crowd.

There was suddenly nothing Megan wanted more than for the evening to end.

And of course, at last, it did.

Morwenna, Joseph, and their crew had cut out early. In fact, that night, the place emptied out just minutes before their last number, even before the bartenders and servers gave last call. Either people were becoming exhausted from so many days of revelry so far, or they were gearing up for the big night to come.

Megan lingered, but Finn seemed engrossed in the synthesizer. She was sorry that Morwenna was gone already. She felt ridiculously alone, and she had no right to, since she was the one who had determined that she had to leave Finn. But she hadn't left him. Not really. She wished she could explain, but then, she probably should have made a point of doing that earlier. But last night . . . he had really terrified her.

He wasn't going to pay attention to her tonight, she decided. And she wasn't ready to beg him to do so. She didn't want to be talked into coming back. Or worse. Be told that she wasn't wanted back.

She looked around but didn't see anyone she knew well. Darren would have been clearly evident in his tree costume, had he remained. And even Mike Smith would have stood out. Neither Sara nor Jamie Gray had remained either.

Megan said good-bye to the hotel workers finishing up at the bar and started out. When she reached the front, she hesitated. The car seemed as if it were acres away. Many of the other vehicles were gone, and the trees planted in symmetrical angles every sixth spot seemed like dead sentinels long deserted by the living.

She could go back in.

She could just walk to her car—or Aunt Martha's car. She could see it clearly enough. She squared her shoulders, determined that she was leaving, and started to walk.

Finn finished covering the equipment and looked to the bar where Megan had been. He hadn't wanted to make a big deal about leaving with her—she might have refused so much as an escort out of the place. He'd meant to keep an eye on her and follow her, but she had been there, just seconds ago.

Adam Spade was sitting there. "Have you seen Megan?" Finn asked.

"Sure, she was here just a few seconds ago."

"She told us all good night," one of the servers called to Finn. "She just went out the main entrance, seconds ago."

"Thanks," Finn said.

He didn't want to look as if he were running, but he hurried out through the main entrance and reached the parking lot.

Looking into the distance, he saw her.

Don't let her be alone at night.

Or in the fog.

But there was no fog.

"Megan?"

He didn't see her.

And as he looked down . . .

A soft, blue swirl was beginning to curl around his feet.

*   *   *

It was when she reached the first tree that the blue mist began to rise.

Just around her feet . . .

By the time she reached the second tree, it was up to her chest. She quickened her footsteps, then instinctively paused, thinking that she was being followed. When she stood still, there was no sound. The air seemed to be dead calm. There was no rustle of the trees. No laughter from other groups of people leaving the hotel.

She turned around to look back. The hotel seemed impossibly far away now, too. Turning again, she saw that her car seemed no closer. Impossible, of course. It all had to do with the fog. She looked back to the hotel once more, assuring herself that there was absolutely no one but herself anywhere near the parking lot, and her car. She wished that even a drunk would stumble out of the hotel.

Her temptation was to go flying back. She swallowed down the ridiculous rise of panic, and even as she turned toward the car once again, she was already walking.

She came to a dead standstill.

There was someone else out. Someone by the car. Someone in a haze created by the fog.

"Megan!"

She wasn't sure if she was really hearing her name, or if she was imagining the sound in her own mind. She couldn't tell who it was standing there, because he was wearing either a cape or a long winter coat. The stance seemed to be powerful, though, and provocative. She was tempted to move forward, to reach the figure as quickly as possible, throw herself upon his . . . power?

She started to move, but stumbled. No matter how strong the urge was to move forward, something was pulling her back.

Screw sanity and reason. She turned, ready to fly back to the hotel. *Screw pride as well.* Someone was going to walk her out.

But this time, as she ran, she did hear footsteps behind her. Coming closer, closer. She looked back. The dark form was gaining on her. It was a blue against the fog, and yet . . . it moved swiftly, coming nearer, nearer . . .

She kept running, suddenly sure that her life depended on her speed.

"Megan, Megan!"

This time, she was certain that she heard her name being called. She couldn't tell from where. It was as if she were running through a sea of thick, silver-blue soup.

She could feel him . . . it . . . *something* . . . behind her. As if tentacles of fiery breath were reaching her, stroking down her hair, touching her, trying to get a grip.

She screamed out loud, for suddenly, it seemed that the form was in front of her, it, or another dark shadow, rising from the mist.

She didn't even know which direction she faced anymore, the fog was so dense. Not dark, like the ebony of the night. Blue. Swirling, though now, there was still no rustle of trees. Nothing picked up a breeze that should have cast dead leaves scurrying as it made the fog twist and whirl.

Spinning again, she choked back a cry. There were eyes in the mist. Burning. Gold, red, pinpoints of fire.

Eyes . . .

Eyes she had seen before. Eyes that had haunted her dreams, her sleeping . . .

Her awakening?

Headlights, flashlights . . . something else. No!

Eyes!

She turned to flee, not knowing her direction, just

determined to fly in the opposite direction of those eerie points of light and fire. Her lungs seemed to burst, her calves to rage with pain.

Hands . . . fingers . . . something real, was upon her, branches, reaching into her hair, trying to wrench her back.

"No!"

The fog was whispering her name; it was as if the fog itself had taken life. And the touch . . . it wasn't real, couldn't be real . . .

But she *felt* it!

Felt hands reaching for her, wrapping around her, but they weren't there, they weren't real, the figure was still just behind her, coming closer and closer . . .

"Megan!"

"No!"

The darkness, real, imagined, fog . . . substance . . . was reaching around her.

"No!"

It was behind her . . .

It was before her.

The dark form before her was now . . .

Racing straight toward her, a thundercloud in sweeping ebony, coming down . . . down . . . nearly on top of her.

She spun to run the other way.

Yet there, in the blue-gray shadow of fog, was the figure that so nearly touched her . . . touched her with icy cold, fingerlike breath.

She spun again, and screamed.

Chapter 14

The dark form before her sailed by. She heard the thud of a collision, or someone falling to the pavement. She cried out again, spinning around.

Almost immediately, the fog began to thin. She could see the hotel, so close in front of her now. She could see the first tree in its aligned spot in the parking lot.

A dark figure on the ground . . .

Rising.

Her breath caught, she backed away, ready to scream again, run pell-mell for that entrance which now loomed so close before her.

"Megan!"

Finn, breathless, his voice very deep, husky. It was him on the pavement. He was stumbling to his feet. "Megan, you're all right?"

"Finn!" She ran to him. The cape he had borrowed from Morwenna's shop was covered in dirt and dead autumn leaves. He rested his hands on his knees as he caught his breath. His dark hair was wildly astray; a few leaves were caught in it as well. The instinct in her heart had taken over; she didn't even pause to reflect on the

fact that he might have been really hurt. She threw herself at him, almost hysterical in her relief that he was
alive and moving.

"Megan, Megan!" His fingers moved gently over her
hair as he cradled her closer, just holding her. As last he
pulled away, anxious to see her. She tentatively reached
to his head, drawing away a leaf.

"Are you all right?" she asked anxiously.

"Fine. Well, bruised and a little embarrassed, since
he got away. But otherwise . . . fine."

"Finn," she murmured, leaning close against the
beating of his heart once again. "You're always there for
me . . . even tonight. You were there for me."

"I would die for you, Megan, and you know it," he
said gruffly.

"And that's incredible . . . we've fought so passionately, sometimes. And even when you came for me . . . I
was afraid at first that I was walking on eggshells, because there are so many other places you could be . . .
or people you could be with. And even when we first
went back, I was so afraid; I didn't want to lose you
again; I wondered if we could ever be as close again.
And now . . . I didn't just walk out on you. Okay, I did,
but it's because I believe that you don't know, that it's
something in your dreams, or even in mine . . . I'm not
making any sense. Except that now, things are so absurdly strange."

"I know, Megan."

"Even right now! This! Who—what was it?" she asked,
searching behind him. Little mists of white fog still drifted
around but not enough to impair her vision. The parking lot, other than the forlorn trees and a few cars, was
empty. "There was someone, right? Something . . . so
strange, the eyes I see in the darkness, but it was just a
man, it had to have been. But I didn't see anyone
clearly, not at all. Who . . . what . . ."

He shook his head with disgust. "I don't know."

"You don't know?"

"Someone strong, powerful," he said ruefully. He looked at her with green, Finn eyes. Eyes she knew well, had known for years. Loved. "I hadn't realized you had left," he said. "So I hurried out . . . to make sure you got off okay. And . . . the fog was out. I couldn't see anything. I stumbled around looking for you, then heard your footsteps and your scream and tried to find you. And then . . ." He shrugged. "There you were, and there he was . . . her . . . whatever. No, had to be a he. Not even a heavy-weight women's wrestling champ could have been that strong. It was like tackling a brick wall."

"Strong—and fast," she murmured. "He's gone."

"Yeah," Finn said ruefully, staring out into the parking lot. He turned and looked at her. "This may be New England, but that fog is damned strange."

She shrugged, unwilling to tell him that she thought so, too.

"Let's go in and report him."

She frowned, balking at the suggestion. "Finn, what are we going to report?"

"That a guy nearly attacked you in the parking lot!"

"But . . . we don't even know what he looked like. I don't, at any rate."

"That's not the point. They need to know that some freak is running after lone women in their parking lot."

"But . . ."

"But what, Megan?" he asked impatiently. "Do you want it to happen to someone else?"

"No, of course not."

He was already heading back in. The Conant Room was empty except for the last of the serving and clean-up crews and a few people at the bar, most of whom who had been in costume, and were now halfway stripped down. Finn walked ahead of her; she followed on his heels. She wondered how she was going to begin to explain that she hadn't really gotten a close look at someone who had almost touched her, and that he had disappeared in seconds flat. She hadn't even known which way he was coming, when Finn had flown by her. And after that, all she had seen was . . .

Finn.

A niggling suspicion crept to her throat, one she refused to accept, entertain, even acknowledge . . .

But it was there, haunting her mind, and she couldn't shut it off.

Finn!

Had it been him chasing her all along, unnerving her, calling her name in that eerie voice in the fog, and all to . . .

Come to her rescue? Make her realize she needed him. Was that why he had been so cavalier all night— his plan had been in motion?

No. She didn't believe it for a second. Finn was never devious. He could be obstinate, stubborn, and fiercely determined; he could even plow his way in somewhere when it was a place or situation where he really wanted to be. But he wasn't devious.

And still . . .

"Theo, there was someone out in the parking lot. Megan was nearly attacked." Finn turned back to Megan, drawing her toward a man sitting at the bar. He was the one who had been wearing the monk's cape and half mask, she saw, as the mask was now next to him on the bar. "You remember—Officer Theo Martin. We met last night during that ruckus up here with good old Marty."

"Yes, of course, I remember you, and thank you so much again for your help," Megan said, accepting the hand he offered her.

"Not a problem. So, what's this? You were attacked in the parking lot?"

"Not exactly." She hesitated. "Finn was there. He . . . tackled whoever it was, and they took off."

"Really took off. Into thin air," Finn said ruefully.

"Adam, have you heard any of this?" Theo said, looking at Megan, but speaking loudly to be heard from his rear.

Adam, the bald bouncer emerged from where he had evidently been stacking liquor bottles below the bar. He was frowning.

"Did he . . . get a hold of you in any way?" Adam demanded.

"No . . . no. Nothing really happened. But Finn thought it was important that we tell you—rather than take a chance that someone else might be attacked."

"We've received some scoop on the girl found in Boston," Theo murmured, still watching Megan. "I didn't say that to frighten you, but all nearby areas have been alerted to what little information they have."

"We've got to get someone out in the parking lot, then," Adam said firmly. "Whether Sam wants to spend any more money or not."

"Hey, he's been raking it in all week; he's had to turn dozens of people away," Theo said. "There are plenty of guys at the station that would be happy to take some off-duty work. Cops can usually use some side work."

"Tartan will have to get on it, whether he likes it or not."

"Megan, Finn, do you all want to come down to the station and file a report?"

Megan glanced at Finn. "Not really . . . because it was all so fast, there's nothing to report. I can't give anything that even resembles a description, and I . . . I was never really touched." *It had felt as if she had been . . . almost. But that hadn't been real, it had just been that she could feel heat, and breath . . . something hovering so very close.* She shook her head firmly. "I don't want to file a report. The only good any of it can do is if someone can convince Sam Tartan that he has to have some security out in the parking lot."

Theo Martin was observing her intensely. "Well, I think we should put the force on alert as well. I mean, who knows, maybe a drunk was just staggering around out there. But with what happened in Boston . . . still, you don't have to fill out a report, Megan. I'll see to it that everyone is aware that we've got to watch out. It's tough. Halloween season. Everyone is dressed as a monster. Hey, even little kids! What happened to adorable little girls dressing up as princesses? Now, they all want to be Elvira or lady vampires. I ran into a kid today covered in old white bandages with enough red makeup on them to make him look like a bloodbath. I asked him what he was, and he told me he was an accident victim. I mean, is that fun?" Theo said with disgust.

"Monsters are big," Finn murmured in agreement. "And guys, thanks. We're going to take off now. And Adam, if you need help convincing Tartan, let me know."

"Tartan can pay, and he should, but don't worry, Finn," Theo said. "If he doesn't fork up the dough, we'll slip someone out here anyway. No one tell him that, though!"

"Not a chance," Megan said.

"Hey, Megan, just be glad you got yourself a wire-muscled blackbelt there, huh?" Adam said. "He can keep down the drunks, the tough guys, and even the things that go bump in the night."

She forced a smile. "Right."

They exited the hotel together.

Once outside, they both stopped. The fog was gone. The moon was huge, flooding the parking lot with light.

"I'll walk you to . . . your car. Or whoever's car it is," Finn said. "Aunt Martha's, I take it. You're staying with her, right?"

"Yes." She hesitated. His eyes were on her. Green. Framed by the dark lashes and defined, cleanly arched brows. That she might have suspected him of staging a rescue suddenly filled her with shame. This was the man she knew, loved. Was terrified of losing. How long would he keep patience with her?

And yet that morning . . .

She had been certain she had been about to die.

"I thought I should go to Aunt Martha's because . . . well, she's so sensible. I know that you suspect Morwenna and Joseph of trying to put a wedge between us. And you're wrong; Morwenna likes you a lot, and you seem to get along fine with Joseph." *And now, look at you and Sara!* she almost added. "Anyway, I just didn't want to . . . well, to feed into any of your thoughts on Wiccans, so I went to Aunt Martha's. But . . . you knew, I guess."

He shrugged. "You weren't with Morwenna, so I assumed you went to Martha's, yes."

"Finn," she murmured. "I didn't walk out. All right, I did walk out, but not like before. I just don't understand what's going on, and I actually left because I do love you, and I'm not angry, or jealous, or anything else . . . just afraid."

"It's all right. I understand."

"You do? Really?"

"Yes."

She stood awkwardly for a moment, then smiled slowly. "In a way, that makes it even harder. Don't be too nice—not when I'm feeling a little like a jerk. At least, it's just two days until Halloween. Then we're out of here. And if the dreams continue, for either of us, we're rushing straight to a psychoanalyst!"

"Go on, get into your car. I'll follow you out to Aunt Martha's."

"You don't have to—"

"Yes, I do."

She shrugged. "Okay."

"And don't worry; I'm not staying. I actually have something of a promise to fulfill this evening."

"Oh? Anything I should know about?" she asked. A

tickle of jealousy found root in her heart. *Was she falling for something incredibly stupid right now? Was his appointment with Sara, or even the blatantly head-over-heels Gayle Sawyer?*

"A promise—and an investigation," he said, grimacing ruefully.

"What are you talking about?"

"I saw the kids earlier this evening, and they were alarmed by something they found old Fallon doing."

"Really? What?"

"Cooking up spells in a pot, or something like that. Anyway, I intend to snoop around the house during the wee hours."

"Finn . . . should you be doing that?"

"Definitely. What if the old fellow does think that he can cook up some evil for Halloween? He could be dangerous, and there are those two children in the house."

"Finn, you've got to be careful," she warned uneasily. "Fallon doesn't like you to begin with."

"Guess what? I'm not so fond of him."

"But still . . ."

"Don't worry about it. If I come across him doing anything weird, I'll simply ask him what he's up to. Maybe he has some perfectly rational explanation for whatever it is."

"Why didn't the kids go to their parents?"

"They did."

"And?"

"They're kids—they got in trouble for sneaking around at night."

Megan hesitated. "Maybe I should go back with you. You're kind of like a big kid sometimes. I may have to keep you out of trouble."

He shook his head, observing her gravely. "Megan, you haven't even told me what I did—or supposedly did."

"Finn, there was no supposed. You nearly strangled

me. You woke in the night like a sex-starved ex-con, and then . . . at the end . . . nearly strangled me."

He stared back at her, spine rigid, jaw hard, eyes almost as shadowy as the strange blue fog that too often came at night.

"There are no bruises on your neck, Megan," he said coldly.

"Finn, I may be the one who wakes up screaming, but you're having some mean dreams, too. I think. I can't figure out what else could make you behave so bizarrely in your sleep."

"Megan, perhaps it was your dream."

"No . . . Finn, I was really terrified of you!"

"As I said, there are no bruises on your neck."

"Finn—"

"Megan, it's all right. I'll follow you back to Martha's, see that you get there safely."

She lowered her head. "All right. Thanks," she murmured softly.

He walked with her to Martha's car, where she determined to drive him to his. When they reached it, she told him miserably, "The oddest thing is, it's sleeping together that's so scary."

"Well, that's great to hear," he said dryly.

She laughed. "I didn't say sex itself. Just sleeping together."

"But it's sex when we're sleeping together," he said.

"We could meet in the afternoon," she said lightly. To her surprise and dismay, he didn't reply right away, but stared out the front window. And as she watched him, she was dismayed by the sudden surge of arousal that raced through her just because he was there. She was far too accustomed to him being *hers*, knowing the scent of him, the strengths of his profile, the look and feel of his hands, the length of him, flesh and sinew, even the way that he breathed . . .

"I'm going to see some folks tomorrow."

"Oh? Who?"

"The people who gave us that great review and got us national coverage. They're from New Orleans you know, but they're on their way up here for Halloween, covering more of the goings-on. Anyway, we're going to meet for coffee."

"Don't you want me to come?"

"You'll see them tomorrow night, I imagine. They're going to stick around a while."

No, he didn't want her to come!

"How curious," she said, studying him.

"Why?"

"Did they get in touch with you somehow?"

"Um, no. I called them."

"You did? Why?"

"Remember the book I accidentally lifted from Morwenna's shop? I still have to pay her for that, come to think of it. Anyway, there was a number in back of the book. I called it—"

"Whatever made you do that?"

"I wanted to say thanks."

Megan wondered if he had hesitated a split second before answering.

"Thanks?"

"National coverage, Megan. Remember?"

"Yes, of course. And naturally, I'd like to thank them as well."

"They're going to be around," he repeated, then exited the car. She felt completely rebuffed, frustrated, and uneasy.

But he paused before shutting the door.

"I love you, Megan," he said softly. "Don't ever doubt that."

The door closed. He walked over, and she heard the sound of the ignition catching in his car. She headed out of the parking lot.

A few minutes later, they reached Martha's. Megan

parked the car, and Finn did the same. He came up behind her, saying, "I'll walk you to the door."

Martha had left the porch light on for her. It cast a
glow of illumination well across the yard, but Finn was
frowning.

"What's the matter?"

"There's nothing but woods behind this place," Finn
said.

"A lot of New England is woods," she reminded him.

"She should have a big German shepherd, or a Rott-
weiler."

Megan smiled. "We're not that far! Aunt Martha has
neighbors—and you know yourself, the hotel is actually
not far from here, either."

He nodded. She touched his arm. They were both
getting ridiculously paranoid. "Do you want to come
in—check in the closets?" she asked softly, half teasing,
half not.

He cocked his head, considering his reply. "I'll come
in for a minute."

Ever considerate, Martha had left the kitchen light
on as well. They walked through the shadows of the
foyer and parlor where Finn hesitated. "Don't stay
here," he said suddenly.

"What?"

"I think . . . it's the woods," he murmured.

She studied him. "Finn, it's Aunt Martha's house.
Apple pie and the American flag."

"I don't . . . I don't know why, but something is bothering me. I think that I really don't like the fact that
we're off the beaten track." He lifted his hands. "And
there isn't even a great big dog. Or an alarm system."

"Because nothing happens here," she said. "Come in
the kitchen. I'll make tea."

She walked through to the kitchen, aware that he
was following her. There were early-American bar stools
at an island counter. "Sit," she told him. When he did

so, she filled the kettle and set it on the stove, then reached up into a cabinet for the tea bags.

"I don't want to wake Martha," he said quietly.

"We won't wake her. Her room is upstairs, on the other side of the house." She laughed softly and suddenly. "Finn! Look at this."

"What?"

Megan swept out a hand, indicating two mugs on the counter beneath the cabinet where she'd been rummaging. There was a note in front. Megan picked it up and read, "Just in case Finn sees you home. Two very special hot chocolates. Add boiling water—and a touch of milk if you like."

"Bless the sweet old bird," Finn said.

The kettle began to whistle, and Megan filled the mugs with the water.

She started to walk by him to the refrigerator. He caught her arm as she walked by, spinning her back to him.

"And where is your room?"

"What?"

"Your room. Martha's is upstairs, and yours is . . . where?"

"This landing. Right behind the kitchen."

"Far away from Martha's, huh?"

She nodded gravely.

"Is there a fireplace?"

"There is."

"Hot chocolate in front of a fireplace. Doesn't that sound deliciously . . ."

She waited for him to go on, certain that he intended to say "sexy," or "sensual."

"Normal?" Finn murmured huskily.

"Normal?" she repeated. "Yes . . . let me put a little milk in them, cool them down. The bedroom is right through there. I guess it was originally a maid's room, or maybe even a pantry. It's charming, though."

"Good."

Megan put milk into the cups; Finn picked them up and indicated that Megan should open the door. She did so, turning on the light.

The room was old-fashioned and as charming as the rest of the house. The bed was a four-poster, the decor was in red, white, and blue, very New England, completely patriotic. The dresser, stand-up mirror, and night tables were the same heavy carved oak as the four-poster.

She watched as Finn set the cups down on the dresser and walked over to the fireplace. Modern day logs, purchased at the local Wal-Mart, were in a stack by the hearth, and Finn quickly set to creating a low blaze. Megan watched him as he did so. He was still so bronze, agile, sinuous in his movements. She found her breath catching, and she had to force herself to remember how he had looked that morning, red-eyed, fierce, the wiry power within his back and shoulders culminating in his hands, long musician's fingers filled with violence as they fell upon her . . .

Or had it been a dream?

Right now, she wanted it to be a dream. He glanced up at her, a lock of dark hair falling over a green eye, the bronze of his features exceptionally appealing as he grinned. "She buys good logs! Nice place. Why didn't we come here to begin with?"

Megan smiled. "Because you didn't want to be forced to cohabit with my relatives if they were as strange as you were expecting them to be."

"Oh, yeah, that."

The fire was stoked. He rose, going for the hot chocolate. He handed Megan a cup, and took his own down by the foot of the bed, before the hearth. The room was carpeted in deep blue except for the tile that immediately surrounded the hearth. There was a thick, plush white foot rug there as well, making a very comfortable place.

Megan brought her chocolate and joined Finn. He sat against the bed, and slipped an arm around her as she joined him. She leaned against his shoulder and chest, feeling the sense of being cherished and secure that she had first known with him, and which had seemed to so abandon her lately.

He stroked her hair, absently staring at the flames. She didn't want him to go, and yet . . .

She was afraid to fall asleep with him at her side, and as much as she might long for him, ache for him, there was something inside her as well, something terrified that she might drift . . .

"Finn."

"Hm?"

"What . . . do you think is happening? Is one of us . . . crazy? Or worse—psychotic?"

"No," he said flatly, and with determination. "I wish there weren't so many woods around here," he murmured.

She smiled, reaching up to touch his chin. "There's a phone on the bedside stand. Hit one, and it dials the police. Hit two—and it dials your cell phone. I programmed it in today."

"Did you?" he said huskily. "Hm . . . would have been nice if you'd picked up when I dialed you this morning."

"Finn . . . you don't understand."

"You're right, I don't, but never mind. I believe that you are really terrified of me, and as painful as that is . . . I'll cope. November first, we're out of here. Back home. And you can lock yourself in a different room until we have a chance to talk to someone. Two more nights. I can be patient."

"I'm not so sure that I can," she whispered softly.

He started to shift, as if he were going to rise.

"I have to get back to Huntington House," he said.

She hesitated. "Can you wait just a few more minutes? I wanted to hop in and out of the shower, really quick. I feel like I have food, fog, smoke, and the smell of booze all over me."

"Sure. I can wait. Go ahead."

She rose. He didn't take the bait. Maybe he figured she really just wanted a shower, or that she was being a real bitch, walking out on him, but playing games as well.

She left him on the floor and walked into the bathroom.

Martha, always a restless sleeper, awoke, not sure what caused her to do so, rather than the fact that her bones were old and creaked when she turned, and almost any little noise startled her.

She lay awake for a moment, paused, then rose, inched her feet into her slippers, and walked to the window.

She smiled benignly, pleased to see that Finn's car was in the driveway.

"Those perfect, charming, young people!" she murmured aloud. There were the problems, of course. Serious, and she knew that she had to keep a wary eye on Finn. But really, they were like an Adonis and Venus, and so very beautiful together.

She was very proud of herself for having left the hot chocolate. It was a way for her to let Finn know that, whatever the problems, he could come to her at any time. Much better her than Morwenna or Joseph!

The yard was richly illuminated. There was so much moonlight, with the full moon just a few days away now.

Ah, well. They were together, as it should be. As it would be.

Martha laughed softly aloud. "Why, old woman, you'd be patting yourself on the back—if you could still reach it easily enough," she told herself in a whisper.

Very pleased with herself, she went back to bed, and slept soundly.

The bathroom was another very nice and sane concession to the modern day. Megan was grateful that Martha was so practical when it came to her home. The old was preserved where possible, and the new came in where it made sense. Martha couldn't have had the bath redone more than ten years ago. The shower stall was marble and tile with a frosted glass enclosure. The sink was a free-standing deep blue color, bringing the scheme from the bedroom into the bath. Megan quickly shed her clothing, wrinkling her nose as she did so—it was true that by the time they left each night, they smelled like the club.

Megan turned on the water, loving it hot. She poured bath gel into her hands from the container beneath the spray, slipped the net sponge from its little hook on the side wall, and began to lather.

She was amazed at the deep spark of sensuality that seeped into her from the heat of the water, the least touch of the netted sponge against her flesh. She was amazed to feel that she was arousing herself as she moved the material over her arms, to her shoulders, around her beasts, down to her belly. It was three in the morning, the world was strangely falling apart, and she was on fire . . . from steam . . . a touch of net . . . the stroke of her own hands.

This was horrible! All she had to do was ask him in. He would come . . .

Unless it was a lie. Unless the violence was real, unless he really had elsewhere to go. Unless he had been doing things like this . . . elsewhere, touching someone else . . . someone like Sara, so small and compact, so tightly configured, so well built, hypnotic, with her powers . . .

The glass doors opened. Finn was there. Naked,

bronze, absurdly beautiful in the most masculine way, and as fully aroused as she was herself, but even more evidently so.

"I take it you wanted me to come in?" he queried.

She saw both the smile in his eyes and the tension in his features as he spoke. The steam from the water rose between them, not unlike the blue fog, and yet . . .

He reached for the sponge. She realized she had been scrubbing herself in a circular motion, low, very low, well below the belly. He took it from her.

"Here, let me do that for you."

He did. Nylon . . . slightly scratchy, erotically abrasive . . . bath gel, slick, oily, foamy . . . moved against her intimately. She clung to Finn's shoulders, pressed against him, his touch, the movement of his hands . . .

She stroked her fingers down the length of his spine, curved them over the muscles of his buttocks, brushed around his hips, gliding the friction of her soapy fingers over the fullness of his erection. The touch of his fingers jerked against her, pressing against an erogenous zone so intently that she gasped out loud, suddenly certain that she was going to fall in the shower.

"Sh!" he whispered, catching her lips in an openmouthed, hungry kiss, then pulling her against him more tightly. "We don't want to wake Martha!"

Dizzy, aching, barely able to stand, Megan returned, "Hey, she left us the chocolate."

"We don't want to give the old bird erotic dreams, eh?" Finn whispered against her earlobe.

"Maybe she'd like a few."

"She's not sharing ours!" Finn said firmly, lifting her against him. It wasn't quite so easy to hold her, keeping her flush with his body, while turning off the shower spray and stepping from the shower stall. Megan had to keep from laughing as he made the stalwart attempt, somehow managing to accomplish what he had set out to do. He carried her from the bath, ready to drop her to the bed. Megan laughed and told him, "Wait!" She reached down to wrench up the bedcover and comforter while he groaned, straining to hold her in the awkward position. But then the covers were stripped and Megan was down and he fell on top of her, then rose slightly, drawing her hands over her head, kissing her again, deeply, with a slow and then frenzied passion, then sliding the length of himself against her, his body creating an absurdly erotic friction, the brush of his lips intent and intimate, over her nipples, the delicate sides of her breasts, sloping over her ribs, caressing her navel, falling below, bringing liquid fire to the flesh laid so vulnerable by his every stroke in the cascade of the shower. She surged up, drew him to her, wrapped herself around him, and lost all sense of anything but the depth of her hunger and passion for him, ultimately him, Finn, the feel of the man, so unique, unique to her, with all the things she loved. The length of his fingers, the scent, so subtle, yet so there, underlying everything. She was aware, incredibly aware, of every movement, every stroke of friction, making her rise to a greater fever, a frenzy, desperate, yearning. Aware . . . and not aware, because she had felt quite so much as if she flew, entered a realm not of the earth, soaring, wanting, hungering, reaching . . . a passion so great . . . a love so strong . . .

She escalated to a climax so volatile that she thought the house, the ground, the granite of New England shook. She clung to him, soaked, hair glued to her face, limbs trembling, heart racing. He held her in return.

Her heart finally slowed. New England became granite once again.

He smoothed the damp hair from her forehead, cradling her against him. Comfort settled in. Security. The sense of being loved, and cherished.

And then . . .

The fear.

She was too blissful. Too glad to be where she was, far too ready to feel that she was his wife, that everything she had felt, fear . . . no, *terror* . . . had been imagined. Power of suggestion. This was Finn, the man she had fallen head over heels in love with the moment she had met him, with whom she had lived, loved with a fever so many times, fought with, made up with . . . adored. Her husband. Her life.

And yet . . .

Those feelings could far too easily change. Had changed . . . there had been this morning, the feel of his fingers around her throat, holding her, the look in his eyes . . .

Don't fall asleep! she thought. *Please, God, don't let him fall asleep, don't ruin this!*

Finn rose. "I've got to get back to Huntington House," he said. He strode across the room, naked and lithe, shutting himself into the bathroom for a quick rinse-off shower.

Just as he had known to follow before, she knew not to follow now.

A moment later he was out and dressing quickly by the light of the fire, taut, bronzed, muscled flesh and lean sinew quickly covered.

He stopped back by the bed, smoothing her hair, kissing her forehead. "I love you," he said.

And then he was gone.

A moment later, Megan followed, hearing his car as he revved it, then sliding the bolt to make sure that the house was securely locked.

Andy Markharm woke in a cold sweat. One more night.

Then it would be All Hallow's Eve.

His small apartment was in a rooming house right in town. He seldom used the old Ford pickup that was so far gone was almost an antique, just like him. But in the last few days, he had begun to feel a greater fever than ever.

There was no traffic in the night. In a matter of minutes, he had come to the cemetery. He parked the old pickup. He'd brought a lantern, but that night, he didn't need it. The moon appeared almost as full as it would in two night's time. Despite the heavy green canopy of the trees, there was illumination.

The ground was more heavily trodden now than it had been just a few days before. He could see it, as he could see the remnants of candles, recently lit.

There were no cars where he had parked, yet as he pulled his pickax from the back of the old Ford, he felt a chill. There were sounds on the air, of course. Leaves rustling in the breeze that swept through such a copse. Just leaves, whispering . . .

He made his way through high grasses, over the broken stones set by the families of even those who had gone to unhallowed graves. The leaves seemed to be sighing, whispering, and then . . . it was as if there was music. Something that touched the air.

Like the blue fog.

Low, swirling, following him, there, wherever he walked, wherever he turned.

Andy, Andy . . . Andy!

The rustle of the trees seemed to call his name.

With greater determination, he moved on.

As he walked, he felt his sense of purpose become a sense of power. Yes, he knew, and by his knowledge, he would be the one to rise!

He fell to his knees before the broken marble statue.

The sound rose . . .

Andy, Andy, Andy!

He staggered to his feet, raising his ax, aware, suddenly, of the movement behind him.

He turned, roaring out. He looked into the sea of the night, and all that moved within it.

He raised the pickax . . .

And again, his cry rose in the night, but the chanting of leaves and breeze rose with the sound, and in time, all was silent.

It was late when Finn returned to Huntington House, nearly four in the morning. In the time he'd spent at Martha's, he'd forgotten his vow to the children. Understandably.

He hadn't felt so good since . . .

Before they'd come *here*, that was definite.

But as he slipped quietly through the front door, he cursed himself for his negligence, despite his deep sense of euphoria and satiation.

He hadn't needed to return earlier.

He was worried about more than checking out what the kids had seen.

Fallon was a scary man. Certainly not in the physical sense. He just seemed somewhat like a lurking crow. And if he did think that he was cooking up some kind of spells, then he wasn't all there. Then there was Susanna—the Wicked Witch of the West. She had just reminded Finn of an old-fashioned and very dour old maid.

She could not be accused of being overly pleasant.

The house seemed totally quiet when Finn came in and closed and locked the main door behind him. He stood still for a minute, listening, but the house was silent. After a moment, he walked through the foyer, into the dining area, and then to the parlor, or sitting room, beyond. The place was nothing more than a ghost town, empty and eerie in the silence and shadows caused by the numerous little night-lights.

He walked through to the kitchen, but it, too, was empty, with no sign of any manner of activity going on. Copper pots and utensils hung from the walls. The gleaming stainless steel sink and counter area—a concession to the modern day—shone in the dim night light. The great hearth, a fixture of the original seventeenth-century house, held a low burning fire, nothing but ash and embers and a bit of glowing red here and there.

Within the next few hours, the fire would be stoked, because apparently, a fire burning in the kitchen—where guests seldom dared wander—was supposed to be part of the hospitality of Huntington House.

Soon, Susanna would be up, getting breakfast ready for her early risers.

Finn walked on through to the side of the house with his lone guest room. He let himself in with his key, closed and locked his own door behind him, and held still for a moment, wondering what was wrong. Then he saw that one of the fragile curtains drifted slightly and he walked over to the balcony area, pulling the curtain away. The doors here were wide open.

A chill of unease shot through him. He stood there for a long moment, remembering that he had closed and locked the balcony entrance. No great mystery. The day maid had certainly come in and opened the doors to air out the room. She had forgotten to close them. Careless on her part, but since it hadn't appeared that anything had been stolen, certainly no big deal. He hesitated, then closed and locked the doors, and, just to be certain, began a complete search of the bedroom and bath. All was empty, even though he grit his teeth with a mixture of dread and anticipation as he wrenched back the shower curtain. Nothing.

He walked back out and assured himself that the balcony doors were secured, then dropped the borrowed cape he was wearing and sat to pull off his boots. He dropped his socks as well, and had started on the buttons to his shirt when he was suddenly certain that he heard a noise from the main house. He hesitated, then rose, barefoot and silent.

He crept back through the house, glancing at his watch as he did so. Four-thirty. Too early for Susanna to be up.

But as he traveled back to the main area of the house, he again heard noise. A soft sound, like a cabinet being carefully closed.

He padded through the dining room, and held still there for several seconds, just listening.

There were voices coming from the kitchen. So soft they might have been imagined—except that they weren't.

He steeled himself, gritted his teeth, and walked toward the kitchen. The heavy old wooden door between the kitchen and dining room—which had stood fully open before, was closed now. Finn set his hand on the antique knob and twisted quietly. To his great relief, though old, it was oiled, and did not screech as he slowly turned it to fully open, and pressed carefully upon the door, bringing it just slightly ajar so that he could observe what went on within.

The great hearth had been stoked back to life; the dark embers were fiery red, and laps of flame were reaching up to touch the huge kettle that was set on a cast iron swing bar.

Susanna was not present.

But old Fallon was certainly there.

He was on his scrawny knees before the huge kettle and burning fire, chanting to himself as he cast powders or herbs into the kettle from a carved wooden casket in his hands. His words were low, very low, but he cast some of the casket's contents into the kettle as he moved his lips, then spoke the same words louder, casting some of the powder onto the fire.

Flames leaped and embers scattered. Fallon kept chanting.

Finn felt his jaw lock so tightly he was afraid he'd soon snap bone. He pushed open the door fully and stepped into the kitchen, angry, and also uneasy, and more irritated with both himself and Fallon that he could be made uneasy by such a display of ridiculousness.

"What the hell are you doing?" Finn demanded.

Chapter 15

Startled, Fallon cried out, dropped the casket, and jumped to his feet, staring at Finn with alarm.

Then his look of fear turned to one of anger and resentment.

"What the hell are you doing?" he demanded huffily of Finn. He pointed a bony finger at him. "Ruining everything you fool! Ruining everything."

"Mr. Fallon, it's obvious you're concocting some kind of evil spell—"

"Don't be ridiculous, you young fool!" Fallon said with such energy that Finn was almost taken aback.

"You're not concocting some kind of spell?" Finn said accusingly.

"Of course, I am. I'm a Wiccan, young man, which is none of your business. And if you listened to anything said, you'd know that Wiccans do no evil—they can't. Evil comes back threefold on a Wiccan, and therefore, true Wiccans would never do evil!"

Finn was amazed to see how sincere and passionately earnest Fallon seemed to be.

"Mind if I ask just what you are doing then?" Finn said.

"Yes, I mind, it's none of your business," Fallon said. But he stared at Finn and shook his head. "A spell, yes. For protection."

"Protection?"

"From the dead, and those not of this earth," Fallon said. Turning away, he hunched back to his knees. He cast something else—green in color, an herb of some sort—into the cauldron. And as he chanted this time, Finn heard the words.

"Potion of magick, have thou the life,
Save us from the evil strife,
Blessed be all those living, and those deceased,
From pain and agony released,
Sorrow and fear have now ceased,
Let them help save us from the beast,
Keep from us the wicked, strong and rife,
Let them not know this life,
Grant us safety, grant us peace
Upon a body, give no lease,
As it is willed, so mote it be."

Finn wasn't sure if he imagined it or not, but it seemed that sparks rose from the simmering cauldron, or from the fire beneath. Fallon kept his head down as if he remained in humble prayer. Then he stood, staring fiercely at Finn.

"If you had a whit of sense in your head, young man, you'd be on your knees."

"Mr. Fallon, I'm not a Wiccan."

"Not a Wiccan, eh? And that would keep you from prayer? I'd thought at first that maybe you had something extra, something special about you. That you were strong, strong enough to keep evil from rising. But you're a fool. Not a Wiccan! So get yourself into one of the churches, or temples. There are but two powers in this world, and you may call the great and the good by the name of a supreme being, a god of all gods, or you may look for peace and kindness in a slew of gentle entities. Evil is the master of the other side, and by what name you call evil, it matters not, it's all the same. Can't you feel it coming, boy? Haven't you seen the fog? Don't mock me, just be glad that I create potions and prayer, and keep this house from evil!"

The old man had to be really crazy. He believed so fully in what he was saying.

Except that . . .

Finn had seen the fog. *Fog.* A weather phenomena. It came and went so strangely. *This was New England, if you don't like the weather, wait a few hours, it will change.*

No, even in New England, fog did not come and go so quickly.

He was suddenly tempted to ask Fallon if he'd heard about a demon called Bac-Dal.

He held his tongue. Here was old Fallon, grumpy, Ichabod-like, stern and straight, like the Pilgrims of old, casting herbs into a cauldron.

He didn't dare trust Fallon.

"Certainly, Mr. Fallon. If your intent is to keep the property safe, then, well, more power to you, sir."

Fallon pointed a long bony finger at Finn. "Don't mock any of it, boy. Like I said, if you've got any sense at all, get yourself into a house of prayer. Whatever kind." He shook his head. "I'll not be seeing you after All Hallow's Eve. And that's a fact."

"You're right. We're taking off first thing the following morning."

"Aye-uh, boy. One way or the other. You'll be gone. Now, leave me be. I run this place. And it's not for the guests to be nosy and invading the kitchen late at night. So . . ."

"Good night, Mr. Fallon," Finn said.

He turned and left the kitchen, walking back through the silent house to his wing, and his room. Once there, he very carefully ascertained that he was locked in.

Fallon's actions disturbed him.

Oddly enough, it was because he believed Fallon. The old man's chants and spells seemed entirely benign, as if he did feel the need to protect the house.

He also wanted to talk to the fellow, question him.

No matter how sincere he had seemed, and how innocent the words of his chant, Fallon wasn't to be trusted. No one here could be trusted.

He was exhausted; it was ridiculously late—or early— whichever way you looked at it. He desperately wanted to sleep; he was afraid to sleep. Megan had left him, but in all good sense, he had to be glad.

Because he didn't know what he did in the dead of the night.

He punched his pillow, determined on getting some sleep.

Megan should have slept well. She was happy when Finn left, as if she remained enwrapped with his warmth. He seemed to understand everything. He loved her.

But she tossed and turned for a long while, and when at last she slept, the dreams plagued her again.

It began with the sound of her name. Soft, echoed in her mind, whispered compellingly, erotically. Like a siren's call, that whisper-breeze of her name could not be ignored. She felt as if she drifted in response, following.

She returned to the forest, and the unhallowed cemetery.

Old Andy wasn't there to tell her tales this time.

The trees created a dark green canopy, and the place smelled richly of vegetation and the earth. She felt the pads of her feet touch down on damp ground and tufts of grass. She knew she was walking to the strange marble statue she had assumed to be an angel, but of course, there, in the unhallowed graveyard, was a demon instead.

She walked through the fog, hearing her name being called. There were whispers all around her. She was afraid to go forward, and yet compelled to do so.

She knew she was being drawn to the statue. There were little markers in the ground, for others who had lived long ago. Spirits seemed to rise like wraiths, or a part of the fog, as she moved. They whispered, sang . . . or chanted. Wisps of the fog, or the spirits, swept around her, and like the voices, urged her on.

She thought she saw faces, and she should know them, but she couldn't see clearly.

"So perfect," someone whispered.

"The voice of a nightingale."

Not that perfect! she wanted to cry. She wanted to tell them that they didn't want her, that the demon Bac-Dal didn't want her.

"In death, so there is life," someone else whispered.

"The time has yet to come," came another murmur.

"But He would touch, He would see, He would know!"

A figure stood before her. She wanted to turn and run, and she managed to stop walking. Megan argued with herself that she was a creature of free will, that she could fight the force that seemed to be carrying her forward. And so she could.

She looked back.

Yet . . . it seemed as if she still looked forward.

A figure, like the first, was behind her. Both wore capes with cowls, dark and swirling as if there were a great wind, but there couldn't be, because the fog didn't lift, it drifted and swirled around her feet.

She didn't know whether to run ahead, or escape, and run in the other direction. She heard her name being called again. Softly, tauntingly. She didn't realize she had begun to move again, but her steps were bringing her closer to the entity before her. Through the blue fog, she saw a blaze of red. Pinpoints . . . eyes. She couldn't really see, but she had a sense of something fetid, rotting, dead. Instinct warned her that she must get away. She was not being held, and yet, it was as if there were arms about her, luring her ever forward. Ivory fingers seemed to dance in the blue light, beckoning.

Megan, Megan, Megan . . .

Then . . .

The creature. The creature she had seen at the museum. The face of a man, but with horns at the temples, a sharp, jutting chin, evil, burning eyes.

Megan . . . !

With a smile, he whispered her name, intimately, as if it were a caress.

She turned at last, running; there was the figure behind her. She must reach it, because help had to come from behind . . .

She ran and ran and ran, and came to a dead stop.

And there he was once again. The figure that had seemed to be behind her . . . but was not. It was the horned creature, who had been before her.

She screamed, seeing him stretch open the great wings of the cloak he wore, ready to entrap her within the folds.

Fingers, yes, touching her now, stroking over her face, her arms, her arms . . . the arms tightening around her.

She screamed, breaking free.

"No . . . I ran away, away. I ran away. To the other!"

The creature began to laugh and laugh. And again the voice came, like an evil caress.

"Don't you see, we are one and the same."

She awoke with a violent start.

Daylight flooded the room. She could hear birds chirping.

She was drenched in sweat. She swung her legs off the bed, eager to reach the bathroom and douse her face in cold water. The room was chilly and she fumbled around with her toes to find her slippers.

She looked down.

Little pieces of dirt dusted the carpet. She frowned, then lifted her feet. The soles were encrusted with earth and bits of grass.

Impossible . . .

She pressed her face between her hands, swallowing back a scream. She leaped up and headed immediately into the shower, furiously scrubbing her feet, because, once the dirt was gone, the impossible image was gone as well. She swore, for the water, whirling into the drain, carried a touch of streaky red . . .

Blood.

She'd scratched the bottom of her foot. She couldn't recall the pain, or the blood on the sole when she had seen the dirt, but then . . . her feet had been dirty. Now, they were bleeding as well, so it seemed.

Had she walked outside in her sleep? Lord, these nightmares were truly getting to be too much. So real . . .

She should have called Martha—told her about the dream, and her feet.

Martha! She wanted to see Martha right away, and feel her practical sense of sanity and reason!

Megan finished her shower, dressed quickly, and raced out of the room. "Aunt Martha!"

There was no answer, just a note on the kitchen counter. "Out shopping, dear—make yourself at home!"

So, she'd have to wait, but she would talk to Aunt Martha, and there would be sense made of it. Maybe she had taken a few steps out when Finn had left last night . . . maybe they had dragged the dirt when they had come in, and she had picked it up from the carpet onto her bare feet then. Certainly, that was the logical explanation.

Finn.

She wished he was with her. She should tell him . . .

Maybe not. He'd been insisting it was her, that she had dreamed things, that he had not. But that wasn't true. He was having dreams as well. Behaving far too strangely.

Better to talk to Martha. To someone with a little distance. She couldn't tell Finn about this, and she certainly couldn't tell Morwenna, who would read far too much into it.

She tried to tell herself again that they must have tracked dirt in onto the carpet.

Ridiculous, and she knew it.

There had been too much dirt for such a simple explanation! Whether she wanted to believe it or not, that was the truth!

But then again—she hadn't been walking in the woods in the wee hours of the morning, that was for certain!

Maybe, she forced herself to admit, she had been sleepwalking, and actually had gone outside, and then walked back in and crawled into bed. She couldn't have wandered all around town, and made it out to the cemetery!

And yet . . .

The vivid memory of the dream was uncannily real.

Despite the late hour he went to sleep, Finn was up and in the dining room by ten. Susanna gave him something of an evil glare, since he had made it just in the nick of time for her to cook, according to the hours listed on the Huntington House brochure. He was pleased to see that though there were no adults remaining in the room, Joshua and Ellie were still at the table, apparently waiting for their parents to go back to their rooms for their coats.

When Susanna was out of the room, he leaned forward and whispered to the children. "Mr. Fallon is a Wiccan. He told me that he was preparing a protection potion for the house."

Ellie sat back in her chair, gaping.

Joshua shook his head doubtfully. "Do you think he was telling you the truth?"

"Well, I heard him chanting one of his spells, and it sounded like a good one to me."

"How come he looks so creepy, then?" Ellie asked.

"I don't know, I guess he's just a creepy-looking guy," Finn said.

"I still think we should keep an eye on him," Joshua said.

"Well, we can do that. And hey, you two, you stick with your folks around here, no matter what. People can be weird, you know. Most people are great, but you know, there are those who would hurt others. And Halloween can be fun, or a little kooky, too, right?"

"Right," Joshua said gravely.

"Creepy—like Mr. Fallon," Ellie said.

He nodded with a half smile. Actually, after last night, his own opinion of Fallon had changed. He had looked like a truly pathetic Ichabod Crane then. Somehow, roles had changed, and Finn hadn't felt like a wayward, maybe dangerous, guest, but somewhat more mature than an old man chanting spells in a kitchen.

He smiled again at the kids. "We'd better hush for now—Susanna is bringing my eggs."

Susanna came back in, obviously huffing and sniffing at the rudeness of guests who came into breakfast at the last minute. Finn smiled at her as sweetly as he could manage.

"Thank you so very much; you're so kind."

When Susanna left again, Ellie burst into laughter. Both children were still laughing when their parents came for them. They looked at Finn, puzzled, but seemed pleased enough to see the kids happy. They all told him good-bye, and to have a nice day.

Finn ate quickly in the empty dining room, then left Huntington House. He walked down to the historic district, and wandered around for a while. When it reached eleven-thirty, he decided to head over to the historic hotel. As he walked, he wondered if he'd actually find Lucian and Jade DeVeau. He hadn't thought of it the night before, but people usually made reservations a year in advance to stay in such a place for Halloween. He doubted that the DeVeaus had actually managed to get in—they had probably been forced to find other accommodations, but they might still have gone there, just to see the place or have a meal.

Or wait for him.

The lobby that afternoon was filled with women and a few men in fancy black dress and cloaks—a Wiccans luncheon was obviously taking place. There were other tourists as well, some gaping at the Wiccans, some trying to pretend that the sight of so many people in cloaks like these was nothing out of the ordinary.

He walked up to the desk and inquired if a Mr. and Mrs. DeVeau had checked in, and he was surprised to hear the clerk reply that yes, certainly, they had checked in late the night before. The clerk would be happy to ring them for Finn. He didn't need to. As he stood there, he heard himself called.

"Finn!"

He turned around.

For a moment, the sight of Lucian DeVeau standing in the lobby was as unnerving as any other event that had taken place since he had come. The man was about his own height. He wasn't dressed in a Wiccan cape, but rather something of a long black railroad duster, increasing his appearance of height, enhancing the darkness of his hair and eyes. Jade walked up behind her husband; she was wearing a long, light wool tailored coat, in black as well, and it created the opposite effect. Her eyes and hair were light, giving her an aura of something almost angelic. *Beauty and the Beast,* he thought wryly. Except that Lucian had the kind of looks that were classic and compelling, hardly the image of a beast.

"Hi," he said simply, staring at the two. Then he walked forward, shaking Lucian's hand, accepting a kiss on the cheek from Jade. "You made it. No problems getting into the hotel? I was thinking about it after we talked. They're booked so far ahead here for the Halloween events. I was afraid you might have difficulty."

"Oh, they were booked," Jade said lightly, glancing at her husband. "Lucian talked with the manager. They were able to find a little room that hadn't been rented because of a few problems. We just assured them we didn't mind. So . . . it's good to see you, Finn."

"Thanks." He hesitated. They had said that they were coming anyway. He didn't know whether to believe that or not. And now . . . he wasn't sure if he was going to be able to talk to them, tell them about the insanity going on that might all be in his head. "Um, thanks for coming," he said.

"We're pleased to be here," Lucian said. He sounded very serious. Not like a man about to enjoy a brief vacation.

Still, Finn found himself answering lightly. "It's an incredible place, of course. They've done a great job with their various events. There are all kinds of stands for children, where they can create jack-o'-lanterns, make Halloween cutouts, and all kinds of other little artistic creations. There are street entertainers, wonderful stores—and great museums here. Geared toward the witchcraft period, and others as well. There are wonderful places that teach about colonial America, and seafaring—the great whaling days, and all. It's truly wonderful."

"Yes, it's a wonderful place," Lucian agreed. "Have you had lunch yet?"

Finn decided not to say that he'd just had breakfast. "No. There are dozens of places to go, of course. And if you're seafood lovers, you've got to try the scrod."

"I've an idea. Let's just start walking and see what we find," Jade said.

"Great."

They left the hotel lobby and headed for the street. The day before Halloween had come, and the place seemed busier than ever. The day was cool and crisp with a slight breeze, stirring up the autumn leaves that lay on the ground. As they walked, Finn pointed out a number of places of interest, then paused. "Sorry. Maybe you've been here before."

"Strangely enough, I haven't," Lucian said.

Finn looked at him. "Not so strange. I'd never been here before. I'm sure a lot of Americans have never seen lots of places in the country. Sorry—are you American?"

"Yes, it's home now," Lucian said.

Before he could say more, Jade broke in. "Someone is waving to you, Finn, from across the street."

Finn looked. Darren Menteith was on the corner opposite them, with Lizzie on her leash.

"A friend?" Lucian asked.

"Well, an acquaintance," Finn said. "A good acquaintance," he said, and explained ruefully, "A fan. Come over, I'll introduce you."

They passed by a group of schoolchildren in costumes and their harried teachers who were trying to keep them all together. As they neared Darren, Lizzie began to growl.

"How strange, she's the sweetest Dane," Finn said.

"Lizzie!" Darren said, distressed as they approached, and getting a better grip on his dog's leash.

She started to bark, her attention all on Lucian. Lucian, however, didn't seem dismayed. He approached the dog, his eyes on hers, his hand extended, and lowered himself to a hunkered down position, touching her head. Lizzie immediately sat, and started licking his hand.

"Wow. Are you a dog trainer?" Darren said.

"No, I just have a way with animals," Lucian told him. "I seem to scare them at first, then get on fairly well."

"Darren," Finn said, hesitating just slightly, "these are friends of mine from home. Lucian and Jade DeVeau. Jade, Lucian, Darren Menteith."

Darren extended a hand, still staring at Lucian. "Pleased to meet you."

"A pleasure," Jade said, and Lucian nodded.

"Beautiful dog," he commented.

"Yeah, thanks," Darren said, still staring.

"Are you from the area?" Jade asked politely.

It seemed as if Darren had to pull his eyes from Lucian's to respond to his wife. "Ah, yes. I am. Is it your first visit?"

"Yes, and Finn is going to show us around some, later," Jade said. "If you've any suggestions, of course, as a native, we'd love to hear them."

"Peabody Essex Museum," Darren said. "Don't miss it."

"Thanks."

"Well, we're heading out for some lunch," Finn said. "Are you coming to the hotel this evening?"

"Wouldn't miss it," Darren told him, but he was staring at Lucian again.

"Good. We'll see you there."

"Yeah, of course," Darren said. "Well, later, then. Come on Lizzie."

Darren started to move on. Finn, Jade, and Lucian did the same. But halfway down the block, Finn paused and looked back.

Darren hadn't gone anywhere. He remained at the corner, Lizzie sitting at his feet. He was staring at them.

Finn raised a hand and waved. Darren didn't seem to notice. He was staring at Lucian once again.

"How about this place?" Jade said.

She had stopped in front of one of the area restaurants that offered back terrace seating, with heat.

"Looks like we can find a quiet corner," Lucian said.

"Ah, sure," Finn said. He paused again, though, before following the other two in.

Darren was still standing at the corner, staring. He hadn't moved. And once again, he didn't seem to notice when Finn raised a hand, and waved.

"Quite frankly, I don't even begin to know what I'm worried about," Morwenna told Megan. "I mean, were anything bad to happen, it should be at midnight, and you and Finn will be playing at midnight, so everything should be just fine. It worries me, however, that I can't be there, but you know that it's incredibly major to us, and I am the head of my coven, and actually, there will be dozens of Wiccans—maybe hundreds!—from across the country taking part in our rites, and I am actually part of the major ceremony here, so . . . still, I wish I could be there."

"Morwenna," Megan said firmly. "You're right. Finn and I will both be playing at the hotel at midnight. We're not off until one, so there's no way we can be in any danger."

Megan wished she had never spoken about her strange dream with her cousin. Morwenna had taken it far too seriously.

"Right," Morwenna said. "Hm." She kept staring at Megan. "Still . . ."

"Still what?"

Morwenna shook her head. "I don't know. It's still all been just too strange. I can't forget what I felt when I did your reading the first day you and Finn were here. And Sara . . . she said the vibes coming off Finn were deadly."

"I thought you liked Finn."

"I do. He's gorgeous. Sexy. Talented. He seems to really love you."

"Then . . . ?" Megan said.

"He's dangerous."

"To me. That's what you keep saying."

"You pointed out to me that he went through a wild time in high school, and that he's taken all kinds of martial arts. Put together a streak of violence with some real training, and you've got a dangerous man. But it's not . . . any of that."

"Then what is it?"

Morwenna hesitated. "A streak of evil."

"You think Finn has a streak of evil?"

Morwenna sighed. "I don't want to think that. And maybe . . . maybe it's not really Finn with the streak of evil."

They were in the back of Morwenna's shop. Joseph, Sara, Jamie, and another girl, Cindy, were manning the shop, and despite the insanity going on in the main part of the store—people suddenly determined that they had to have a "real" witch's cape for Halloween night—Morwenna didn't seem in the least dismayed that she was taking time out.

"What on earth are you talking about?" Megan demanded.

"I don't know myself. Something creepy. Maybe not believable. But then again, we all know that there's good and evil. So, if we believe in magic at all—"

"Morwenna, make sense."

"Okay, Miss Catholic," Morwenna said. "You believe in God, right?"

"Yes."

"Then you must believe in the devil."

"Morwenna, I'm one of those people who happens to like church. The music, the words, the sense of healing. I don't believe in every bit of doctrine, I think that many things taught are parables, and like many people believe, I think that, if there is a hell, it's just the absence of God, or goodness, or peace, or whatever."

Megan spoke with assurance, fully aware that she was lying. She had seen the creature in the unhallowed graveyard, and she had seen it again, in her dreams. By day, all of it seemed silly. But when the darkness came . . .

"Finn has been wonderful," she said firmly. "Last night . . . I was nearly mugged in the parking lot, and he was there. He didn't insist on my coming back to Huntington House, he just followed me back to Martha's. And he was the one who insisted on leaving."

Morwenna frowned. "You were nearly mugged?"

"In the parking lot."

"Did Finn catch the guy?"

"No . . . he disappeared."

"Disappeared? Like—into thin air?"

"Almost. They fought . . . and the guy was gone."

"You saw him? You could describe him? If so, you should call the police right away. They're afraid that the guy who murdered that poor girl in Boston might be a serial killer. One of those lunatics who kills by the full moon. Which is tomorrow night, you know. Were you able to describe the guy?"

Megan shook her head, feeling more uncertain all the time. "No, I didn't get to see him."

"Could Finn describe him?"

"I doubt it. The fog was really heavy."

Morwenna stared at her a long time.

"What?" Megan insisted.

"Are you sure someone was out there—other than Finn?"

Megan fought to keep from trembling. *No, she wasn't sure! She'd had her own fears the night before. But there had to have been. She couldn't believe that Finn . . .*

"Why would Finn need to mug me in the parking lot?"

"Maybe he was afraid that you were really through

with him, that you would refuse to talk with him alone, be with him alone. Once he pretended to save you . . . well, you'd have to trust in him, right?"

"Morwenna, I am getting the most crossed vibes from you in history. You like Finn. You and Joseph are friendly with him, even when I'm not around. But you're suggesting that he's immorally devious, and might even have stopped by Boston on his way to reach me in Maine just to take a night out and commit a horrible murder!"

Morwenna looked distressed. "That's just the point— I'm receiving the most mixed vibes myself—from Finn."

"Morwenna, you're my cousin, and I love you. But I love Finn, too. So if you want to cast around unfounded suspicions, don't do it with me!"

"All right, all right, sorry . . . it's just that—"

"Don't!"

"No, what I've been getting at in a roundabout way is that you both need to start looking into past history. I mean, let's face it, your lives—your dreams, at least— have been ridiculously weird. All right, here it is—"

"No! I don't want to hear anything ridiculous."

"You have to. Because I think that Finn just might be a demon."

"A demon!"

"Right. You've really got to read some of the old things I've come across. If—"

"Morwenna, I've got to go." Megan stood angrily, staring down at her.

"No, wait."

Megan leaned upon the desk, staring hard at her cousin. "My husband is not a demon!"

"Megan, please—"

Furious, Megan turned. She didn't note the way that Joseph, Jamie, Sara, and even the new girl, watched her as she left.

*   *   *

The restaurant was fairly full, but out on the terrace, there was seating available. And there was a corner, secluded from the other tables by palms that must have been carefully tended by the owners throughout the winter months. The hostess had been bringing them to another table, but the mere suggestion from Lucian that the secluded seating would be better had brought about the change.

They all ordered coffee to drink. Finn didn't give a damn about what he ate, but Lucian and Jade studied the menu, and it wasn't until after they'd ordered and their coffee and water had been served that they both gave their full attention to Finn and the matter at hand.

With both of them staring at him, he suddenly felt ridiculous. "I . . . well, I hope you two were really coming here, because I probably shouldn't have called you. Anything I have to say is going to sound really ridiculous."

"Oh, we like the ridiculous," Jade said, glancing at her husband. "What's been going on, what made you call?"

He shrugged. "As I said on the phone, dreams. I would imagine that Freud could explain it all away easily enough. Except that . . . well, it seems that Megan and I are both having them, and if I understand my wife correctly, they are frighteningly similar."

"What's happening in the dreams?" Lucian asked.

Finn hesitated again. "I'm either hurting or killing my wife."

"Ah," Jade murmured.

"Ah?" Finn repeated.

"The dreams started when you came here?" Lucian said.

Finn nodded.

"But nothing—*nothing*—unusual happened to either of you before then?" Lucian asked.

"No," Finn said honestly, then he frowned, and paused. "I—actually, yes."

"What?" Jade said.

"I'm afraid to even say this, because . . . well, you'll understand in a minute. Megan and I had been separated. Misunderstandings—normal misunderstandings, nothing to do with dreams—and I drove up to Maine to talk to her. I'd been driving really hard and I wound up stopping in Boston . . . and I wasn't drunk or anything, but I must have passed out in a pub. I woke up on the street, being prodded by a cop. I've never done anything like that before in my life. It was as if I just lost the time, and any memory of having gotten from the pub and down the street. I chalked that up to being exhausted and road weary. But, I guess you could say it was bizarre." He hesitated. "I hate to mention it, because that was the same weekend that young woman was murdered in Boston."

"Ah," Lucian murmured this time.

"Hey, don't 'ah' me there. I know myself. I never saw that girl, much less murdered her."

"We're not suggesting that you might have done so," Jade said gently. "But it's interesting. Go on."

Finn lifted his hands, feeling flushed, wondering what in hell had made him mention the entire Boston episode.

"Nothing, really. Just dreams. And then . . ."

"Then?" Lucian said. "Go on. What was the 'then' that made you call us?"

"Bac-Dal," Finn said flatly.

"Bac-Dal," Jade murmured.

"Well, you've heard of the 'demon,' of course," Finn said, "since you have a chapter devoted to him in your book."

"Yes. But my book didn't make you call," Jade said.

Finn shook his head. "My wife's cousin is a witch. A

Wiccan. She was all excited and said that I had to go to a bookstore and read this old text about a man named Cabal Thorne who came here, not long after the witch hysteria, and intended to bring Bac-Dal to life. No one wanted to cry 'witch' or 'Satanist' because so many innocent people had just suffered. So, apparently, I guess, people here got together and murdered Cabal Thorne and buried him in unhallowed ground somewhere without the local authorities knowing about it. Or maybe they knew about it, and sanctioned it. According to his own writings, he murdered a young woman. He had gained so much power that he just walked into her home, took her with her parents' leave, and then murdered her. For the blood that he needed, I imagine. Or the sacrifice, or whatever."

"Well, what do you think?" Lucian said, looking at Jade.

She shrugged, and turned her attention to Finn. "I'd like to find out more about this Cabal Thorne. Can you take us to the bookstore or wherever it was that you learned about him?"

"Sure."

Their meals arrived. Lucian and Jade had opted for the special of the day, fresh Maine lobster.

He'd had the scrod. Ridiculous, but it's what Megan would have ordered.

"Tell us more about the people you've met here," Lucian urged him.

"About the people here . . . well, as you can imagine, there are many. As I said, my wife's cousin is a Wiccan. Morwenna and her husband, Joseph, own a witchcraft store, and of their employees, I've come to know a girl named Sara—who tried to convince me that I was the most evil being in the world, and now thinks she's helping me anyway, for some reason. There's also a young man at the shop named Jamie, who seems to be all right. My wife has a distant relative living here, too—Aunt Martha. She's the epitome of the stereotypical New Englander, sound sense, logic, all that. Megan is staying with her, out at her place. That's the family. The Wiccan and her place, and her total opposite. Aunt Martha seems to think that they're all commercial, cashing in on Salem's reputation. I'm trying to think of anyone with whom I've spent time. Huntington House is managed—along with Susanna McCarthy—by a fellow named Fallon. I caught him cooking up Halloween herbs in the kitchen last night. Says he was making spells for protection, but he scared the daylights out of a couple of the kids in the place the night before. I don't know . . . I fell for his story. Could have been wrong, he is definitely a weird man. Susanna cooks, supervises staff such as the day maids, and takes the reservations. She's a dour old sort—amazing that they keep people coming back all the time with those two in charge. Who else . . . ? A guy named Sam Tartan hired us for the hotel, and he's got a body guard. Guy's name is—believe it or not—Adam Spade. Let's see . . . ah. My wife has an old friend here. Mike Smith. He runs the new museum, down-to-earth type. No-nonsense guy. I should like him. I don't. The girl running the ticket booth for him is Gayle Sawyer, and she's a strange little thing, looks Ivy League by day, and Goth by night. There's a cop who really helped us out one night when a guy got drunk and frisky at the bar—Theo Martin. And he has a brother, Eddie—the guy with the bookshop where Sara brought me to read about Cabal Thorne. They're identical twins, by the way. Let's see . . . there's old Andy Markham. He's the one with whom it all started, I think. When we first arrived, we went to one of his 'storytelling' sessions. That night, Megan woke up screaming. Then Fallon came to the door, apparently certain that I was beating her. The thing is . . .

318   *Heather Graham*

it's like the dreams never stop. And . . . you'll see tonight. There's also this fog . . . okay, so it's New England. There's often fog. But this is one strange fog."

"What about Huntington House?" Lucian asked.

"I told you about Fallon and Susanna."

"What about the other guests?"

"Well, unless they're hiding people in the basement, I only know about two other couples, Brad and Mary—mid to late thirties, they're the ones with the children, Joshua and Ellie. The other couple are in their late twenties, maybe early thirties. John and Sally. She's very pretty, and they've both been pleasant. I think all of them heard Megan screaming that night, but they seem to believe she really did have a nightmare." He hesitated, then shrugged. "Because Megan's family lived in this area for generations, rumor spreads fast. Before we split up, we had a fight. In truth, Megan hit me with a loaf of bread. By the time the story traveled around, I was a wife beater, and the bread was a bottle of wine, or some such thing like that. I'm not sure who talked, but you know, maybe Aunt Martha, maybe Morwenna or Joseph . . . anyway, by the time we actually checked into Huntington House, I think we both had a reputation, in old Mr. Fallon's eyes, anyway."

"Rumors will spread," Jade said, moving spinach around on her plate.

"And actually, there are so many people here now," Lucian said with a shrug, "you've probably talked to dozens that you don't even remember. But let's go back. When we met with you in New Orleans, you'd been married, you'd split up—and you'd made that trip to Maine, via Boston, to find your wife?"

"Right." Finn said, staring at him. "Is that supposed to mean something?"

"I don't know," Lucian said. "Maybe." He hesitated a minute. "You had no connection to this area, though, before you came here then—or through here—at that time?"

"No," Finn said, shaking his head. "I'd never been in Salem. I know that. Not even as a child, or an infant. Wait—I might have been in Salem. I drove to Maine from Louisiana, coming through the Boston area, and I stopped somewhere soon after for lunch. But as to a connection? If you can call ordering a hamburger a connection, I might have one."

"But you and Megan had been married a while, right?"

He nodded. "Yes. So . . . ?"

"And everyone knew that you were married, right?"

"Everyone? Well, everyone who knew us knew that we were married. We didn't hide it, or anything. So? I'm not sure that anyone else would care about our marital situation. Is that important in any way?"

"Again, I don't really know," Lucian said. "More coffee anyone? Dessert? Because, if not, I'd really like to get to that bookshop."

Morwenna was in the basement, standing by the altar.

Candles burned.

Head bowed, she stood in deep reflection.

She stared at the flames, burning around her, narrowing her eyes, letting the light filter, and then diffuse.

She lowered her head.

There was a change . . .

She felt it. And, of course, it meant that they would have to make changes as well.

Tonight . . .

Chapter 16

Irritated with Morwenna and far more uneasy than she wanted to allow, Megan idly wandered through the streets, smiling at the kids at the play stations, enjoying their costumes.

She wished that Aunt Martha had made it back to the house that morning, but after whiling around for a few hours with nothing to do, Megan had called for a cab and come into town.

And now . . .

She wondered where Finn was. In town somewhere. Maybe meeting up with the reviewer and her husband. She wished that she were with them. They'd been a nice couple, and the woman, Jade, had certainly done good things for her and Finn.

The day was cool, but not cold. She bought a large mocha from one of the coffee bars and wandered toward the common. She was sitting on a park bench when she saw Darren, throwing a Frisbee for Lizzie. As the dog caught the Frisbee, Darren laughed, and moved toward someone, calling out. Megan frowned, shielding her eyes from the sun, curious to see if she knew the person with Darren. She thought she heard a woman's voice, rising, saying his name. More curious, and glad to give thought to something other than her own strange dilemma, she looked around the area surrounding Darren's position, intrigued that he might have a girl-friend. But the woman with the voice she had heard was nowhere to be seen, not through the different clusters of people in the common. Megan couldn't see anything at all except for the family group that was greeting one another warmly almost directly in front of her bench.

But a moment later, Darren was out in the grass, throwing the Frisbee again. He saw Megan, and waved. A few seconds later, he and Lizzie came running toward her.

"Hey!"

"Hey, Darren, how are you?" Lizzie, knowing she was wanted and loved, got a little carried away and crawled up halfway on the bench, halfway on Megan. Laughing, Megan hugged the dog.

"Lizzie! Down, girl!" Darren said with dismay.

"She's fine, don't worry, I love her," Megan said. She scratched Lizzie's ears and looked at Darren. "Where's your friend?"

"My friend?"

"I thought I saw you with a young woman," Megan said.

Darren stared at her, and slowly shook his head. "No. You must have been mistaken."

"Oh, sorry. I guess so."

He laughed. "I wish. No girlfriend at the moment."

"Well, you're young, you know. Your entire life is ahead of you."

"Right. Like you're old."

She laughed. "I have a few years on you!"

"Not that many." He grinned, joining her on the bench. "But then, alas, you're married anyway, right? You're still married, huh? Or really married, I should say."

"Yes, I'm really married, and still married. Why?" Megan said.

"Oh, I just saw your husband earlier."

"He does go places without me," Megan said dryly.

"He was with a couple."

"Ah, yes." She still wondered why he hadn't wanted her to be with them from the start. "They're . . . friends. From back home."

"I see," he said, staring at her. He didn't see. "How come you're not with them?" He asked pointedly.

She was irritated by the question and tempted to tell him it was none of his business. But she knew that her own mood might have been better, and there was no need to offend Darren. "I . . . needed to run into Morwenna's this morning," she said. She forced a casual smile. "I'll catch up with them later."

He nodded, staring past her. "Hey, look, there's Mr. Smith."

She turned to see that Mike Smith, a brown bag in hand, was heading onto the common. Since it was a pleasant day, he had probably opted for a lunch hour outdoors.

"You two know each other?"

"Of course. Students do frequent museums, you know," he said, grinning. "And it can be a fairly small place, you know." He turned and called out, "Hey, Mr. Smith!"

Mike had been preoccupied with his thoughts, apparently, but his head jerked up when Darren hailed him. He smiled, coming in their direction.

"Hey, I went in to see the new exhibit the other day," Darren said. "It's great."

"Thanks. I worked hard on it." He smiled down at Megan. "Hey, Megan. I don't know, but this seems strange, seeing you alone in the park."

"Oh, well . . . I was just . . . sitting. It's really a beautiful day."

"Yeah, I guess I thought the same."

"It's a beautiful day, for the end of October," Darren said. "But I think I've worn Lizzie out. Or she's worn me out. I'm going to get going. Hey—see you tonight, Megan."

"Thanks—it's been really nice for you to come every night. Especially since students tend to be on a budget."

"Hey, I got a free CD," he said grinning, then saluting, he walked off.

"Nice kid," Mike said.

"Yes, he seems to be."

"Smart as a whip, too."

"That's good to hear."

Mike nodded, watching after Darren. "He's going into architecture. Hope he stays around here after he graduates. You should see some of the horrors they come up with for new buildings in the area." He stared at his brown bag, then at her, smiling slowly. "Have you still got some time? Or are you supposed to be meeting your husband somewhere?"

"I have some time. Why?"

"Well, I've lost my appetite for canned tuna and wilting lettuce. Thought maybe I could talk you into having some lunch with me."

She hesitated. If Finn found her, he might be furious.

But Finn was off with the couple from New Orleans. And she hadn't been invited. And she was out here, sitting alone, because she'd actually gotten into an argument with Morwenna—defending Finn.

"Sure. Lunch sounds great."

"We're on, then!" Mike said, pleased. With a flourish, he tossed his brown bag into a garbage bin. He caught her hand, bringing her to her feet.

"I know a great little place," he told her.

* * *

Eddie seemed exceptionally pleased to meet Jade and Lucian; he had a number of Jade's books, Finn quickly discovered; and in a matter of minutes, Eddie managed to discover that Lucian was fluent in many archaic languages as well. In fact, Eddie seemed incredibly impressed.

They all wound up in the back of the store with Eddie pouring through old tomes, finding just the ones he wanted himself, and scratching his head and thinking each time Jade or Lucian asked a question.

"Here's one that I keep under glass at all times . . . I barely touch the pages. It's handwritten, Old Norse, written by a Viking explorer who went down through Finland, Poland, into Russia, and into the Near East," Eddie said, coming in with a volume that was obviously an incredible collector's piece, the binding thick leather with etched writing on the cover. "I've had a few of the pages translated, but not many. The book is far too delicate. I don't think it will do us any good, unless someone can read Old Norse, but with your interest in the books, I thought you'd at least like to see it."

"My God, it must be worth a fortune," Finn said. "Eddie, perhaps you shouldn't even take it out from underneath the glass."

"I read Old Norse," Lucian said. "Eddie, I will be extremely careful."

"You read Old Norse?" Finn said skeptically.

"Yes." Lucian stared at him with a shrug. "I've spent a number of years studying languages."

"He's moved around a lot," Jade explained.

"Ah."

Lucian poured over the text, looking through pages, his fingers light against the nearly transparent paper.

"The explorer's name was Erikson, I know that much," Eddie said, taking a chair near Lucian where he sat at the back desk. "That's one of the first really excellent pieces I ever acquired. An old man here was going out of business while I was in college. I helped him sort out his stuff for sale and disposal, and he allowed me one piece for the help. This is the one I chose."

Lucian glanced up at him. "You could probably retire and move to an island on this one book alone," Lucian told him.

"I could, yes. Except that I love these books, and I love my store, and I don't need to retire," Eddie told them with a grimace.

Lucian nodded and gave his attention back to the text. "Erikson talks about coming to a village where the people kept an altar and on the full moon each month, offered up one of the village maidens. They were instructed by what Erikson calls a black priest, and they were promised peace and prosperity within the village, as long as they obeyed the commands. When Erikson and his men arrived and ransacked the village, they were warned by the black priest that they would all die, since his leader was determined on stealing the young woman intended for the next sacrifice. Erikson and one other man left the village to explore another valley. When they returned, their leader, and the forty-odd men who had been in their number, were dead, throats slit, tied upside down to poles, drained of blood and life. One of the ancient village women convinced them that they must escape, saying that Bac-Dal had come." Lucian looked up at Jade. "Had you come across this story in any of your reading on the demon?" he asked.

"Demons aren't real," Finn reminded them quietly.

Lucian looked at Eddie. "You really do need to put this back now. What I'd like to see is anything at all that you might have about this man Cabal Thorne, and what supposedly happened here in the very early seventeen hundreds."

"Will do," Eddie told him, excitedly on the hunt. He

picked up his Old Norse tome as if he were handling a premature infant, tenderly, and with reverence. "You're sure you're done with this?" he asked Lucian.

Lucian nodded. "Thank you," he said gravely. "It was a privilege to read."

"Wow. And you can read it," Eddie said, shaking his head. "I know some languages, but Old Norse . . . wow. All right, let me see, everything I can find on Cabal Thorne."

"Maybe you should start by showing them the book you showed me the other day. The one Sara read from."

"The one written by Cabal himself. Yes, you should see that. It's an incredible piece," Eddie said, and went to get the book.

Finn looked at Jade. "You wrote a book—with a section on demons. Apparently, there are plenty of people who do believe that they are real."

"Yes," Jade said, glancing at her husband.

Finn leaned forward "All right, I believe that people cause the evil in the world. Because of their beliefs. Here, in Salem, no one was practicing witchcraft. Jealousy and envy and whatever other factors caused whatever happened. The girls went into convulsions and fits—brought on by tales and stories, and who knows? Bacteria in the wheat. The point is, there was no witchcraft, but that didn't mean that people weren't tortured, or that they didn't die. Obviously, Cabal Thorne was a nut case who believed in demons, and committed murder, believing he could bring a demon to life. Surely, a rational man would have known that stories about demons were like stories about Roman gods and goddesses, or mermaids, and the like."

They both looked at him without replying.

"Men do evil," he said softly. "A man killed that girl in Boston. I think that there are powers, all right. Maybe someone has been drugging our drinks. Maybe the power of suggestion is greater than we're willing to

accept. Supposedly, hypnotism can do amazing things—
convince people that they don't want to smoke, and
that they're going to eat less."

Lucian eased back in his chair, crossing his arms over
his chest. "You definitely believe that something is
going on. You called us, remember?"

"Here!" Eddie said, coming back into the room with
Cabal Thorne's handwritten tome. "I've actually only
read some of it. The language is often archaic, and the
handwriting has such flourishes that it's often difficult
to decipher what he was trying to say. Exactly. Of
course, from the start, and certainly modern day, it's incredibly important to remember that there's a huge difference in being a Wiccan or a Satanist."

"Absolutely," Jade murmured softly as Lucian accepted the book.

Eddie stood over his shoulder. "There's a slip of
paper on the page that Sara read the other day, the one
that got Morwenna going."

Lucian went to the page, read silently for several seconds, and then aloud. "'Of all that is needed, these
three are of the greatest and utmost importance—the
blood of the sacrifice, the blood of the anointed, the
hair of the anointed.' "

"What do you think he means by anointed?" Jade
asked.

"I'm not sure," Lucian murmured.

"Blood of the sacrifice sounds easy enough," Eddie
mused. "The slaughtered lamb—or, in Cabal Thorne's
case, the blood of his victims."

Lucian read aloud again. "'And all who would honor
He who is the God of Darkness, remember that All
Hallow's Eve, that which falls upon a full moon, is a
night when the elements of the spirits and those who
roam the netherworld are strongest, and therefore, it
can be as well, the Time of The Coming.' "

"Well, we know that the guy was a crazy, sadistic, murderer," Finn said. "He thought he could bring a demon to life. What better time than to do so than during the full moon? And All Hallow's Eve."

"Well, right," Jade said dryly. "That part seems fairly evident." She glanced at Lucian, who looked up from the book, and then at Finn.

"Lost any hair lately?"

"Am I going bald? I doubt it. The gene for hair loss is supposed to come from the mother's father, right? My granddad had hair thicker than weeds until the day he died," Finn assured them.

"Megan hasn't had a haircut here in Salem, has she?" Jade asked.

"Megan . . . a haircut? No."

Jade looked at Lucian again. "There are brushes . . . the shower. Everyone loses hair on a daily basis."

"I would think they'd need some solid strands."

"What are you talking about?" Finn said. "Megan hasn't—" He stopped dead in the middle of his sentence. The words Lucian had read repeated in his head. *Of all that is needed, these three are of the greatest and utmost importance—the blood of the sacrifice, the blood of the anointed, and the hair of the anointed.*

"What?" Lucian said.

Finn stared at them blankly for a moment. "This is . . . ridiculous, I think. But . . . the first night that we were playing here, there was some kind of a monster decoration in the hall. You know, a creature. And it had branch-like fingers. Megan walked beneath it and her hair tangled in it." He shook his head, shrugging then. "I got tangled in it myself about twenty minutes later. And I'm sure more people were caught in it—the creature was taken out before the night was over. I'm willing to bet a lot of people complained."

Lucian and Jade looked at one another again.

"You know, wait. This is really kind of ridiculous. That would be awfully elaborate, don't you think?

Getting some kind of a huge, creature-decoration kind of thing into a hotel hall, and then having it disappear in the middle of the night? It had to have been put there by the hotel, right?"

"Maybe not."

"Then the whole thing about the blood," Finn said. "Megan hasn't cut herself, she hasn't run into anything, suffered no injury."

"What about you?" Jade asked pointedly.

"No!" he said, scoffing at the idea. Then he paused again, chills seeping through him that he denied with a deep and silent scream from within the core of his body. "Yes. There was a dragon in Morwenna's shop. You know, a collectible piece for display. I picked it up, and . . . bled like a stuck pig," he admitted.

"Hm," Eddie commented gravely.

"That doesn't make any sense at all. Seriously. Think about every bit of legend and lore out there. A guy is never the sacrifice. It's always a vestal virgin, or the beautiful blonde—someone like Megan," he said dully.

"The blood of the sacrifice—there's no real tense there, past or present," Jade said. "The blood of the sacrifice could be blood obtained before the main rite."

"Someone sacrificed in that sense is usually dead," Finn said.

"Yes," Jade said.

"At least Megan and I are both alive and well. So far," Finn commented. He leaned forward, elbows on his knees. "This is what I'm getting. If there is something to get. There is someone out there who has read all this bull about Bac-Dal and Cabal Thorne. Apparently, Cabal Thorne was not successful at raising the demon, because people came after him. He was, by his own admission, a very bad man, a murderer. He was killed silently, outside the law, because the people didn't want to be accused of any injustice again—most of them probably realized that they had just executed a large number of innocent people, having believed that they were in league with the devil. It seems possible that this nut has targeted Megan, and that they know something about hypnosis, or suggestion, the power of the mind, or something like it. Split Megan and me up, and she becomes more vulnerable. Make me look like a dangerous man, and when she is used for whatever their heinous intentions may be . . ." He paused, swallowing hard, refusing to believe that Megan could become the victim of the insane murderers. He lifted his hands. "Well . . . make me look like a wife beater, a crazy, jealous husband . . . and I take the fall if something terrible happens to her. Maybe it's time to call in the police."

"And tell them that you're having dreams?" Jade said quietly.

Finn exhaled on a long breath. He shook his head. "Yet I'm the one who lost the blood, and the hair."

"You're sure that Megan hasn't suffered a cut, or anything like it? A good pin prick on the finger?" Jade asked.

"Not to the best of my knowledge," Finn said. He hesitated. "Unless she cut herself last night, after I left her. This is all crazy, though. At first, I was upset because of what was happening between us. Now, I'm afraid for her life. I don't believe that you can bring a demon to life, but I do believe she might have been chosen for some kind of ritual killing, and that I'm the one intended to do life in a maximum security prison for the deed." He rose suddenly, agitated. "And I don't know where she is right now, which is suddenly scaring the hell out of me. Excuse me."

He turned away from the group around the table, pulling out his cell phone and punching the speed dial to connect him to Megan. She answered on the third ring. "Megan?"

"Finn. Hey."

"Where are you?" He asked the question tersely.

Despite the reassuring sound of her voice, he was afraid for her.

"About a block and a half in from the wax museum and the cemetery," she told him. "I ran into Mike at the park. We're having a bite of lunch."

"Great." He tried to keep the grinding of his teeth from being audible. He should just be glad that she was with Smith, in a crowd, alive and well—safe for the moment. He was still irritated.

"Where are you?"

"Just perusing an old bookshop."

"Did the writer and her husband get in?"

"Yes, they're with me." He glanced at the two. "I'm showing them around a bit."

"Want to meet up?"

He glanced at the desk, and the threesome around it. Before he could reply to Megan, Lucian said, "Jade and I need to study some more of the stuff in here. Why don't you go meet her?"

"How much lunch have you had so far?" he asked Megan.

"We've just ordered."

"Order me some coffee. I'll meet you. What's the name of the place?"

Megan told him. He rang off. He stared at Lucian, wondering how the hell he had known what Megan had said to him. Maybe he'd heard her.

"We'll see you tonight, at the hotel," Lucian told him.

He nodded. "I had thought you might want to go by Morwenna's shop as well."

"We'll find it," Jade said. "Eddie can point us in the right direction."

"All right," Finn said. "I don't mean to run off, but—"

"You want to be with your wife; we understand," Lucian said.

Finn turned to Eddie. "Hey, thanks."

"I'm having a great time here," Eddie told him, shaking his head with pleasure and casting a glance toward Lucian. "The guy reads Old Norse! Thank you for introducing us."

"My pleasure," Finn said with a grin. "All right, then. I'll see you later. Oh, and hey—Eddie's twin brother is a cop."

"Maybe we can talk to him later, too," Jade said.

"He's a good guy. But he doesn't believe in demons, either," Eddie assured them.

"Well, thanks again, to all of you," Finn said, turning to leave.

"Finn." Lucian called him back.

Finn turned.

"Remember, this is the last day before Halloween."

"I know."

"And midnight, All Hallow's Eve," Jade said.

"Midnight can't mean too much of anything," Finn told her. "Megan and I are playing tomorrow night. We don't get off until one."

"You're definitely scheduled at the place?" Jade said, sounding just a little startled, as if that didn't fit into things.

"Yes, we're definitely scheduled. For the Wiccans around here, it's the time of the high holy day, or whatever. But for the entertainment world, hey, it's the time to be working."

Jade nodded thoughtfully.

"Later," Finn said, and left them.

For some reason, the troubled look in Jade's eyes seemed to go with him. *It had to be good, then, that they were working. As long as they were in a crowded hotel hall, together, in a crowd of a couple of hundred, they had to be safe.*

The question was, of course, safe from just what?

Dreams.

No. People. Crazy, sick, people who thought that they could sacrifice others, and bring back demons.

He moved more quickly. The urge to be near Megan, to protect her . . .

Die for her, if need be!

. . . was stronger than ever.

Morwenna called Sara to the back of the shop.

"What is it?"

Morwenna hesitated. "I want you to take over for me tomorrow night."

"What?"

"There are things that I'm going to have to do . . . I'm worried. About the way things are going. With Megan."

Sara shook her head strenuously. "Morwenna! I couldn't . . . I can't—I'm just not you! You're known, you're respected . . . Morwenna, you have to lead tomorrow night, there's information out there, there are people who have come from all over the country! You have to be there."

"There are other people doing rites that have been publicized tomorrow; the head witch of Salem is doing a morning rite. Yes, people know about our midnight services, but . . . if I'm not there, it won't be the end of Wiccans in Salem. But Sara, you do have something special. You could fill in for me. You're young, but you speak so well, you've read so much, you know so many of the really beautiful passages . . . you could be me."

"You are the important person, doing the important service!"

Morwenna shook her head. "Some things," she said softly, "are just more important than others."

"There's nothing more important than tomorrow night."

"Yes, there is."

"Morwenna," Sara said firmly. "I can't. I mean it. I can't!"

Morwenna sighed. "Sara—"

"Morwenna, you've got to find someone else. You have to!"

"Sara—"

"Morwenna, I mean it. Tomorrow night . . . well, it's a learning experience for me as well. I'm new—I'm young. Too new, and too young. And tomorrow night, as for myself . . . there are just no guarantees. I'm dead serious, and truly sorry. If you want to fire me, go ahead. But I can't fill in for you tomorrow night."

"You're a different coven, of course, but you work for me—"

"Morwenna, like I said, you'll have to fire me. I can't, and I mean, I can't."

Morwenna shook her head, disheartened. "I'm not firing you. But you've got to help me. There's been a change. I must . . . I must be with Megan."

Sara sat down in front of Morwenna. Morwenna had been reading the Tarot cards.

The Grim Reaper was face up in front of her.

"I'm really sorry; I do have my own agenda," Sara said. "But . . . I'll help you think. We'll come up with something."

Megan didn't know what had induced her to tell Mike everything she had told him. She hadn't, of course, told him everything, but enough so that they had really gotten into talking. Mike knew a lot of old lore as well as history, and he didn't laugh at Megan at all, but told her he believed the story about Cabal Thorne having come to Salem to raise the demon, Bac-Dal, was certainly based on some kind of truth. He thought it was nearly criminally cruel for Andy to have taken her out to the unhallowed ground to tell her that a demon was after her.

He didn't believe in demons, and agreed that the

dreams she was having had to have something to do with the many impressions she received during the day.

"That old Andy Markham! So he said, 'Bac-Dal wants you'? "

"That's what he said, exactly."

"That old fool!" Her hand lay on the table. He covered it with his own and told her seriously, "Megan, there are no such things as demons."

"But there are such things as bad people."

"Sure. But I think that old Andy may be crazy, but do you think he's a bad person? You know, you can take ghost tours here and hear about all kinds of bad things that have happened to people. They'll show you all kinds of pictures and tell you that rain spots are ectoplasm and stuff like that. There are plenty of horror stories that take place in real life. But that doesn't make those involved bad people. Take old Andy though— he's been telling his tales the longest. You know, Salem wasn't all this great big place where tourism ruled everything. It's only been . . . what, maybe twenty, thirty or so years that everyone has cashed in on history. But Andy . . . he was just a storyteller from the start, that's what the old folks say. He was a teacher when he was young, and loved to set up campfire tales and stuff like that. He started believing his own schtick. That's all there is to it."

Megan smiled. "I never thought of Andy as dangerous himself. Just scary."

"What things do to the mind is scary," Mike said. "Don't let him get under your skin."

His hand remained on hers. Both their heads were lowered.

"Did you order my coffee?"

Megan's head jerked up at the sound of her husband's voice. Inadvertently, she jerked her hand back. She didn't know why in hell she felt guilty when she looked up.

"Finn. You made it. Yes, I ordered the coffee—the waitress said she'd bring it as soon as she saw you so that it wouldn't get cold."

She thought his smile looked a little forced, but he acted casually.

"Thanks. Hi, Mike."

"Hey, Finn, good to see you."

Mike offered him a hand across the table. Finn shook it, and sat in the chair at the end of the table.

"Where are your friends?" she asked.

"Reading," he said, giving her another smile and glancing at Mike. He didn't want to say too much in front of a third party, she realized, and dropped it, despite the fact that she was dying of curiosity and still feeling somewhat left out.

"I have some friends in from New Orleans," Finn said to Mike. "A woman who does travel books, guides, things like that. So . . . they're off, happily exploring Salem. How was lunch?"

"Good," Mike said. "Seems like a place that will make it. Some here do, and some don't."

"Like everywhere in the world," Finn said agreeably.

The waitress brought his coffee. Finn thanked her and brought the cup to his lips, but then paused, looking out the glass window to the street.

"What?"

"I don't believe it."

"What?"

Mike was staring at him, too.

Finn shrugged. "There's Mr. Fallon, walking around with a big bag. He's been doing some tourist shopping, I guess."

Mike swung around to look out the window, too. It was true. Fallon was standing in front of one of the shops with a big sign that advertised itself as a witchcraft store.

"Who'd have thunk, huh?" Mike said dryly.

"So everyone gets into it a little bit," Megan murmured.

"Not everyone," Mike said. "But, hey, most people who come here do so for the history—and the fun of it. Moms buy their daughters all kinds of jewelry in those shops, and some of them carry beautiful little Victorian dolls and things like that. Cute books, and oils—lots and lots of people get into the scented oils, whether they believe that they do anything or not. I had a lady in the museum one day who had bags full of mortars and pestles—and not for witchcraft. She needed them because she had five kids and found out they were great for science projects."

"The commercial world is the commercial world, right?" Finn said.

"Oh, yeah. And it's okay. One of the haunted houses is run by a really great guy. He starts off his little bit by telling the kids that it's all just for fun, and the entire 'scare' factor is done by someone running around in front of them in the darkness, making things bang and bob out. But if anyone gets really scared, he just stops and escorts them out. Fear is usually in the mind," he said, offering Megan an awkward little smile again.

"Fear can be real and sensible, too," Finn said flatly. "Megan, did you tell him that you were attacked in the parking lot last night?"

Mike stared at her hard. Funny, she had said so much, but nothing about that. Maybe because she was still smarting from what Morwenna had said. *Could she say for sure that anyone else had been there? Anyone other than Finn?*

She looked at her husband in the light of day. She'd known him to be angry at times, temperamental, determined, impatient, passionate . . . and tender. She couldn't look into his eyes and believe that he didn't love her, almost too fiercely, at times.

She gritted her teeth, absolutely determined to shake off the unease that Morwenna had awakened in her.

Her husband might be many things, but not a demon.

"I was stalked, more than anything. I wasn't hurt, but Finn did get into a tussle with whoever it was."

Mike looked sharply at Finn. "You went to the police, right?"

"We didn't actually have to go to the police; a cop who comes in all the time was there. They're going to set up more security at the place."

"You've got to be really careful," Mike said gravely. He looked at Megan, and seemed uneasy. "You know . . . they haven't caught that guy who killed the girl in Boston. And we're awful damned close here."

"A murderer who struck in Boston almost a month ago could be anywhere in the country now," Finn said, "but that's beside the point. Every young woman out there has to be extremely careful because at any given time, there's more than one psycopath in the world, preying upon the vulnerable, which usually means children and young women."

"I'm careful," Megan said.

"You really shouldn't go anywhere alone," Mike said. "Anywhere. There's strength in numbers, you know."

"I'm careful," Megan said. She didn't know why, but she felt as if Mike were warning her about Finn as well—he didn't suggest that she cling to her husband at all times, but rather seemed to suggest that she needed lots of numbers around her.

"There," Mike said, "look, they've got it on the television again."

There was a TV set over the bar, set to a local news station. The volume had been low, but a young bartender had a remote in her hand, and she clicked the volume higher. The newscaster was repeating words they had just exchanged, warning that people needed to be extra safe this Halloween, and saying that the police in Boston had no new leads on the murder committed there.

As they watched, she went on in a slightly dramatic tone to mention a more local situation.

"An apparent hit and run has our local police searching for the perpetrator of what may prove to be a deadly accident. Mr. Andrew Markham, local storyteller, was found on an embankment off US1 this mid morning by a banker on his way to work. Police believe that he was struck and that the driver paused long enough to drag him off the road, but that he was then deserted by the offender. The driver might well be guilty now of manslaughter for leaving the man to die. As yet, no news has been given out as to what type vehicle may be involved. Mr. Markham was brought to the hospital in critical condition, and remains in a coma as of this newscast. Anyone with any possible clue or information is asked to call the police or our crime stoppers number. Sadly, the doctors doubt if Mr. Markham will survive his injuries. Police are imploring the public for any information, however slight, they may have."

The news being the news, the young woman went on in a cheerful voice to give a list of the activities available for children in the following two days.

Mike, Finn, and Megan all stared at one another.

"The poor old bugger!" Mike said.

Megan knew the blood had drained from her face.

There had been no accidental hit and run, she was certain.

Andy had been struck on purpose. Mike, despite Finn's presence, covered her hand again. "He's an old man. He was walking where he shouldn't have been walking."

Finn was staring at her.

She'd never told him about her morning excursion with Andy.

She couldn't be absolutely certain that there had been any-one else—other than Finn—out in the parking lot last night. And this morning . . .

She didn't really know where her husband had been.

Finn had been in Boston when the girl had been killed there.

Ridiculous.

She looked her husband in the eye. "I'd like to go to the hospital, Finn. And see Andy."

Finn frowned. His eyes seemed guarded. "Megan, the old fellow scared you to pieces the first night we got here with all his tales. We barely know the man."

"If he's in a coma, they're not going to let you in," Mike pointed out.

"That may be true," Megan said.

She still believed that Andy Markham was in a hospital because of her.

Or because of what he knew. Which still came back to her. He had tried to warn her.

She stared hard at her husband, praying she wasn't going to be afraid just to be in a car with him. And yet, if he absolutely refused her . . .

"Finn, I'd like to go to the hospital."

He hesitated. Too long, she thought. Then he said, "Sure, Megan, we'll go. But I think Mike is right. They're not going to let us in."

"Take me anyway."

"I don't suppose it would hurt if you just went by."

"We'll get the check," Finn said, and rose.

"Finn, even if we're just sent away, I'd like to go by."

"As you wish, Megan. As you wish."

Chapter 17

At the information desk, as Finn expected, they were told that no one except immediate family could see Andy Markham.

Megan was distressed, and looked at Finn. "Maybe we could at least buy flowers and leave them for him."

The woman on volunteer duty at the desk was middle-aged with short, curly red hair and a gaunt but sympathetic-looking face. She cleared her throat and told them. "I'm sorry. They won't allow flowers in the intensive care unit. Perhaps if you come back in a few days, he'll be better, and in a regular room."

"What are they calling his condition right now?" Finn asked.

"Critical but stable."

As Finn watched Megan, he knew she was certain that Andy Markham was never going to get any better.

"Perhaps we could buy a card and write a get well note in it," Finn said.

Megan glanced at him with a quick smile of appreciation. "We'll do that," she said softly, though again, he was certain his wife believed Andy would never read the note. Still, it was something that could be done.

"I'll go buy a card in the little gift shop, and be right back," he said, and turned to leave Megan by the desk.

The shop was small. It took him only a minute to find an appropriate card. When he returned to the desk, however, Megan was gone.

Panic seized him. It felt as if skeletal fingers of iron were wrapping around his heart. For a moment, he couldn't breathe. Then, controlling himself seemed the greatest effort he'd ever made. His fingers nearly bit through the counter when he leaned against it to ask the redhead at the information desk, "Where is my wife?"

He must have concealed his fear with greater effect than he had imagined, for she didn't scream or shout for the police. She frowned, as if aware of his underlying tension, and answered him as pleasantly as she could. "Martha came by for her."

"Martha? You know Martha? You do mean my wife's Aunt Martha?"

"I know Martha, of course—it's a small town. Most residents come here with their aches, pains, and accidents. Martha is friends with most of the doctors—and she volunteers here as well." She looked as if she didn't want to say more to him—as if the hospital was engaging in policies that might not be quite fair—but then she sighed and explained, "Martha may be the closest thing to next-of-kin old Andy has. They're not related, but they've known one another for years. Bickered as much as anything, but Martha came in as soon as she heard about Andy, and the doctors believe a friendly voice can sometimes break into the mind of a person in a coma. So . . . Martha took your wife up for just a second."

Finn exhaled, staring at her. "He's not going to make it, is he?"

"I'm not the doctor," she said softly. He was surprised, especially in his present mood, that she seemed to look into his eyes and be willing, despite herself, to talk to him. She shook her head and told him, "Andy's an old, old man. He received some terrible injuries. Being thrown by a speeding car . . . it's kind of like being beaten by a dozen lead pipes, you know. Anyway, it's all in the hands of God, now."

"Thank you," Finn told her.

She smiled at last. "Take a seat in the lounge there. She won't be but a minute. My friend Dorcas is the nurse in charge of Andy's room—no one will be in there for more than a minute or two, I assure you. I'd tell you to go on up, but Dorcas would be risking her job if any more people tried to get in, especially if Andy does . . . well, you know. If things don't go well for Andy."

"I understand," Finn said, and he did. But he leaned against the counter idly, and when a visitor came in to ask for directions to the maternity ward, he carefully gazed over the counter. He was glad to see that the computer screen was drawn to a list of room numbers.

He pretended to push away from the counter, take a seat, and glance at a magazine. But as soon as the redhead's attention was taken again by a new visitor, he stood and headed for the elevators.

Efficiency was the order of the day in Dorcas Brandt's arena of care. Megan found herself suited up in a matter of minutes—Andy didn't have any kind of a contagious disease, but apparently at his age and in his condition, pneumonia could be the final straw. Masked and gowned, she entered the room with Martha and Dorcas.

Martha, a glaze of tears about her eyes, was still silent as she came by Andy's bedside.

Andy was a maze of tubes. Thin, almost transparent little lines helped him to breathe. An IV brought sustenance into his veins and kept him hydrated. A monitor watched his heart. Both of his eyes were blackened, or so sunken that they appeared to be so. Amazingly, he had suffered no broken bones—he had simply been bruised from head to toe and knocked unconscious. He had never come to, but had sunk into the coma, despite every effort made to revive him in the emergency room. But his heart was still beating, and his lungs were working on their own. And, Dorcas had assured Megan, there was plenty of activity going on in old Andy's mind.

He looked like hell.

There were stitches running across the top of his forehead; his white hair had been shaved away from that area of his skull. His cheeks were cadaverous.

"Andy, you silly fool, what were you doing out on the road like that!" Martha said softly. She glanced at Dorcas, who nodded to her. Martha gently took his hand. "Andy, you've got to wake up, let us know you're all right."

There was no movement from Andy. Not a flicker of his eyelids.

Martha stroked a finger down the too apparent vein in his hand, then moved over to whisper to Dorcas at the rear of the room. Megan moved forward. She bit lightly into her lower lip because she felt a sting in her eyes as well—if she'd never met the man, she would have been moved by his condition.

"Andy, you're a fighter. And they need you around here, you know," she murmured. Feeling somewhat inadequate—and something of a fraud, she certainly wasn't a lifelong friend—she took his hand as she had seen Martha do.

"Come on, Andy, you've got to make it."

She felt the slightest flinch against her fingers, where he touched her hand. Her eyes were drawn there, as if she could thereby verify the movement. Nothing. But when she glanced toward his face again, her breath caught in a sudden wheeze; her heart seemed to stop.

His eyes were open. They stared at her, and somehow *beyond* her. He seemed to be looking at something beyond the room.

He moved his lips.

She couldn't hear his words.

She moved closer against him, and heard what didn't even sound like a voice, more like a mechanical rasp.

"Bac-Dal wants you. I must be there. Will be there. The evil must be stopped. The evil . . . there! Bac-Dal wants you."

Megan dropped his hand, her jaw working as she backed away from the bed.

"Martha! Martha . . . Dorcas. He's moving, he's speaking!" she said. She turned to the women.

Both instantly ceased their whispered conversation and hurried over to the bed.

"There—" Megan began.

There. Andy's eyes were closed. His lips were closed as well. He lay just as he had lain.

Dorcas opened one of Andy's eyes and checked it with her pin light flashlight, drawn from her nurse's scrubs pocket. She opened the other, checked his pulse, and stared at the monitors that surrounded the bed.

After a moment, she shook her head, and stared at Megan hard.

"No, dear, he couldn't have spoken. And if he moved, I'm afraid it was a simple reflex. His condition is completely unchanged." She stared at Megan as if wondering if she were a hopeful idiot, or someone trying to create havoc for an unknown reason.

"But . . . I saw his eyes open. I saw his lips move. I heard him," she insisted.

Martha set a hand on her shoulder. "What did he say, dear?"

"He said—"

Megan hesitated. With Dorcas staring at her—and with whatever reputation she might have already gained in town with her nightmare screaming—she wasn't going to tell the truth. Or what she believed to be the truth. Looking at Andy now, it did appear as if he'd never moved. Frankly, he looked as if he were already dead. Those parched lips couldn't have formed words.

But they had.

Very afraid, she still hesitated.

"I don't know what he said," she lied. "I only know that he spoke."

"Who the hell is that?" Dorcas demanded, looking past Megan, and more than a little irritated by now.

Megan swung around. Finn was outside in the hallway, staring through the glass windows. He was looking at Andy and didn't see Dorcas, and then Martha, and herself, staring out at him.

"My husband."

"Doesn't anyone understand the concept of a *waiting* room?" Dorcas demanded. She was a gaunt woman herself. Her white shoes seemed huge against her skinny ankles. She was tall, though, and despite her fragile-looking frame and the fact that she had to be nearing sixty, she had the appearance and demeanor of a woman who was tough as nails.

Dorcas looked back at Andy again, shaking her head with sympathy and concern. She gazed at Megan again. "You just want him to be okay," she said with greater patience. "You want him to speak. Sometimes, we imagine things. In fact, when interns start in the morgue, they're often convinced that we've made mistakes in the wards, because the body . . . the body is filled with so many gases, and death brings on changes that create reflex action. Sorry," she said wincing. "I really didn't mean to mention the word morgue. Andy may make it. But he's got to get through tonight. Please, let's go on out. Your husband is making me nervous. He looks like a giant transformer or something, about to meld through the glass."

Megan tried to smile. She couldn't.

They didn't believe that Andy had spoken.

She knew that he had. At least, she thought she knew that he had. She was amazed she wasn't shaking outwardly because it seemed that every fiber within her was trembling. She had fought down a moment of sheer terror, and now wondered if what was happening meant she was losing her mind, of if she was the target of a truly evil entity. Either way, she was in serious trouble.

Dorcas was urging her out of the room. She went. She nearly crashed into Finn just outside the door.

"You all right?" he asked her.

In the strange hospital light, it appeared that there was a strange gleam in his eyes. A niggling thought tore into her mind. Andy had been staring not at her, but *beyond* her. Out the glass windows. Where Finn had probably already been standing.

She braced herself and fought the insanity in her mind. She loved him. What was love? Faith, trust. They had learned that lesson. But love might well be defined as insanity as well, wanting someone so badly, that the truth didn't matter, as long as it could be denied. Morwenna had warned her about Finn, Finn had been a creature in her nightmares, Finn had been in Boston most probably on the night when a terrible murder had been committed.

Finn had saved her from an attack last night.

From an invisible attacker.

Stop! she urged herself.

Finn didn't even understand what was going on himself.

"Megan?" he said.

Martha came out behind her. Megan didn't have to reply right away. "Finn, dear, how are you?" She stood on her toes, giving him a kiss on the cheek, which he returned.

"Martha, how are you? I'm so sorry. I didn't realize

you and Andy were such good old friends," he told her sympathetically.

"Oh, actually, we're good old bickering enemies," Martha said wryly. "But we've both been around forever, so . . . of course, I care for the old coot!"

Finn nodded, looking at Megan again.

"Martha, now, you and your family are cluttering up the ICU halls," Dorcas said firmly.

"Yes, yes, we're gone. And thanks, Dorcas. Come along, children," she said, and slipped her right arm through Finn's, her left through Megan's. "Dorcas has been patient enough."

"How's he doing?" Finn asked as they walked to the elevators.

"Holding on, anyway," Martha said. "Megan thought he said something, but when Dorcas checked his vitals, there was no change whatsoever. What did you think he said, dear?"

Megan shook her head.

"Dorcas was right. I must have imagined that he opened his eyes . . . that he spoke."

"But said what?" Finn inquired that time.

Was he worried that Andy might have said something that could have implicated him . . . ?

In what?

"I really don't know. Just a mumble. Maybe my name," Megan said with what she hoped was an offhand shrug.

Finn was frowning as he stared down at her.

The evil . . . there! Andy had said. And he had been staring beyond her. At the glass windows to the hallway. Where Finn had come to find her. He hadn't stayed in the waiting room, even when the volunteer woman had surely told him where she had gone.

It was crazy.

A little pinging noise indicated the arrival of the elevator. A woman in a wheelchair cradled a brand new baby while her husband and friends stood around her bearing balloons announcing that the newborn was a boy.

The three of them congratulated the new mother, and the elevator reached the bottom floor. As they exited, Finn set his arm around Megan's shoulders. She somehow suppressed a shudder. Again, she thought that she was crazy. Her husband would never want to hurt her. How could she even begin to believe such a thing—over and over!—when they could share time such as they had last night? And how could she believe that she loved him so deeply when she could suspect him of evil?

The happy new parents, the baby, and their entourage moved down the hall ahead of them. Megan listened to their light talk and laughter.

"Well, have you two had lunch?" Martha asked.

"Yes, we were eating when we heard the news about Andy," Finn told her. "But if you're hungry, we'd be happy to accompany you somewhere."

"No, no, I'm an old bird, I lunch early when I'm on my own," Martha said. "It's just that Megan is looking a little peaked—I was hoping that you were keeping up with your meals, and therefore your strength, young lady!"

"I'm fine," Megan said, determined that she would play the part. "I was just upset to hear about Andy. A hit and run is such a terrible thing. Are they sure, though, that it was a hit and run?"

Martha arched a brow. "Well . . . that's what they're saying. He was found on the side of the road. I guess . . . well, what would it be, other than a hit and run?"

"An assault," Finn said flatly.

Martha looked horrified. "Who on earth would assault Andy? I don't believe the police are even considering such a possibility. He was found with his wallet and personal effects—the old codger wears a good watch and a signet ring worth quite a bit of money. I don't know anything about police business, but I'm sure they checked out the scene. Now, come on, you two! Let me worry about Andy. You both look dreadful. It's a sorry state, but you two hardly know him. You've both come here, you've done all that you might, when unfortunately, there's really nothing anyone can do, other than his doctors, and they're going on a wing and a prayer as well. Finn, would you like to come back to the house? Megan, honey, are you coming with me now, or your husband?"

Megan closed her eyes for a moment, fighting a wave of dizziness. She lowered her head, biting into her lip. Fury suddenly filled her. No. Finn wasn't guilty of anything. She did love him, and she wasn't going to lose him. And she wasn't going to be a coward, neither was she going crazy. Whatever the hell was going on, she intended to fight it.

She considered going with Martha, since the news of Andy's condition had completely erased her earlier discomfort when she had awakened from her dream—and found her feet dirty. Maybe a long talk with Martha would be good.

But it seemed more important then to be with Finn.

"Thanks, Aunt Martha, but I'm really fine." She slipped her arm through Finn's. "We have some friends in town. I think we're going to try to find them before it's time to get ready for work tonight."

"All right, kids," Martha said with a smile. "You two take care."

"We will, thanks," Finn called to her.

They watched Martha walk to her car. Then Megan looked up at Finn. "So what is going on with you and this couple from New Orleans? Do you think I could see them as well?"

He smiled. "We'll head back into town and try to find them."

He led her out to the car, opened the passenger door for her, then went around and slid into the driver's seat. He started up the car. They were halfway back into town when he asked her, "You know, the others may believe you, but I don't. What did Andy Markham say to you?"

She stared straight ahead. "Didn't you hear Dorcas? He couldn't have said anything. His condition was totally unchanged."

"Bullshit," Finn said.

Startled, she looked at him. Then she stared out the front window again. "I don't remember, exactly. Except that he said, 'Bac-Dal wants you.'"

Eddie was out of the room. Lucian and Jade now had a selection of old books, new books, and manuscripts laid out before them.

"What do you think?" Jade asked Lucian.

"I think that some well-read Satanists are planning on bringing Bac-Dal to life, and that they intend to use Megan Douglas as his final sacrifice, or . . . I don't know. Maybe they intend to use her as a gift when he first arrives." He ran his fingers through his dark hair, picked up one of the manuscripts again, and gnawed on the eraser of the pencil he'd been using to scratch down some notes.

Jade nodded. "It should be easy then. Find out who the Satanists are."

"Yeah, everyone wears a T-shirt," Lucian said dryly.

She smiled. "There are a lot of Wiccan shirts around, and the usually heavy metal stuff."

He shook his head. "The problem is . . . it isn't going to be easy at all."

Jade leaned forward on the table. She eyed him carefully. "Haven't you had any more . . . feelings? Intuitions?"

He shook his head, frowning.

"But . . . you should *know* more, shouldn't you?"

"We're playing in a different league here," he said quietly. "I believe that this is real. I believe, as well, that Megan was fingered long before they came here—why, I don't know."

"But it was Finn who disturbed you."

"Yes."

"Do you think they're using him?"

"I don't know. The 'they' is so vague right now. And the thing is . . . 'they' are being protected by a strong force. There is nothing that I can see or feel." He lowered his voice. "Eddie could be in on it, and I wouldn't know. Someone found out about the Cabal Thorne attempt here to bring back Bac-Dal. They know that the timing is right, the full moon on Halloween, and more than that, they found the archaic writings—spells and rites—that are used, to bring a demon to life." He hesitated, shrugging. "They've made first contact, and though the demon isn't back in the flesh, apparently he can produce some power from beyond. His followers have already opened a vent. Most of the ancient peoples believed that there was a very thin veil that parted the living from the dead—or such other entities as spirits, ghosts—and demons. Create a crack in that veil ahead of time, and you get the power to see that everything is done on Halloween night, when the veil is at its finest, most vulnerable point."

"What do we do?" Jade said.

He smiled. "You, keep reading. I'm off."

"Off?" she said, sitting back, somewhat offended that he planned to leave her.

He kissed the top of her head. "You're a journalist, my love. You know how to sift through material to get to the important facts. I'm a . . . hm. I'm a people reader. I'm going to go to try to read a few people."

"Hey—you're the one who reads archaic languages!"

"I don't believe we're going to find what we need in an archaic language," he said. He started to smile, but his smile faded. "We're out of time, Jade. Halloween is tomorrow."

She looked at him and nodded slowly. "Happy hunting," she told him, and turned her attention back to the manuscript before her.

Finn managed to find a space to park on the side of the common.

"Where are we going?" Megan asked him. "Do you know where your friends are?"

He shrugged. "Morwenna's," he said.

Megan didn't particularly want to go back to Morwenna's shop.

"What makes you think that they're there?"

He shrugged. "I know they were going to go there. So we'll give it a try." He frowned. "What's the matter?"

"Nothing."

She didn't intend to tell him that Morwenna seemed convinced he was the cause of all ills. She reminded herself that she was going to be a fighter. She wasn't going to lose her husband—or her mind.

"Let's go to Morwenna's."

The shop was crazier than ever. Jamie, though, immediately escorted them in, then resumed his post as door guard.

There were so many people in the shop that neither Morwenna, Joseph, Sara, or the other two young people they had working that day could do more than glance up at them. Oddly enough, Finn, however, seemed to know exactly where he was going. He headed toward the rear of the front area, near a rack with capes and cloaks. Of course, it wasn't difficult to see Lucian DeVeau. He was, if anything, taller than Finn. Very dark, and good-looking. He drew attention immediately. He greeted Finn as he saw him weaving his way through the crowd, and offered a quick smile as Finn brought Megan forward.

"Megan, great to see you again," he told her.

"And you, of course. You and your wife have done incredible things for us, with your reviews," Megan said.

"You'll have to tell Jade that; I don't write the reviews," Lucian said. "But I'm glad." He had an armful of the little herb packets that were sold at the store. Each offered instructions such as, "Place in the pocket for wealth," or "Burn for True Love," or "Protection from Evil." They seemed rather silly, but then, Megan realized that she did cross herself with holy water every time she went into church.

"Let me just pay for these; we'll get out of the shop and talk," Lucian said.

She nodded.

"We'll be outside," Finn said.

He started to take Megan's hand, but a heavyset woman jostled between them and Megan waved him on out, indicating that she was following. She had almost maneuvered her way to the door when cool fingers landed on her arm.

She turned around. Morwenna was staring at her. Her eyes looked wild.

"Who the hell is that?" she demanded.

Megan frowned. She hadn't realized that Morwenna had noted them talking to Lucian.

"A friend from New Orleans," she said cautiously. "Why?"

Morwenna shook her head strenuously. "He's evil. Really evil."

"Morwenna!" she protested. Then she laughed, looking back. "Evil? He's just *wicked* good-looking, as they say around here. Sure he hasn't jangled your chains a little?"

"I'm married."

"So am I. And I can still tell you, he's damned good-looking. A bit exotic. Seductive, don't you agree?"

"Don't laugh at me. I mean it—he's evil. I can tell. Megan, you've got to be careful. I really feel that you're in danger now. Why is this guy here? I'll bet Finn brought him up."

"He and his wife are reviewers—"

"Oh, that's bullshit!"

"Morwenna," Megan said patiently, pulling her arm free. "He's a friend!"

She forced her way the rest of the distance to the front door, aware that she had somewhat rudely jostled a number of customers. She didn't care. She was already hating the little doubts that were trickling into her bloodstream again.

Finn waited for her just outside.

"It's a zoo in there, huh?"

"It's almost a zoo out here, too," she said. The streets were crowded. Little Salem was beginning to look like New York—highly decorated—at rush hour.

Before Finn could reply, Lucian came down the steps from the entry. She wondered if he had decided to forego his purchases, thinking that he couldn't possibly have gotten through the line at the cash register so quickly. But he was carrying a bag with the shop's insignia, so he had managed to make his purchases.

Maybe Sara, at the cash register, had thought that he was evil as well, and somehow managed to add up his items without causing a stampede among the other customers.

"It is crazy out here," Lucian said.

"There must be somewhere to go that's quiet, where we can talk," Finn said.

"Actually, Finn, if you don't mind, would you go and get Jade? She's still at the bookshop. I'd like a few words with Megan. Meet us at . . ." He paused, looking down the street toward the mall. "The second coffee shop."

"We'll never get in," Megan warned.

Lucian smiled. "Sure we will."

Finn looked hesitant for a moment, as if he were unsure as to what he should do. Then he squared his shoulders. "Look out for my wife, huh?" he said lightly. "I'd die for her . . . or kill for her, for that matter." He turned and started down the street.

Lucian looked after him for a long moment. "He really loves you."

She didn't know what to respond; he really was a total stranger. She felt something odd around him as well, though not a terrible premonition of any kind of evil, as Morwenna claimed to sense.

She just felt . . . odd. And wary, of course, but that could certainly be said to be natural.

"Shall we?"

They started down the street.

"So . . . things have been odd here?"

"Things . . . yes."

"It started off with the nightmare?"

Megan paused, and then shrugged. Apparently, he knew everything. "The nightmare . . . the feeling that Finn was trying to kill me. Yes, all the odd things." She glanced at him. "What I guess you don't know is the latest. There's an old fellow here who tells ghost stories, and . . . well, I've had a chance to talk with him a few times. He warned me about this demon. Bac-Dal. And he keeps telling me that Bac-Dal wants me. Crazy." She waved a hand in the air. "But last night, he was apparently struck by a hit and run driver. He's in the hospital in critical condition."

"Someone warning you . . . hm." They had reached the coffee shop. He opened the door for her. The place was packed. Lucian DeVeau went to the harried host. He pointed to a table in the back, which was occupied. It appeared that they had just been served. One of the women at the table looked up and noted them at the host's stand. She smiled vaguely, then nervously looked back at her cup.

Lucian stepped back by Megan.

"We'll have a table in just a minute."

She arched a brow, but to her surprise, the group drank their hot coffees, teas, or cocoas with remarkable speed.

"Mr. DeVeau?" the host said politely.

There had certainly been others in the line ahead of them, but no one seemed to notice that they were being seated out of line. In fact, people smiled at them as they walked by to take a seat at the table for five.

"That was rather remarkable," Megan commented.

He shrugged. "Mind over matter," he said lightly. "What will you have?"

"Straight coffee. It's going to be a long night."

He gave their order to the waitress who seemed to materialize at their table, then leaned forward. "So this old man has been warning you about Bac-Dal?"

Megan actually tried to hesitate. It was very strange. He didn't seem evil at all to her. Nor did he seem like a stranger, which meant she should be all the more wary. It didn't work. She immediately found herself saying things that she shouldn't have.

"Finn doesn't even know this, but . . . I went to meet him one morning and he told me the tale about Bac-Dal, and this man named Cabal Thorne who had come here long ago. Apparently the townspeople—with help maybe from some other religious group—managed to kill Thorne. They weren't going to have him arrested, not after the witch debacle. So they killed him. And then . . . later, one night when after we played . . . he was there again. This morning, when I heard what happened to him, I was . . . wow, strange, I was overcome by this terrible guilt. As if he were in the hospital because of me. Because he's tried so hard to warn me."

Lucian nodded. The coffee arrived. He pleasantly

thanked the waitress, but didn't speak again until she was gone.

"You don't believe it was an accident that landed Andy in the hospital."

She stared at him. "No."

"And you and Finn went to the hospital, and they let you see him?"

Megan smiled at that. "I ran into my aunt—Martha, with whom I'm staying right now. She's been in Salem forever, knew the nurse on duty, and managed to get us in."

"And what happened then?"

Unease filled her. The way that he was looking at her . . . he knew. More than Finn had known, that something had indeed happened.

"He's supposed to be in a deep coma. But I could swear that he came to and . . . and talked."

"Exactly what happened?"

"He told me again that Bac-Dal wanted me. And it was very strange, because he wasn't really looking at me, it was more as if he were looking through me . . . and Finn was looking in at us through the glass windows all the time—oh, jeez!" she broke off with a gasp, amazed and dismayed at what she had just said.

He smiled slowly, a dangerous smile. "It's all right. You two are in trouble here. And you do need help."

"My husband isn't . . . Finn isn't cruel, or a killer, or evil," she said. Great. She was explaining all this to a man she didn't know. A man Morwenna had termed "evil" himself. "Of course, neither of us believes in demons or things that go bump in the night," she tried to add lightly. "It's all the power of suggestion," she went on quickly.

He raised a hand to her. He smiled again, that slow rueful smile. "I don't believe that you're being plagued by the power of suggestion. You see, there are plenty of things out there that go bump in the night. And I'm sure that there really are demons, and your life may depend on your belief in them."

Despite the fact that Eddie Martin's store was as crazy as Morwenna's Wiccan shop, he didn't at all mind the fact that Jade DeVeau was still at his desk, browsing his manuscripts. He inclined his head when Finn entered the shop, indicating that he should go back and find Jade at his leisure. Finn felt badly about having taken over his business area, but he didn't want to leave Megan alone long with Lucian DeVeau, though he didn't know exactly why. The guy had his own beautiful wife, and the two seemed so compatible, they were almost as one.

Jade didn't see him arrive at first, she was so engrossed in what she was reading. It was a bound book, not ancient, but very old.

"Jade?"

She looked up, startled. Her eyes narrowed as she looked at him—almost suspiciously—and he wondered what she had found.

"Hey," she said, her forced tone belying her manner.

"Lucian sent me to get you. He's with Megan down at the coffee shop." He paused. "I'm supposed to collect you, and we're supposed to meet them. He somehow got some ladies to inhale their coffee. We have a table, and need to meet."

"Of course."

But she stared at him, not closing the book.

"What is it?"

"Your name."

"What?"

"Your name is in this book."

"What?" he repeated, coming around behind her.

"It's an account of the events of the Cabal Thorne killing . . . a diary. The writing is very confusing, hurried." She looked up at him, studying him. "I keep reading it all over and over again, but I can't quite tell if *Finnegan Douglas* was among the citizen vigilantes, or . . ."

"Or?"

"The Satanists," she said flatly.

Chapter 18

"I'm telling you, it's impossible!" Finn said vehemently, both hands surrounding the large coffee cup that held his extra large cappuccino. "Look, I know that we go back, way back, in Louisiana. I have my great-great grandfather's Civil War diary. He put together a militia outfit, and when things got bad, wound up being commissioned as a captain in the regular army. He was killed at the Battle of Cold Harbor. You can look him up—his name appears in any number of southern Civil War museums! He was a Dixie-singing Rebel, for fact."

Jade nodded. "We believe you, Finn. But the Civil War started in 1861. The events here preceded that by nearly sixty years."

Finn leaned back, staring around the table.

He had seen the passage that referred to a Finnegan Douglas having been in the area when it was "rumored" that a vigilante party had taken care of the "perceived" evil of Cabal Thorne. And, like Jade, he had been unable to determine if the writer had referred to the said Douglas as having been among Thorne's followers, or the vigilantes. The writer had been scornful of any of the proceedings. Having escaped an accusation of witch-

craft himself by timing alone, the author of the words, a
man named Ethan Miller, was writing from hearsay, and
the script had been so full of "thees" and "thous" and
other strange spellings that only Jade's deciphering had
made any of it clear to him at all.

"My name isn't Finnegan, by the way. It's legally just
Finn. Finn Douglas." He flushed slightly, then grimaced.
"I have a middle name—Beauregard. I'm telling you,
we're as Southern as pecan pie."

Jade shrugged. "Maybe it's just a coincidence."

"It's not a coincidence," Lucian said flatly.

Megan leaned forward suddenly. "You know, I've just
realized—this is beyond insanity. Finn, you were right.
We need to get the hell out of here."

He turned and looked at Megan. Her eyes were on his,
bright and determined. They all looked at her. "Finn
wanted to leave before. I had it in my head that we were
imagining a lot of things. That we were totally vulnerable to the power of suggestion. Then I thought—I thought
that something was wrong with Finn. Then me. Then
both of us. But what would be crazy would be to stay here!
Whatever one believes—if there are or aren't demons—
there are people capable of torture and murder in the
world, we all know that. So, since I seem to be a target
for whoever or whatever, the intelligent thing to do
would be to get beyond range of it."

No one replied to her right away. Finn stretched his
hand out across the table.

Jade cleared her throat. "I think they may be right."

"It would seem the logical thing," Lucian agreed.
"But I don't know. I just wonder if they can really be out
of reach. We don't know exactly what is happening. So
far, most of what is going on happens in dreams. You
can't run away from dreams."

"The dreams . . . are all the same. When I have them,
I'm being . . . attacked. When Finn has them . . . I guess
he sees himself as some kind of god or being walking

through adoring crowds to take . . . kind of a sexual prize, I guess."

"One fear that I've had," Finn admitted, "is that the killing in Boston may be related to what's going on now. Say our coven of Satanists arranged for her murder. Well planned, since I don't know how anyone here could have known that I was in the city! Then," he hesitated, not looking at his wife, "say they wanted to make Megan another sacrifice. They've caused a rift between us, so I'd make a good fall guy for both killings."

Lucian sat back in his chair, studying Finn. "You've got an interesting point right there. How could anyone know that you were going to stop in Boston? Most drivers would get through the big, traffic-riddled city as quickly as possible. And, if I understood you right, you felt as if you were actually compelled to stop off in Boston."

"I don't even remember," Finn said with disgust.

"Someone has some kind of mind control, that seems clear enough," Jade said

"All right, hold up," Megan said with practicality and determination. "What exactly is a demon?"

Both Lucian and Finn opened their mouths, but then stared at Jade.

Lucian gave her a crooked smile. "You wrote the book."

Jade shrugged. "The term 'demon' comes from the Greek 'daimon,' and what it actually means is 'replete with wisdom.' In some societies, a demon may be considered either a good or evil spirit, and some people believe that they are just mischief makers. In the Middle Ages, there were a number of Christian demonologists, and they classified various demons, had them serving different princes of evil, and so forth. Exorcism dates back to the early sixteen hundreds. In the days of the witch hunts—across Europe—it was believed that demons could gain human form and that they were terrible sexual molesters. A succubus was a female demon who came down to seduce men. An incubus took on the male form and seduced women. Demons are supposed to be sterile, and yet, they were able to impregnate women by drawing upon the semen of living men, and making it their own. There are all kinds of accounts of demon molestations, including a number which have to do with haunted houses, or with poltergeist activity. Usually," she said ruefully, "these cases turn out to be either the longing or loneliness of certain living souls."

Jade shook her head. "But . . . it sounds as if demons are as laughable as the thought of old Rebecca Nurse really being a witch practicing black arts."

"No, that's just it. Say Rebecca Nurse was innocent of any kind of witchcraft—malignant or benign. That doesn't mean that there aren't Wiccans—your cousin is one. And by the fierce of avowal of modern day Wiccans, no evil is done in the practice of true Wicca. But hell, the rites of Satanism can be very similar. And some self-proclaimed witches have been evil people—take Aleistar Crowley."

"He was still just a man," Jade said.

"Probably," Lucian agreed.

"So what you're saying," Finn interjected, "is that most reported cases are invented, or hallucinated. But that doesn't mean that the real thing isn't out there somewhere."

"Exactly," she said softly.

"I don't know if I can believe any of this," Megan said softly.

"Well, I do know this," Jade said. "Whatever you decide about leaving, *don't* tell anyone."

Megan looked uncertainly at Finn. "Don't you think the sooner we tell Sam Tartan the better?"

"Megan, he's not going to give us a reference once we don't show up tomorrow night no matter what," Finn said flatly.

"Don't say anything, and don't worry about it," Lucian said. "It won't matter."

"How can you say it won't matter?" Megan asked.

Lucian shrugged. "Midnight is when things are going to happen. You're scheduled to play at midnight. I can guarantee you, someone has other plans. Whatever they are, I don't know. But they don't intend for you to be playing at midnight. The witching hour."

Megan glanced at her watch. "It's nearly six! We have to get ready to go in."

"We don't start until nine, Megan. We're fine," Finn said.

"We should still get going. You can drive me to Martha's first, then we'll stop by Huntington House, and be at the hotel with time to get a quick bite before we start." She looked at Lucian and Jade. "You'll be there tonight?"

"Oh, yes, certainly," Lucian said.

"Safety in numbers," Jade added.

"Remember, don't say anything. To anyone," Lucian warned. "Whether you choose to go, or stay, make sure you don't give anyone advance warning."

Megan looked at Finn. He smiled his assurance to her. "All right," she said softly.

They hadn't asked for the check, but their waitress came by, and Lucian insisted on offering his credit card. They started out of the coffee shop as a foursome.

"We probably won't be there until elevenish," Jade told Megan. "I want to go back to the shop and try to find out what else I can."

"Sure." Megan smiled at her. "Are you going to dress up? You should, you know. It's fun. A lot of Morwenna's Wiccan friends frown upon the ghoulish costumes, but to most of the people, they love the chance to be famous folk, living or dead, and monsters."

"Maybe, we'll see."

"You could do Frankenstein's monster and his bride—Lucian is so tall," Megan said.

"We could," Lucian agreed.

"Hey, he'd make a great vampire, too, huh?" Finn asked, setting his arms around his wife's shoulder, as he, too, smiled at the friends who were practically strangers—and yet, a very sudden and odd lifeline as well.

"A vampire. Hm," Jade murmured. "Maybe we'll just come as Wiccans. We'll see."

"Come just as you are, if you choose," Megan said. She hesitated, then gave Jade a quick, fierce hug. "Thanks."

"It's our pleasure to be here," Lucian assured her.

Finn thought there was something underlying in the words, what, he couldn't tell.

"Someday, you may need to give us a hand," Jade said lightly. "Hey, we'd all better get going."

She waved, and turned with Lucian back toward the direction of the bookstore. Finn led Megan down the street, since they were several blocks from the common and the car.

"Nice folks, huh?" Finn said to Megan.

She looked up at him after a moment. "I can't believe some of the things I said to him."

"Oh?" Finn queried, startled by a sudden little jab of jealousy.

"No, I mean . . . most people would have thought I was crazy. Wait—do you think they might be crazy? I mean, you say the word 'demon' and they don't blink an eye or give so much as the hint of a smile. Maybe they're dangerous themselves? Crazy people who think that they're magicians, or . . . or . . . I don't know! Maybe they've been doing occult articles and have begun to believe in their own fantasies. Maybe . . . Finn, maybe they're as crazy as everything else going on."

Finn didn't answer her right away. Her fingers cinched around his. "Finn?"

"Let's hope they're legitimate," he said softly. "They seem to be all we've got."

She walked along in silence beside him. An eerie sensation seemed to scrape against his neck and he suddenly stopped, turning back.

"Megan."

"Yes?"

"Don't look now—I mean, really, don't stop and stare! But there's a guy behind us in a long brown duster who just stopped to light a cigarette."

"So . . . ?"

"I think he was standing outside the coffee shop."

"I'll pretend to fix my shoe."

Megan did so, dropping down. She stood again, linked her arm with his, and started walking.

"Well?"

"I don't think I've ever seen him before."

"You sure?"

"Pretty sure. He's not as tall and dark as you and Lucian, but . . . pretty darned cute. I'd have noticed."

"Oh."

She laughed at his tone.

"Don't tell me you don't still notice cute girls?"

"I give more attention to dynamite women."

She was still smiling. He was glad she could still do so, and startled when she said, "Maybe we're beginning to get the entire trust thing right again."

"Maybe."

She grew serious. "Honestly, I don't think I saw that man outside the coffee shop. But then again, I wasn't really noticing people."

The car was right ahead of them. Finn was glad.

No matter what Megan had said, *he* had noted the man before.

And he was damned convinced that they were being followed.

"Finn," Megan said suddenly, pulling back.

"What?"

"I want to . . . I want to stop by the church down the street for a minute."

Finn paused. They had just reached the car. Going to the church meant backtracking, and taking up time he wasn't sure that they had. "You want to see Martha—but you want to stop by the church first?"

"Finn, please, it's important to me." She squared her shoulders. "I'm going with or without you."

"You know I'm not letting you go anywhere alone."

She smiled, and turned. He quickly caught up with her.

Despite the crowded streets, Megan managed to keep up quite a pace. But when they reached the church, she hesitated on the steps and turned back to him. "Are you coming in?"

Finn stared up at the building. It wasn't particularly old—certainly not from the seventeenth century, more likely the nineteenth century or even early twentieth century. He wasn't sure why, but as he approached, he felt a strange burning sensation.

"I'm coming, yes," he said, surprised by the irritated tone that came from his lips.

Megan frowned, but started on in. She hesitated again at the door, as if afraid that it would be locked. The door opened, and she entered.

Finn, still feeling somewhat hampered and on fire, stood at the door. It was a church; yet he was disturbed to feel that he shouldn't enter, that he didn't have the right.

No.

That he *couldn't* enter.

Megan walked on in. An eerie feeling assailed his spine. He turned. The man he had seen watching them at the coffee shop was on the street, apparently engaged in conversation with a group of costumed children.

Finn gritted his teeth and walked in.

Megan stopped by the little font at the entrance, crossing her forehead with holy water. Finn came up to her. "Do it," she said.

"Do what?"

She sighed with impatience and dipped her own forefinger into the holy water and quickly drew a cross on his forehead.

He staggered back, stunned by the burst of pain that threatened to split his skull. Megan was unaware. She was already walking down the aisle to the pews directly before the altar. Finn stumbled forward, catching hold of the backrest of the nearest pew, trying to steady himself. Black waved before him. He had to grasp each pew to move forward, to reach Megan.

Finally, he came to the pew directly behind the one where she knelt. He nearly fell into it, then down to his knees. He didn't bow his head so much in prayer as he did because he could no longer hold it upright.

"Are you all right?"

Startled, Finn looked up. He hadn't heard the priest arrive. The man was probably about forty, well groomed, his priestly attire immaculate. He had concern on his face.

"Halloween," the priest said wryly. "It gets crazy out there. Um. We create our demons, huh?"

"Yes."

"There are services here tonight and tomorrow and the next day—All Saints' Day, you know."

Megan turned. "Father, could you bless us both?"

"No," Finn heard himself mutter.

The priest was studying him strangely. Almost as if he wished that he could back away, but would not do so.

"Father?" Megan said.

"Are you Catholic?" he asked her.

"Yes."

"And you?" he said to Finn.

The pain was pressing horribly into his temples again. *I'm whatever she wants me to be!* he wanted to say. *Catholic? Am I anything? Have I ever really believed in anything?*

"Please, Father," Megan said.

He kept staring at Finn, then at last turned to Megan. "It would be best if you came to the service tonight."

"We can't. We're working."

"Ah. Tomorrow, then."

"Please. Before tomorrow."

"Come to the altar, then."

They both knelt before him. He set his hands upon their heads, and said the words of blessing.

Finn bowed his head, gritting his teeth, fighting the explosion of pain that erupted within his head.

The priest drew his hand back quickly when he was done, and seemed to favor it, as if his palm had been burned. He spoke to Megan. "Go with God, child."

Finn, desperate now to reach the cool air outside, was already hurrying down the aisle. He was vaguely aware that the priest told Megan, "I'm Father Mario Brindisi. Please, if you can, come to Mass tomorrow. And . . . if you need me, call me."

Finn burst out onto the street.

As he did so, the pain cleared from his head. Megan joined him. "What was the matter with you in there? You were so rude!"

"Head . . . headache," he said.

"We'll buy some aspirin, then!" she said angrily.

He gripped the rail going down the concrete steps back to the street, and paused. "No . . . no, it's all right now. We've got to get moving, if we're going to make work on time tonight."

Megan was still staring at him. He forced a smile and grabbed her hand, and hurried down the walk. The staggering pain was gone, but . . .

He could still feel a burning. In the shape of a cross, right on his forehead. *Tell her, tell Megan!* he thought.

No, he couldn't have her running from him. Not now. Not when he was convinced that she was in so much danger.

Again, he forced the smile, winding his fingers more tightly around hers. "Happier?" he asked her.

"Yes," she said simply.

Smiling as well, she kept pace with him and they hurried back to the car.

He looked around, certain that they were still being followed. But he didn't see the stranger who had been watching him.

He was still certain that the man was near.

Lucian spent the late afternoon roaming the streets of Salem as any tourist might. With little time left, he stopped by the newest museum.

He stared at the building a long time, then walked toward the ticket counter. The woman on duty was dark haired. He could see the many piercings in her ears and face, devoid now of jewelry.

Gayle Sawyer.

As he reached the counter, she opened her mouth to speak, then fell silent, staring at him. He smiled.

"One, please."

She nodded.

He looked at her a very long time before entering the museum.

Prowling the halls, he came up a seventeenth-century oil. It was titled, *Signing the Devil's Book*.

In the painting, three women clad in nothing but transparent strips of a gauzy, floating material cavorted about a fire in the woods, surrounded by horned, tailed creatures. In the background an imp or satyr stood, holding a plume and an open book. A plaque by the side of the painting described the belief that witches made pacts with the devil, and that he or his minions would seal the bargain with carnal activities, often in the woods at midnight.

He moved down the halls. The museum was well done. Fact was presented well, and the viewer could be transported back to somewhat comprehend a different mindset. One large plaque stated that there were cases in which—though there may have been no devil summoned, no soul sold—the apprehended man or woman might have been guilty according to the laws of the day. The very practice of witchcraft in any form was a capital crime, and therefore, sticking pins in dolls, burning herbs while cursing, or any such other such activity was clearly illegal.

He moved on. There were scenes of mass burnings in Europe, and a diorama of the events that had occurred at Salem.

As he stood studying the tableaus, he listened as a man gave a lecture to a group of tourists, recounting the possible causes of the hysteria. The man giving the lecture was dressed somewhat casually in dockers, a tailored denim shirt, and a tie. He wore a name tag that identified as Mike Smith, Curator.

Lucian fell in with the crowd. As the man continued to speak, his eyes fell upon Lucian. He drew them away, but found himself looking at him again.

And again.

Once, he lost his train of thought, and had to be prompted by one of the children on the tour.

Still, he was an excellent historian, and his speech was good, drawing a round of applause when he had finished. Several people stopped to talk to him, many with questions about details regarding the events.

Lucian waited patiently.

At last, they stood alone in the room. The man at last shook his head and smiled ruefully. "Do I know you?"

"No," Lucian said, stepping forward and offering the fellow a handshake, which was absently accepted. "I don't think we've ever met. My name is Lucian DeVeau. Thanks for an excellent education on the witch trials."

"You're welcome. Glad you enjoyed it." He was still frowning, as if he *should* recognize Lucian.

"Actually, I think we have mutual friends," Lucian said.

"Oh?"

"Finn and Megan Douglas. I'm from New Orleans."

"No Southern accent," Mike Smith commented.

"I've lived all over."

"I see."

"Well, thanks again. Great speech."

"Sure. Thank you." He stared at Lucian, then seemed to recover himself. "You should come again. We've got other exhibits." He shrugged. "Halloween week, all anyone wants to do is rehash the witch thing, but our maritime exhibits are great, too. We've halls on early settlements, and many other areas that are well worth a look."

"I'm sure. I'd love to come back, since it seems to be closing time now."

"Yes, I'm afraid it is."

"Thanks again," Lucian said, turning to leave.

"Hey!" Mike called after him.

Lucian turned back.

"I take it you'll be going to watch Finn and Megan play tonight?"

"Probably. I won't be around the entire night, but if you're going, I'll see you there."

"Great."

Smith sounded anything but enthused. Lucian exited the museum. The girl, Gayle Sawyer, was still at the counter. She stared at him as he passed. Her mouth worked, but no sound came.

Smiling, he waved and walked on.

* * *

Megan absently answered her cell phone, holding it to ear as she buttoned her blouse.

"Hello?"

"Megan. It's Mike."

"Mike, hey, how are you?"

"Good, good, thanks."

"Guess what? I did get to see Andy. My Aunt Martha was there, and she was friends with the nurse, and we got in for a moment."

"How's the old codger doing?"

Megan hesitated, then decided that she just wasn't saying anything more about her belief that Andy had spoken, not even to Mike.

"Holding his own," she said.

"Good, good," Mike told her. Apparently, he was preoccupied. "Megan, are you alone?"

"Kind of," she said, glancing toward the closed door to her room. "Finn is in the parlor, talking to Aunt Martha. Why?"

"Well, I don't think that your husband likes me very much, that's all. And I don't want him to think that I'm interfering. I don't understand this myself—I just felt that I had to call you."

"Why? What is it?"

"Um, listen, this is going to sound really strange, but . . . I just met someone who said that he was a friend of yours from back home, and . . . I don't know. I don't even know how to say this. You know me—I don't believe in any kind of weird crap—but . . . the guy gave me the creeps."

"Lucian," she murmured. "You must have met Lucian."

"Megan, like I said, this is just the strangest thing, but I had to call you. I don't mean to offend you, or insult you or anyone who really is a good friend, but . . . well, especially in your current state of mind. Watch out for this guy. There's something that's not quite right about him. I sound like an idiot, huh? Anyway, I'm just calling because I'm your friend."

"Thanks, Mike. He is—" she hesitated briefly. "He is a friend. But thanks for the warning. And I'm watching out all the way around, okay?"

"Sure. I'll be there tonight. I'm going to watch out for you, too."

"Great. Thanks.

Darkness fell early in the fall in New England. Despite the nearly full moon and the illumination pouring from street lamps and shops, it seemed as if it had deeply penetrated Salem that night.

When Lucian returned to the bookshop that night, Eddie was behind the counter with a gaggle of customers waiting to pay for their purchases. Despite that, he was yawning. He was probably tired as all hell, Lucian figured, considering the fact that during the week preceding Halloween, the shop opened early, closed late, and was probably busy throughout the hours.

Eddie, however, saw him, grinned, and inclined his head toward the back.

Lucian found Jade still pouring over volumes and journals.

She lifted her head as he entered, grimaced, and stretched. She, too, yawned.

"I don't think that I can read anymore," she told him.

"Come across anything you need me for?" he asked.

She gazed at him dryly. "No—everything was in English. Kind of English, anyway. It's just that the few people who were writing just didn't comprehend the proper use of pronouns. And they used different pronouns. I found another reference to a Douglas, though. And there are several references to a Merrill—which was Megan's maiden name, right? Merrill is easy to pinpoint. She had an ancestor who was an outspoken opponent to the proceedings, but one who was so involved with the church at the time that he apparently escaped persecution, despite his opinions. Heck, that could have been witchcraft right there, the way accusations were flying around here back then. It's easy to presume that this same man, Jacob Merrill, was with the group who went out that long ago Halloween night and took part with the mob that killed Caleb Thorne. So, if there is a cult now attempting to bring back Bac-Dal once again, Megan would certainly make what they consider to be a perfect offering or sacrifice for their demon. She really is in danger."

"Maybe they should leave," Lucian commented. "And maybe you should go with them."

"Someone is going to die on Halloween night, if nothing is done," Jade said softly.

He shook his head. "I'll stay."

She lifted her chin. "You're dealing with something new here yourself, and you know it."

He shrugged. Taking a seat on the corner of the desk he told her, "What bothers me is the passage about bringing Bac-Dal back. The three things needed—the hair, the personal possession, and the blood. Why would those be needed before the rite—if the rite was just to be a sacrifice?"

"And why would these things be happening to Finn as well as Megan?" Jade said. "Actually, he's the one who cut his hand on the dragon in Morwenna's shop. According to our conversations, they both lost hair to that creature thing at the hotel the first night they were playing."

"Maybe they're both supposed to die," Lucian said.

Jade shook her head, sitting back. "That doesn't make sense. I agree with Finn. What does make sense is the concept that she's to be an offering to this demon. 'Bac-Dal wants you.' That could mean he wants her alive in a sexual content—especially if you listen to their stories about their dreams—or else he wants her alive, and then dead. The murder of the girl in Boston could have provided the blood they needed first, and more—Finn went through Boston that night. He was *compelled* to stop there. So, here they are in Salem—obviously at odds with one another, since—no matter how discreet they've been, locals will know that he stayed at Huntington House while she moved in with her aunt. Megan's body is found—and Finn winds up accused of both murders. And certainly, there would be evidence planted to assure that he was convicted."

Lucian had been idly turning a pen forward and backward and studying the practiced movements of his hands. He looked at Jade then.

"Maybe."

"It makes sense. Unless, of course, Finn is evil, doesn't know it, and did murder the girl in Boston, is a disciple of Bac-Dal, and has brought his wife here to be sacrificed."

Lucian arched a brow. "That does remain a possibility."

She stared at him, frowning. "You mean . . . he may already be under possession by the demon, or something like that?"

"As I said—it remains a possibility."

Jade closed the book she'd been reading. She shook her head. "The answer is here, somewhere. I don't believe that Finn Douglas can be that dual—even if possessed by a demon."

"He does have a certain charm," Lucian commented dryly, but he was smiling, and Jade knew it.

"When he talks about Megan, you can see . . . he would rather die than ever hurt her."

"People don't always have that choice."

"I think you're wrong," Jade said.

"Maybe I should have sent you out to meet people," he said.

"Oh?"

He shook his head. "Either everyone I've come across is as pure as the driven snow, or the protection Bac-Dal can provide is immense. I'm managing to do nothing but make people wary."

"No hint of anything from anyone?"

"No," he said, and stood. "I'm blinded here, in a way I've never been before."

"You got us a room in an overbooked hotel," she reminded him. "And I hear some ladies downed their coffee quickly; that's for certain."

He smiled dryly. "We wouldn't want to have to wait for coffee."

"Coffee now would be good."

"It would be, but why don't you keep at it a little longer?"

"I'm just about cross-eyed now," Jade said.

He grinned. "Just about doesn't cut it." Then he said seriously, "Tomorrow is Halloween."

"I know," she said. "And I'm still missing something. Lucian, do you think that back in the early seventeen hundreds, when the people attacked Cabal Thorne . . . were they part of the Alliance?"

"Maybe. I don't know. I wasn't here in the seventeen hundreds," he said lightly.

"Brent is here, you know. He called me."

"Yes. I'm aware of that."

"Of course. You would be," she murmured.

There was a slight tone of sarcasm to her voice, but he didn't note it. He lifted his hands, distracted. "This should be . . . hell, between us all, it should be easy."

"But it's not."

"No, and it's not going to be, because . . . well, it's strange. It's kind of like fear, which can exist in the imagination with devastating effect. So much that is going on is in the mind—the dreams, for instance. You can't hunt down and destroy a dream. And what bothers me more than anything is this . . . this veil that exists. Like the blue fog. You don't always know what you're seeing through it. Let's assume it is the demon. And then the high priest, or priestess, who came across all the right rituals to bring Bac-Dal to life. Whichever, however, there is an incredibly strong power than can enter into the world of the mind. I'm afraid that we could capture a dozen followers who are merely on the fringes, and there would be a dozen more to take their places. The thing is, we've got to get to the absolute root of what is going on."

"And then?"

"Then, I believe, we'll need to know the right rituals ourselves to counter everything that is going on. I've got to leave. And you have to keep reading, and bear that in mind—that our strength may not be sufficient, despite the fact that we could mow down dozens of people. We're going to need to do all the right things, not barrel in like an army."

"Where are you going now?"

"It's getting late—places to be, people to see. If I don't come back for you in an hour, head on to the hotel without me. I'll meet you there."

"Lucian!" Jade rose, calling his name. But by that time, he was already halfway toward the door.

Jade sat back down at the table, staring at the array of written material before her. She picked up an old volume, but set it back down again.

"The necessary items," she murmured softly to herself. "Hair of the victim . . . blood of the victim . . ."

Finn Douglas had hurt himself on a dragon in Morwenna's shop. A decorative "monster" had ripped hair from the heads of both Megan and Finn. Personal objects could have easily been acquired from the two as well.

Jade gnawed on a pencil eraser.

She glanced at the store phone on the desk, then decided against it, reaching for her shoulder bag and digging into it for her cell phone. In a few moments, she'd found Megan's and Finn's cell phone numbers, but decided against dialing as well, and hoped that, when she'd interviewed them two weeks earlier, she'd had the sense to put both their cell numbers into her own phone.

She had.

She dialed Megan's number. Megan didn't answer with "hello?"

"Mike?" Came Megan's voice again. "I've got to get going, Finn is waiting."

"Megan, it's Jade."

"Oh, Jade. Hi, I'm sorry. I thought you were a friend calling back. Is anything wrong?" Megan asked. "Or, more so than before, I should say."

"No. I was just wondering—Megan, have you hurt yourself while you've been here? Just a scratch, anything?"

There was a long hesitation on the other end.

"Megan?"

"Well, this is a little weird. And it's very strange that you should ask . . . wait, just a minute. I'm going to close the door. I'm at Aunt Martha's packing up . . . Finn is just outside." She was gone for a second, then returned to the line. "I didn't want to say anything to him. For several reasons, a few I'm still sorting out myself. But I dreamed last night that I was walking in the woods, and this morning, when I woke up . . . well, my feet were dirty and I had cut the bottom of my left. It's nothing, really, just a scratch, as you were saying."

Jade stared at the phone.

"Jade?"

"I'm sorry, I'm here."

"Please, don't say anything to Finn."

"No, no . . . I've one more question. Are you missing anything?"

"No. Yes! I lost it when we first got here."

"What?"

"A bracelet. A really beautiful bracelet that my father gave me. A claddagh bracelet."

"Ah."

"How about Finn?"

"Did he lose anything, do you mean?"

"Yes."

"Not that I know of, but . . . Finn can be careless sometimes. He goes through guitar picks by the dozens. Of course, those wouldn't really be lost because he expects to use them up just like tissues. Jade, why are you asking all this?"

"I don't know yet. I'm just trying to get to bottom of what's going on, figure it all out."

"You'll call me back if you think of anything . . . if we should know anything that you've found."

"Of course! And we'll be there tonight. Maybe a little late, but we'll be there."

"Great."

"I'll let you go now."

"Thanks. See you later."

Jade pushed the button to end the phone call, staring thoughtfully at her cell. A sound drew her attention to the doorway.

She looked to the outer room. There were a number of customers browsing the shelves.

And Eddie Martin was striding away from the door area.

He'd been listening to every word she had said.

Chapter 19

Finn carried Megan's bag out to the car.

Martha stood in the parlor, smiling, and yet Megan thought that she still looked uncomfortable.

"It's all right, really," Megan told her.

"Honey, I'm sorry, I'm just worried about you. I like Finn very much. And I may be old, but I certainly see your attraction to him. It's just that . . . there's never any excuse for violence," she said very softly, speaking as if she wished she could mind her own business.

"Finn has never been violent. With me," Megan amended.

The way Martha stared at her, she found herself explaining further. "If that story about defending myself by crashing a wine bottle over his head reached you, no such thing ever happened. He never attacked me. I was just angry and hit him with a loaf of bread."

"But you said that you're having strange dreams—"

"I had the strangest one here last night. In fact, I think I went sleepwalking out your front door."

"Megan, no!"

"Cut my foot and everything," she said dryly.

"Does Finn know about it?"

"No, and don't say anything. It was just a scratch. I don't want him insisting I sit all night. I've been walking on it all day and it's fine. Oh, Martha, I know you're worried, but we're going to be fine together. We've talked a lot of things out."

Martha shook her head unhappily. "You're going to leave on November first, right when we could have spent some real time together."

"Right now, Aunt Martha, I want to get home to New Orleans." She hesitated. "You come and visit us! Then we'll have some real time together."

"It's just terrible that you've come home . . . and been so unhappy here."

"I haven't been unhappy here. Just—stressed," Megan said. Martha still looked so depressed that Megan put her arms around her and hugged her tightly.

"Maybe tomorrow," Martha suggested, "you and Finn could both come here for dinner before going to the club. Halloween night. No restaurant in town will be able to make anything decent—it will just be too crazy."

"I think we'll just be too crazy," Megan murmured. Lucian had warned them not to say anything about leaving. But this was Aunt Martha.

Martha was studying her keenly though. "Um. I see. You're going to bolt out on Sam Tartan, huh? Megan, have you seriously thought about what that will do to your careers?"

"We're not bolting out on anyone," she lied blithely. "I just want to say a real good-bye now, in case we don't get time together tomorrow."

"You really think you should go back to Huntington House with Finn? Maybe you should have both stayed here," Martha said firmly.

"We'll be fine," Megan said. She wished she believed it.

Finn came back to the door for her. "Ready? Martha, you know, you've been wonderful. To both of us. Thank you so much for everything."

"I'll see you two sometime tomorrow," she said stubbornly.

Finn gave her a kiss on the cheek. "Sure. Megan, ready?"

She hugged her aunt tightly again. "I love you," she said. Arm in arm with Finn, she walked out to the car.

As they drove, she looked over at him. "We've got one small problem, you know."

"Hm?"

"What about the equipment?"

He stared ahead for a moment, then turned to her with a rueful smile. "Nothing is worth our lives, or our marriage," he told her. His fingers curled around hers where they lay on the seat.

Megan smiled. The world around them was dark out here by Martha's, yet she suddenly felt she could see the light at the end of a very long tunnel.

The shift was changing at the hospital. There were three shifts of nurses each day, but it didn't matter who came on, when Dorcas considered herself to be the authority on her ICU patients.

Janice Mayerling, twenty-eight, attractive—and with an actual life outside the hospital, thank you very much—listened to Dorcas, trying to control her temper as the other nurse gave her a long list of commonsense instructions having to do with Andy Markham.

Janice didn't really know Andy—she had recently moved to the area, having heard that the hospital was in need of registered nurses and that they paid well. She hailed from Connecticut, not so terribly far, but far enough, and close to New York, where the world might be somewhat insane, but constantly so busy that there

could be no silly fixation with one period of history, as
there was here in Salem. She didn't mind working tonight
because she was off the next night, which meant that
she had Halloween to party.

If you were going to live in Salem, you had to take advantage of a good party night.

"A lot of people around here think that they can say
they're next of kin to old Andy, and they'll try to get in.
You don't let them. I already let Martha see him for a
minute, hold his hand, talk to him. There was no change.
A flu bug can kill Andy in seconds flat. Quite frankly, I
doubt that he'll make it anyway, but he always was a
good old codger, despite his flights of fancy, so we're going
to do our best to see that he lives. Understand?" Dorcas
demanded.

That was it.

Janice did lose her temper. "Dorcas, I don't know
about you, but I do my best to see that every patient in
my care lives!"

Dorcas stiffened down to the soles of her nurses'
shoes. "There's no call to get uppity, Janice. None at all.
I'm stressing that this patient needs extra attention."

"Martha, it's an intensive care unit! Our patients are
here because they need extra care."

She wasn't going to back down. Neither was Dorcas.

"I had best come in tomorrow and find out that
Andy is alive and still holding his own!" she warned.

Janice bit her lip. The third floor nursing supervisor
was coming down the hallway. She wasn't going to stoop
to a brawl in front of the woman.

"Good night, Dorcas," she said firmly, and turned
away.

She waited until Dorcas had finally departed and
went in to check on old Andy Markham. IV running,
vital signs weak, but steady. He would still be termed
critical, but stable.

It was going to be a long night, Janice thought.

She went to read the rest of the doctor's notations at the nurses' station. "Trust me, Dorcas, the old bugger will still be kicking when you come in tomorrow," she muttered.

She frowned, suddenly, a shiver ripping through her as the lights seemed to dim, as if giant bat wings had swept through a corner of the hospital.

"They've got to fix that air-conditioning!" said Toby Wyatt, hugging herself where she sat at the phone station.

"And the lights," Janice agreed. She hesitated, then set down her notes and walked back down the hall to look at her patient, Andrew Markham.

No change.

She was still . . . cold.

And little shivers still seemed to trickle down her spine, one after the other.

Finn showered and changed at Huntington House.

Megan had been sitting on the bed, waiting for him, but when he came out of the bathroom, she wasn't there.

He dressed quickly, and went into the dining area and then the parlor, looking for her. Sally, the pretty young blonde, was sipping tea, minus her husband. She smiled at Finn. "Hi, how's it going?"

"Good, thanks. Have you seen my wife?"

"Actually, yes. She was in here getting a cup of tea. Strange, too! Susanna walked in and saw her, and nearly dropped the tray she was carrying, she was so startled to see her, though why she should be startled to see a guest, I don't know. Anyway, Megan, your wife, helped her pick up the mess she made, got her tea in a to-go cup, and headed outside. I think she wanted to talk to Mr. Fallon, because he had come through the parlor before going out to water some of the plants by the house."

"Thanks," Finn said, and turned quickly.

"Hey, we'll be there tonight!" she called to him.

"Thanks, we appreciate the business," he told her, calling over his shoulder. He didn't know why, but he didn't want Megan alone anywhere near Fallon.

When he came out the front entry, though Megan was on the walk, Fallon was nowhere to be seen. He hurried to Megan. "Hey! You scared me. And I'm not so sure you should go looking for Fallon on your own. The old fart is creepy."

Megan smiled. "I think he's all right. Just a Wiccan."

"Oh?"

She kept smiling.

"So . . . ?" he queried.

She lifted a tiny velvet bag.

"And what's that?"

"It's a little satchel of some stuff called burdock," she said, and went on to explain, "It brings luck—and wards off evil spirits."

"You really think a little bag of stuff can help?"

"It can't hurt."

"You got it from Fallon?"

"Yes."

"Are you certain that it is the stuff called bird-whatever?"

She laughed. "Pretty certain. I've seen it at Morwenna's."

He nodded. "Okay, if it makes you feel better."

"Actually," she said, "it does." She stroked his cheek. "I'm wearing a pretty little medieval cross I picked up at a shop today, too. One or the other might just kick in."

"Sure," he said.

But he wondered unhappily just how many vulnerable young murder victims had been found clad either in their gold crosses or Jewish stars.

"We'd better get going," he said.

* * *

From the window of Huntington House, Susanna watched Megan and Finn go around to the parking lot. When they were gone, she hurried outside.

At first, she saw no sign of Fallon.

Then he came ambling around the house, the garden hose in his hands.

She marched over to him furiously.

"What the hell were you doing?"

"Taking care of business," he snapped back at her.

"You stay clear of those two," she warned.

"You mind your own business, woman, and let me tend to mine," Fallon said.

"You steer clear of them!" Susanna persisted.

"I know what I'm about," he told her angrily, and turned on the hose. He didn't spray her, but made it darned obvious that he would, if she got in the way of his watering.

"I'm warning you!" she said, turning to walk away.

"Don't *you* warn *me,* woman," he said.

She swore at him then, but she was certain he didn't hear her. The old fool—always determined to have the last word.

The hell with him.

She marched back into the house.

Fallon could dig his own grave, if he so chose.

It was a full house.

The dance floor was packed.

Every table in the place was taken.

Costumes had grown more bizarre. A giant spider with twinkling colored lights at the end of each foot roamed the room, every spider leg issuing from the shoulders of the man beneath batting everyone he walked by. Black cats abounded among the women, but

then, the black costumes were mostly very good, and
very sexy.

There were witches galore. If Morwenna was out in
the audience, she was surely about to have apoplexy by
now. There were many stereotypical costumes, hag
noses, broomsticks, tall pointed hats, striped hose beneath jagged hemmed skirts.

One woman had done an incredible job with face
putty, creating huge warts and a nose that dipped to her
chin.

There were also fairies, princesses, harem girls, and a
number of women in far more beautiful costumes.
Wings were plentiful that night, and, like the legs of the
spiders, they brushed those in the crowd. A number of
wings were bent already.

There were monks, lots of them. Grim reapers, and
more—brown capes and cowls worn with masks were
easy costumes, and they, too, littered the dance floor.

Theo Martin had kept his word as well. Finn didn't
know if Sam Tartan had put some money into it or not,
but there were a number of police officers, in uniform,
just outside the doors, as well.

At their first break, Megan told him that she was
going to take a look around and see if Morwenna and
Joseph were there. He set about changing a guitar
string, looking out at the crowd as he did so.

There was a grim reaper standing about fifty feet from
the stage, talking with a Barbie doll. He didn't know the
man, didn't think that he did, at least, and yet something
about him was vaguely familiar. A sense of unease filled
him, but then, he realized, that didn't mean a damn
thing because he was always uneasy these days.

Still, there was something. Maybe it was in the way he
was standing. He took a longer look at the Barbie doll,
but she appeared to be college age, and he was certain
that he had never met her.

Tonight, he didn't see anyone he knew—or at least, anyone that he *knew* that he knew. In all the nights they had been working, he hadn't begun to see so many fantastic costumes.

He gave his attention back to the work at hand.

"Hey, how did it go at the bookshop?"

He looked up. He didn't recognize the girl in front of him. She was dressed as a witch, and she had gone all out. Wickedly pointed hat, green makeup. "Sara?" he said incredulously.

"Yeah. Well?"

He didn't answer. He still just stared at her. Then he asked, "Sara, isn't your costume against your beliefs?"

"I was feeling like a rebel," she said dryly. "Well?"

"It's all going really well, thanks," he told her.

She came closer to him. "Well, I'm glad to hear that, but you've really got to watch out."

"Why is that?"

"Your friends from New Orleans . . . they may not be your friends."

"Oh?"

"He was in the shop today. Look, Finn, I admit to being afraid of you, right? There's something really off with you. But I can tell you, too, that your friend Lucian . . . well, there's something really off with him."

"And how do you know that? Did you read his palm or his cards?"

She shook her head, then lowered it. "I know because . . ."

"Yeah?"

She stared at him again. "When he looked at me, I would have gone anywhere with him."

"He's got a wife. He tried to seduce you?"

"No," she admitted. He thought that she was blushing, but it was hard to tell, since she was wearing green makeup. "But," she continued, "he could have made me say anything, do anything. I think he's dangerous, and . . .

tomorrow is Halloween night. He's dangerous, and you're dangerous. I know that you're dangerous, Finn. I don't believe that you mean to be—you just are. You're the chosen, or something."

He watched her, remembering the great hostility he had felt toward her, and the almost ridiculous desire to seize her sexually, assault her. Right now, she just seemed like an ordinary young woman dressed up for a Halloween party. But she also seemed sincere.

"You should lock yourself up somewhere," she told him.

"Thank you," he said gravely. "I'll give that my deep consideration."

"Finn, I'm serious. You see, I looked at Megan tonight while she was singing, and . . . she had an aura around her."

"An aura. What does that mean?"

"It means she's going to die," Sara said, and turned and walked away, back into the crowd.

He watched from the shadows.

And just before midnight, it happened.

The door to the ICU room opened and closed. The person in scrubs, cap, and mask entered slowly, bootie-covered feet moving silently across the room.

He waited.

The person moved to stand over the bed, looking down at Andy Markham. Seconds ticked by.

Then the person moved around to the plugs that connected to the monitors and oxygen system.

And bent down.

"No."

Lucian stepped from the shadows and said the single word. The person spun around.

To his amazement, he saw that it was Aunt Martha who had come to do old Andy Markham in.

* * *

Finn was watching for her anxiously when Megan returned to the stage.

"What's the matter?" she asked him.

"Nothing," he told her. "Nothing at all."

"You're lying."

He shook his head. "Are Morwenna and Joseph here?"

"If so, I haven't found them," Megan said. She was certain her cousin and Joseph would show up tonight. She watched Finn curiously, because he seemed to have gained a shade of pale. Still, she decided not to press the point. "It's getting late, but I'm sure Morwenna and Joseph will show up. Unless they're just too tired. Hey, I did see Theo Martin at the bar. He's not on duty tonight, but he told me he's keeping an eye on things anyway; people can get crazier and crazier the closer it comes to Halloween. Even just rowdy, you know? He was telling me that sometimes the local college boys like to pretend to be 'haunts' during some of the tours on these days, and that they can pretend some pretty silly things, that get people hurt—like trying to break into places, wearing sheets, and coming out on balconies. One kid dressed up like a ghost and fell out of a second floor window of one of the historic buildings last year. Luckily, he landed in some bushes and only broke his leg. But thankfully, Theo took our stalker in the parking lot last night very seriously, told Sam he had to hire a few guys and the cops would provide extra on their own. So, there are several extra guys here and around the parking lot tonight."

Finn nodded. "I've seen a few of the uniformed cops."

She smiled. "So why are you so white?"

"We need to get back in the sun for a while, that's why," he said lightly. He glanced at his watch. "Our time is up. Let's do our set."

Megan picked up her mike and looked out at the crowd as Finn announced their next number. There was a grim reaper standing very close to the stage. He had on a cowl that almost completely obscured his face, and still . . .

She could see his eyes.

She shivered.

It appeared that his eyes glimmered in the dark. Like those of a cat.

Or a wolf.

Martha stood still, staring at Lucian, but not seeming to see him. She wasn't even surprised that he was in the room, a stranger.

"What are you doing?" he asked.

She kept staring at him.

"Martha!" he said, and waved a hand in front of her. She didn't blink. He snapped his fingers, and at last, her lids rose and fell.

She took a look at him. Her eyes widened in sudden terror. She opened her mouth as if she would scream.

"No!" he said again, very softly.

The scream died on her lips, but her distress became very apparent. "Who are you? What am I doing in here? Oh, my God—Andy!"

"Sh. Andy is all right. The question is, what are you doing here?"

"I—I don't know!" she said with dismay.

In a few minutes, someone in the hospital would realize that there was a commotion going on in an intensive care room. "Let's get out of here, shall we?" Lucian said.

She stared at him, still trying to figure out who the hell he was, but aware as well that she was dressed up and in scrubs and in a room where she shouldn't be, not at that time of night.

He opened the door quietly, ushering her out.

The night nurse, Janice Mayerling, was standing in

the hall. Right in front of the room. She was staring into space. She didn't see them, despite the fact that they walked right in front of her. Lucian motioned to Martha to move down the hall, toward the elevators. He tried the same routine, waving a hand in front of Janice's face, to no avail. He snapped his fingers directly in front of her eyes. She blinked, shaking her head, pretty face knit in a frown of bewilderment, quickly masked. She stared at Lucian. "Sir, who are you? What are you doing here? Visitors are not allowed to roam around in this wing."

"I'm not here," he said quietly. "Get in with your patient; stay with him."

He turned and walked down the hall to join Martha. Though still distressed, she seemed to have stiffened up with solemn Yankee resolve.

"Who are you?"

"Lucian DeVeau. I'm a friend of Finn's."

"Finn," she murmured. Her eyes widened again. "Megan . . . she's all right?"

"They're both fine at the moment. The question right now is you."

A deeper dismay and confusion filled her eyes. "I went to bed!" she exclaimed, lowering her voice as the elevator arrived and she looked in to make sure that it was empty. "I went to bed; I fell asleep. I woke up here. Oh, my God! I hope it isn't Alzheimer's!"

"I doubt it," Lucian said.

The elevator came to the ground. "I—I don't understand any of this at all," she said in deep frustration. "I don't remember . . . I don't remember getting out of bed, coming here . . . I don't even remember waking up. And I'm in . . . I'm in scrubs!"

"So that's it—you don't why you're here, you don't remember getting here, driving here, anything?"

She shook her head. "Why would I come here? I saw Andy this afternoon. Oh, this is so frightening. But . . .

you! Why were you in there?" she asked, her confusion turning to suspicion and anger. "I don't know you— and I don't believe you know Andy. How did you get into that hospital room?"

"I don't matter in this," he assured her.

"You could have hurt Andy!"

"Martha, let's get back to you. I stopped you before you could pull the plug on Andy's oxygen supply."

"I would never do such a thing!" she protested adamantly.

"But you would have come to the hospital and dressed in scrubs to sneak into his room at night?"

Martha, looking mortified, hurried to the exit. She pushed open the door to the outside, inhaling deeply as if the night air could clear her mind.

She didn't look at Lucian, but gasped. "I had a dream! I remember the dream. Andy was in it. He was some kind of a monster and he was calling to Megan. I could hear him, and his voice wasn't at all old and decrepit, it was compelling, commanding . . . even seductive. And I remember in my dream that I was trying to get to him, to stop him before he could hurt Megan!"

Her eyes turned to his, as if wondering if he could verify such a strange dream, but then she squared her shoulders again. "This is ridiculous! Andy wouldn't hurt Megan, and I never usually have dreams—oh, it's all this stuff with Halloween, and the shenanigans of all our local Wiccans. Or the college pranksters. I'm going to see a doctor first thing in the morning. This is so dangerous. There's my car. I drove here. I might have killed someone!"

"I'll see you home," Lucian said.

"You'll do no such thing. I don't know you—for all I do know, you could be a maniacal killer. You'll get yourself out of here, before I call the police."

He arched a brow slowly. "You're going to call the police and tell them that we were both in Andy's room?"

She blushed to the roots of her silver-white hair, then lowered her head. She met his eyes.

"You're going to go home, and back to bed," he told her. "And that's it, back home, and back to bed."

Her eyes were locked with his. "Back home, and back to bed. Of course."

"And you're going to drive carefully."

"I'm going to drive carefully."

She stared at him a moment longer, then became determined. In no-nonsense fashion, she walked toward the parking lot with long strides.

At twelve-ten, the fire broke out.

Finn was on the acoustic guitar, Megan was singing.

The electric connector on the stage suddenly exploded, the noise as deafening as thunder, sparks flying to the ceiling and in every conceivable direction.

Screams rose in an instantly cacophony.

The electricity went as terrified workers and clientele alike dashed, pushed, prodded, and ran through the darkness.

Finn dropped his guitar.

"Megan!"

There was no answer.

Chapter 20

"Finn!"

Despite the bursts of sparks and the small fires instantly breaking out across the room, the darkness seemed overwhelming.

Then, as flames began to lap around in the velvet ebony of the room, the sprinkler system came on, creating more havoc.

People were being trampled.

Someone was yelling for calm; some people were shouting that others were being hurt. The words did nothing to stop the stampede.

Megan found herself being pushed and shoved, caught up in the crowd. She was shouting herself, but no avail. Panic was ensuing

"Stop!" she insisted, feeling elbows gouge into her.

There was no help but to continue to be propelled forward.

She thought she heard Finn shout her name; she tried to reply, but there was so much noise, he couldn't possibly hear her trying to shout in return. Obviously, some of these people knew where the exits were, and she was being jostled along in that direction.

A surge of flame suddenly shot up from the area of the stage. Her heart seemed to catch in her throat for a moment, but she knew that Finn couldn't still be there. He, too, was somewhere in the crowd, being forced toward an exit. The emergency signs to guide them out should have been more prominent, but by now, smoke was filling the space, obscuring even the glow of the signs.

Megan decided just to allow herself to go with the flow.

But then her foot fell upon something that was obviously a human limb. She yelled out in fury and gave a fierce shove back to the person trying to force her forward and bent down, groping blindly to help the fallen person up. She felt coarse wool, limbs, and then a hand. Fingers curled into hers and she strained to pull upward. The person came.

But then, the grip on her hand became a vise. And a whisper sounded against her ear. "Stay with me!"

Firmly guided, she made her way through the throng. By then, she was coughing and choking; her eyes stung terribly.

They burst out a door, smoke billowing out along with them. Frantic yells continued to sound; even outside, milling people were bumping into one another, every one trying to get farther and farther away. Shouts sounded from everywhere.

"It's going to explode! The whole place is going to explode."

"Get away, get away, get far away!"

"Someone planted a bomb."

"It's just an electrical fire!"

"There's no bomb!"

"Calm down!"

Sirens blared through the night; the fire department was on the way.

Megan was still jostled forward, and still blinded, for

the darkness, combined with the smoke, and the fog that curled low over the ground combined to create a thick pea soup of the night.

She felt her hair pulled, her elbow jostled.

And then . . .

Along with all the other sounds, a whisper.

"Run, Megan, run."

Then laughter. A soft, eerie laughter, right at her ear.

The person in the cloak and cowl still had her hand. In a death grip.

"We've got to get farther. We've got to get away."

"No, I have to find Finn!"

"Finn's all right. We've got to move out!"

"Who the hell are you?"

She tried to jerk away. The grip was relentless. She couldn't see the person's face. The voice was deep and raspy.

"It's all right, Megan, it's me. It's Mike. Please, let's just get far enough away in case there is an explosion. Finn will get out, he'll know you're out."

"No!" she said insistently. "Finn will be looking for me; he could run back in!"

Apparently, Mike didn't hear her. Someone pushed her from behind, forcing her forward. Mike took advantage, jerking her hand hard, running.

Propelled and dragged with equal force, Megan found herself tripping across the parking lot. They were heading past the cars, she saw.

And toward the woods.

Megan had gotten off the stage; Finn made certain of that. Despite the sparks flying and the flames leaping up around the area, he crawled on his hands and knees over the entire area of the stage, praying only that he wasn't electrocuted in the process. People were running into the dais there, falling, crying out. He could hear a voice, begging for calm. It sounded like Adam Spade. It wouldn't be Tartan, Finn thought bitterly. Tartan would have been the first person out of the building.

Someone fell hard against the stage. Finn found an elbow and lifted whoever to their feet. He was rewarded with a dazed, "Thanks!"

"Get out, buddy, get out!" Someone told him.

Another small explosion rocked the stage. Finn rolled backward to avoid the flames. Landing hard on the dance floor by the stage, he ducked beneath it quickly to keep from being trampled. Despite the tangle of legs rushing past, he managed to roll out and get to his feet.

The acrid smell of smoke filled his nostrils. The smell of it definitely indicated an electrical fire, but he knew that his sound system had been in excellent shape. So . . .

"Move, move, move! The fires are growing!"

They were, which seemed impossible, since the sprinklers were now dousing the entire place. Caught up in the exodus, Finn became determined to move with the crowd, shouting Megan's name all the while.

Feeling the temptation to give way to panic, he gritted his teeth, telling himself that Megan was capable and smart; she had been caught up in the flow of the crowd, just as he was himself. When he found an exit, he would find Megan.

Still, fear set in. All this hokum about dreams and demons. And the greatest danger they were coming to face was a fire. A very real danger. Not something out of the mist, or the imagination.

A fire that had started on the stage.

A fire set on purpose?

He thought back to the afternoon and remembered what Lucian had said—that they wouldn't be playing tomorrow night. They were scheduled to play, but they wouldn't be playing, because midnight was the hour.

The hour when a demon could best return to earth.

"Megan!" His voice roared over the spray of the sprinklers, the screaming, the thumping, the crashing of objects around him.

A few minutes later, he burst outside.

Into something worse than darkness.

A true shadow realm, for smoke had combined with the ceaseless fog that seemed to haunt the place, and all that was visible was a field of shadows.

"Megan!"

He called her name.

"Finn!"

Faint . . . the answer so faint, and yet, he was so certain he heard her. From where? From the direction of . . .

He whirled around.

"Finn!"

He thought he heard her again. Real? Imagined? He didn't now.

He had no choice. He ran in the direction of the woods.

"Mike! Stop, I mean it!" Megan said determinedly. She jerked hard on his hand, forcing him to come to a stop.

"Megan, we have to have distance!" he insisted, jerking her hand again.

"We've got distance. We're nearly in the trees."

"I am not going to let you kill yourself!"

He started to move again, jerking her along. But suddenly, in the midst of the fog, he came across a barrier and crashed into it so hard that he drew Megan along with him.

It was another man in a brown cape, the hood so far over his face she couldn't begin to see it.

"Let her go," he said firmly.

"I'm trying to get her out of here, you idiot!" Mike claimed.

"Are you?"

He reached for both their wrists, jerking. Megan was instantly freed from Mike's hand.

"Thanks. If you'll excuse me, I'm going back," she said flatly.

"No, Megan," the man said. "You're coming with me."

He had lifted his head somewhat.

Ice filled her heart. She had seen him before. He was the man Finn had said was following him. Who had stood outside the coffeehouse, watching them. His hair was a dark sable color; he wore it on the long side, like Finn. He was muscularly built, but his eyes were his strangest feature. They were a strange green, almost yellow.

It was the color of his eyes that unnerved her most.

"No, I'm going back," she said, and turned.

His hand fell on her shoulder, and he spun her around.

"You're coming with me."

"The hell I am!" Great. She kept pepper spray in her purse, but, of course, her purse was back at the hotel—burning up somewhere, probably.

And she wasn't a weakling.

But neither could she hope to win against this fellow's apparent force.

"Leave her alone!" Mike shouted.

"You don't know me, but I'm a friend," the man said.

"A friend, right!" Mike protested.

"Get out of the way."

"You're not taking her anywhere!"

The man pushed by Mike effortlessly. He made a move to come at the man, assault him. The man let out a sound that was chilling . . . a warning, but not a warning, a snarl that seemed to fill the night. She was dragged along as he walked through the fog, not blinded at all.

Gritting her teeth and bracing her strength, she coughed and choked. "Wait!"

When the fellow turned, she kicked him. With all her strength. He loosened his grip.

Megan saw her chance. She turned to run back toward the hotel. In the fog, she couldn't tell the direction at first. She heard her feet clip on the pavement.

Then, a tongue of fire suddenly lapped into the night sky. She spun around, realizing she had been running in the wrong direction.

And just as she did so, she felt a rush of wind. Someone coming, seeming to be all but part of the wind. She kept turning, listening to the fall of feet on the pavement.

Darkness seemed to blacken even the murk of the fog, as if giant wings had unfolded before her.

And as it encompassed her, she heard her name again.

A whisper.

"Megan . . ."

As Finn ran, intent only on finding the direction in which Megan had gone, he crossed over the asphalt of the parking lot. The sounds of sirens, shouting, and cacophony began to fade the farther he ran.

"Megan!" he screamed her name, into the night.

Then he paused, gasping for breath, bracing his hands on his knees as he bent over, fighting the pain in his lungs. He listened intently, praying that he would hear her respond.

Megan did not shout back to him.

But he became aware then of other sounds.

Footsteps . . .

A rush of them, running . . . coming in his direction.

He straightened, spinning around.

Figures began to emerge from the fog. One, two, three, four, five . . . more. They were all clad in cloaks, some brown, some black. The cloaks were hooded. The people

clad in them were wearing masks as well, most of them
simple plastic, the kind that gave them all a faceless
quality.

He was so furious and desperate that he was ready
for them.

When the first man rushed him, his timing was pre-
cise. He kicked out in a split second, taking the man
sharply in the jaw with the butt of his heel. A screech of
pain ensued, but even before it had died out, others
were rushing him.

At that point, instinct took over. Two came at him,
and again, the years of martial arts training paid off, for
he was able to throw out a punch and a kick at the same
time, once again eliciting gasps and cries of pain. The
one man was down, doubled over, the other was staggering.

But there were more.

Finn fought, and fought well, adrenaline and sheer
willpower his main strength. But while he jabbed and
lashed out as another two came forward for a frontal assault, someone jumped him from the back. Someone
heavy and powerful. He whirled, seeking a tree against
which to slam his assailant. Someone else came to the
side, using both his arms to snare Finn's one. Another
attacker fell to capture his arm.

He still had his legs, and he used them with brutal
dexterity. But even as he did so, he knew he was bound
to go down. He could only take on so many of them for
so long a time. Adrenaline could not sustain him forever.

One of the furious fellows he had first kicked came forward then, and delivered a blow to his chin that caused
blackness to spin with a few pinpricks of stars before his
eyes. "You'll have to kill me, you asshole!" he raged.

"He's not supposed to be harmed," someone else
yelled.

Finn gathered all his strength, freed an arm, and lashed out with a solid kick again.

"Fuck that!" the man with the lethal jab roared, coming forward again.

Finn braced for a jawbreaking swing, but it never came.

The man was picked up cleanly and jerked away from him. The guy must have been two hundred and fifty pounds, at least, but he was picked up as if he were a feather. He was tossed aside.

He couldn't see his sudden ally, but he knew the fight wasn't finished. He used the surprise his attackers were feeling, and jerked free. He elbowed the man at his right side so fiercely that he was almost certain he heard a rib crack.

The man grunted in agony, falling halfway over. "Get up!" the man on Finn's back ordered his fallen comrade, but to no avail. The one who had been at Finn's side staggered into the fog, into the safety of the nearby trees. Finn again gathered his resources, ducked, and pulled, sending the man from the rear flying over his head to land with a thud against something on the ground.

Others flew at Finn again.

He kept spinning, fighting, struggling, but in time, he thought, it was going to end. There were only so many blows he could take before he went down himself. Only the thought of Megan, out there, somewhere, without him, kept him moving. They weren't going to win. They couldn't have her.

And still . . .

When it seemed a total loss, he became aware that bodies were flying all around him. His volunteer ally had an incredible strength. Finn wasn't about to give up his own fight; there had been too many of the caped and cowled figures after him.

And then, he took a jab at someone standing in front of him. Someone in a long black cape, no hood or cowl.

"It's all right!"

A hand fell on his wrist, stopping the blow he would have sent flying. "It's me," Lucian said.

Finn stopped and stared, shaking then with it all over, and furious. He looked blankly at Lucian.

"You!"

"Yeah, sorry, I suspected something would happen, but the fire took me by surprise. I shouldn't have been so late getting here."

Finn took that in, still studying the strange new friend who had made men fly through the night. For himself . . . he had to bend over, grasp his knees, and gasp in every breath. Finally, he could talk.

"Yeah, well, thanks . . . you came. We still should have gotten the shit beat out of us, you know? What the hell—did you work for Jackie Chan or something, spend time training with Ali?"

Lucian shrugged. "You can hold your own yourself," he told him. "Good thing."

Finn heard a moan, startling him from his concentration on Lucian. He saw that one hooded figure who remained on the ground. Walking to the man, he flipped him, staring first at the mask, then ripping the mask from his head. By then, Lucian was at his side.

"Know him?" Lucian asked.

"No . . . yes. It's one of the kids working in a novelty shop near Morwenna's witchcraft store," Finn said. "I've never exchanged so much as a single word with him." His temper flew again and he bent down. "But we're going to exchange a few words now!"

He went to take the kid's shoulders, shake him back to consciousness. But Lucian's hand landed on his arm.

"You don't need to strangle him, or tear him up."

"I want to know what's going on. I want to know where Megan is!"

"He won't know."

"What the hell are you talking about?"

"I don't think he's going to know," Lucian said calmly. He hunkered down as well, taking the man's cheeks between his long fingers, and rolling the head back and forth. "Hey!" he said.

Eyes opened slowly. The pupils were huge in the darkness, totally disoriented, and then filled with panic. The boy struggled backward on his elbows, staring at Finn and Lucian.

"What do you want? Take my money—it isn't much. I've got a watch, though. A good one. Take what you want, and leave me alone . . . hey, please! Don't . . . don't hurt me. Please."

"Hurt you!" Finn said incredulously.

"What's your name?" Lucian asked him.

"Peter Davis."

"What were you doing with that group of thugs?" Lucian said.

"What thugs?" the kid inquired.

"You were with a whole group of people in similar costumes. And you all came and attacked my friend here," Lucian told Peter.

Either the kid was a great actor, or he was being truthful. He stared at Lucian with sheer amazement. "I wasn't with any group of people in similar costumes! I opted for the cloak and mask tonight because it was easy. I had to work late." He shook his head, still in confusion and fear. "I came in really late, and then . . ."

He stopped speaking, more confused.

"I remember . . . a fire. Yeah . . . the fire. I remember running from the fire."

"Bullshit!" Finn roared, about to go for his throat to shake either sense or truth out of him.

But Lucian put a restraining hand on his shoulder. "He really doesn't know," he said quietly.

"I don't know anything, honestly, and I sure as hell

don't know what you're talking about!" Peter said
pleadingly. He took a second to survey his surround-
ings. "I must have run here from the fire. Was I hit on
the head? No, man, my jaw hurts . . . and my ribs. Feels
like I was gored by an elephant."

"You attacked me," Finn told him.

Peter shook his head, staring at Finn. "No man, not
me. Hell, look at me, I'm a nerdy little guy, I'd never attack anyone."

Lucian offered Peter a hand; he came slowly to his
feet, still groaning.

Finn would have doubted that Peter's lack of memory could be possible, except that he had seen the kid's
eyes.

And suddenly he remembered that he didn't have
time to sit here and try to force the kid to say something.

He didn't know where Megan was.

"Let the kid go," he told Lucian, fear trickling through
him again. He was suddenly certain as to why he was attacked, and that was all that mattered. "Or do what you
want. I've got to get back there. They've got Megan."

"If you don't let me go this instant, you are going to
be so sorry!" Megan warned.

Blackness had given way to the night, but they were
removed from the scene, hurrying down a dark road.

If he heard her, the man gave no sign.

She was being half dragged, and half led. The man
had a grip of steel on her right arm. Panic was beginning to set in again.

She reached into the pocket of her skirt for the little
bag of burdock she had gotten from Fallon earlier in
the day. Still doubting her own sanity, she managed to
pinch a few pieces from the bag and throw them at his
eyes.

He frowned, looking down at her as if she were crazy. Either burdock really had no effect on evil spirits, or this was just a regular guy with some superhuman strength.

"What *are* you doing?"

The angle of his face was just right. Unfortunately, she was right-handed, but she still did her best to deliver at least a painful blow to his jaw.

He swore; his grip didn't lessen in the least.

He came to a dead stop, staring at her. "I'm trying to save your life, you idiot!"

"Don't save my life; let me get back to the hotel."

"Megan, I can't do that. You're in danger there."

"Let me be the judge."

"You have to come with me. I'm a friend."

"Like hell you are."

He wasn't going to release her. He was an oddly striking man, six feet, maybe six-one, sandy-haired . . . clean-shaven. Respectable looking.

Ted Bundy had been charming, so history reported.

She stared at him another moment, then cast her head back and started screaming at the top of her lungs.

He swore again, telling her to stop.

To add to his dilemma, she dropped. Just dropped. Dead weight, she went to the ground.

He swore again.

But this time, he bent down and scooped her up, throwing her over his shoulder. Her nose crashed into the wool of the coat.

She opened her mouth to scream again but he had started running.

Fast . . . like the wind. They might have been loping, as if she had been tossed over the back of a thoroughbred, or a greyhound.

There was no way she would go down without a fight. She kept trying to scream.

To claw at his back. But through the wool, her nails couldn't begin to reach flesh to rip. The wind rushed by her.

She tried to see.

But now, a cloud had covered the moon. The fog was thicker than ever.

She was flying at a steady pace . . .

Into an ebony hell.

"Wait!" Lucian told him firmly. He caught Finn's arm, since Finn was ready to start running again.

"What! Megan is in danger!" Finn shouted, his sense of urgency rising.

"You can't go back to the hotel; Sam Tartan will just have you arrested for arson."

"Arson!"

"The fire began on the stage—with your equipment."

"But that's bull!"

"Of course, it's bull. But Tartan will have you arrested. Finn, think. They want you and Megan separated. Get the police in on it, and you're in a jail cell and Megan's . . . out there. Somewhere. Vulnerable."

"I have to find her!"

"We'll find her. But you have to listen to me."

Finn stood still, teeth grating so hard they could have snapped. "Who the hell are you?" He demanded furiously. "What are you? How can you keep knowing any of this. Shit! How the hell do I know that you're not a major part of it? How did you throw people around like that? Yeah, you're right. I know something of what I'm doing, but that was a crowd against us. Damn it, tell me now just who—or what—you are."

Lucian stared back at him. "You don't want to know," he said quietly. "But this is the truth before any god every honored—you have to trust me now. We're the only friends you've got."

"Megan—"

"I know where Megan is."

"Take me to her—now!"

They were going deeper and deeper into the woods. They'd followed the road—to exactly where, Megan didn't know—and then turned off.

Her captor came to a halt, drawing her back over his shoulder, and setting her down in front of a tree. She would have stood, except that her limbs didn't seem to be working, and so she sank against the bark as he set her down.

He hunkered down before her. She stiffened, ready to fight again. She eyed him carefully, ready to fight with her mind. *He was one of them. He was a liar; he had been held in reserve. She was to be some kind of a sacrifice to Bac-Dal, and this man was going to see that she was kept prisoner until tomorrow at the midnight hour. But that meant she had time to get away.*

"Are you all right?" he asked.

Her eyes narrowed. "Oh, yeah, I'm just fine, you asshole. You've abducted me like a sack of meat, thrown me all over, forced me here against my will, but I'm just fine."

"Look, you haven't met me, so you won't believe this. I am your friend. And you have to trust me for a few minutes now. We're almost at what we believe to be a safe house. I need to make sure that there's no one around the area. Can you stay here, please—I'm begging you—for just a few minutes?"

She looked at him. There was something about him. She wanted to believe him, wanted to trust him.

He'd abducted her.

They were in the woods . . . deep in the woods. And tomorrow was Halloween. She was insane if she trusted him.

But then again, his eyes held some strange power . . .

And emissary of a demon would have power, right? Logically, she didn't believe in demons. But hell, logic was gone, and evil was out there.

She shook her head. "I can't trust you! I need to get to Finn."

"Megan, Finn will come to you, I swear it."

So earnest, his words were so earnest. He stood then, as if determining he had to trust her. He disappeared into the woods, silent as a cat in the night.

Finn will come to you.

Right. Finn would come to her. Because someone else had kidnapped Finn. And everyone would believe that they had disappeared on purpose, afraid of repercussions from the fire which had surely gutted half the hotel. It had all been so well planned out.

Lucian had said that something would happen. That they'd never be playing at the hotel at midnight on Halloween.

So . . .

Had Lucian caused the fire? Mike had tried to tell her that Lucian was evil. Mike had tried to help her tonight. Maybe they had been drawn into the dead heat of the fire while trying to escape the smoke.

She set her hands upon the tree trunk, trying to use the support to help her to rise. She came to her feet.

But then she paused.

She could hear . . . footsteps?

Soft crunching . . . like something moving the dying leaves of autumn that littered the forest floor. Someone was coming. Someone moving stealthily. Creeping up on her, slowly, carefully.

A hooded figure, bearing a knife held high, burst into the clearing, running straight at her.

Megan screamed in terror and turned to run.

From behind her, she suddenly heard another scream. She turned, and heard a fierce, deep snarling sound.

She turned back.

The fog had settled over the clearing. But she thought she saw . . .

A dog.

A giant dog. Ripping into the caped entity that had been running toward her with the knife.

"This is insane," Finn said. They were in Lucian's rental car, curving around a winding road in the gray darkness that not even the moon could penetrate. "Why would Megan have driven out here?" He looked at Lucian suspiciously. "I don't care who or what you are, but if anything happens to Megan, I'll find a way to kill you before I die, so help me."

Lucian cast him a glance that was chilling. "We're trying really hard to save your fool lives—and others as well, since the rebirth of a demon could be deadly to hundreds of people for decades to come."

"Why would Megan be in the woods?" Finn insisted angrily, refusing to be cowed, no matter the ice fire in the guy's strange eyes.

"I have a friend who went to see that she wasn't taken," Lucian said.

"Great. You have a friend. And he can throw people around the woods as if they were pebbles as well?"

"She's safe with him."

"In a cabin in the woods?"

"Obviously, yes—they were trying to take her tonight. So, obviously, yes, my friend went to make sure he could take her before they could—and he checked out the cabin in the woods to make sure he could find a real safe house."

"This is just so much bull!" Finn accused him, his growing fear for Megan giving him the adrenaline and strength to fight both his instinctive fear for himself, and the words that were being said. "Dammit, Lucian, who are you? What the hell is going on? This has got to be some really insane murder plot. Demons, shit! *What* are you?"

Lucian stared at him, his own temper obviously at a peak.

"You want the truth? The absolute truth? Hell, yes, there are demons out there. Demons, boogiemen, monsters, and more."

"And how do you know that? How do you know that for fact?"

"How do I know?"

The car jerked to a halt at the side of the road.

"How do I know? Because I'm a fucking vampire, and my friend is a werewolf. There, you've got in a nutshell. Now, can we try to get to your wife? Or do you want me to prove what I've just told you?"

Chapter 21

"Stop. For the love of God, please stop!"

Megan felt the wind at her back; he was behind her again. He could leap up her, injure her, any second.

Keep running? Run until she could run no more? Wouldn't that be the instinctive thing to do, the way to win? Fight on and on until . . . there could be no more fight.

But something in the tone of the words caused her to halt. The man had just stopped a maniacal assassin from coming after her with a razor-sharp blade. Or had he? Maybe it was all part of an act, and as Mike had said, they shouldn't trust the outsiders any more than they could trust anyone in the town.

Yet, it might be more prudent to prevent injury, and still, there remained that ring of honesty; this man had evoked God's name. Would the real enemy have done so? Perhaps yes, the better the deception.

A cold breath seemed to touch her nape. She was caught anyway.

She came to a dead standstill. To her amazement, the man crashed into her; they both stumbled forward, and then down.

He was quickly up on a bended knee, and staring down at her, talking quickly rather than offering any force. "My name is Brent Malone. I'm a friend of Lucian and Jade. There are others with us, and we believe that you are in serious trouble, far worse than you've even imagined."

"I imagine that someone wants me dead, what could be worse?" she demanded.

"There are worse things, believe me."

"Who was that man back there?" she asked, and added determinedly. "Is he dead?"

Brent Malone shook his head. He looked as if he should have been a rock musician himself, with rather long, sable dark hair. Then again, he was tall, wiry, well-muscled, like a laborer, or lightweight boxer. Unnerving all way around.

"He's not dead."

"Who was he?"

"It doesn't matter."

"What do you mean, it doesn't matter? He tried to kill me."

"I don't think he intended to kill you."

"He was running around with a butcher knife, coming straight at *me*, but he wasn't supposed to kill me."

"I don't think so. He was supposed to scare you. Just as the fire was supposed to send you into hiding."

"Why?"

"Because," he said flatly. "We don't think that you're supposed to die until tomorrow night."

The shivers that swept into her somehow made her believe that his words held a ring of solid truth. "All right, so I'm not supposed to die until tomorrow night. And I'm meant to go into hiding—where, of course, 'they'—exactly whoever 'they' may be—will be able to find me when others can't. But the situation is looking pretty serious to me right now. I don't know you, and you're expecting me to trust you. I don't know what's happened to my husband—between you and Mike, I've been taken so far from the scene of the fire that I may never find Finn. And Finn . . ."

She stopped, a sudden tie in her throat preventing her from speaking further. What could be worse than someone wanting her dead?

Finn, possessed by some outside force, being the one who wanted her dead!

"Lucian is with Finn; I am certain," Brent said, as if drawing on deep reserves of patience as he spoke. "Listen to me, please, because I can't let you go, and I don't want to hurt you."

"Fine. Then you need to tell me just exactly what happened back in the woods, and why it shouldn't matter who was doing the attacking. Wouldn't he have been part of 'they'?"

"No. Most probably not. Everything happening now is just a teaser, and the people provoking you tonight are just vulnerable to the suggestion of those in power, while those in power will not risk themselves or their identity until the time is right."

"Great. You apparently have a dog, and the dog brought the man down for you. Where did the dog come from, and where did it go now?"

She was terrified, but determined that her speech would be matter-of-fact.

"Let's take it slowly for now, huh? The man in the woods is alive, but dazed, and not one of the main Satanist group, I don't believe. I saw him delivering mail earlier today, so he was most likely just out to party tonight. Tonight was intended to destroy the possibility of you and your husband being surrounded by a crowd of hundreds tomorrow at the midnight hour. And yes, probably, to cast suspicion upon the two of you as well, to bind a rope more tightly around Finn's neck—make it appear as if he might be an arsonist on top of all else. I believe you were to have wound up in the custody of the Satanists, with Finn in a rage at the police department, but maybe under arrest himself as well despite your disappearance—after all, plenty of people in the town knew that you two were at odds, your own relatives believe that you're afraid of him. Please listen carefully, and I'm begging you to believe me. There are a number of us here. We're part of something we call the Alliance, and we . . . we try to keep down some of the murder and destruction in the world caused by such people as those who are trying to bring Bac-Dal back into the world."

Megan stared at him blankly.

"I swear, I'm telling you the truth."

She struggled for words. It wasn't difficult to believe that a group of people might be evil, that they might intend to do murder for a diabolical ritual.

It was more difficult to really believe that a demon existed, and that it could be brought back. And yet . . .

There were the dreams.

He extended a hand to her. She took it slowly, eyes on him warily as she came to her feet. "Where's your dog?" she demanded again.

"The dog?"

"Don't play me for a fool! I saw a huge dog over the man with the butcher knife."

"Actually, you only thought you saw a dog," he said.

"I know I saw a dog."

"You saw a wolf."

"A wolf? So where is it now?"

"Occupied. If you should happen, though, to speak to anyone not in our immediate circle, don't mention the wolf. It will never hurt you, only protect you. Please— the place we've rented is just ahead."

She wasn't sure what to do. Go with him to a remote location in the woods and perhaps play right into the hands of the evildoers?

A shiver rent down her spine. *She might as well. This man could kill her here and now and be done with it.*

But that wasn't part of the plan, was it? She was supposed to die tomorrow night, at the stroke of twelve.

"Please."

She nodded, because there was nothing else she could do. He would force her to go with him, no matter how polite he was trying to be.

"Your husband will come there," he told her.

"If Finn isn't there, I'm leaving," she said with a determined show of bravado.

"He'll be there. Just give it a little time. That's all I'm asking."

"He'd best be!"

The man smiled. "Jade is there, and my wife."

"And your wife? I see, she's part of this Alliance as well?"

"Her name is Tara. And there are others. Rick and Ann. Maggie and Sean Canady."

Others.

The perfect coven?

"Great," Megan muttered. "A dark cabin in the woods. Let's go."

"This area isn't Salem, but would have been Salem Village four hundred years ago," Lucian said.

Finn still stared straight ahead. They had parked the car, not wanting to bring it too close the actual cabin that Jade had rented late that afternoon. He hadn't been able to speak since Lucian's last outburst. He felt stunned, not real, as if he were walking in one of his own nightmares. It was too much to assimilate, far too much to believe, at one time.

But when Lucian twisted a key in the lock and they entered the cabin, Megan was there. She was sitting in an upholstered rocker before a roaring fire, a cup of something in her hand, staring at the flames. She looked as dazed as he felt himself. There was a beautiful woman with reddish hair and green eyes in the chair opposite her, and a handful of people sitting at a table in the dining room that attached to the parlor area.

He gave the others no notice at first.

"Megan!"

Her name croaked from his lips. She jumped up, spilling the cup of whatever she had been drinking, and with a glad cry, came flying into his arms.

He held her, feeling as if it was just the two of them against the world. And looking around the room, he was still dazed.

In all, they equaled ten. Himself and Megan. Lucian and Jade. Another fellow of an average-tall height, another man of about forty-something, one with deep brown hair of a shaggier length, and one who was light, with piercing blue eyes, who had the ability to appear tall, even when sitting.

Finn held Megan close to him, staring at the group around him. He felt fiercely protective, determined to hold her against the world, though he felt his spirits sinking. *If these people were not what they claimed, he was dead, and he had lost, because he knew he couldn't hope to win any battle against them, certainly not by himself, here in the woods. He had already seen what Lucian could do, and though he hadn't asked the man to prove his words, he had no doubt that he had been speaking the truth.*

Feeling defensive as well as far more than dazed and confused, he went on the offensive, looking around the room, catching the eyes of each individual before moving on.

"All right," he said coolly, "which one is the werewolf?"

"Werewolf?" Megan gasped softly.

"That would be me."

The man he had seen waiting outside the coffee-house came forward. He was the one with the dark hair and unusual green eyes.

"Werewolf?" Megan repeated. She seemed to have lost some strength and he held her more tightly.

"Want to explain what the rest of you are?" Finn asked tightly, but politely. "Rick Beaudreaux, vampire," the blond man with crystal blue eyes said. "Vampire."

"I'm Ann," his wife, said one of the women, a very elegant, chic woman with dark hair and ice-light eyes said, with a very French accent on the two words alone. She shrugged then with a rueful smile. "Simply human."

The auburn-haired beauty who had been sitting across from Megan rose then, walking to him, offering him a hand. "Maggie Montgomery Canady, human now, and my husband, Sean." She indicated the dark-haired fellow who was graying ever so slightly. "He's a cop in New Orleans. Honestly. He can show you his credentials. That might make you feel better."

"Yeah, it might, except that credentials can be forged," Finn said.

The man with the extraordinary height spoke up then. "If we wanted to cause you any injury, you'd be dead already," he said. "Ragnor Wolfson. Vampire. My wife, Jordan." He indicated the petite woman at his side.

"How do you do?" she said politely.

Megan was almost dead weight in Finn's arms. He thought that she might be about to pass out. Apparently, they hadn't shared this information with her earlier.

But Megan didn't pass out. She stood taller.

"Vampires," she said, and looked at Brent Malone. "And a werewolf. Hence the dog I thought I saw, naturally. And the moon is very nearly full."

"I don't need a full moon," he murmured.

"And you all!" Her gaze swept over the room. "Could you explain this with a little more detail? You simply think you're vampires—like those cults who believe that drinking blood will make you more powerful. Or you are vampires? And if you are vampires—shouldn't we be running from you faster than from any demon in hell?"

Lucian came before them. "Obviously, we don't intend you harm. As Ragnor said, you'd be dead now if we did. We don't need to practice any rituals, have a full moon, a certain date, or any of these other small details going on here."

"But," Megan said, "how do you exist then?"

"Not on the human populace," Ragnor said impatiently, rising. "But we can, suffice to say that not one of us is a vegetarian."

"We're wasting time," Tara said impatiently. "If we're going to get to the bottom of this in less than twenty-four hours, we need to get started now."

Finn shook his head. "I don't understand. If there are so many of you in this Alliance thing, and you have such great powers, why don't we just go in and clean out the Satanists?"

"Good idea," Sean Canady said. "Except—do you know exactly who they are? And even if we could pick off the fringe members, most likely, whoever has the contact with Bac-Dal, the high priest or priestess, surely has the power to add to the number needed if necessary."

"You see," Jade explained, coming closer and slipping her arm through Lucian's, "contact has been made. So whoever the person is, he or she has a certain strength already."

"One that I can't actually combat," Lucian told them.

"I'm confused," Megan said. "Very, very confused."

"It's not going to be a battle of simple strength," Lucian told them. "There are powers that have been set loose, and they've been set loose through ritual. We're going to have to fight back in the same way."

"Don't you see? Everything that has gone on tonight was staged—but none of the starring characters were in on the act. Bac-Dal has given his servant certain powers—like the power of mind control."

"What we need to do tonight is read," Maggie said, rising from her position at the fire. "Sean has gotten into the police files on the Internet, searching for past criminal activity involving the citizens of the area, but none of us think that we're going to find anything. Except for information on that recent murder in Boston, which we think is related to what's happening here now."

Finn felt instantly defensive again. "I didn't kill the girl in Boston."

"Probably not," Sean agreed.

"But," Lucian said, "you were there. And you felt the power, forcing you to stop in Boston. And you awoke in the morning—having lost hours of time."

Finn shook his head vehemently. "That doesn't matter. I don't believe that this mind control can make a person do something so horrible. I'm not a killer."

"Someone killed her," Lucian began.

"Not me!" Finn insisted furiously.

"Lucian isn't saying that you did murder her," Jade said. "Just that you were meant to be there when she was killed. That way, others would be suspicious of you." She exhaled.

Jordan Riley, a petite woman, but one with incredible dignity when she stood, spoke up calmly. "The big pot of coffee is done."

"Coffee. I think I need a straight shot," Megan muttered.

Jordan smiled. "Yes, but coffee is what we need right now." She extended her hand and Finn saw what they had all been doing around the table.

Jade had somehow managed to "borrow" a large bundle of books from Eddie Martin's shop. "We need to get every clue out of this that we can."

Ann Beaudreaux headed toward the kitchen. "I'll bring in the coffee. Please, don't despair when you see the amount of work we've got to get through. Tara and I are cousins . . . our grandfather is a part of the Alliance as well, and he is Paris now, a bit too old to travel well, but he has a wealth of research material on the occult. He'll be working on this as well."

"I've got to go," Rick said suddenly. "Old Andy has been left alone at the hospital too long now as it is."

He inclined his head toward Finn and Megan, and excused himself to get out the door.

Lucian indicated chairs at the kitchen table. "Have a seat. We're going to start by going through everything that has happened since you've come."

Megan looked up at Finn. He stared back at his wife and shrugged. "What else are we going to do?"

"This has to be one of our dreams," she whispered.

He shook his head. "Neither one of us is waking up," he told her ruefully.

"First off, this is very confusing," Jade said, ushering them to their chairs. "We know that certain rituals call for a blood sacrifice, hair, perhaps an object belonging to the person, and blood of 'the anointed.' We know that Megan lost a bracelet; a Halloween decoration at the hotel relieved you both of some hair. Finn—you were cut by a dragon in Morwenna's shop." She hesitated. "And Megan, you dreamed about walking in the woods at night, then awoke to find that you had cut your foot, and that it appeared as if you'd really been walking through dirt."

"What?" Finn demanded.

Megan looked at him. "I didn't want you to know. I didn't want you to worry any more than you already were."

"They have everything then!" he murmured, threading his fingers through his hair.

"Except us. They don't have us!" Megan reminded him.

"They don't have us," he agreed softly.

He looked around at the group surrounding them. Great. He'd been afraid to trust anyone in the area. Anyone.

So here they were now, surrounded by . . .

Monsters.

An alliance. What did they call themselves? Good monsters? Monsters 'R' Us?

It all had to be a nightmare.

"I think," Tara said, "that Jade's discovery of your name in the old texts is very important, maybe a key to the whole thing, Finn."

He shook his head. "I don't know anything about any ancestors having been here in the sixteenth or seventeenth centuries. And we know that Megan's were."

"The warning Andy Markham had was for Megan," Ragnor pointed out. " 'Bac-Dal wants you.' "

"But we still have the Douglas name in the records," Jade said. "And that could mean one of two things."

"All right, shoot," Finn said.

"The first is that your ancestor might have been part of the Alliance at that time—it is a loose-knit organization that has been in existence since . . . well, the beginning of time, probably. People really only come in contact with one another when it becomes necessary," Tara told Finn.

"I still don't believe I had an ancestor back here then," Finn protested.

"Right. And before this week, did you believe in demons, vampires, or werewolves?"

Finn shrugged, and almost smiled. "Point taken." He looked at Jade. "You said that there were two possibilities. What is the other?"

"That you are really the one chosen by the demon,

you were manipulated to kill the girl in Boston, and you are the evil meant to steal the life and soul of your wife."

Morwenna was hysterical.

There was nothing on television except for news regarding the fire at the hotel.

Amazingly, no one had been trampled or burned to death. Dozens of people had reported to the local hospitals suffering from smoke inhalation.

That was all to be expected.

What drove her to distraction was the fact that police were looking for Finn and Megan Douglas, who had disappeared, and were wanted for questioning in regard to the fire.

Despite the fact that it was three A.M. and she'd had almost no sleep lately, she couldn't allow herself to wallow in fear and anxiety. She had to be productive, move, do something.

She paced in her bedroom.

Finally, Joseph let out a sound of vast impatience. "Morwenna! Obviously, they're hiding out, lying low."

"Something has happened to them, someone has them. I know it."

"Maybe they're running, knowing full well that the law is after them."

"Finn lit the fire!" Morwenna exclaimed suddenly. "That bastard. There's something wrong with him. I've known it . . . he lit the fire. He's going to kill my cousin."

"Morwenna, the cops are looking for them."

"Everyone is looking for them," Morwenna muttered, glancing at her husband.

"I need some sleep," he said.

She bit her lower lip, staring at him. "Sorry," she said.

But she didn't get back into bed. She ran to the

shop, keyed it open, and gathered supplies. Then she headed down to the basement, and her altar there.

She arranged herbs upon the altar, and took out her book of spells. She closed her eyes, praying fervently.

In time, images formed in mind. Trees, swaying beneath the moon. Natural carpets of green grass, leaves, trees. Paths lit by stars.

Tinged by fog.

Very low fog . . .

Creeping slowly across the terrain, as if the fog were a personality itself, as if it looked, searched . . .

She froze suddenly in the midst of her deep concentration.

Someone was standing behind her.

She felt the chill against her neck.

She turned, lifted her chin, seeing who had come.

"I know where they are," she said.

"Really?"

"And there's no time. I've got to get to Megan.

"My God!" Megan breathed.

The group around the table stared up at her.

She shook her head. "I'm sorry . . . I was reading a factual account about Catherine Montvoisin, La Voisin, as they called her. For years she arranged for 'black' masses during the Sun King's reign in France, and apparently, half of the aristocracy wound up involved. She had a home for unwed mothers, and the infants were sacrificed at the altar and their blood was dripped over the attendees so that they might achieve their goals through the power of Satan. The king's favorite mistress, Madame de Montespan, was reputed to have allowed her body to serve often as the naked altar of living flesh for the proceedings."

Lucian looked up at her, a grim twist to his lips. "La

Voisin went to the flames, singing," he said. "And it's true, if you look at history, the monsters you'll find in human form are endless. Gilles de Rais was a soldier, a statesman, a warrior who stood at the side of Joan of Arc, and then he went on to murder hundreds of children—a crime he confessed rather than face the torture before execution."

Finn slammed his own book shut. "I found chapters on Anton Szandor LaVey, the Black Pope—who defended Satanism and condoned no acts of violence," he said, shaking his head. He stared at Lucian. "We're finding nothing here to help." He hesitated. "I admit that I am reeling; it's still incomprehensible to believe that you all what you say you are, and I don't understand how that can be, or what your Alliance can be, but . . . this is simply insane. The best thing to do, I believe, is simply get Megan out of here. Get her as far away from these people as possible, whether they're planning a blood sacrifice, or the real rebirth of a demon."

There was silence for a moment as they all looked at one another.

"He could be right," Tara said softly.

"Maybe a few of us should just start getting both of them out of here," Jade said to Lucian.

Lucian hesitated. "I'm not sure why, but . . . I don't think that will help us."

"If they don't have Megan, they can't shed her blood," Finn said flatly.

"Perhaps you're right," Lucian said slowly. "But . . . you mustn't go unarmed against these people."

"You're going to get us guns?" Megan said.

"I don't think that guns will do you much good," Lucian said. "No, there are other weapons. Keep reading; give me an hour, and I'll return."

He rose. Jade frowned, looking up at her husband.

"Keep reading. Our greatest power is going to be in

what we know," he said. "Ragnor, if you'll come with me?"

The tall man rose, watching Lucian thoughtfully.

"What is your plan, Lucian?" Tara asked.

"I think we need to keep an eye on our friends and neighbors," he said lightly. "I'll need his help. I have to break into a church, you see."

Finn rose as well. "I'm coming with you."

"Finn, perhaps you shouldn't," Megan murmured uneasily.

But Lucian studied him, and seemed to come to a firm conclusion. "Actually, I could move much faster without you, but . . ."

"You could be recognized and arrested," Megan persisted.

Finn walked over and kissed her lips lightly. "It will be all right." For a moment, he seemed uncertain himself, but then he said, "You'll be all right, as long as you're here."

Jade came over and set a hand on Megan's shoulder. "Finn will be all right with Lucian."

Then Finn frowned as if doubtful. "Megan—"

"I will be fine here," she said.

"Stay with these . . . people." He gave the last word just a bit of hesitation.

"Let's go," Lucian said.

Martha watched the news, feeling ill. She hadn't been able to go back to sleep.

She hesitated a long time, watching the story repeat, repeat, and repeat again.

Then she stood. It was time to go out again, come hell or high water.

* * *

Megan yawned. She glanced at the clock over the mantel. Six in the morning. Light would be coming soon.

They were no longer gathered around the table, those who remained. Sean Canady sat at a laptop, sipping coffee and studying the files he brought up, barely blinking. Occasionally, he would say something to Ann, who would come over and follow his train of thought, and refer again to one of the many books they had. Jordan had curled up on the sofa with a number of ancient pages, while Jade sat at the other end of the sofa, looking at others. Ann and Tara were studying books of spells, while Maggie seemed to prowl the place like a jungle cat, going from the men to the women, making suggestions here and there, and offering insights to their research. Only Brent Malone remained at the table. He'd taken a notepad and was jotting down a list of what had happened, and what they had learned, trying to make sense of exactly what was planned.

Megan sat in the chair facing the fire.

Maggie brought her another cup of coffee, then sat across from her, cradling her own cup and staring at the fire.

"Maggie," Megan said worriedly.

The other woman looked at her.

"Are they going to be all right?" Megan asked in a whisper.

"They? Who?" Maggie asked. "If you're worried about Finn, believe me, he's safe with Lucian."

"Actually," Megan said, "I wasn't worried about Finn at the moment. I was thinking about Lucian, and Ragnor. It's almost light."

Maggie smiled. "Some of what you see in the movies is true; some isn't. They won't turn to ash once the sun rises. Their strength is greatest at night. But don't worry."

"And then, I started thinking after they left. A vampire is going to break into a church?" Megan said.

Maggie hesitated. "Lucian is very fond of churches these days. He wasn't always. Lucian is definitely a man on a mission, since he, more than any of us, feels a need to atone for the past. He's old, you see, very, very old. And he wasn't always on this side of the good and evil question." She hesitated. "Men have created most their own devils, you know. And as you might have discovered, the power of the mind is one of the greatest strengths in the world. Take the entire Wiccan/Satanism dilemma. Wicca was the religion of the ancients. A celebration of nature. There were feasts for the harvests, for the home, for the time of reaping, the time of sewing. Way back then, the Wiccans, or Wise Ones, knew no such thing as Satan. But then the Middle Ages came, and Christianity, and there were men within the church who began to believe in the 'Evil Eye,' and supernatural, or magic acts done out of malice. And as you've seen, there were those who then twisted practices of the old magic into a defiance of the Christian rites, and prayed to Satan, the God of Darkness, using many of the ancient pagan beliefs as well. True Wicca offers no harm; Satanism celebrates debauchery, and allows men the opportunity to let loose all the demons within them. The ancient Greeks believed that everyone had a guardian daimon, or demon. And there were some great philosophers who believed that demons were within all of us, that demons were the parts of our souls who longed to lash out, cut, slash, and cause harm within the world. The point is . . . what you believe is what gives you strength, whether it's to do good, or evil. You have a deep faith. Cling to it. It's important. That doesn't mean that you won't trip or stumble along the way. But at the worst of times, don't give up your faith in all that is good. It may be the final salvation."

Megan smiled. "I'm still not sure I believe in werewolves—but I believe I saw a giant dog standing over a man who would have cut me to ribbons tonight."

"Ah, and there . . . you have said it. You *believe* that you saw a giant dog."

"So . . . I didn't really see a dog?"

Maggie smiled mysteriously. "He's a wolf, silly, not a dog."

"Maggie!"

"A great deal remains in the heart and the mind of the observer, always," Maggie said simply. "And then . . . well, beyond it all. Most people believe in a divine being, in one way or another. Study religion, and you'll see that gods and goddesses—from the ancient Roman, Norse, and so on—usually have counterparts throughout human belief. Perhaps there's really one place to get at the end of life here on earth, but many paths that may be taken to get there. I personally believe in the soul, and that what lies in the soul is what makes us what we are. And it's why a vampire can learn not to kill, and why he can enter a church at will, and wear a crucifix when he feels the need."

"You've learned all this from observation?" Megan asked.

Maggie shook her head, smiling secretively. "Actually, I was a vampire."

Megan frowned. "But you're not now?"

"No."

"You were a vampire, or you believed you were a vampire?"

Still smiling, Maggie shook her head. "I was a vampire. I admit, I'm the only person I know who ever was a vampire, and gained mortal life again. But you see, that's because there are powers out there greater than evil."

"And what are they?"

She laughed aloud. "Goodness—of course. Love, and belief in our fellow man, and so on." Watching Megan frown, Maggie waved a hand in the air. "It's a very long story, and we've got far too much to worry about tonight. However, to make that long story short, remember that strength of will, love, and the fight for good over evil can all be very powerful."

"Hey!" Jade exclaimed, suddenly looked up from her reading. "I have found the name Douglas mentioned again," she said.

They all stared at her.

She read from the volume on her lap. "'And among those in attendance was the outspoken one, he who called out, Finnegan Douglas.'"

Ragnor departed on his own; apparently, he and Lucian had agreed that Andy Markham might well be a key to the truth, and Ragnor was impatient that he should be watched.

Finn drove alone with Lucian as they headed into town.

"I came to church with Megan before we went to the hospital to see Andy," he told Lucian, staring ahead into the street. "It was painful. I thought that my head was going to explode."

"Did you see a priest?"

"Yes . . . Father Mario Brindisi."

"Were you blessed?"

"Yes," Finn said, staring at Lucian curiously.

Lucian only shrugged.

Finn hesitated. "All right, let me put it this way. I thought I was going to die, the pain was so great when I was in here. And with everything that has happened . . . no matter what I say, no matter what denials I give, I'm afraid. I'm afraid that I . . . that I might have killed the girl in Boston, that I might . . . that I might hurt someone. That something is happening to me. So . . . if it comes to a point when I may hurt someone . . . anyone . . . Megan, specifically, you have to stop me. By whatever means it takes. Swear to me that you'll do that."

Lucian turned to look at him at last. "Trust me. If you threaten Megan or anyone around you, I'll bring you down faster than you can blink. All right? Let's see how you fare in church, huh?"

They found parking easily enough; it was still early morning, and despite the havoc of the fire at the hotel the night before, the majority of the populace was still gearing up for a big night.

As they approached the church, Finn fell back, feeling the pounding begin in his head. Lucian opened the door easily enough, and stepped inside. As Finn faltered, Lucian stepped back, slipping an arm around him to help him in. Finn gritted his teeth against the agony that assaulted him.

"You'll make it," Lucian said firmly.

Half dragging Finn down the aisle, he came to the front of the church and lowered Finn down into one of the pews. He paused in front of the altar for a minute; Finn, though nearly blinded, watched him, and watched his lips moving. Then Lucian moved. Finn hadn't heard a thing, but apparently, Lucian was aware that the priest had come into church.

"We need your help, Father," Lucian told him.

The priest stared at him a long time, then said, "I can do nothing, you know, without the approval of Rome."

Lucian shook his head. "You're afraid."

"Of you? Yes, that I am. Very afraid."

Lucian shook his head. "Father, you are afraid on so many levels. We need your help. But I understand if you can't give it. I will ask you to turn a blind eye, though, to the theft I am about to commit."

Father Brindisi nodded slowly. Then he walked back toward Finn. By then, Finn knew that his features were totally devoid of color. He and the priest stared at one another. He heard Lucian moving about the church, taking what he required.

Then suddenly the priest stiffened, and seemed to

grow. He reached out a hand to Lucian. "The holy water. Hand me a vial."

Lucian did so. Father Brindisi lifted the vial over Finn's head. "Father, protect thy servant. Let him walk in Thy way. Protect him and strengthen him from evil."

The water dropped onto Finn's head. He felt as if he had been shot. He fell to the floor, doubled over in pain. The priest did not stop. He implored God's mercy. Finn could hear the words of the prayer growing stronger and stronger.

A burst of pain knifed through his skull.

He blacked out cold.

The shift at the hospital had changed. Janice's replacement, a woman Martha didn't know well, had come on. She explained herself politely, said that Dorcas had thought it an excellent idea for her sit there, as next of kin, and talk to Andy.

But the new nurse—a Miss Matthews—disagreed. "No one is going in there during my shift. The doctor has already been in. There's been no change, and he didn't say a word to me allowing anyone in to hold his hand or any other such nonsense!"

"I must get to Andy!" Martha insisted.

"Andy is in a coma!" Miss Matthews said. "And you're not going in there. Not while I'm on duty!"

Martha should have been calm, serene, and hard as nails, totally determined. But her emotions were fraying. "I must. I must see Andy. Get him to talk, to wake up—talk in his sleep, whatever! He knows something. Don't you understand? Haven't you seen the news? My niece is going to be accused of arson. There has been something going on since she arrived, and Andy, bless his old soul, is part of it! Please, Miss Matthews, the doctors have said that he might respond to the voice or the touch of a friend."

"No one gets in!" Miss Matthews said firmly.

"Well, you're going to have to call the police to get me out of here," Martha said firmly.

"You think that I won't call the police?" Miss Matthews demanded, aggravated.

She turned to the phone on the counter.

Martha looked up and down the hallway. They were alone; the nurse on duty who should have been at the desk was away, either attending to a patient, or, more likely, making coffee, or going for a snack out of one of the machines.

There was a heavy clipboard on the counter.

Martha picked it up.

She was amazed by her own strength as she knocked the bitchy little pinched-nose Miss Matthews hard on the head.

The nurse crumpled to the floor without so much as a whimper.

Martha set the clipboard down and headed for Andy's room.

Megan sat before the fire, trying to read, but despite herself, growing exhausted. The others had gathered back around the table again. She had thought that if she was going to read, she'd remain comfortable. They knew one another—it seemed that at times they even thought alike. One could begin reading a passage, get stuck, and find a friend right there, deciphering the words. They were growing excited, as if they were on to something, but so far, they weren't making any sense to her.

She and Finn were evidently the ones in danger, so she was determined that she would keep moving in her own defense as well.

But exhaustion was taking its toll. She didn't think that she'd actually slept through an entire night since they'd come here. And last night . . . at the least, it had been rent with dreams. So as she watched the flames, she felt her eyes grow heavy.

The fire could be so pretty, fascinating, compelling. Little tongues of flame rising in so many colors, with such strange and ethereal contrast. Brilliant golds, deep maroons, startling blues. Twisting, rising, combining.

Despite herself, she felt her eyes close.

The flames continued to dance, blurring, and then receding.

She didn't realize that she had fallen asleep, and strangely, that thought was with her, even in the dream.

She walked . . . and walked. Lulled by the colors in the flames. Lulled by a voice, by a face in the fire, by a deep, rich tenor in the whisper of her name that beckoned and compelled. She knew him, trusted him, loved him . . . and she would go.

Walking . . . casting off her shoes, for they were annoying, and she needed to feel the sensual, deep, gritty feel of the earth itself beneath her feet.

She was touched by the fog, the mist. And it was sweet. A gentle caress.

Too late, she saw the figures arranged before her. They were part of the mist that surrounded the house, deep in the woods, but they took shape quickly.

She opened her mouth to scream, but one of them was behind her. A hand, holding a cloth dipped in some sweet-smelling liquid, clamped tightly over her nose and lips before she could do so.

She tried to assure herself that it was nothing more than a dream, that she would awaken.

Except that she suddenly knew. It wasn't a dream.

She fought, squirmed, kicked.

Someone swore soundly.

"Shut up!" Someone else said.

"The bitch caught me, right in the family jewels."

"Shut up!"

They were real. Real flesh, blood, muscle, bone. What-ever had come over her face was stealing consciousness, and she fought hard from slipping, in a frenzy of violent energy now, determined that she must escape.

Someone else howled.

She had nails, and she knew how to use them.

But consciousness was fading quickly. Her limbs went limp; blackness swirled before her, and she kept trying to blink, desperately trying to remain awake.

Once, when she opened her eyes, she was aware of being in a car, thrown into the backseat, covered by some of the rough-textured cloaks her assailants had been wearing. She felt nauseated, certain she would be violently ill.

But then the blackness came again . . .

When she awoke, the fleeting light of the New England fall day was already fading . . . or gone, or covered by the canopy of green. She knew where she was.

Ah, yes, she knew where she was! An unhallowed cemetery, deep in the New England woods. But no one else would know. Because she, like a fool, hadn't told Finn about meeting Andy. Had she told anyone? She couldn't remember. Maybe Mike.

But Mike . . .

Mike had tried to take her away from the fire. He might be one of these people, despite his stalwart disclaimers against any belief in witchcraft . . .

He never mentioned Satanism!

No, she knew where she was, but no one else would know. And she was no longer in the realm of dreams, this was real!

From somewhere, she could hear a soft sobbing, and whispers.

"You've done a good job," a voice whispered. "So good that if . . . well, if you weren't needed, I'd let you go. Ah, but you are needed, a perfect sacrifice."

The sobbing was muffled. Whoever cried was gagged.

Megan frowned, certain she recognized the voices, but couldn't quite place them.

She tried to move, and realized that she was tied down. She tried to open her eyes very slowly, just a crack.

And when she did . . . looking up . . . she started to scream.

Chapter 22

"You're going to get arrested, you know."

Martha almost screamed in surprise. The last thing she'd imagined finding in Andy's room was a man coming from the shadows.

"Who are you? What are you doing here?" she demanded.

"Who I am doesn't matter. What I'm doing does. Why are you trying to kill Andy?" the man demanded.

"Kill him?" Martha said incredulously. She shook her head. "I don't want to kill him! I want to find out where my niece is!"

"Oh?"

She backed away from the man uneasily. "You—you—haven't hurt her, have you?"

"She's safe," Martha was told.

Martha crossed her arms over her chest, afraid, but more afraid that night would be coming again, far too quickly.

And it was Halloween.

"Do you have a name?" she demanded indignantly. "Who you are may not matter, but if I am to address you, a name is handy."

The man smiled. "Beaudreaux. Rick Beaudreaux."

"And you're from New Orleans?"

"Yes."

"How did you get in here?"

"I was a cop—once."

"And that's supposed to make everything all right?"

"No . . . it just means that I know some procedure, how to get in . . . and out, of certain places. I've been guarding Andy. I don't think that you intend to guard him, Martha," Rick said.

"I have to get him to talk!"

"It's my understanding that you were here before. And that you meant to harm him."

Martha sighed impatiently. "I might have been here . . . but I wasn't really here. Not willfully. Not to hurt Andy. I mean, really, he'd do me no good dead!"

"So . . . ?" Rick said, leading her onward to an explanation.

"I don't know you," she said pointedly.

"No, you don't. But since you're the one who just attacked the nurse, you're going to have to trust me."

"You don't even begin to know what's going on here—"

"Trust me on this for sure—I do."

Martha let out an aggrieved sigh. "They think that Megan and Finn might have caused that terrible fire," Martha said. "But she didn't—she would never do such a thing. And Finn . . . well, no matter how strange things may be, he wouldn't do it either. Not purposely, anyway."

The fellow in the room was strange. And frightening. Something about him wasn't quite right. Martha inhaled deeply. "She's safe, you say?"

"Yes."

Martha walked past him to Andy's side. "I . . . don't believe it. I don't feel it. I've been such a fool all these years. Insisting that nothing out of the ordinary can be true when I've ... sensed there was something ... going on. All these years. I thought that Morwenna was such a ninny with all her hokum hocus-pocus, but ..."

She looked at the stranger standing closer to her now. He looked like the boy next door. The tall, blond, star quarterback–looking spic-and-span clean boy next door. She knew she'd never seen him before, but he seemed to know who she was, and it was true, he definitely seemed to know what was going on. She swallowed hard, not knowing who to trust.

"Andy has always talked. He's told his stories for the tourists, of course. But ... he's been convinced, for years, that something was coming. And with all the various things that he's hinted at ... I'm afraid. And afraid that it has to do with Megan. And some of it may be my fault. When they were married, she and Finn, of course, I was proud as a peacock. I went around showing everyone the pictures. And Andy got mad at me! I thought he was crazy as an old coot at first, and I *wanted* him to be crazy. I ignored him and got mad at him every time he tried to talk to me. He knows something. I'm not here to hurt Andy—though I came before, and didn't know it. One of your other friends was here before, apparently! That's why I had to come back. If I can get him to wake up, he can help."

"I told you—Megan is safe."

Martha shook her head vehemently. "I don't think that she is. You may think that she is, and that you and your friends can protect her. But there's something that's not right yet."

"We'll never let them hurt her," Rick said flatly.

"You don't understand. I don't think they want to hurt her."

Rick Beaudreaux frowned. "You think they mean to kill Finn, and not Megan?"

Martha shook her head. She inhaled deeply, then exhaled. She looked out anxiously into the hall, but it was still quiet.

"They don't mean to kill either of them physically," she said softly.

"What are you saying?"

"I don't know . . . exactly. Oh, even with Megan and Finn here, and at odds, and feeling strange, I just refused to believe any of it! But now, since Andy was attacked—and I'm certain he was attacked!—I've started going over everything that he's said, and what it could mean. I don't know if I believe any of this myself, but when Andy rambled . . . it was something about Bac-Dal wanting Megan, but the point is, Bac-Dal must come back in a human form. They plan to kill Finn, yes, his essence, his soul, whatever you would call it. And allow Bac-Dal to become Finn. I think that the demon has already seeped into his skin, that he has caused the dreams, that . . . he will become Finn. And then I'm afraid that . . ."

She paused, tears flooding her eyes.

"I'm afraid that then, Megan will either be his initial entertainment, and then a sacrifice to him, or . . ."

"Or?"

"Someone else, someone who wants to serve Bac-Dal, will take over her human form as well, and the Megan that I know and love will die upon the altar, just the same as if her throat were slit there, and her blood flooded the earth."

From darkness, Finn came to in another world.

A world of fog.

He was striding through it, boldly, walking naked upon the verdant earth, and aware of the deep, sensual smells of the forest. The fog touched erotically against his bare flesh, and bit by bit, as he moved through the

swirling zone of strange, eclectic pleasure, the soft, curling brush of the mist became that of delicate fingers.

He was escorted as he moved. Women shadowed his
every step, stroking him, praising him. He knew that he
walked to a certain place, and that, when he came
there, the greatest glory would be waiting. Creatures of
unearthly beauty seemed to float before him, taking
shape in the swirling mist, beckoning. He had to follow,
enticed, seduced, because each stroke against him
seemed to bring him closer and closer to a point of
power so orgasmic that he would be able to seize the
world, every delight within it, every carnal pleasure,
along with the sheer ecstasy of total command over all
that lived and breathed . . .

He came to a halt, for the altar was before him. A
wraith with long hair came directly behind him, rubbing against his back, teasing his flesh with her hair, her
hands, drawing them down his body, seizing hold of his
erection, stroking. Another came before him, offering
up a knife that gleamed despite the shadows and fog.

*Take it, take it, take it . . . she's there, take her, seize her, do
what you will. Then spill the blood of the innocent, taste it as
well, come, come, come . . .*

He moved forward, and he could see her, Megan,
hair like a web of spun gold and silver, careening down
the side of the altar. Her flesh, prone, tied . . . her throat,
so beautiful, and more, the length of her form, so well
known to him, but new now, stroked as well by misty
hands, offered up to him, and yet . . .

There was screaming, muffled, from somewhere . . .

The sacrifice, the blood sacrifice . . .

He didn't know if the sound came from elsewhere . . .

Or from Megan.

Sean Canady sat back, staring at the computer. "It's
ridiculous. Well, ridiculous, but then again, I'm afraid,

not out of the norm. They really have nothing, absolutely nothing, on who might have murdered the woman in Boston. I've been into the case files, even the files that are only supposed to be for the eyes of the police task force involved, and they haven't managed to get a thing from witnesses. She was with someone in the bar—but not a soul could even begin to say if he was light or dark, tall or short . . . black, white, Hispanic, Asian—nothing!"

At her husband's side, Maggie looked up. "Finn was there," she murmured.

"Yes, but, he might not have done it, even if he's been affected by the demon. Anyone could have reached Boston from here in under an hour. A man could have even gone to sleep for the night, slipped out of his house, killed the girl and disposed of her remains, and made it back in time to wake up beside his wife in morning," Sean said.

"Hey, hey! I've got it!" Jade exclaimed, nearly jumping from her seat. She looked at the others with her eyes afire with pleasure and triumph. "Finn's ancestor was not trying to bring back the demon! Look . . . the ink here is smudged over, and it's from an old book of eighteenth-century ghost stories, but, listen! 'Though my grandfather did not see the deed done, he heard that it was the Douglas, well aware of such heathen activity through the ancient stories of his Highland family, who drew the blade, and slew the man who would have willingly come to share his mortal being with the Demon. And thus, Cabal Thorne died, and with him all hopes of evil!' "

"It all makes sense then," Maggie said. "Finn's ancestor destroyed Bac-Dal's hopes of coming back before. And Finn was lured to Boston—and then here—for revenge as well as for convenience."

"So it would seem," Sean agreed.

"Megan will be pleased to learn that," Ann said, smiling, and looking to the chair before the fire.

Ann leaped up. "She's not there!"

Sean, too, came to his feet. They all stared at the chair.

"Megan!" Brent Malone called.

Tara rushed to the door leading to the cabin's bedrooms. She flicked on the lights, calling out as well. "Megan!"

"Son of a bitch!" Brent swore. "The front door is ajar."

"You mean . . . she just stood up and walked out, with all of us here?" Jordan inquired incredulously.

Sean began to swear softly, berating himself.

"Hell, you're not to blame. You're human," Brent said bitterly, starting out.

"Wait!" Sean told him. "We can't fly off like idiots now. We have to use logic to find her. And we have to keep a tight control on our communications. It's coming down to the wire."

Brent didn't reply. He looked toward the door, his senses now on keen alert. "Someone is coming . . . Rick is back. But he's not alone."

Sean strode toward the door, throwing it open. Rick was indeed back. He was accompanied by an attractive older woman.

And he carried a very old, unconscious old man in his arms, handling his weight easily, but having a bit of trouble with the dangling IV.

"Where's Megan?" the old woman asked anxiously.

They all stared at her.

A look of horror filled her eyes, along with a flood of tears, and she slumped to the floor.

Finn paused, despite the pressure on him, the hands, not just enticing him, but pushing him ever forward.

The sound . . .

Megan.

She was calling him back . . . or protesting his move forward. And for a moment, he felt nothing, not the evocative lure of the flesh, nothing, for she was finer than anything that could be taken elsewhere, except that . . .

She was what lay ahead. She would be waiting for him. He felt the whisper of reassurance in his ears; yes, Megan was the prize.

The seduction began anew . . . yes, yes, oh, yes, just keep moving forward, just keep feeling the soft fingers, moving so fluidly against him . . .

Then . . .

Finn screamed himself, for in the midst of his growing, erotic pleasure, the soft cool feel of fog and feathery fingers against his bare flesh, he suddenly felt as if he had been immersed in a tidal wave of fire. He jerked up.

He hadn't been doused in fire.

Rather, water. He was drenched, from head to toe. It was dripping into his eyes.

He was still in the church, stretched out on the floor before the altar, and both Lucian DeVeau and the priest, Mario Brindisi, were bent over him.

Thank God!

Because he knew now that . . .

It would be Megan, but not Megan. Megan until the hurt began, and then . . .

It made no sense, but he knew. He wasn't being lured to his wife. They were both meant to somehow pay.

"You've brought him back, Father," Lucian said.

The priest nodded, not proud of his achievement, but relieved.

Finn scrambled to his feet, nearly knocking over the two men who had hunkered before him. He stared at them with wild eyes.

"I think they have her," he said sickly.

Lucian stared at him, frowning. As he did so, his cell phone began to ring. Still staring at Finn, he answered curtly into the phone, "Yes?"

He listened, then said, "We're on our way now. I have the items from the church; make sure you have what you need from the spell shop."

"Son, you need the Word of God," Father Brindisi said, looking white and pinched.

"Father, these people have taken their spells and incantations from both the old pagan religions, and from the church. And so we will need both as well to fight them."

"God first!" Brindisi said.

Lucian stared at him.

"Oh, hell!" the priest swore. "I'm coming with you!"

"Where is she? Could you see her?" Lucian demanded of Finn.

"She's in the woods."

"Where?"

"I don't know."

"There are woods all over New England!" Lucian exclaimed.

"You're the vampire—you're supposed to know. You're supposed to read minds—"

"We're up against a demon," Lucian said levelly. "A creature well versed in slipping into thoughts and the conscious and subconscious. Think! You were with him, or he was with you; Bac-Dal was in your mind. Where?"

Finn stared back at him, so tense he thought that his bones would shatter. "I don't know!" he grated out. Then, "But I think I know who might."

Lucian stared back at him. "Smith—Mike Smith. The curator at the new museum?"

"Megan was confiding in him, I'm certain. And . . . he knows this area like the back of his hand. I personally think he's a smarmy asshole . . . and I'm going after him."

Fist clenched at his sides, Finn went striding out of the church.

Megan kept screaming. It was above her. The statue of the horned being. And it was still just marble and stone, but now . . .

The eyes moved. She was certain. The face had a life of its own. It was leering at her, laughing at her. It had been set at the end of the altar where she had been tied, and she could feel it reaching for her. The stone hands, or hooves, did not move, but she could *feel*. It teased, it invaded her indecently, it suggested everything that was evil, as if it ravaged her intimately, touched with its eyes alone . . .

And when she had first opened her eyes . . .

The face that had seemed so alive had been a parody of Finn's own.

The museum had closed.

By then, the trick-or-treaters were all over the streets. Little witches, ghosts, goblins, movie stars and rock stars, princesses and more, ran about the streets, laughing, shrieking, crying out.

But as Finn paused in front of the museum building, raging against his impotence, he saw Mike Smith.

The man was hurrying away down the street.

At a distance, with all the kids between them, he suddenly looked up. He saw Finn.

And he started to run.

Finn, with Lucian at his heels, tore after Mike, finding a lung-bursting speed unlike any he had ever known in life before. Smith had a good lead on him.

But not enough.

Finn tackled Smith with the skill of one of the finest

line blockers ever to grace NFL history. Smith went
down. Finn straddled him.

"Where? Where is Megan?"

"What the hell are you talking about? I tried to get
her to safety. Some other asshole swept her away from
me. What are you, a fool? I'd never hurt her, never in—"

"Where the hell is she?"

"I don't know! Don't you get it! I did see her after
the fire. I tried to get her away. But there was someone
else there—"

"Tell me!" Finn raged. He was about to set his hands
around Mike Smith's throat, but Lucian set a hand on
his shoulder, drawing him to his feet.

"Finn!"

Finn let out a breath. Lucian drew him up, then
reached down to bring Smith up to his feet as well.
"Megan has talked to you. What we need to know is if
there is anything she might have said about her dreams,
or any of the strange things that have gone on."

"Now!" Finn grated.

"While we're walking. We've got to get back to the
others," Lucian said. "Come on—I've already got the
priest headed for the car."

He pushed Mike ahead of him, eyeing Finn. "Half
strangling him isn't going to help right now. We have to
find out where they are and then—"

"We need the police," Finn said.

Lucian shook his head. "The police can't help us
now. What we need is to find out where we're going—
and then each one of us needs to play his or her part."

"Part—in what?"

"Our counter against the Black Mass," Lucian said.

It was just a stone statue. The image of Finn faded,
and Megan saw that the statue had been set at the end

of the altar, as if it would come down on top of her any minute.

Her scream, however, had brought someone running. A face popped above hers.

That of Gayle Sawyer. "Ah, Megan! You're awake. How nice of you to join us."

She wasn't surprised to see the girl. She wondered if Mike, too, was in on this.

All the little piercing points on Gayle's face and ears had been filled in. She wore little silver upside down pentagrams, rams' heads, and horned gods, all about her face.

Megan pulled instinctively against the ropes binding her to the altar. Gayle saw her efforts and smiled. "They're good and tight. Our priest knows how to tie knots."

Megan was terrified, so much so that she was afraid she'd black out again. It wouldn't help her any. Neither would fighting with Gayle, but she thought that anger might sustain her until . . .

Until she died, or help came.

"You know, you're going to prison. And some biker woman who killed her husband and five other jocks is going to rip your face to pieces."

Gayle laughed. "I'm not going to prison. Once Bac-Dal has returned, his power will keep us all safe."

"So, you think that Bac-Dal will return. You don't know what you're up against."

"Those ghost busters from Louisiana? Don't be ridiculous. Sure, they've had some success, but we didn't send anyone against them who wasn't entirely expendable."

"You will be dead, or you will go to prison," Megan repeated.

"Nope!" Gayle said cheerfully. "Nope, I won't."

She walked down to the end of the altar. Megan

could barely raise her head, but she did. She was covered in something of an altar cloth, a huge piece of fabric with the inverted pentagram embroidered on it. The statue was at the end, and before it, a knife. Sharp, with a curved blade. A sacrificial knife.

Gayle picked it up and smiled at Megan. She took two slow steps back to Megan's head. Laughing, she put the blade against Megan's throat, teasing it along her jawline. For a few moments, Megan couldn't help but feel the chill of fear. Then she smiled grimly. "You are such a child, Gayle. You know that you can't mar me in any way. I won't be the sacrifice that your Bac-Dal demands if you cut me."

Gayle instantly pouted, her eyes growing dark, and Megan knew that she had hit upon the truth, but it gave her little comfort.

"You're not the sacrifice, you silly twit!" Gayle told her.

Megan held still, staring at her.

"You're not to cut me, and you know it," she said, pretending she understood far more than she did.

"All right, so you won't be cut. But you'll die in pain anyway! When midnight strikes, and the priestess sheds her old skin to take on yours, the agony you'll feel will outweigh any little prick of the knife!"

Megan blinked rapidly, trying to hide the fact that she hadn't the least idea of what Gayle was talking about. But Gayle smiled. "Ah! Clever girl. You didn't really get it at all, did you? It's been so much fun, watching you and Finn. You've been so mistrustful of him. Shame, shame. That's no way to have a marriage! But admit it . . . hasn't it been great? The demon has gotten into his soul now and then, and I'll bet he's been a fantastic lover. Down and dirty, huh? What a pity. When he's truly come into being, he'll no longer be Finn, and you'll no longer be Megan. So you'll never get to know what it's really like, but . . . think of it this way. You've had a hell of run of it, the life that you've led. And you should feel privileged, you know. Your bodies will go on—I imagine that as Bac-Dal and his priestess, you'll dress better." Gayle laughed delightedly at her own joke.

As she laughed, someone came to her side, and slipped around Gayle's back, grinned down at her as well. "Peek-a-boo! Ah, Megan, you don't look so famous now, you know," Sara said. "You look . . . well, all right, you look pretty good. All that blond hair flowing off the table. That white look of terror on your face—makes your eyes look so blue!"

They were all startled by a sudden scream, followed by a hard, slapping noise, and then a moan. Megan's head had jerked around at the sound.

Sara giggled. "Morwenna!"

"Morwenna!" Megan breather in horror. God. Finn had mistrusted her so much! And here she was . . .

"She'd figured something out, you see. We hadn't really decided on the blood sacrifice for tonight, but . . . well, Morwenna could have caused some real trouble. You should have listened to her—okay, so Finn himself isn't evil. But with the demon in him . . . he surely did emit some bad vibes. Then, he started trusting me. You know, I could have had him a few times, Megan. I could have made him cheat on you while he was still himself. Of course . . . there will be time later. Not at first, of course. The priestess, cloaked in your blond hair, will want him. But in time . . . we'll all have our turn. And just imagine, once the priestess has entered your body . . . well, you just can't begin to believe the things you're going to want to do. They certainly won't be calling you a little prude—or a little blond angel!"

"Sara! Get over here!" Someone shouted.

"Gotta go. It's rather fun to torture Morwenna. She is going to die, you know. She'll be the final sacrifice to make the transformation take place. Originally, we weren't going to use Morwenna, but you know, she has more perception than I thought. She wanted me to officiate with her coven tonight! Can you imagine? There you go—she just wasn't perceptive enough!"

Sara left, but Gayle remained, staring down at her. Megan forced herself to glower at Gayle, determined, at the least, to unnerve her. "You really don't know what you're up against."

Gayle shrugged. "Maybe your ghost busters do have some special powers. But not greater than His. Not greater than Bac-Dal's."

"Really? Because I think that your Bac-Dal intended to split Finn and me up from the time we first arrived . . . you know, to make both of us so much more pliable and vulnerable. We've been stronger than you anticipated."

A flash of anger burned in Gayle's eyes. "So he's not a pushover—we never thought that he would be. His ancestor's blood does run in his veins. But you know, in Boston, he still blacked out. The priest wound up having to commit the murder himself, but . . . Finn himself is afraid that he killed the girl. Murdered her slowly . . . so, Finn's poor soul will be tortured as he tries to enter his heaven!"

"Finn didn't murder her!" Megan said triumphantly.

Gayle frowned. "It won't matter. None of it will matter."

"I think that it will. And I think that you will go to prison. What? No one is ever going to find Morwenna's body? And you're mistaken if you don't think that our friends have certain powers. They will find this place. And they'll see to it that the police get their hands on you."

"The police?" Gayle said, grinning again.

A man in a one of the hooded black capes came toward her. She felt a sinking sensation. It was Eddie's brother, Theo.

"Did someone call for a cop? Here I am!"

"I sincerely doubt that the entire police department is tainted. I'm assuming that your coven has thirteen members? There are lots more cops out there than that!"

"You know, I'm itching to slap you, and that won't leave a mark at all!" Gayle threatened.

"Okay, Gayle, enough," Theo said then, impatiently. "We've still got work to do. Just knock her out again—we don't want her screaming at the wrong time. And hell, do something to shut Morwenna up, will you? She'll wake the dead from hallowed ground a mile away!"

Theo walked off impatiently, still managing to swagger in his black robe.

"Night, night, Megan!" Gayle said. She had pulled a handkerchief and little white vial from the pocket of her cloak. Megan twisted her head aside, but knew that it was to no avail.

"Wait!" Megan implored her.

"What?"

"Well, you're truly having a good time torturing me. Probably you wanted to live my life. You think that you could have had Finn . . . but then he didn't do quite what you expected, did he? You might have managed to befriend him, but no matter how seduced he might have felt, he didn't touch you, did he? You wanted to be a rock star yourself, and you wanted someone like Finn, someone tall, charming, so damned good-looking, hardworking, artistic—and successful?"

"I'll have whatever I want for serving Bac-Dal!" Gayle retorted.

Megan couldn't help but smile, because she sensed the slightest hesitation in Gayle's words.

"But let's face it, you're having fun torturing me. So who else that I've trusted is in this coven of thirteen?"

"I'll give you a few," Gayle said.

"Old Mr. Fallon?"

"Oh, no, the silly old buzzard! He's a Wiccan, and a plain old grouch!"

"Mike?"

Gayle smiled. "It's more fun to torture you by not letting you know—especially about your old buddy Mike! I'll give you a few. You know that charming young couple staying at Huntington House?"

Megan swallowed hard. "Not the family! Not the kids, not—"

"No, they're just run of the mill tourists. The pretty pair. John and Sally. They came all the way to be here and serve just for tonight!"

So now she knew five . . . John and Sally, Theo Martin—the cop!—Gayle and Sara. All of these people, so many she considered friends . . . or at the least, fairly normal acquaintances.

Normal!

Nothing was normal.

And she knew as well that Morwenna was innocent, and intended as a sacrifice. She longed to talk to her cousin, to ask her forgiveness, to help her . . .

There had to be a way out.

"Who else?"

"Darren, of course. Though Lizzie has proved to be an absolute wretched familiar for him. She just loves people too much. And, of course, you should have figured Sam Tartan. He was so totally important, making sure that you and Finn arrived here, safe and sound."

"You keep talking about your priest and priestess—who are they?"

"You'll find out tonight!" Gayle said playfully.

"Wait—you shouldn't kill Morwenna."

"You're going to give us advice? You can't save her, you know. A stranger, snatched from the street elsewhere would have been better, but . . . Morwenna's such a pain in the ass, why not kill her?" Gayle demanded.

"She'll be missed. And you're in danger, playing with fire, taking her. Joseph will be irate, coming after her."

"None of this is going to be your concern," Gayle said blithely.

"Even if Theo is a cop, you must realize that there will be repercussions."

"Don't worry—someone will be left to take the fall. And listen, cutie pie, even if an army of FBI agents showed up, it wouldn't matter. Because once we begin, the circle will be protected by a power stronger than any earthquake imaginable. And once Bac-Dal comes back . . . he'll see to it that a corpse is there to be guilty of any murders committed, and that the cops see everything the way that he wants. You see, you are the one who doesn't comprehend what you're up against! Which reminds me, I do have work to do."

She brought the handkerchief to Megan's nose again.

Megan started instinctively to turn her head away.

"Make it easy on yourself!" Gayle said, as if finding some small bit of empathy for her captive.

Megan pretended to submit to what would be most merciful. She didn't try to hold her breath completely, but she tried very hard to inhale just one or two shallow breaths. She wanted the drug to wear off quickly so that . . .

So that what? The ropes binding her were so tight she could barely budge her arms or legs. She was freezing, naked beneath the embroidered altar cloth. Somewhere nearby, Morwenna was being tortured, probably for trying to help her.

And Finn . . .

Finn was out there. Finn's ancestor had come to kill a murderer and prevent the return of a demon; he had not been an evil man. And neither was Finn. And he was with those who could help. There was hope.

There was always hope . . .

The world was spinning again, but Gayle already

thought her completely out. She had turned away because there were others in the woods, and they were very busy. Arranging for . . .

The stroke of midnight.

Chapter 23

Finn sat white-lipped and tense, anxious every moment that they sat in the cabin.

Andy had been made comfortable on the couch, and Martha sat by his side, holding his hand, talking to him.

Lucian sat behind her, on the arm of the couch.

Mike was at the table insisting that Finn must know everything that Megan had told them, about the dreams, about the horned god, about Finn being . . .

Weird.

Father Brindisi sat at the table with Mike, seemingly incredibly uncomfortable. At length, he stood and walked to the fire, then asked Finn if he had a cigarette.

Finn gave him one, and Brindisi turned toward the flames.

"I am acutely uncomfortable here," he said.

Finn shrugged. "Well, Father, we are in the company of wolves, as they might say. A vampire must surely make a man of the cloth uncomfortable. I can assure you, learning such details about the man has not always made me feel warm and cozy."

Father Brindisi looked at the fire, shaking his head.

"I know. You don't believe it," Finn said.

Brindisi smiled. "No. You're mistaken. I believe wholeheartedly in God, the one great God! But as I believe in His goodness, I know that there is evil in the world as well. There is very little that I will not believe— or else see in the realm of the possible. There is something more . . . Perhaps it is the fact that I'm going to officiate at a Mass to counter one that is meant to summon a scion of the devil, I don't know. But something here . . . isn't right."

The door opened. Ragnor stepped in. "I've found them," he said quietly.

Finn rushed over to him. "You've found them? Megan?" he asked. "Why didn't you bring her; why didn't you seize her away?"

"Because it wouldn't have done any good; it would have done nothing but warn them," Martha said dully from her perch beside Andy.

"The graveyard!" Mike Smith said, staring at Ragnor and jumping from his seat. "What an idiot I've been! Of course!"

They all stared at him.

Then Lucian left his seat on the arm of the sofa and walked to Ragnor. "A graveyard?" he queried.

Ragnor glanced at Mike. "Yes."

"I should have thought of it immediately," Mike said. "There's only one . . . rumored to be unhallowed. There's really nothing there, some broken old statuary, but . . ."

Finn felt a flicker of anger and jealousy, compounded by the depth of his fear. He strode toward Mike again. "The cemetery. Yeah. You should have known all along. Why didn't you? Are you sure that you—a man so attuned to science, and scornful of the occult, suddenly believing!—aren't running the whole show? Maybe you're enjoying every minute here. You'll just accompany us to the right point—and become part of the Black Mass?"

Mike stared at him angrily. "I would never hurt Megan."

"You wouldn't hurt her, because someone is supposed to become her. But, how about it—were you willing to hurt a woman in Boston—slice her to ribbons before you killed her?"

"No!" Mike protested. "Look, I'm trying to help you here."

"Finn, I think he's legit," Lucian said.

Finn spun on him, swallowing hard. "You think. Well, Father Brindisi here is somewhat uncomfortable."

"Because a demon is living inside *you!*" Mike countered.

"This isn't getting us anywhere," Ragnor said quietly.

Finn stared from Ragnor to Lucian. "You're vampires, so you say. With powers. Well, I've seen something of your powers. Why don't we just go there and rip them to shreds; hell, we've got a werewolf here— let's just go chew them up. Because I'm not sure just who we can trust here."

"Finn!" Jade said softly. "We can't do that, you've got to understand. It's all begun already. And you know it, because of your dreams. We could kill a dozen people, and if we don't kill the right ones, and if the spells are completed, you'll be dead. Your body will be walking around, but *you'll be dead.*"

Finn knew she was telling the truth. He lowered his head for a moment, then looked at Lucian. "Kill me. Make me a vampire."

"I don't do that," Lucian said.

"Why not?"

"Because I don't know the final repercussions in the end."

"And we don't know that we can stop any of this, even with a priest. So make me a vampire. At least then I won't become a demon, and I'll be able to really fight for Megan."

"That's impossible," Lucian said.

"Why?"

"There isn't time. You have to die, you see. And even if I kill you quickly, you won't come back in time. Not to save Megan."

Finn lowered his head for a minute, gritting his teeth. He looked around the room. He had to trust the people—and *beings*—who were with him. There was no other choice.

He stared at Mike. "You who suddenly know so much—who's behind all this? Morwenna? The old crone from the hotel? Who?"

"I don't know," Mike said evenly. "I can only tell you that I'm not. Who the hell knows about the others?"

"We're wasting time, and we don't have a lot of it. Let's go," Lucian said. "Father Brindisi, are you ready? We must cast down our own circle of magic as soon as we come near their unholy altar."

"Please don't call it a circle of magic. It's a circle of holiness."

"As you wish, Father."

Martha stood, wringing her hands. "Do I come with you?"

"No," Lucian said.

"But . . . she's my niece!" Martha said.

"No," Jade said firmly, grabbing her papers with chants and incantations they would need. "There are ten of us—Finn and Mike. That makes twelve. And Father Brindisi, as our priest, makes the thirteen. Martha, you stay here and tend to Andy. He may still pull through. Or waken to say something that we'll need to know."

Martha looked unhappy, but she stayed where she was.

As they walked out of the house, Lucian set his hand on Finn's shoulder. "You're going to want to run to

Megan. You can't do it. You have to stay in the circle of power we create, do you understand."

Finn nodded.

He understood.

He just wasn't sure that he could do it.

Megan didn't allow anyone to see that she was awake. When she first came to, she tried to move her wrists, desperate to free herself. But they had been bound so that the rope wrapped around the bottom of the altar. No matter how hard she tried, she couldn't budge the ties binding her. At one point, she bleakly wondered if she should have let herself be knocked out completely. Soon, she'd have to accept the fact that she was going to die. Painfully—if this was all true. If someone really could say all the right incantations, do the right thing, steal her body and send her soul to purgatory.

Her wrists and ankles chafed. Good.

She'd leave the high priestess or whatever in sad shape.

Night had settled over the copse in the woods completely. The full moon rode high in the sky. She didn't know the time, only that there was a bevy of activity going on. A great circle had been formed around the altar, and a chalk pentagram, upside down, had been drawn, the altar resting between the two points of the star shape. She still didn't recognize everyone walking around her because they were all clad in the black robes and cowls. They talked freely to one another though, thinking that she still slept.

Someone arrived in the copse then, and all the figures who had been hurrying around went rushing to him, going down on their knees, kissing the hem of his robe.

"All is in readiness?" he inquired. "Where is the sacrifice?"

"The blood of the last moon is in the chalice on the altar," a figure told the newly arrived man. "Morwenna remains bound to the tree . . . and Megan awaits Bac-Dal, as instructed. However . . . you know that the Douglas is still with his friends?"

"And that is perfect. For he will change as he should, and those who would have interfered will die quickly, ripped to shreds by Bac-Dal's power, and we will all be rewarded."

The newly arrived man, the high priest, Megan presumed, walked to the tree where Morwenna, now silent and slumped, was bound. He paused long enough to kick her. But she had been drugged, and all he received for his efforts was a moan.

He strode to the altar then and looked down, smiling. "Hello, Megan. I can see that you're awake. It will all be over soon. Hm. You always were a pretty piece of baggage, hm?"

She knew the voice. Far too well.

"Joseph. What a shock. Couldn't stand the fact that your wife was liked better than you, or that in a Wiccan society, she was simply far more important and powerful."

"Megan, you are a bitch."

"Joseph, I should have known."

"How would you? I'm just your cousin's husband. A good Wiccan. Following her every word. And listening to her rant and rave this last week! God, how I laughed inside!"

"You're going to rot in hell, Joseph."

"Not until I've had one hell of a good life here, baby. Bac-Dal is real. You've met him. He's been in your husband already."

"But you're the one who committed murder. Because not you—or your Bac-Dal—could make him do so."

"Megan, you're going to die."

sneering faces at them as he held the dog's collar, as if he could send Lizzie out to crunch into their throats. And there . . . an old hag! It was Susanna from Huntington House. And then the couple! John and Sally. The nurse he had seen at the hospital . . . Dorcas. Theo Martin, the cop—*and* his brother, Eddie! A huge bonfire blazed from the center of the pentagram, and they cavorted around it, sneering at him, as if incredibly entertained that they had been leading them along all the while.

Lucian elbowed him. He forced himself to keep repeating the prayers they spoke. But he was counting. Sara, Gayle, Susanna, Brad and Sally, Darren, Eddie, Theo, Sam Tartan, and there . . . the old asshole who had acted like a lecher at the bar, and his wife. Two more. They needed two more.

One . . .

The man in the black robes at the altar.

But . . .

There. Walking from the woods. A small figure in a black cloak and cowl, just like those worn by the priest at the altar.

She came forward, crying out.

"Great Bac-Dal! Tonight, we serve you. We offer you flesh, blood, and carnal pleasure. We implore your coming into our world! And first, we offer up the sacrifice of the flesh!"

Finn fell silent again, horrified as he saw two of them break away from the fire. Finn felt ill. There was Morwenna, hog tied on the ground. As the newcomer spoke, she grabbed up a knife at the end of the altar, and walked toward Morwenna.

"No!" Finn roared.

"Oh, God, oh, God, oh, God!" Mike Smith breathed in terror at Finn's side.

As the newcomer brought the knife to Morwenna,

the newcomer grasped the Morwenna's head, dragging it up so that the newcomer could slice her throat.

But then she paused, casting back her cowl with pride.

It was Aunt Martha. Attractive old Aunt Martha, who had claimed that she didn't believe in evil, then pretended that she had to admit to something, and that she was trying to help . . .

The pride and gloating on her face were incredible.

From the altar, Megan screamed. It was a terrible cry, rising in the night. It was horror, protest, revulsion, fear . . . and fury.

"No!"

Martha laughed.

Father Brindisi was reading from the book of exorcism, begging God to cast out evil demons. Jade led half of them in chanting from a book of spells.

"Fools!" Martha raged in a loud, clear voice. "Fools! You think you have power! Vampires, you are but the refuse of the earth! Bac-Dal, your moment has come! You have entered the servant of your vessel, Finn, the descendant of the man who has delayed your coming." She cackled out a laughter so chilling that Finn felt goose pimples rise on his flesh. "Finn, He is in you, and you will come forward!"

A rush of fire filled him, just as if he had really been lit on fire. He could hear nothing then, only a chanting like a music, pulling him forward.

The fog swirled on the ground. Swirled from his own feet. Someone touched his arm, and he shook off the hideous restraint with the power that surged through him. He walked forward.

Jade threw salt before him, seeking the power of the earth to hold him. He knocked her aside. Father Brindisi raised a cross above his head, gibbering away in the name of God.

But he stepped from their circle, ripping off his coat, freeing himself from the material of his shirt.

They were touching him. The women were touching him. Lauding him, praising him. They kissed his flesh . . . fell behind him, their lips falling upon him even as he walked away, falling upon the earth where he had stepped. Blood thundered and raged through him. He felt a hunger, unlike anything he had known before.

And a surge of desire . . .

To kill.

Take the knife, rip open the woman's throat. Drink her blood, bathe in it, and then . . .

The prize on the altar would be his, in a new life, one of raw carnal pleasure and sheer power. The world would fall to his feet.

"Come, great Bac-Dal! Take the blade, and we will share in this woman's blood, and when it is done, the mortal coil will be yours, and youth will be mine, as my soul, ever ready to serve your least desire, shall root within the youth and beauty upon your divine altar!"

Yes!

Bac-Dal was within him. Great and powerful. He was Bac-Dal. Supreme. His fingers itched to caress the knife, to rip into flesh, to drink the blood of life.

He moved forward, slowly, for there was no rush, just great pleasure.

He reached the priestess, the crone, an old woman now, but with a soul that had sought to serve him, planned, for years . . . she would take on the beauty of youth, the vigor, the passion, and together . . .

His fingers closed around the knife.

He was Bac-Dal!

Morwenna was shrieking for her life, fighting the hands that held her. Megan strained wildly against the ropes that bound her, shouting, screaming until she was hoarse. She could hear the priest, his words growing more desperate, and she could hear the others, their voices rising in the spells of nature and the earth . . .

Finn was going to kill Morwenna!

Another voice entered into her mind. Not a voice that tried to rise above the others, just a voice in her head.

Call out to him, Megan! Call out to the man, the man you have known and loved, call to him loudly, with everything in your heart and soul.

It was Lucian's voice. And she knew, no matter what the power of their supernatural friends, she and Finn had to fight and win this battle. Bac-Dal might have blocked much of the "sight" that the vampires usually had, but still, they had known somehow, suspected Martha, even. But it had to have come to this, to her, to Finn.

You must call out to him, stop him, somehow, now.

Call out!

And so she did.

"Finn! For the love of God, *Finn!*"

The knife was in his hands. It was he now who had Morwenna by the hair, jerking her head upward so that the blade could easily access the white flesh of her throat.

"Finn, dear God, dear Lord, *Finn!*"

He let go of Morwenna's hair. He turned to Martha, and smiled. He walked to the altar where the priest remained at Megan's side.

"Joseph—you asshole!" he said clearly, scornfully. Then he sent his arm flying, knocking Joseph to the side. He raised the knife above Megan. His eyes met hers.

The sacrificial weapon came down, slicing the ropes that bound her to the altar.

Joseph came to his feet with a roar of fury, racing toward Finn, who was taken off guard, and the two went flying to the ground together. Martha let out a cry of anger as well and came racing forward, anxious to grab the knife.

Megan saw her running toward Morwenna, still tied and vulnerable.

But Martha couldn't reach her because there seemed to be a flurry of darkness, and Lucian was at her side, wrenching the knife from her.

Screams rose from everywhere.

Megan leaped up from the altar, then staggered and fell—her ankles were still bound. She struggled to free herself.

Mayhem seemed to have broken out.

She clawed the ropes from her ankles and stumbled up. Joseph lay flat on the ground, knocked unconscious. Megan grasped the wooden altar for the strength to stand. As she did so, she saw Gayle Sawyer come running forward, an oak branch in her hand. She was ready to crash it down with all her strength on Finn's back.

Megan found strength. Twisting, she jabbed her fist into Gayle's stomach with all her might. Gayle screamed and fell.

Megan looked down at her, and wrenched the branch away. "Guess what, bitch?" she said softly. "You'll never touch him—in any way!"

She felt a whir of air behind her and spun around, the branch now raised as a weapon in her own hand.

It was only Mike Smith, handing her his coat to cover her nakedness. She smiled at him. White as a sheet, he tried to offer her a smile.

Sara, across from the bonfire, started to shriek, tear at her hair, and run into the woods. They wouldn't get far. A whir in the darkness, a flap of wings . . .

Those who ran would quickly be caught.

Theo Martin was raging that he was still a cop, and he'd see that they all rotted in jail. He didn't speak long, though, because Ragnor just shook his head in disgust, and went over to flatten him.

It was just the mop up. The main battle had been fought, and won. And now, since their friends had such unusual power, the end would be quick and clean.

But then . . .

There was a terrible cry of rage.

Martha had risen again. And she had retrieved the sacrificial blade. She went rushing at Finn.

"Help him!" Megan shrieked, seeing that Lucian was striding around the pentagram on the ground, destroying it, and its power.

He'd never have time to reach Finn.

Yes, God, please! She thought. He was a vampire, he could reach Finn . . .

But he didn't need to. Finn was ready, kicking out and hitting Martha's arm.

They could all hear the crack of bone.

The knife flew up, and down. Finn caught it, and grabbed hold of Martha, bringing it to her throat.

But there he paused.

"No," he said softly. "You will *not* make a murderer out of me."

He tossed Martha from him. And then, the copse was silent. Some of their enemies had run, and would be easily caught.

A few were lying dazed or unconscious on the dirt of the forest.

Lucian had freed Morwenna, who had first dissolved into a flood of tears, and then risen in silence.

Finn turned to Megan. And he came across the forest floor, as he had in dreams. He reached the place by the altar where she stood. And he pulled her to him, gently, tenderly. They just stood there, holding one another.

She started to shake. Then she whispered softly.

"They saved us! A priest, and a pack of vampires, and a werewolf, and their wives!"

He pulled away from her, just barely. Enough to see her eyes.

"Dear Lord, yes, they helped. We wouldn't be alive without them. But you saved me, Megan. I heard your voice, when I could hear nothing else."

She smiled, allowing herself to fall against him.

She was vaguely aware then of Morwenna, still shaking, wrapped in someone's huge coat, and walking, shaking still, until she stood over Joseph.

"You pathetic, jealous, dickhead, prick!" she cried, and kicked her husband's fallen body. Megan thought that her cousin was going to collapse.

But she didn't. She lifted her head and turned toward the circle where Father Brindisi now stood in silence.

"I'm so sorry, Father Bridisi, please, please, forgive my language!" she said with dignity.

Father Brindisi grinned. "God forgive me, Morwenna, but I was thinking along the exact same lines!"

They heard the sound of sirens in the night.

"Cops," Mike Smith managed to say.

"You have mental power?" Finn asked him, grinning.

Mike shook his head. "Cell phone. I thought it was time we called them."

"And time a few of us slip away," Lucian said. "You are all right now, right?"

"I think," Finn said. "We'll all be all right—if the woods don't catch fire."

Lucian turned, kicking dirt upon the bonfire. "Help me," he told Finn.

Finn joined him. It seemed, as the dirt flew up and fell upon the flames, that fog, not smoke, rose above it.

And for one terrible moment, Megan thought that she could see the burning eyes and horns of the demon, Bac-Dal, outlined there, in the fog.

More dirt fell upon the flames.

Smoke rose, and dispersed, and the fog was gone. An eerie sound seemed to rip through the night.

Something like a scream. A cry of pain and rage.

Fading, as the remnants of fire became nothing but ash.

And then . . .

The strange shriek in the night was gone.

There was only the blare of the sirens heralding the police vehicles that were coming quickly now, roaring through the night.

Epilogue

"Put your money where your mouth is!" Sean Canady told Finn.

"You bet I will. I see your quarter, and I raise you fifty cents!"

"Wait a minute, will you!" Jade said. "I'm still in this game."

"And me!" Megan said determinedly.

"Sure," Sean said, still staring at Finn. Neither man noted the others at the table; they were intent upon beating one another.

Jade tossed her money in. "Gambling. It becomes such a silly testosterone thing for them!"

"Read 'em and weep," Sean said, throwing his cards down. "Full house."

Finn smiled, the thrill of the challenge hard in his eyes. "Four tens!"

Sean swore, casting down his cards. Finn started to rake in the change.

"When will you boys ever learn!" Jade groaned. "I happen to have four ladies." She started to reach for the change.

Megan laughed. "Well, you've all got me beat. I was in it for the bluff. Jade, take it away."

"Excuse me, will you?" Morwenna protested. "I have, beyond a doubt, the winning hand. The aces—all four of them, my friends."

They all sat back and stared at Morwenna. Sean looked at Lucian, who had folded early, then at Finn.

"Can you imagine? Four queens in one hand, and four aces in another, in the same damned game? How the heck did you manage that, Morwenna?"

"Witchcraft," she said serenely, taking in the change.

Megan laughed, rising from the table, and beckoning to Finn. They were out at Maggie's plantation, close enough to home, but . . .

They were staying with Canadys for the next week or so. It was good to be with trusted friends, for the moment. Especially in such a plantation house. They had plenty of room.

And Morwenna . . .

She had really needed a break from home.

"We're going to take a breather on the balcony for a minute," Megan told the others. "Finn, er, wants a cigarette."

He slipped an arm around her shoulders. "Thought you wanted me to quit completely," he said.

"I do. But . . ."

They walked outside. A month had gone by. For the two of them, it had been a good month. But Megan worried about Morwenna, who had later told her that she had never even suspected that Joseph had hated the empowerment of her coven, and loathed her for the power she'd had in the community.

Not only had her husband been betraying her with the women in the coven she hadn't known existed, he had left her to commit murder in Boston, come back with the blood on his hands, and she hadn't even known.

And then, of course, he had tricked her into finding out where Megan and Finn were.

Not to mention the fact that he had intended to make her a blood sacrifice to his demon god, Bac-Dal.

But Morwenna was thriving in New Orleans. She had decided that she wasn't going back to Massachusetts. Not to live.

"So . . . why are we out here?" he asked her, sweeping his arms around her and pulling her to him.

"Just to feel the night breeze."

"Ah."

"And . . . I was thinking."

"Yes?"

"No one really understands what happened. With Father Brindisi's testimony, it came out that Joseph and Martha were Satanists who had formed a coven to force others to submit to their demands. And Martha is dead now," she said, her tone bitter. Rather than accept her defeat, Martha had hanged herself in jail before the day had ended.

One way or the other, she had intended to be done with her "earthly coil" that day.

Joseph, the police had decided, was a psychotic lunatic.

And the others . . .

All would be tried for attempted murder, and for complicity. Every single one of them faced long jail terms. The news coverage on the "cult" had been sensational, and so, since the trials were still coming up, the exact venue had yet to be decided, but mostly likely, they would be moved elsewhere in Massachusetts.

They knew that they would have to attend as state witnesses. They didn't know where or when as yet. For all offenders, the future boded dim.

Except for Lizzie, the Great Dane. She now had her

own doghouse on the Montgomery plantation, here in Louisiana.

"What are you getting at, Megan?"

She smiled. "Not now—not right now—but I want to go back."

He arched a brow to her.

"New England is one of the most beautiful places in the entire world. And despite the tragedies that have occurred in Salem, there's something special there as well. Terrible things have been averted, too. I want you to see my home as I really know it, filled with splendor and history and wonderful things! I got a letter from Mike, too."

"I hope he's doing very well," Finn said sincerely.

"He's been spending a lot of time with Father Brindisi—he's thinking of going to seminary. But what's important is this—Andy Markham has come out of his coma. I have to go see him, Finn. And thank him."

"We have to go see him, and thank him."

"Then, there's Mr. Fallon. He's been very ill, and could use some visitors. He worked with Susanna every day, and just thought that she was a nasty bitch! Apparently, when she was arrested, he had a breakdown. So we should see him."

"Of course."

"There's also Adam Spade, just another nice guy. Adam has taken over the store for Morwenna, because she's not sure when she'll go back. We should check in with him."

"We should."

"I spent some time with him, but I'd really like to thank Father Brindisi again myself. And what's really important is that . . . I want what I love back. I want the beauty, the fun, the respect for true Wicca . . . the belief that people around me are just living, going along like the rest of us, and not all part of a conspiracy. I need that back. I'm not letting a core of evil ruin my home for me, and everything that is so wonderful about it."

"I agree!"

"So . . . we have to go back."

Finn pulled her tightly against him.

"Whenever you want!" he said softly.

"Really?"

"You bet."

She leaned against him happily. Sometimes, she still doubted herself all the things that had happened. It was all too impossible. But then again, she was very good friends with a number of vampires now, people who insisted that she and Finn were really part of their Alliance. Vampires. And a werewolf, of course. Different, but not to be forgotten.

They were just so damned *normal.*

"But for right now . . ." Finn murmured.

"Yes?"

"I'm having this vision . . ."

"Oh?"

"There's a great expanse, and I'm trying to cross it. And I'm on fire, because I know that you're waiting. There's a feel in the air, like a caress, and I'm hungry, starving, I have to reach you."

"Like a demon lover?" she murmured, joking uneasily.

He shook his head, smiling. "No, just like the man who loves you more than life itself . . . and of course, wants you right now with every bit of *natural* but ardent, fevered, passionate, lustful desire in his very human body."

Megan smiled, feeling his fingers moving lightly, insinuatingly, down her ribs.

"Let's go say our good nights, shall we?"

There was no fog that night as they left the balcony. And later . . .

He walked across their darkened room to her.

And he was everything. The man, the perfect man, who loved her. Which was all they had needed, Lucian had said.

There were many powers on earth.

None as great as the power of love.